Praise for
Ice Shear

"Cooley's writing has an easy flow . . . the pacing is excellent and the storyline so engrossing that it's difficult to believe *Ice Shear* is a debut novel . . . Cooley's characters are bursting with vitality, practically leaping off the page." —*Los Angeles Review of Books*

"Excellent debut . . . a strong, fast-paced narrative and an intriguing heroine propel the believable twists in a plot involving politics, a burgeoning meth industry, and biker gangs."

—*Publishers Weekly* (starred review)

"Cooley's high-energy plot keeps the surprises coming. She is an author to watch." —BBC Books

"This promising debut delivers a fast-paced, engaging rural thriller."

—*Booklist*

"Cooley makes it a gripping ride all the way."

—*San Jose Mercury News*

"As chilling as its title, a small-town police story that grows and grows into the bigger themes of power, corruption, and cover-up."

—Andrew Gross, author of *Everything to Lose*

"Captivating, original and brilliant. Seamlessly natural—*Ice Shear* shines with the remarkable confidence and authority of true talent."

—Hank Phillippi Ryan, author of *Truth Be Told* and an Agatha, Anthony, Macavity, and Mary Higgins Clark Award–winning author

ICE SHEAR

ICE SHEAR

M. P. COOLEY

WILLIAM MORROW
An Imprint of HarperCollinsPublishers

A hardcover edition of this book was published in 2014 by William Morrow, an imprint of HarperCollins Publishers.

FIRST WILLIAM MORROW PAPERBACK EDITION PUBLISHED 2015.

Designed by Jamie Lynn Kerner

Art on the title page and the chapter-opening pages © argus/Shutterstock, Inc.

Library of Congress Cataloging-in-Publication Data has been applied for.

ISBN 978-0-06-230072-0

15 16 17 18 19   OV/RRD   10 9 8 7 6 5 4 3 2 1

For my mother and father

Some time when the river is ice ask me
mistakes I have made. Ask me whether
what I have done is my life. Others
have come in their slow way into
my thought, and some have tried to help
or to hurt: ask me what difference
their strongest love or hate has made.

I will listen to what you say.
You and I can turn and look
at the silent river and wait. We know
the current is there, hidden; and there
are comings and goings from miles away
that hold the stillness exactly before us.
What the river says, that is what I say.

WILLIAM STAFFORD, "ASK ME"

ICE SHEAR

CHAPTER 1

My OPTIONS WERE LIMITED.

On the one hand, Ned wasn't driving drunk. And he seemed so peaceful curled up in the backseat of the Ford Escort. Under the gentle glow of the streetlights he looked like an apple-cheeked toddler instead of a forty-five-year-old with gin blossoms.

On the other hand—the frostbit one—I'd be shirking my duty as an officer of the law if I let Ned sleep off a drunk in the back of an unheated vehicle. He'd pulled his Buffalo Bills pom-pom cap low over his eyes, but his threadbare army jacket wasn't going to cut it. Overhead, the Hopewell Falls Saving Bank digital clock blinked: 17 degrees. Several bars on the display were broken, so the real temperature could be as low as 10 or as high as 19. All were too cold.

Of course, the deciding factor was that, well, it wasn't his vehicle. Our one and only bus driver, Janelle DuMaurier, owned it. After his numerous license suspensions Ned spent quite a bit of time on her bus, so I'm sure they were great friends, but Janelle had a bus driver's value for schedules and wouldn't appreciate it if Ned made her late for work. If I didn't roust him now I would have to move him in an hour when Janelle came downstairs and found an uninvited guest. Plus, I'd have to do paperwork.

I rapped on the window. The pom-pom didn't move.

The door handle was iced over, and I pulled three times before it gave. The hinges' screech bounced off the empty predawn streets. Ned slept through it. Ned slept even as I opened the door, his head sliding down the blue vinyl, leaving a trail of saliva. Before he ran out of door and spittle, I squatted, made a basket of my arms, and caught him. He jerked awake.

"Shit, man," Ned said. He pulled the knit cap up over his brow, rumpling the red, white, and blue bison, and blinked up at me owlishly. "S'cold."

"That it is, Ned." The smell of beer—fresh Genny Cream Ale on his breath, stale Genny Cream Ale dried into his clothes—came off him in waves. He grinned toothily at me, and I found myself grinning back. Ned had a good heart, although not paired with the sharpest mind. Resting one hand on my holster, the other on my radio, I said, "You can't sleep here, Ned."

"C'mon! S'not fair. You told me not to drunk drive! Drunk driving's bad."

"On that"—I took a step back out of range of the beer smell and his spittle—"we are in agreement."

"I know! I'm so not drunk driving. And last time, you told me not to sleep on the street or you'd put me in perspective, protective . . ."

"Protective custody."

"Yes!" Ned looked at me like I was a genius. "And I'm not. And hey! This's my car! My private property! And it's not American to tell me not to sleep in my own property—"

I put on my stern face. "Not your property, Ned. It's Janelle Du-Maurier's Ford Escort. Your Honda is the next vehicle up."

Ned took in the Ford, its full ashtray, its PROGRESS, NOT PER-

FECTION air freshener, its Kleenex box hidden under a doll's pink crocheted skirt.

"Oh."

"Oh, yes," I said.

Ned clambered out of the car, fished out his keys, and, holding them an inch from his face, flipped through them to find the one that would open his Honda. He missed it twice. I snatched the ring out of his hands.

"C'mon, June. Gimme!" he yelled. "I wasn't gonna drive. Just gonna sleep."

"Too cold." I unlocked his trunk, facing a sea of empty beer cans. Ned would make a killing at the recycling center if he ever remembered to go. I dropped the keys in, watching them bounce off Rolling Rock bottles before settling in a nest of crushed Pabst cans. I slammed the trunk closed.

"You can pick them up in the morning when the locksmiths are awake." I held out my hand. He grabbed his hat. I struggled to keep from laughing. "Give me your phone, Ned."

"C'mon, June. Gordon'd give me a break."

"You know he wouldn't." When Gordon—my dad—trained me after I'd joined the Hopewell Falls PD, he'd used the time we cruised around to explain the city. With the exception of two summers spent with my mother in Florida after my parents' divorce, I'd spent all of my first eighteen years in Hopewell Falls, so I knew most of the residents. He'd skipped the statistics because I'd already read up: On average we had one murder per year, but plenty of domestic assaults that stopped just short. Seven rapes in the last year. A higher-than-average number of burglaries committed by people out of a job and out of options, or people so high they couldn't think of any.

Instead, Dad focused on the personalities. He explained that Ned was mostly harmless, ID'ing him as a fall-down drunk rather than one of the nasty, belligerent ones. By the time Dad retired, aka had the massive heart attack, I knew which people were loitering for loitering's sake and which people were loitering with intent.

"Phone," I repeated. Ned pulled the cell out, bobbled it, and then dropped it, sending it skidding across the sidewalk. I told him to stay put. I weighed 120 and Ned probably twice that, and lifting a drunk off an icy sidewalk would take the rest of my shift.

I knelt and fished the phone out of the remains of a snowbank, gently brushing black ice off with a gloved finger.

"Your wife?" I asked.

"Nah. She gets pissed when I drink. C'mon, June."

"Call someone to give you a lift now, or we'll have to call someone in several hours for bail. Who's your best friend?"

"C'mon. He's asleep. Don't bother him."

"How courteous." Drunks always have strange ideas regarding politeness: they can throw up on my shoes but don't want to put a friend out. I flipped through the names. Ned had his mother listed three times, but I tabbed past. Her funeral had been last May.

"I'm cold," I said, which was true, but Ned dithered, which made me cranky. "Pick."

"Fine. Pat. But he's not going to like me waking him up."

Pat's number rang three, four times, and I resigned myself to spending the rest of the morning doing paperwork instead of pulling an early go. On the fifth ring, a scratchy voice answered.

"Pat!" I said loudly, calling over Ned's shouted apologies. I shushed him to keep the neighbors from calling in noise complaints, not that I needed to worry. Except for a few stalwarts like Janelle, most of the apartments were empty, little demand for converted Victorian rooming houses in a town with no jobs. "Pat, it's June Lyons. Sorry for disturbing you, but I've got your friend Ned down here, outside of Smitty's Pub. He's impaired by drink, I'm sorry to report, and I might have to PC him. Yeah, again. Unless you're willing to pick him up at the Dunkin' Donuts in the next twenty minutes. Work for you?"

A grunt sounded in my ear and the line went dead. I handed the phone back to Ned, who was still whispering, "Sorry." His life must be one long apology.

"C'mon, Ned." I gave him a smile. "I'll buy you a doughnut."

We scuttled down the icy sidewalks past his car and my cruiser to the Dunkin' Donuts, where Susie had my usual waiting for me: coffee and cruller.

"June," Susie said, her smile faltering as she spotted Ned trailing behind me.

"Susie," I said, "Ned here will take a large coffee and a"—Ned pointed to the top of the display—"and a chocolate with sprinkles."

Susie reached to the upper row, the seams on her salmon-colored uniform straining. I remembered her wearing that uniform when I was in high school, twenty years ago. These days, the capped cuffs cut into her biceps, and snag marks creased the fake crinoline apron where the cash register opened against her abdomen again and again. Susie placed the coffees and doughnuts on the counter.

"He's not going to throw up again, is he?"

"Nah," I said. "He wouldn't do that to you, would you, Ned?" Ned grabbed his food and parked himself at the table closest to the bathroom. "And if he does, he'll come back and do floors for a month. How much do I owe you?"

"No charge for you on night shift. You know that."

"But you do charge for drunks waiting for a ride." I appreciated that Susie would like me to come around more, not less, during these long nights, but I don't think she hoped that Ned would, too.

"Well, if you insist . . . that'll be a dollar fifty-five."

Counting out my change, I found only a dollar forty-five. I searched my pockets for another dime, digging out a paper clip and a seashell Lucy had given me before my shift, but no change. I pulled out my wallet. "Since I'm using my card, gimme a dozen to bring back to the station. I can be the big hero today."

A rush of static crackled from my radio, and the night dispatcher's voice rang through the room: "C-12, what is your 10-20?"

"Dunkin' Donuts, Lorraine, picking up a homicide kit"—using the radio code for the doughnuts. "Anything called in?"

"Channel seven, June." I switched over to the unrecorded channel. "Nothing called in. Will you be bringing jelly?"

"Affirmative," I said, as Susie dropped a raspberry filled in the box. "See you in thirty. I'm out."

While the cruiser warmed up, I took a bite out of my doughnut, swallowed it, and held the rest in my mouth while I backed out of the parking lot onto Mohawk Street. The car was dirty enough that I wasn't eating anything that touched its seat.

My cell rang. I rummaged through the side pocket of the cruiser's door, jabbing my wrist on a pencil as I retrieved the phone, and I parked and spoke without checking the display, knowing it could only be one person.

"Hi, Dad."

I heard him swallow his coffee. "Busy night?" he said finally.

"Quiet night, actually. Doing one last lap. Lucy up?"

"The kid's been sleeping since you kissed her good night. She's over that damn cold." As he spoke, a light three houses down flicked on and a woman drifted to her sink, coffeepot in hand.

"She ready to go back to school?" I asked.

"Yeah. She misses those friends of hers, and if I have to spend another day with a six-year-old who's not sick enough to nap, I'll lose my ever-lovin' mind. Want Luce to call you before school?"

"No." I felt small and a little mean, but I wanted more than a phone call. "I'm doing one last pass. I'll be home around seven thirty or so and can walk her over to the bus. And hey, if she's up to it maybe we can ice-skate after school." I had taken Lucy to the rink the previous week. She had never been on the ice, and it was my first time since college. I fell as often as she did, her ankles arched in on rented skates. "I think she liked it."

"Hmm," Dad grumped. He never liked me on skates, convinced I went too fast and would crack my head open. He liked his grand-daughter on them even less. "I'll pick up helmets for you two speed demons."

"Dad, I spent the whole time skidding across the ice on my ass, and Lucy was primarily interested in the concession stand. We don't need helmets."

My father sighed. "Want me to hold breakfast?"

"Nah."

"You sure?"

"Yeah, I'm sure. But thanks." Dad had been amazing since Kevin died, but sometimes he acted like I couldn't raise a child, let alone make my own breakfast. Kevin, Lucy, and I had moved back to my hometown three years ago after Kevin's cancer had lasted (and lasted and lasted) long past his disability and my ability to take care of a sick husband, a daughter, and a job. Dad had offered me a spot on his force: "Jeez, June. You're an FBI agent. Seriously, you think you're going to fail the Hopewell Falls civil service exam?" The job paid the bills and kept me sane through Kevin's death.

I decided to make a peace offering in the fight Dad didn't know we were having. "Hey, we need anything? I'll stop at Price Chopper."

"Nah, we're good. Stay safe, and get yourself home."

During the conversation, the rest of the world awoke. More houses lit up, the cops on the day shift sounded over the radio, and traffic picked up. I half slid and half drove down the Manor Avenue hill toward the Mohawk River, the sun rising over the Taconic Mountains in Vermont. The greenish gold spread warming the hori-zon. I couldn't remember a time when it wasn't winter. Just the idea of sunshine was wonderful.

Turning left, I could see Harmony Mills in the distance. The buildings were long empty, no longer needing the waterfall's energy to power the industrial looms or the Erie Canal to ship gloves, shirts, and collars to such exotic places as Rochester and Cleveland. The inactive mills continued to dominate the city: they took up a huge chunk of downtown real estate, and people were always gossiping about who might move in and restore Hopewell Falls to its former glory. The "former glory" mostly consisted of being named an All-American City in 1947, when Harmony Mills last operated at full steam. Everyone talked about how if we gave a tax break to a high-tech company, built a new park, or attracted an Internet café, young people would come back and renew downtown and draw congregants to keep the churches from closing. That seemed unlikely: We lived in an area our former governor called "like Appalachia," a comparison that was unfair to Appalachia. West Virginia had job growth seven times our measly 0.2 percent, and our population had dropped as the jobs disappeared. New York City, only three hours away, might as well have been on another planet.

A jolt of excitement rushed through me as my tires rumbled over cobblestones. The pavement had worn away, exposing the roads from the last century—or the century before?—and the vibrations that shook the cruiser were my signal that my shift was almost done.

I'd almost reached downtown when I saw Jackie DeGroot. The teenager was currently caught, her silver jacket snarled in the chain-link fence that kept people away from the river. She twisted left and right, like a cigarette wrapper blowing in the wind. I couldn't tell if she wanted in or out.

I slowed and rolled down my window, the cold hitting my face like a slap. The microphone on the cruiser didn't work, so I yelled to her. "Jackie!" She didn't respond. I turned off the car and repeated myself. "Jackie! Shouldn't you be getting ready for school?"

Still no reaction. I parked and approached her cautiously. She appeared healthy. The puffy coat, big jeans, and Timberland boots that were popular right now kept her warm, but unfortunately were ideal for concealing drugs or a weapon. I was pretty sure this wouldn't be more than a talking-to and a ride to school, and I'd still be home in time to walk Lucy to the bus.

I touched Jackie's arm. She jumped like she hadn't seen me coming. I cataloged her responses. Her eyes weren't dilated, but she was disoriented. Drugs? Shock? Injury?

"Jackie." I kept my voice low and soothing. "Let's get you someplace warm. You okay? What're you doing here?"

Jackie's face was red with tears and streaked with heavy black eyeliner. Her earrings bobbed as she pointed wildly, the chained hearts snagging in the fleece of her hood. I reached over and unhooked the hearts before Jackie tore her earlobe. I searched where she pointed, toward the waterfalls. The Hopewell Falls weren't visible from here, hidden beyond the cliff that rose above the river. I struggled to maintain my composure even as Jackie pointed again and again, pulling until her jacket ripped away from the fence.

"Well, that solved our problem," I said and smiled, trying to make eye contact with her, but she stared through me, back toward the falls.

I guided her over to the cruiser. "Okay, Jackie, you're not tracking right now. Did you take any drugs? You're not in trouble, but I want to help you." Jackie started crying again. I kept my voice firm. "How about I get you settled and go investigate whatever's on the other side of this fence. Okay?"

Jackie nodded, her chin trembling, taking great gulping breaths. I called for backup, and continued to try to coax answers out of Jackie, but she was disturbingly silent. Pete arrived in two minutes, having just started his shift. He contemplated the snowdrifts that led to the river.

"I don't want to do my whole shift in wet pants," he said apologetically.

I would've given him shit about that if Jackie hadn't been there. "You take Jackie. I bet getting her fixed up will take more time than it'll take me to walk over, evaluate the scene at the river, walk back, and write up a report."

This arrangement suited Pete. I crawled through a hole in the fence. Looking back, I saw Pete shrug as he comforted a sobbing Jackie. I pushed through the snow. Only a foot deep, the drifts were hard, having melted and refrozen into ice. Even in the dim light, I could follow Jackie's trail, picking her footprints out from among the knots of tracks, both animal and human, that covered the area, identifying places where Jackie had fallen and stood back up. I still thought the drugs she'd taken were going to be the reason for this trip, but I had to know what had scared her out of her mind, even if it was just a hallucination.

I reached the edge and paused, taking in the waterfalls. Usually the power impressed me, the Mohawk River dropping in a rush before being subsumed into the mellow Hudson. Today, I was amazed at how absolutely that power had been stopped. I didn't see even a trickle of water. The river glistened, and the falls had frozen in midmotion. Facets of the ice-covered river mimicked the current, tumbling over rocks and ledges, forming ice shelves in some places and waves in others. I followed the path of the river down, down. At the bottom, where the water would normally hit and form mist, were icy breaks—spikes—pointing up. As I surveyed the whole scene, my breath caught.

Impaled on one of the spikes was a girl.

CHAPTER 2

Up in town, it hadn't seemed that cold. Down here on the frozen river, the wind stung my ears, and if I spoke, a layer of frost glazed my cheeks. Thankfully, there was little reason to speak, out on the ice with the dead. Well, the dead and Norm, but he kept his own counsel.

The coroner, Norm Finch, had been on his way to 7:00 A.M. Mass at Saint Agnes when I made the call. He arrived first, and the two of us waited for the techs, paramedics, and detectives outside the crime scene perimeter I had marked out in the snow. A bear of a man, Norm didn't mind if I used him as a windbreak.

"I hate the young ones," he said.

Water froze quickly along the edge of the river, rocky steps slowing the current, quickly stagnating into ice in the winter months. To the left was Hopewell Falls, a ninety-foot wall of water that dropped abruptly. During mild winters, it didn't freeze at all. This winter hadn't been kind, and an ice shear formed where the ice from the falls was repeatedly ripped open and reformed against the stagnant shelf, creating a line of spikes that rose like dragon's teeth out of the ice-covered river. She lay on her back, left leg jackknifing under her right one, her torso arched up around one of these points.

The woman's cherry-red jacket was unzipped, revealing a T-shirt that spelled out I'M AMERICA'S SWEETHEART in rhinestones across her chest; still readable, which was surprising, considering the injury. Snow drifted against the angles of her body, blurring the line between the woman and the ice, curling around her elbow and nestling in the crook of her broken leg. Around her the frozen river rose and fell. She appeared adrift.

Her long, dark blond hair spilled out around her, whipping up when the frequent gusts hit it, its movement in sharp contrast to her absolute stillness. A wash of blood from the gash in her forehead blurred her features, but I put her age between eighteen and twenty-five. I was pretty sure she had got the head wound when she was alive, and was dead before she'd landed. Between that and where she was found, I called it in as a suspicious death. The crime scene unit would get here soon, along with the ADA and Dave Batko, our town's one and only detective. For now, I could think.

I edged along the outside of the boundary I'd set, examining the scene from every angle. I eyed the cliffs, and raised my hand. It wavered in the strong winds, and I forced it straight, charting the possible trajectory with my eye. I took a step to the left, stopped, raised my hand again, and I knew. "There."

"Hmm?" Norm said.

"There. That's where they threw her from. The cliff kind of hangs out, jutting." Norm shielded his eyes and looked to where I traced the arc in the air, following it down until it stopped where the girl lay. "It would be a clean drop from there, so she would hit the river instead of landing on the banks."

Norm shrugged. After twenty-five years handling all the bodies on this edge of the county, death held no excitement for him. He had seen everything, and knew almost all the victims, most of whom had come to peaceful ends. Norm did his job well and with little remark; little remark, except for those he thought had their heads up their asses. "Do you think the boys stopped for Egg McMuffins on their way here?"

As if summoned, the paramedics and crime scene techs crested the hill, followed by Dave Batko and—shit!—the DA, Jerry Defoe. I'd assumed, hoped, really, that it would be one of the ADAs on call. Dad had spent ten years ranting about Jerry, who always hesitated when Dad thought a conviction was a gimme. Politics being the Irish-American blood sport, Dad had made a lifelong enemy of Jerry when he failed to endorse Jerry for his DA run. When Dad had his heart attack and retired, Jerry decided to keep up the payback, aiming it at me.

In his haste, Dave kept slipping down the hill, the paramedics a few steps behind. The two techs struggled behind with cameras, lab specimen bags, and bottles. They arrived at the river's edge streaked with snow. Jerry, trailing behind, stepped only in spots that had proved secure. Jerry's gray pinstripe was snow free, but he was heavily winded.

The paramedics, eager to declare her dead and get out of the awful weather, moved quickly across to the victim. Dave lurched slowly sideways, like Frankenstein. The ice was so thick his caution was unwarranted. He had been a nose tackle in high school but, unlike a lot of other football players, hadn't aged into fat. I remembered him, an immovable object who stood on the field and let the opposing team run into him.

"Glad you called me!" he yelled cheerily. "You know how we Slavs love a good impaling!" He slowed as he got close to the young woman. His face remained impartial, his voice steady, but he swallowed three times before he spoke. "God, the vic, she's . . . destroyed."

I pointed to the spot I'd charted. "I think she was thrown from there."

"Oh, please." Jerry sneered. "I cannot believe you called me down for this. I think the brain surgeon we got here decided to drown herself in a river that had less running water than a bathtub. She should've done it in the comfort of her own home. It would have worked better, and a bathmat is easier on the knees."

"That's correct." I was furious, both for myself and for the girl, but kept my voice even. "But there's no blood from the *gaping intestinal wound,* which means she died before she hit the ground. They killed her up above, and tried to dump . . ."

From behind Jerry, Dave gestured wildly. He looked like he was miming cutting his throat, but after a second I realized he was signaling me to zip my lips. These days, it seemed I always had to give up responsibility for cases that should have been mine, and smile as I did it. I walked to where the paramedics huddled over the body, wrote down the time of death, and trained my face into the impassive expression I'd used when interrogating witnesses for the FBI. At least my training helped with something.

"So, Norm," Jerry asked, turning his back on me, "any idea who our jumper is?"

Norm watched the techs demarcate the line of broken ice that arced out from the body, doing weapons analysis on a stalagmite. He didn't look up.

"No. Ask June," he said.

I explained that we had no wallet or purse and, so far, no other way to identify the body.

"So'd those fibbies teach you anything of value when you were on their payroll?" Jerry asked.

Every time I seemed a little too uppity, Jerry would bring up my time in the FBI. As far as he was concerned, I was an overtrained snob who was a gross incompetent—really the best of all possible worlds. Too furious to do the smart thing, I argued.

"Well, they did teach me not to let myself be prejudiced in any way when approaching a case."

I was going to pay for the comment, and I didn't care. Jerry was a small man, who tried to make sure I felt smaller. He pursed his lips, ready to spew forth misery.

"You know," Dave said, not looking up from his notebook, "radios are for shit out here. Lyons, why don't you head up and brief everyone."

Dave was backing me up, in his way. Jerry couldn't abuse me if I wasn't there, so problem solved, right? But in being nice, he got the same results as Jerry did being cruel.

I skidded along the ice toward the river's edge. Above I could see Pete marking a path, orange flags flickering in the wind. At the bank, a tangle of roots from a tree washed away by the river jutted out at the river's edge, a perfect toehold. I heaved myself up.

The cold air stabbed my lungs, and I drew the air in hard to get the oxygen I needed, another reminder that I was no longer in peak condition. My ponytail caught in a branch. I yanked my head forward and wrenched free, leaving behind three long blond hairs. I heaved up until I was level with Pete, who hauled me up the last few steps, both of us panting.

I considered the tableau before me. The men down on the ice continued to investigate the case, while I stood above, useless. Their voices wafted up, indistinct. Dave and Norm huddled over the woman and seemed to be ignoring Jerry. *Good,* I thought meanly.

"Who's the girl?" Pete asked.

"I was going to ask you. Jackie didn't say?"

"Jackie didn't say much of anything. Mostly she cried. She cried a lot." Pete shook his head. Someone as low key as Pete might not understand hysterics, even if they came from a teenage girl who'd found a dead body. "I ended up calling her dad, and he came down. She calmed down some once we told her there was only one body down there. Dave had someone run them both to the station, let 'em warm up."

Not my case, I reminded myself. I pointed up along the path he'd marked. "I should go."

Pete viewed the rest of the trip down with skepticism. "Geez, I don't know why I'm doing this. You know we're going to have to airlift Jerry out of there."

"Don't worry. He'll blame it on the body. Or me. We've already ruined his day."

I crested the hill. Two techs stood at the edge of the cliff taking pictures of the footprints, confetti-colored tape marking different tracks. Traffic control was going to be *fun*: the main artery to Albany was down to one lane, turning everyone's fifteen-minute commute into an hour. A yellow bus drove past on the way to Holy Trinity, and I could see small faces pressed against every window.

Lucy! I hustled to my cruiser and pulled out the cell. Zero calls. Knowing my father, he'd probably called the station first, expecting Lorraine to have a handle on what I was doing now and what I would be doing next. He wasn't wrong. I gave a brief update to everyone and radioed Dave. No response. He'd claim he couldn't get reception, but really he was avoiding me. To be *nice*.

I slogged along the side of the road, pressing face-first against the fence every time a vehicle passed, the cold metal a relief against my anger-red cheeks. A flash popped down on the ice as the techs recorded every distorted angle of the woman's body, and then another flash at the edge of the road. Onlookers had gathered and were peering over the edge, some with camera phones. I scanned the crowd. A couple of teenage girls with toddlers perched on their slim hips pointed at the scene, and the ladies coming back from early Mass had their heads together, talking. Then there were the boys, scaling the fence and dropping, or getting pulled off by their friends, showing off. They didn't respect the dead because they had no fear of death.

Below, Norm was zipping the victim into the black body bag. The girl disappeared except for a few strands of gold hair that were caught in the zipper, blowing in the wind.

CHAPTER 3

I EXPECTED A QUIET KISS-OFF at the station. That was fine. I had done good work, the best I could, but it seemed that Dave was now fired up for me to type up my report and pulled me off traffic duty. Still, I appreciated it when Lesley put a caller on hold so she could yell, "Good job." Lesley handled dispatch and the desk during the day. Lorraine's twin, she had her sister's nasal, flat tone. The two provided a certain reassuring continuity on the other end of the radio.

The squad room was uncomfortably crowded. This was hard to accomplish. The station was built when the population was closer to fifty thousand than fifteen, and now half the room was cordoned off with paste-colored dividers to store unused desks. With high ceilings, no windows, and few warm bodies, the remaining space was usually more than enough for our shoe-leather-and-gum operation. It sometimes echoed. Today, the crowd forced me to hug one wall, avoiding the day shift guys as well as the county and state law enforcement folks who occupied most of the desks, including my own.

In the corner, Chief Donnelly briefed a couple of local reporters. He avoided giving chairs to what he affectionately called "the vultures," lest they stay too long. I caught his eye over a reporter's shoulder and he arched a formidable eyebrow at me. His version of a smile.

Halfway to the women's locker room, I ran smack into Jackie DeGroot, her hood pulled low, almost to her nose. Her father escorted her, rubbing her back gently, his calloused hand swishing softly against the nylon of her jacket.

"I need it!" she said, flouncing out of her father's reach. The swishing stopped.

"I'll buy you another one, sweetheart. A better one," he said.

"But Ray won't have my number! What if he needs me?!"

Chuck DeGroot smiled apologetically at me. I knew that smile well. I would give it to people in restaurants when Lucy was a toddler and, having dropped a French fry, mourned its loss for a long time, at top volume.

Chuck held himself close to the wall so I could slide past. This didn't leave much room. I had slim hips and no breasts to speak of, but Chuck was almost as wide as he was tall, and the buttons on his Carhartt jacket snagged on my radio. By the time we had disentangled ourselves, Jackie was already at the door.

"Dad!"

Chuck's apologies echoed down the hall, following him out of the building. I had taken two steps when I felt a sharp tug on my arm, Dave yanking me into the chief's office and slamming the door behind us. Propelled forward, I crossed the room in five steps, using the momentum to put the desk between us. Facing off with Dave, I tried to match the ferocious expression and crossed arms of the first police chief, whose portrait hung behind me. I thought I did a pretty good job, even without the muttonchops.

Dave tried to smooth down his hair, but his wiry black curls defied his efforts, sticking up in odd directions. Finally he gave up.

"Look, I need your help," Dave said.

"Really? More traffic control?"

"Lyons, you know I wasn't pushing you out. Jerry needs to be managed."

"By managing me."

"C'mon, Lyons. Things go faster when he thinks he's calling the shots."

Good intentions counted for a lot with Dave, but not with me. "He *was* calling the shots. I was out."

"No. You were first on scene, so you're in no matter what. You stay with me on this, solve this case, and you will be *made*."

"Oh, really."

Dave took a step toward me. "I got the dead girl's name."

I wasn't surprised. Dave often charmed information out of people, presenting himself as just one of the guys, and criminals often confessed much more than was good for them. People he'd jailed had invited him out for beers on more than one occasion, and he sometimes accepted with a shrug: "They paid their debt to society, and hey, who am I to turn down free beer?"

"This case, it's about to get big," Dave said. "Bigger than me. Bigger than us." He leaned forward on the desk. In the gentle light of the milk-glass pendant lamp, the circles under his eyes, always there thanks to his Ukrainian heritage, looked cavernous.

"It's Danielle Brouillette," he said finally.

"Brouillette?" Fingers of fear ran down my spine. "Like Amanda—"

"Yup. The dead girl was the daughter of our representative to Congress, Amanda Brouillette. Jerry's working with some local party bigwigs to pass the word on to higher-ups in Washington, who will be on hand when DC Metropolitan breaks the news to the congresswoman."

God, I loved Albany politics, where even a death notification was a chance to schmooze.

"And our friends in the press know something's up," Dave continued. "The Schenectady and Troy papers had someone over here before I got back, and the *Times Union* guy will be here shortly. As a bonus, the FBI will be arriving in an hour to explain to us how to do our jobs, since obviously we can't be trusted to investigate the murder of a federal official's daughter. Cluster. Fuck. We need to interview the husband fast."

"The congresswoman's husband?"

He walked around the desk, bumping shoulders with me. "You are going to love this: Danielle was married to the brother of Jackie's boyfriend."

"Ray?" I asked.

"Yeah, he has a brother, Marty. . . ." Dave's shoulders sagged, and even his mustache drooped. "Wait, how'd you know?"

"Jackie mentioned him in the hall."

Dave grimaced. "Great. Hope the papers heard it, too. What else did she say?"

"She didn't say it to me. More like *near* me. She was saying Ray wouldn't be able to contact her."

"Oh, wait till you see what Chuck gave me." He opened the phone that sat on the desk. Over his shoulder, I watched him flip through the texts. The four most recent were from Ray. The message at 6:38 A.M. read, "cnt mAk it. wiL caL l8r." At 7:37, another text: "CaL me xoxoxo," followed at 7:48 with "whr R u? CaL me." A final message at 8:45 read, "DIS shit iz feckD ^ CaL me," which Dave translated as "This shit is fucked up. Call me."

Ray sounded delightful, and I wondered if his brother was equally charming. I knew I hadn't seen Danielle's wedding notice, which I assumed would make the front page, and I had to wonder if the Brouillettes weren't thrilled with their new in-laws.

"What's the husband's name?" I asked. "Family name?"

"Jelickson." Dave spelled it out. Not one of the local family names, and generally people moved away from, not to, Hopewell

Falls. "Guy from California she married when she was doing the college girl thing out in L.A. From what Jackie says, Danielle washed up and dragged the husband back with her. I got the address of the guy, and since you are on this—"

"Until Jerry wants me off."

Dave sniffed in the air. "Aww . . . do I smell a martyr burning? I'm sorry I tried to be nice to you. I promise not to do it ever again. But you are on this, which I know would make you happy if you would stop bitching long enough to appreciate me and all I do for you."

He had a point.

CHAPTER 4

I WAS GREETED BY TWO FISTS.

While Dave drove, I downloaded the Facebook app and searched for Danielle and the Jelickson brothers. Danielle was easy to find. Her page was "friends only," but I could see her picture. The girl on the screen barely resembled the victim I'd found this morning. She was driving, the blond hair caught midflight in the draft of an open car window, more straw than gold. She seemed to be suppressing a smile, and her lips quirked up on the left. Most striking were her eyes: blue green, meeting the photographer's gaze, not watching the road. I showed the picture to Dave at a stop sign.

"She's a knockout," he said.

"How professional," I said, hunting for the Jelicksons.

"It's not like I asked her out for an ice cream soda, although to be fair, she doesn't look much like a soda kind of girl."

Marty had opted out of Facebook—I liked him already. Ray had been hard to ID at first. His user picture was two fists, with THUG

LIFE Sharpied on the fingers, the black block letters uneven. Thankfully, unlike Danielle, he didn't protect his page. His updates were an endless string of getting ready to party, partying hard, and recovering from partying, but in his photo album I hit pay dirt. There were several pictures of him shirtless, baggy jeans belted low with boxers peeking out, his scowl and crossed-arm pose undermined by his skinny arms and concave chest. There were also pictures of Harley motorcycles; colossal men, bandanaed and bearded; a hand-drawn marijuana leaf; and a string of photos of Ray with Danielle. Danielle wore a white A-line dress with draping at the neckline, the loose fabric creating a deep V, the round globes of Danielle's breasts emphasized with glitter. The shots were from a phone, the angles all from arm's length and above, the two of them flashing Vs at the camera and taking swigs out of a flask, and laughing lots.

Dave pulled up in front of a row house that looked like it belonged in Belfast, not upstate New York. One of several hundred hastily thrown up in the last century for garment workers, Danielle's house was without adornment, reflecting the grudging spirit in which it was built. Block upon block of the brick boxes listed to the left, as if trying, and failing, to escape the shadow of the mill. The random tacked-on wooden porch added to the haphazard quality of the neighborhood, and made me feel disoriented.

I balanced on Danielle's bowed porch. Dave knocked three times, and with each rap the whole structure shook. I grabbed a post, but my glove slipped, picking up a coating of paint chips. The sounds of a video game rose from inside.

"Where've you been?" a male voice called. "You forget your key?"

The door swung open. My first thought when I saw the young man in the doorway with his slate-blue shirt buttoned tight at his neck and wrists was "prison," but a security guard patch was stitched to the arm, and a tie was tucked in the breast pocket. His blunt-cut blond hair was short, almost military.

"Martin Jelickson?" Dave asked.

"Yeah?" Marty crossed his arms, and the fabric pulled tight across his chest and arms. Behind him, Ray sprawled on the couch, game controller forgotten on his lap, ignoring the sound of people dying on-screen. The boy had straight hair, a bit long, sun bleached at the tips but growing in brown. He wore a wifebeater under a too-big leather vest, which made him look even smaller.

"Martin, we're the police. I'm Detective Batko and this is Officer Lyons." I nodded at him. "May we come in—"

Marty widened his stance, filling the doorway, blocking his brother from view. "Have a warrant?"

Dave dropped his voice into a low rumble, private tones that the husband of the deceased deserved. "Martin, we are unhappy to inform you that your wife was found dead this morning."

Marty stumbled back. Dave reached out to steady him, but Marty whirled out of Dave's grasp, ready to swing. I grabbed my baton. He saw me and paused, panting as if he had run a race. His expression hardened, and he stalked over to the couch, collapsing on it.

Ray twisted toward Marty. Unsure where to put his spider-thin legs and arms, he touched the sleeve of his brother's shirt. Marty pulled away.

"Marty, man—"

"Don't." Marty clamped his mouth tight, blue eyes flashing silver.

"Are you Raymond?" I asked the boy.

He jutted out his chin. "Yeah, whatta you—" His voice broke high, childish, and a blush spread over his face and neck. "What the fuck do you want?"

"Let me get you both some water," Dave said, crossing through to the far door. With a few more inches free, I edged forward into the room. The space had too-big furniture and heat so high sweat popped on my brow. There was a veiled scent of cigarettes, as if someone had smoked outside but left the door wide open, or had quit recently, leaving years of the smell soaked into the walls and floorboards. A sagging brown couch dominated the whole far wall and encroached several inches into the kitchen doorway. Remote controls were lined up on the water-ringed table, and two books, their corners squared, sat next to them: *Alcoholics Anonymous* and AA's *Twelve Steps and Twelve Traditions. The GED for Dummies* was wedged between the couch and the recliner, and *Friday the 13th* and *Halloween* were alphabetized on the DVD stand.

Ray propped the water Dave gave him on his knee, his legs thrust wide, staring into space. Marty drank three huge gulps, pulled a coaster out of a box on the table, and put the glass down on it before speaking.

"Accident?" Marty said.

Ray jumped in. "Or some serial killer? Like Freddy Krueger?"

"Ray, we'd like to talk to your brother first," Dave said.

"C'mon, Ray." I waved to the bedroom. "I'll keep you company."

Ray didn't move until his brother nodded, yanking a Game Boy out of the overstuffed couch cushions and ambling out. I followed, stopping in the doorway. A heavily spiced perfume permeated the bedroom, not the light grassy scents popular with the girls these days, but something heady and dark. I watched Ray flop across the unmade bed, pausing to reach under his stomach and yank out a woman's leopard-print sweater, which he rolled into a ball and tucked under his head. He saw me watching and buried his face in the sweater, inhaling deeply.

Two diamond-shaped patches were sewn into the back of his vest: MC, standard fare for a motorcycle vest, and something I hadn't seen since my FBI days, 1%.

I got closer—surely I was mistaken. But no, there it was: 1%

meant outlaw gang. Strands of white thread and small tears hop-scotched across the leather, where an insignia had been sewn on and pulled off roughly. I was studying the outline when Ray looked up.

"Leave me alone. Pig."

I wanted to pin him to the bed and make him tell me his club. Maybe later. Back in the doorway, I tried to give Dave the high sign, but his back was to me and I didn't want to risk tipping off Marty.

"I have rights," Marty said. "You'll tell me what happened to Dani. You have to."

"We'll tell you," Dave said kindly. Perhaps Dave's lack of knowledge was good right now. There were no immediate threats, and he could be the sympathetic ear, and one of us on full alert was plenty.

Dave absently sat down in the recliner that jutted out from the corner, and promptly stood back up: it was covered with clothes. He settled on the couch.

"Her death was suspicious, so we're doing a full investigation," Dave said. "Marty, can you give us a breakdown of your movements since you last saw your wife?"

"Went out to eat." Marty talked fast. "We do that a lot. Our landlord cranks the radiators so we don't like to use the oven. All our plants died, you know? Plus, Dani isn't much of a cook." He unbuttoned his sleeves and pushed them up absently, revealing a flaming skull tattoo.

I knew that ink from my time on the FBI's Metro Gang Task Force. Abominations.

The Abominations were one of the big five of outlaw gangs: Hells Angels, Pagans, Outlaws, Bandidos, and them. Mostly the Abominations stuck to the West Coast. Why was he here? I scanned the room for weapons, signs, anything.

"Anyway, she *wasn't* much of a cook. Not bad—not a problem—just no practice. So we ate over at the Purple Pub. Then she dropped me off at work. Then she took the car since she was going to pick up some shit . . . a new shower curtain, I think . . . at Target." He breathed deeply, breaking up his rushed speech. "So where'd you find her?"

"What time did Danielle drop you off?" Dave asked.

Marty seemed to consider the question. "Nine thirty? Or thereabouts?"

My suburban mom radar tingled. A lie, I thought. Target closed at nine.

"And did she return from those errands?" Dave asked.

"Yeah. Ray said so. Want me to get him? Ask him?" A live wire exposed, Marty jolted into unfocused action. He barreled toward me, and I lowered my center of gravity, ready to intercept.

"Marty, you're the important one here," Dave called, patting the seat next to him. "C'mon, tell me what you did next." Reluctantly Marty returned. I checked Ray, who hadn't registered anything, only the top of his head visible.

"I'm security at the state capitol building in Albany." Marty held up the sleeve of his blue shirt with the state insignia. "Ten P.M. to six. Dani picks me up."

"Last night?" Dave asked.

"Couldn't reach her." Marty pulled out his phone and tabbed through the messages. "Last text from her was at two forty-eight."

Dave held out his hand. "Could I see?"

Marty held the phone close, hiding the screen. "You got no warrant."

"You're right. But we're trying to investigate here and, well, it would help." Marty gripped it tighter for a moment before tossing the phone in Dave's lap.

I watched Marty as Dave read the messages. He dropped his face on his forearms, but there was no shaking. No fear. His breathing was normal and his skin was a healthy golden, so no shock. Dave walked the phone to me. A few texts from Danielle, stopping at 3:00 A.M. Marty had sent more texts and called both her and his brother at five thirty and six thirty.

"You left at six?" Dave asked. "What happened to—"

"No, see that's the thing. I ended up staying late because the next guy—guy who's supposed to take over—called in. Car problems. Asked me to cover until seven, and the asshole didn't show up until ten. So I called Dani. No answer. Called Ray. He said she was having an early breakfast with her dad." His leg started jittering. "Did her father do this? He was always trying to . . ." Marty reached out, like he was searching for the word with his hand. "God *damn* him."

Dave kept the information he gave Marty about the Brouillettes vague, saying only that they were in DC.

"But he could've come back. He's got a plane. He'd do anything to keep Danielle. I mean the first time we met he tried to punch me out."

Dave tapped his pad twice. "Could you explain, Marty?"

"I was helping her move out of her apartment in L.A. She and I had become friendly. . . ."

"Where?" Dave asked.

Marty faced his bookshelf. He touched four books, and I began to think he wasn't going to answer. Finally he said, "AA. And before you start thinking all kinds of crazy stuff, you gotta know Danielle was just checking it out. She says she didn't have a problem, and I believe her."

"And you?"

Marty moved the Charles Portis so that it came after the George Pelecanos. "I did. Before." He turned to face us. "I've been clean and sober for almost four years."

"That's very cool, man," Dave said, sincerely. "You should be proud. So tell me more about your run-in with Phil."

"So me and a buddy are loading up a truck with stuff to take to her dad's plane"—he said it nonchalantly, as if everyone had their own plane—"and Danielle and her dad are going at it, him telling her all the things she's not going to do when she's back under his roof, blah, blah, blah. And he grabs her, and I put down the dresser I was holding because I got a problem when things get physical."

Generally I found that bikers liked nothing more than getting physical. I watched him closely, but didn't see any tells that he was lying.

"But Danielle," Marty continued, "she's so mad, she's blazing, and she shakes him off. She looks like she's going to punch him out, no kidding, throwing up her fists and dropping low, even though she weighed maybe a buck ten. And it's pretty clear where she learned that move—he's got the same stance. Craig is standing there with his thumbs up his ass—"

"Craig?" Dave asked.

"Yeah, Craig Madigan, the Brouillettes' pilot. He's trying to pat Danielle's shoulder, and Danielle is shaking him off so she can get a better shot at her dad. I'm ready for a punch-up, but instead of screaming at him she just backs up to me and says, sweet as pie, 'Can I go home with you?'"

Dave didn't look up from where he was writing. "And you said?"

"I said, 'Sure thing.' My stepdad was a fucking bully, too. Phil, he turns on me, comes at me swinging, but I'm bigger and got him pinned before I had to fuck him up. Craig is following Danielle around like a puppy, begging her to stay calm, but she was firing with both barrels, telling her dad to leave, telling him she didn't care if he cut her off. I let Phil go once he promised to go quietly, and suddenly it was me and Danielle against the world."

Pacing, Marty tripped over a woman's black patent-leather boot that peeked out from under the coffee table. He picked it up, found the second, and lined the pair up against the wall. His hands shook, and he knelt down so that he could get the heels square. When he spoke again his voice quavered.

"Look, I'm trying to help out here, but I don't understand how something that happened last year is more important than my wife being dead." Through clenched teeth he added, "I know how this stuff works. Tell me what happened. Where was she?"

"She was on the river," Dave said.

"Wait, what? On the river? Not in?"

"The water's frozen," I said, "and based on what I saw—"

"What you saw. You. So *you* found her." Marty seemed to see me for the first time. "What . . . did she suffer?"

"No suffering," I said, telling him how I found her. Marty flinched, so I paused, picking my words carefully. "Injuries were sustained . . . from the fall." I thought that was a diplomatic way to phrase Danielle's gutting. Since I had his attention, I asked him a question. "Tell us about her, Marty. We need to know Danielle."

Marty sputtered protests, but his desire to help, or maybe the chance to talk about his wife, won out. "She was smart. Not book smart—she hated school, and they hated her right back—but she could think fast. And she was really, really beautiful.

"She moved in with me after the blowup with her dad. We weren't a couple, at least at first. I didn't want to sleep . . . didn't want to be romantically involved . . . with someone who felt like they owed me. And she said we should wait, until we could come together as equals."

It was hard to believe any guy would take a woman in out of the kindness of his heart, especially one as pretty as Danielle. The skepticism must have shown on my face.

"No, it's true. I was trying to be of service, and it's not like I got nothing out of the deal. She let me read all the books from her classes, and she was cool when my dumbass brother"—he thumbed in the direction of the bedroom—"came down for the weekend from my folks' place. And when she couldn't make rent, she gave me her furniture. Nice stuff her dad bought her. I didn't have any, so that worked out." He ran his finger along the ripped piping of the couch cushion. "Should have brought that stuff with us when we moved out here, but she thought her folks would set us up. . . .

"Anyway, she made up a bunch of work experience and talked her way into a waitressing job at a high-end place. She offered to move out, but . . . I liked having her around. It's just . . . I'd been on my own for a while, and to have someone . . . someone like her . . . around . . . She was smart—she thought fast, faster than anyone. We were both flat busted, and we'd do free stuff, like walking around Japantown talking about all the crazy shit that came into her head. Her honesty, it made me want to tell her things. She listened." He paused, a smile on his face. "'An adventure in adulthood,' she called it. Her folks, she loved them, but she felt like everything they gave her had strings attached, and the stuff and money and experiences, it was almost too much to be grateful for. She wanted to reunite with them, not as a kid crawling back to her parents, but like a responsible adult who owned her mistakes. I got that."

"When did you get together, exactly?" Dave asked.

"Last spring. Summer is when we got together. July."

"You got married in July?" Dave asked.

"No, October. When we were moving back. She thought it would make it easier. Like her parents would have to like me and her if she married me." He clenched his jaw. "Told her it wouldn't happen, and I was right: it didn't."

"You had reservations, but you married her anyway?"

Marty shrugged. "Not about marrying her, but moving back? Yeah. But she had this way. . . . I've seen people get married where they hate each other's guts three seconds after the wedding, but her thing was that if two people . . . if the two of us . . . found each other, loved each other, we should do it."

I knew that feeling; I'd felt it one time in my life, with Kevin.

"And I wanted her"—Marty's voice cracked—"and a new life, a do-over. More than anything. But starting over in this town, when there's no jobs or nothing? Not easy. Not possible."

"Thank you, Marty. You were a huge help," Dave said. "If you could come with us—"

Marty jerked up. "Fuck. Of course. All bullshit!" he yelled. "My wife dies, gets murdered, and you take me into custody." Marty stood and paced, closer and closer to the bedroom door. "You motherfuckers should have told me I'd need a lawyer."

I took hold of his arm with two hands, spanning his biceps. He tried to shake me off, but I gripped tighter, his muscles spasming under my hand.

"No," Dave said, confused, and I regretted not clueing him in about Marty's gang affiliation. "No! You're next of kin and we need you to identify the body."

Marty deflated, but I kept alert, like when I arrived at the scene of a car accident. The debris has stopped flying, but the engine might blow at any second.

"I can do that. Ray'll need a minute."

"Ray can stay here with Officer Lyons," Dave said. I smiled benignly, like a babysitter. Marty didn't believe it for a minute, and I stopped pretending.

"Christ. Fine."

We trailed him into the bedroom. A phone was ringing, and Ray pulled one out of his pocket, talking in a low voice.

"Great. Let's hope that's not Jackie," Dave said.

Damn it. Trying to keep Marty from spinning out, I'd left Ray alone, and now look what happened. Dave's comforting pat on the back didn't help. I pointed to Ray's patch and in a low voice said, "Outlaw gang." I explained the Abominations, and the code of outlaw motorcycle clubs—destroy—while Marty explained things to Ray. Ray had no interest in what his brother was saying.

"Dad." Ray waved the phone at his brother. "He wants to talk to you."

Marty didn't answer. Walking back to the hallway, he pulled on a wool cap and coat and slung open the front door. I shivered as frozen air washed over me.

Marty marched out the door onto the porch.

"You ready?" he asked Dave.

Ray spoke quickly on the phone as he followed his brother outside.

"Marty!" Ray called.

"Enough. I can't talk." Marty crashed down the steps, not looking back.

"Dad says to keep my mouth shut."

"Dad's right," Marty called over his shoulder. "Keep your mouth shut."

"He said not to trust the fuckin' LEOs." Ray seemed oblivious to the two law enforcement officers he was insulting, barreling on. "Dad says he and Mom are going to come."

"Well, I can't *stop* them." Marty waved Dave along. "Shouldn't we go? Now?"

Dave and Marty crossed the street. As they approached the car, Marty walked to the back door, his arms behind him as if handcuffed, momentarily confused when Dave waved him around to the front. Dave made an illegal U-turn toward downtown. Marty sat with his face pressed against the glass, eyes closed, his back to Dave. Like every suspect and victim in a homicide, he'd lost all privacy.

CHAPTER 5

I STOOD AT THE FRONT door and watched as Pete, Bill—a cop who also worked the day shift—and a crime scene tech slowly walked toward the house. Between the frigid air at my front and the hot air at my back I expected a nor'easter to open up over me.

"My parents are coming," Ray said.

"Oh, good," I said blandly. "Will they be here soon?"

The tech, an Asian woman half the size of both men, struggled with three brown vinyl evidence cases, each the size of a television set. She jerked the cases close to her body when Pete offered to take one.

Ray said no, as if I'd asked a really stupid question. I wondered if he'd picked up that tone from Jackie or if she'd picked it up from him. Maybe it was what had brought them together. "They're in California."

"Really." I waved Pete, Bill, and the tech past Ray into the kitchen to start their work, pretending that I didn't care what came out of Ray's mouth.

"They're pissed." Ray snorted as he plopped down on the couch. "They're so mad."

"Mad?"

"Marty's acting like a damn fool, trusting you pigs. I'm keepin' it real, you know what I'm sayin'?"

Was this Ray keeping secrets? This was going to be easier than I thought. "Really?" I prompted.

"Oh, yeah. And Dad knows it, too."

"How old are you, Ray?"

Ray grinned. "I'm a man. Seventeen last July, free and clear in New York. School's *out*."

I flipped through their videos. Horror movie, horror movie, oh, hey, *Fight Club,* which was a bit of an existential horror movie. "Marty's your guardian?"

"Yeah, he wanted me to go to school and shit, you know, but Danielle, she told me I didn't have to, that I could take the GED, like her." He laughed and slapped his thigh. "You better believe I was done."

"Sounds like you really liked her."

I listened as Ray explained how he and Danielle had bonded during his weekend visits to L.A., both of them protecting Marty, who, the way Ray described it, was a babe in the woods. The source of Marty's newfound naïveté was apparently Alcoholics Anonymous.

"Marty went all soft when he moved to L.A." Ray shook his head. "I know they met in AA, but Danielle wasn't stupid like him—she got away from those AA culties as soon as they signed her card for the judge. She beat that rap. She and I understand each other." He smiled, and I couldn't bring myself to point out that he was still talking about Danielle in the present tense.

"Danielle get picked up for drunk driving?" I asked.

"Nah, some stuff that went down at her school." I asked him more about it, and he shrugged and said, "Stuff."

"She didn't ever go to trial or nothing," he added. "And she knew Marty was acting like a damn fool, but she married him anyway."

"Were those wedding pictures I saw on Facebook? I wasn't sure, since Marty wasn't in them."

It didn't register with Ray that I was snooping on his Facebook page. "Yeah, Dani and me needed to take the edge off with all those straights. She gave me this cool flask for being best man." He pulled the flask out of the pocket of his cargoes. It was red enamel with black flames running up the side. "So we didn't invite Marty. Plus, I can't be seen with him in public. He's shunned by the club. Don't get me wrong, I stand *tight* with my bro, but I have my rep, and the Abominations don't stand for traitors. Danielle used to say how bad it was that he walked away from everyone who had his back—his family and his brothers in the club."

I nodded at his leather vest. "That's where you got the cut. It's nice."

"It's Marty's. He don't wear it no more, so it's mine."

I heard a crash from the kitchen. I tripped in the kitchen doorway, catching my toe on two of the four layers of linoleum that were curling back at the entrance, but righted myself and surveyed the scene: Bill standing in the middle of smashed china, Pete squirming by the door that led to the backyard, and the tech, who looked ready to beat someone to death with an evidence brush. Everyone was miserable, and our surroundings didn't help. The walls were lined with green-gray cupboards that coordinated with the linoleum three layers down. The Jelicksons didn't do much housekeeping, and I could see why: this dinge was ground in.

"Problem?" I asked.

"This idiot"—the tech targeted Bill—"knocked over the dish drainer with everything in it!"

Bill gestured at plates with dried spaghetti and fifteen cups balanced precariously in the sink. "Do you think the stuff in the drainer has anything to do with what's happened in the last twenty-four hours? Or even the last week? You're overreacting."

I thought he made a good point. The tech did not. "And what's under those broken dishes, hmm? There could be footprints or other trace evidence, and you . . . you people have destroyed it." The tech's voice was rising, and if she meant to strike terror into Bill, she seemed to be succeeding.

"I bet the footprints are still there," I said. "A few pieces of glass aren't changing that."

"There's footprints in the backyard," Pete said, pointing out the window. "A bunch of them."

The tech pushed him aside. "Okay, don't go out there. I'm going to retrieve my kit and pull some imprints."

"I'm going to glance out the window," I said.

"Fine. At least *pretend* not to taint the evidence. Here—" The tech handed an evidence bag to Bill. "Sweep up the glass before you track in new dirt from the living room. Wait, I forgot the sterilized brush in the van. Don't move!" and she rushed out, pointing at each of us as if to freeze us in our spots.

"So, hey, should we go out into the backyard?" Bill asked once the tech had slammed out the front door. The three of us cracked up. "Hey, Pete, two cups were in there, right?"

"Yep. And two saucers."

"Cups and saucers?" I inspected the Fruity Pebble–crusted bowls in the sink. "How civilized. Bill, did you already bag up the garbage?"

"I did not." He snapped his white gloves theatrically and opened up the door under the sink. "Urgh. Haven't emptied this in a while." I took a step forward, my boots sticking to the unwashed floor. The garbage was much as I expected: rotten banana peels, coffee grounds, and a few dozen cigarettes, all Camels but some with crimson lipstick marks coating the tips. Two tea bags sat on top.

"What are you doing?" the tech demanded from the doorway. "God! You people! I knew I would regret not working at the crime scene."

"You claimed it was too cold down by the river," Pete said.

"I know what I said. I also didn't expect to be assigned the *clown* police. Are there another twenty-five of you ready to spill out of the cruiser?"

In the next room, Ray laughed.

I stood in front of the tech. "I'm sorry, but what's your name?" The woman was maybe a half a head shorter than my five feet ten. I was surprised. She projected tall.

"Anastasia Lin."

"Anastasia, look—"

"Call me Annie."

"Okay, Annie, we all want the best information from this crime scene, and you are definitely the authority. But you aren't the person in charge here. I am." Pete and Bill nodded. "Tell us how not to get in your way while you collect evidence, and we'll tell you how not to hinder our investigation."

"I can't do my job. It's the secondary scene, but they didn't send over nearly enough people to do this properly. We need at least two more techs—"

"Well, you have three officers here and two more in the vicinity. Give us some direction. We can all move forward faster."

"I don't suppose you could all stand very still and not touch anything?" Annie said, but with no real bite. She flapped her hands at Pete. "This one could take the bedroom. Grab something with DNA on it so we have a comparison for future sampling."

"Or any pertinent evidence," I added.

"Yes, yes. And the other one could take the bathroom. And that leaves the living room for you, so chop-chop."

"Actually, Annie, I'm going to stick with you."

"Oh, *fine*."

"Bill," I said as he shuffled past, "you take the bathroom and the bedroom, and, Pete, keep an eye on our little friend," tipping my head in the general direction of Ray.

Annie held out a camera.

"Can you use this thing?" she asked.

"I can."

"No, I mean really, can you take shots that would be usable in court?"

"I *can*."

The two of us cataloged the kitchen. Annie was pretty nice when she wasn't talking. I appreciated her methodical approach, especially since I knew both of us wanted to race to the backyard. My part of the search mostly consisted of holding open evidence bags while Annie documented what she found, but I didn't mind; so much police work—*good* police work—consisted of watching, taking careful notes, and waiting around. Lots and lots of waiting around.

My favorite assignment back when I was in the Bureau was out in the Palm Desert, conducting surveillance on a Central American gang with Ernie Aguilar and Jerzy Fernandez. Jerzy, who everyone called Bear, was a half-Polish, half-Salvadoran agent who worked deep undercover with the Maras and was assigned as the inside man on our desert operation. Discretion came naturally to him—he very rarely spoke. A big guy who always wore flannels buttoned tight around his beefy neck and wrists, he gave Ernie the nickname Tigger and threatened to duct-tape him to a wall if Ernie didn't sit down and shut up. After that, Ernie always referred to the three of us, our team, as "Lyons, and Tigger, and Bear."

I was proud of my work on that operation, which resulted in sixty-seven state and federal convictions. Of course, my work mostly consisted of listening to a surveillance feed in a tin shack and doing buys undercover as a meth-hungry tweaker. Kevin found that hilarious, suggesting I keep my one-inch-of-roots bleach job and running his finger over my fake tattoo, a heart with a dagger through it, drawn fresh daily to look faded, like the black ink had washed into my blood. I wished I could see it again, wished I'd kept some evidence of that time and the work, and Kevin's hands on me.

"Are you coming?" Annie demanded, holding the back door open.

A small deck made of untreated pine jutted over the yard, which was dominated by an old tree stump. Multiple sets of footprints tracked back and forth in the snow to the coffee-can ashtray balanced on the railing. A third set led down the steps and across the yard to the fence that bordered the alley that was a straight shot to the river. Halfway across the yard, a deep indentation ran parallel to the footprints. Someone had dropped and dragged Danielle. I could make out the sweep of long hair and where her arms had spread wide, a bleak snow angel. Blood marked the path.

"There's been some melting. Can you cast the molds?" I asked.

"Of course I can." Annie thrust out her chin, but she dropped it slightly as she pointed to the first footprint. "Just not that one. Or that one," she said, pointing to the next one. "Oh, but this one!" and Annie smiled to herself as she pulled out her molding kit.

"Annie, do you need help here?"

She rolled her eyes.

"Well, then, I'm going in and finish my interview with Ray." Annie waved me into the house. "They are sending a few more techs over from the river."

"Oh, great," Annie grumped. "More people to destroy my scene."

"Aren't they your peers?"

"Colleagues, not peers," she sniffed.

I found Pete in the living room with Ray, both with game controllers in their hands. On-screen, a man crashed his car into a pole, and several women in miniskirts pulled him from the vehicle and beat him until he was lying senseless on the ground.

"You suck at this," Ray told Pete gravely. "For serious, yo."

Pete shrugged. I waved him over to the bathroom. Bill was returning a box of tampons to the cabinet under the sink, stiff armed and with gloves.

"So?" I prompted once we'd all crowded in.

"Nothing of interest," Bill said. "I've got a brush with her hair, for DNA. Clothes were all over the floor, but Ray says they're always like that. I did brush for prints. Nothing interesting."

"How 'bout these earrings?" Pete pulled an evidence bag out of his pocket containing a pair of two-inch hoops, blinged out with stones running down the front curve. "I was straightening the afghan and found these tucked behind the couch."

"The finest zircon," Bill said.

"Not zircon." Pete waved his finger in a circle next to his own ear, indicating hoop earrings or, possibly, craziness. "I mean, assuming these are the same earrings that were out at Franklin Jewelers right before Valentine's Day, two weeks back."

"Why were you at the jewelers'?" Bill asked. "Need a new string of pearls?"

"Me and Delia were looking at rings."

Bill hooted. "Delia?! Who you have been dating for three months?"

I gave Pete a sympathetic smile and he continued. "Yeah. And shut your stupid face about that. I tried to get Delia to try these earrings on, for a joke, you know. Anyway, she wouldn't, because she was afraid she'd lose one and owe nine thousand dollars."

"Which means the pair"—I suddenly became afraid *I* would drop one—"are worth . . ."

"Eighteen thousand dollars," Pete said.

Bill and I whistled. That was the starting salary for a cop. Without overtime, of course.

"Husband better have scored," Bill said.

I held the earrings up to the window. I liked shiny objects, and they glittered brilliantly, even through the plastic.

"Your turn!" Ray yelled from the next room. We agreed that I would take Ray, Bill would start the search of the car, and Pete would go help out Annie.

"Can I have a soda?" Ray asked as I entered the living room. He glanced up, noticing the bagged earrings, and frowned. "Give those to me. They're mine." He blushed, but held his hand out insistently. "They're Danielle's. Give 'em to me."

"I wanted to ask you about them. We thought they might be evidence."

"They're not. She's rich and has rich earrings. Hand 'em over."

He had a point. These earrings could not be linked to the commission of the crime. He grabbed them out of my hand as I held them out, shoving them in a pocket of his pants and snapping the button. He stared ahead at the TV, where it was player two's turn.

I went into the kitchen and stood in front of the fridge. Orange juice and mayonnaise sat on the top shelf, some wilted greens on the second. Soda filled the bottom shelf.

"What kind do you want?" I called.

"Grape!"

I smiled as I grabbed one. Lucy would have chosen the grape, too.

When I returned he was frantically thumbing a text. He blushed when he saw me. "One of my girls," he said. "Jackie."

I handed him the drink. "Got a lot of girlfriends, Ray?"

He popped the tab and gulped down the soda, letting out a huge burp when he was done, his lips stained purple. "In California. They're way hotter there."

I picked up the controller and pushed the button. The vehicle on-screen lurched forward.

"So," I said, pulling my on-screen car over to the side of the road to make a drug deal. "You sleep out here?"

"Mos def." Ray burped again. He giggled. "You're sitting on my bed right now."

"And you're sitting in your closet." He shifted around in the nest of clothes.

The police on-screen tried to stop me, and gave chase when I gunned it onto the expressway. "When's the last time you saw Danielle?"

Ray was back in gangster mode. "I don't have to answer you. I don't have to answer anything." The leather of the vest bunched up as he crossed his arms.

"True. But I think you might have seen her last, and I assume you want to help. I mean, from what you said before, the two of you had a bond, right?"

Ray seemed to consider the question. "You're supposed to stop and beat up the hos. More points."

"Thanks for the tip"—I swerved around the group of prostitutes, crashing my car—"but I prefer not to." I sent my guy running for the pursuing cop car, grabbed the cop's gun, and commandeered his cruiser. Police business.

"So, can you tell me when you last saw her?"

"Before I went to bed, okay?"

"And no one could have come in or out the front door without waking you up?" I fired my stolen gun back at the police car that was now in pursuit.

"That's right."

"And the back door?"

"That's, that's possible." He dropped the controller and quickly grabbed it up again. "That's probably what happened, okay?"

"But she told you she was going to meet her dad for breakfast."

Ray was rocking back and forth in the tan recliner, oblivious to the fact that he was banging the wall every time. "She told me that before. I woke up, she was gone, and I figured her dad picked her up. I went out, got my brother—"

"What time did you go to bed?" I asked.

"I don't know."

"Guess."

"Midnight or one, okay?" He bobbled the game controller before bouncing it between the chair and the wall. As he scrambled to reach it, his drooping pants revealed Homer Simpson boxers peeking out from beneath the biker vest. When he sat back he was breathing hard. I let myself crash on-screen, and watched as a cop pushed my guy down on the hood of the vehicle.

Ray was still huddled up in a ball.

"Your turn," I said.

Ray picked up the controller. He hit a bunch of keys at once and the car started to fly.

"That's cool," I said.

"I know all the cheats. Wait, catch this." His speech was a charming mix of farm boy and gangster. He didn't do either well. "I'll show you how to get a really big gun, for your turn, you feel me?"

"I feel you," I said. "So the Abominations. Pretty hard core."

"They are. They're in the Bible. *Serious* badasses."

Somehow I doubted that the Bible spent much time on outlaw motorcycle gangs. "I didn't realize they were in New York."

"They're everywhere. They are legion." He swung his arms and the vehicle on-screen made a sharp right.

"Do the Abominations, or any other gangs, have anything to do with Danielle's death?"

"No!" His on-screen car skidded off the road. "No, nothing like that!"

Dave and Marty walked in. Marty moved quickly across the room, standing in front of his brother. "You okay, Ray?"

"Yes. They're stupid. They should leave." Ray threw his controller on the floor. Marty grabbed him up in what looked like a headlock but I realized was a hug. Marty's muscular arm completely encircled Ray's head. Marty whispered to Ray, Ray responding yes softly, before Marty pulled away. "Look," Marty said, "do your thing here. I'm going to trust you for now, trust you to find Danielle's killers. My folks'll be in tomorrow to pick up Ray—"

Ray's head bobbed over Marty's shoulder. "Did you talk to Dad?"

Marty didn't acknowledge Ray's question. *An indirect lie,* I thought. "—after the funeral. Which I need to plan."

"Absolutely," I said. "But I have one follow-up question for you. Ray, the earrings?"

Ray looked stricken. "What?"

"The earrings in your pocket. Can you show them to your brother?"

After fumbling with the snap, Ray slowly pulled the earrings out of his pocket and handed them to Marty.

"Was she wearing these," Marty asked, "when she . . ."

"No," I said quickly.

Marty continued to study them. Even in the dim light of the living room the earrings had a real sparkle. Finally he said, "But she wore them?"

"Ray says so."

Ray nodded. The brothers didn't look at each other.

"Well, I guess the earrings are hers. Were hers. You taking them?" I told him no. Ray looked ready to reach over and grab them back, but Marty folded the bag and gripped them tightly.

Dave and I left the brothers in the living room for some solace, if not solitude. In the backyard, we found Annie pulling a finished cast out of one of the footprints.

"Annie!" bellowed Dave, grinning broadly.

Annie jumped. "Don't do that!"

"What? We're old friends," Dave said to me. "Annie and I did great work together on that string of B&Es last spring. We understand each other."

"Shut up," Annie said.

· "Did you get a footprint?" I asked, figuring the less time spent on social niceties—did Annie have any social niceties?—the better.

"Three!" Annie pointed to two bags and a box. "And I was about to tackle that drag mark."

Dave jumped off the porch and over the footprints. "So, we're just in time."

I paused for a moment, looking at the tracks. There were footprints away from the house, but not toward. The killer had come in, or been invited, through the front door.

I jumped over the fence. Midcalf on Dave, the snow was up to my knees. We all approached the imprint, and Annie crouched down.

"Aha!" Annie pulled a hair out of the snow. I held out a bag for her. The three of us settled into a happy pattern, finding hairs, drops of blood, and even a piece of fabric. While we worked, I explained to Dave that I had suspicions about the earrings. We arrived at the edge of the fence, which was made of flat wooden planks of varying widths and in a range of shades of drab, depending on the water damage. The planks were woven unevenly through poles, and the gaps provided toeholds.

Annie hit the fence. It vibrated out three houses on each side. "She went over here!"

"No shit!" another tech yelled back. "Something got dragged, all the way down past the power plant to the river."

"Any blood?" called Dave.

"A little. Any blood over there?"

"Yes!" shouted Annie.

"Anything else?" yelled a voice.

"Don't we have radios we can use?" I asked.

Dave stood on his toes and peeked over the fence. "Radio if anything else comes up, guys. And you," he said to me, "why don't you go home for a few hours?"

I looked at my watch: noon. I felt strangely energized despite going on hour thirteen. Still, it would be good to catch a nap and play with my daughter.

"I'd like to see Lucy," I said.

"Yeah, I'm so going to owe her after this," Dave said. "Tell her she's got a trip to Hoffman's Playland coming to her when things thaw out. Roller-coaster rides and skee ball till her arm falls off."

I smiled. "She'll keep you to it, you know."

"She's a tough one . . . just like her mom." He waved me away. "Get lost, and be at the station at seven. We got a meeting with the chief, Jerry, and Special Agent Hale Bascom, our liaison from the FBI."

Hale? At the mention of his name I shivered, my guts feeling like they'd turned to ice. Hale and I hadn't seen each other in eight years. During that time, he was off being a badass in Homeland Security, so we never crossed paths professionally, and he steadily ignored the e-mails Kevin and I sent, even as Kevin's illness progressed and Kevin's desire to connect with Hale became desperate. My last e-mail to him three months before Kevin died probably got me knocked off Hale's Christmas card list: "Hale, I appreciate that you are an overgrown adolescent, but Kevin needs you right now, and there's not a lot of time. I have no idea why you stopped talking to us—or maybe it was just me—but whatever the reason you need to get over yourself and call him. Give a dying man the peace he needs."

He never called.

"June? Is Hale Bascom a problem?" Dave asked, a worried look on his face.

I waved him off, promising to be at the meeting at seven sharp.

Inside, Ray was again playing the game, hopping up and down in the chair. Marty spoke low into a phone, plugging his other ear to muffle the sounds of the game, his face like one of the granite cliffs along the Hudson.

"I know it would be good to get some help from the fellowship right now, but it's just . . . the AA meetings aren't the same. I just can't connect with the people in the rooms out here." He caught me watching. "Look, man, I appreciate you taking my call, but I gotta go. I'll call you later." He was silent for a moment. "Thanks for that. She was something else and"—his voice broke—"I don't know what I'm going to do." Listening again, he started laughing. "Fine. I'll get my ass to a meeting."

"You out?" Pete said, startling me. I'd been as lost in Marty as he was lost in his conversation.

"I'm out," I said, as Marty hung up the phone.

Marty snapped his fingers in front of his brother's face until Ray swatted him away. "We should eat."

"Marty, we need you to stay clear of the kitchen for a little while longer," I said.

Marty sighed. "And of course none of you could arrange to feed us." Before I could protest he continued, "Can we leave? Go get something?"

"McDonald's!" shouted Ray.

"No. Real food," Marty said. "Bob's Diner, up by the arterial." He turned to me. "That okay with you?"

I said yes. The two of them didn't wait, crashing down the stairs two at a time, sending the whole porch shaking as they waved away my offer of a ride. They turned right, and I headed across the street, where Bill sat in a cruiser.

He rolled down the window as I approached. "Ride? Dave's taking your car."

"What fine collaborative police work." I climbed into the passenger seat. I had plenty of room: the cruiser was new and outfitted with a laptop terminal, not that the city could afford the computers.

We made a U-turn, passing Marty and Ray as they trudged along. Marty rested his gloved hand on his brother's neck, guiding and comforting. I could see neighbors watching the brothers, some openly but most half hidden, peering from behind curtains or through gaps rubbed in the condensation from the ancient steam radiators. The neighbors didn't want to get hauled into this murder, not when they had troubles of their own. Outsiders caused *this* trouble. As long as it didn't touch them, they were fine.

CHAPTER 6

CHIEF DONNELLY'S LONG-SERVING WOODEN chair creaked under the strain of his aggrieved suffering.

"Can we get another seat in here?" he said.

"And put it where?" Jerry demanded.

Much as I hated to admit it, Jerry was right. The office comfortably sat three, and five exhausted people were a strain. I felt rested having spent the afternoon with Lucy, drifting in and out of sleep on the couch with her nestled next to me. Usually she wouldn't have sat still that long, but I let her watch SpongeBob and she was riveted.

Perched on one of the deep windowsills, I felt lucky to avoid the crush around the desk: Chief Donnelly, Jerry, Dave, and Special Agent Hale Bascom. I couldn't see Hale's face from my seat, which was fine with me. I had hoped never to see him again. I slid backward on the sill until my shoulders were pressed against the window. The chill seeped through all four layers of clothing I was wearing.

"The Brouillettes wish to have the body released," Jerry said, brandishing his cell phone, a proxy for the congresswoman and her husband. "They want to have the wake tomorrow night."

"We want to accommodate any parents of a murdered child," Dave said. "But the truth of the matter is that the coroner might need to keep the body up to forty-eight hours. A case this high profile—we can't afford to make any mistakes."

"And do these plans sit right with your partner?" Hale asked. I slid forward and faced him. The first of what no doubt would be a cadre of feds, he appeared every inch the FBI agent: fit body in a no-longer-required black suit, undoubtedly made by a tailor who'd worked with his family for six generations. Close-cropped hair, so conservative you wouldn't know he artfully applied product to tame the cowlicks. He had a handsome face, with a square jaw, and intelligent green eyes. The only thing that was out of place with his G-man image was the lips: full and currently set in a half smile.

I addressed the room. "The wake will be a good place to meet those close to her, people who might—"

"Officer Lyons," Jerry interrupted, "is assisting on an as-needed basis. Correct?" He glared at the chief.

"The Bureau would like to request," Hale said, "that she be assigned as a full-time liaison on this case." Hale's voice sounded rough, the southern accent absent, but I knew it would come out the moment Hale wanted people to trust the dumb good ol' boy.

"Any particular reason?" Jerry asked.

"I'd think it would be obvious. However, to state it plainly: With the FBI's involvement in the case, it would be good if we could have someone on your end who understands what information our agents need. And when."

Great. Hale had announced to the room that he wanted me on the case so that I could spy on my fellow officers. Dave seemed fine with my new role, nodding along with everything Hale said.

Jerry was having none of it.

"As the person responsible for prosecuting this case, I need to ensure that we have the best possible—"

Ignoring Jerry, Hale stood and motioned me up. He raised his right hand and signaled for me to do the same.

"Repeat after me," he said: "I will support and defend the Constitution of the United States against all enemies, foreign and domestic"—I found myself speaking the FBI oath from memory, sometimes speeding ahead of him—"that I will bear true faith and allegiance to the same; that I take this obligation freely, without any mental reservation or purpose of evasion; and that I will well and faithfully discharge the duties of the office on which I am about to enter." I took a deep breath. "So help me God."

Hale winked at me, and I couldn't help grinning at him. He sat back in his chair looking like he'd had his cake—as well as Jerry's—and eaten it, too.

"I've deputized Officer Lyons. Y'all can decide whatever you want, but June Lyons is currently an agent of the U.S. government."

Jerry protested. "I—"

"Guess that's settled," Chief Donnelly said. "Anything else?"

Chief Donnelly, Jerry, and Hale stayed put to discuss communication with the state authorities. Dave twisted his bulk left and then right, maneuvering out. I followed him into one of the interview rooms.

Whistling "Here I Go Again" by Whitesnake, he spread his notes across the table.

"Told you, told you," he started singing, his long legs brushing mine under the low table. I organized the interviews from the river, interviews with Marty and Ray, statements from neighbors, and crime scene information. I heard a sharp rap at the door, and in walked Hale.

The interview room was meant to inspire claustrophobia in suspects. When Hale took a seat at the table, his shoulders brushed mine. He pushed his chair back as far as he could, which was only a few inches.

I decided to quash any idea that my role would be FBI informant. "So, Agent Bascom, any questions about our findings after your earlier briefing? Any gaps?"

"Nothing you and your colleagues"—Hale nodded at Dave—"haven't already identified."

"I was assuming that if the FBI was planning to investigate, perhaps we hadn't considered an important angle. Do you think she was kidnapped?" Dave watched the two of us as if we were players at a tennis match.

"Not a kidnapping, no."

"Anything related to the charges she faced in California?" I fished.

"I'm not aware of any charges against Danielle." He rested his hand on the back of his neck. "Marty, however, is a whole other matter."

He was right. When we'd done a search on Marty's name, a series of federal charges from three years ago came up. Newspaper articles breathlessly recounted how the good looks of this "Rebel Without a Cause" hid a dangerous drug lord and killer. Marty had been facing serious time for the large-scale production and distribution of meth, and RICO charges related to being a fully patched member of the Abominations, one of the big five outlaw motorcycle gangs. In photos, Marty craned his head away from the flashes, more often than not being dragged along by a special agent.

"Our case," Hale said, "was going to send Marty away for a good long while, and take down the Abominations' whole operation."

"But your witness disappeared?" Dave asked.

Hale sighed. "Without a trace. It killed us to lose that one. We had spent years cultivating Big Dog—real name Reginald Davidson—as an informant. Finally we got everything lined up just the way we wanted and bang, he was gone. Disappeared. And when we interviewed his wife in her brand-spanking-new condo with the Mustang parked out front, she claimed he ran off with some floozy to Costa Rica."

"You think Marty killed him?" I asked.

"We had Marty locked up tight, but Marty's dear daddy is head enforcer of the Abominations, the guy that keeps the other outlaw bikers in line."

Based on the patches that had been stripped from the vest and from Marty's refusal to talk to him on the phone, I'm not sure how "dear" daddy really was, but Dave bolted up in his seat. "The head enforcer who's on his way here?" he said.

"The same one," Hale said. "But don't worry, his record is clean."

I couldn't believe it. "No arrests?"

"None. The man's far enough up the food chain that he doesn't get his hands dirty."

"So, he's under federal investigation," Dave said.

"No investigations are ongoing." Hale leaned back in his chair and stretched, rubbing the back of his neck, and something clicked.

He's lying. I heard Kevin's voice in my head as clearly as if he were still alive next to me. It was ten—no, almost fifteen, I realized— years ago, the year the three of us first met. Kevin, Hale, and I sat at a table in Shea's, the bar popular with students from Quantico. Kevin wore a powder-blue suit; I wore a white prom dress and pig's blood. I was Carrie and he was my date.

"You're a natural," Kevin said, straightening his curly blond wig. "With your cornflower blue eyes and blond hair, you were made to play Carrie."

"Plus you're pretty flat chested," Hale added. I kicked him under the table.

The night was our first outing after "the disaster." Hale winked at us, saying he would be right back, the knob attached to his belt jangling against his buckle as he bolted from the table. He was costumed as a door this Halloween, which involved little effort and the opportunity to waggle his eyebrows and invite people to "turn his knob." Right now he was talking to Missy Fenwick, a petite redhead who was tan all year round. I tried to push down the jealousy rising in me.

"Who's going to trust an FBI agent named Missy?" I knew how petty I sounded.

"Don't worry," Kevin replied, "she has a long and illustrious career of undercover work in prostitution trafficking ahead of her. As does Hale." As if sensing that we were talking about him, Hale raised his beer at us. I groaned and mashed my face against Kevin's shoulder.

"He's lying," I heard Kevin say.

"What?" I picked my head up. I rubbed some of the fake pig's blood off his suit, dabbing it with beer, but he grabbed the napkin out of my hand and pointed at Hale.

"Look. He's rubbing the back of his neck while he talks to Missy. After living with the man for two months I know. He always does that when he's lying."

Through the rest of the conversation, Hale rested his hand against the back of his tanned neck.

I couldn't help myself: "He's lying a lot. You're completely right!" A weight lifted off my shoulders and I smiled for the first time in a week. "You're so observant. Have you considered a career in law enforcement?"

Kevin laughed, and adjusted my tiara.

"You'd be surprised at what I see, June." His breath was warm against my ear.

"June, anything else?" Hale said, smiling at me as if we were old buddies.

I shook my head to clear the cobwebs. "Yeah, our victim. You folks really don't have anything, even word of mouth, about what went down at college?"

Hale sat back and rested his hand on the back of his neck, and I struggled not to belt him as he said, "I know she was expelled. I know there was a civil suit, but the terms of the suit are confidential."

"We'll ask the Brouillettes tomorrow," Dave said. "You'll be there, right?"

Hale nodded.

"Lyons and I will be stopping by the coroner's bright and early but will meet you there." Dave stood and stretched. He had a long torso, and his shirt pulled out of his pants, revealing a pale soft stomach with a trace of dark black hair. "For tonight, we're done."

I raced into the squad room, aware of Hale's light quick step behind me. The room was busy, even at 10:00 P.M. A state trooper and Pete had phones to their ears and were typing notes into computers. Both the desks and the computers were ancient: the desks were brownish gray metal, from the fifties, and were almost completely taken up by the computers, which were grayish brown plastic, from the midnineties. The congresswoman had posted a big reward for tips leading to the capture of her daughter's killer and the calls were flooding in: fifty thousand dollars was almost two years' salary for most people in the area. Lorraine was up front on dispatch, fielding phone calls. "Please hold. . . . Please hold. . . . Oh, Lesley, wait till I tell you what our lordship, Jerry, said when he came in. Hold on a sec. . . . Hopewell Falls Police Department, please hold." The radio next to Lorraine was silent, which was good; one big crime was more or less our limit, manpowerwise. I wove my way back toward the locker room, stopping in front of Pete's desk as he hung up the phone. "Anything good?" I asked. Pete gestured to three blinking lights. "Apparently our girl went to a party. *Last year.* Apparently she went to a lot of them. Also, she went to college in Los Angeles. Also, she went to high school." Pete made a show of checking his notes. "Also, grade school."

Pete's phone rang again. "Hopewell Falls Police Department Tip Line, this is Officer Sheehy, how can I help you?"

The women's locker room had been carved out of the men's in the seventies, when they first let women on the force. No more than two women served at any given time, and when I joined, there were zero; the last female officer had retired three years before I started. Lorraine and Lesley tended to keep their bags and coats up with them at dispatch, so I had the place to myself. They didn't put in a lot of effort, installing a wall of pale yellow lockers and showers. Rather than rewiring the lights, they cut out holes near the ceiling where the fluorescents ran from one locker room into the other. No one could see any part of the other room, even when standing on a chair; I had tested. You could, however, hear everything. Sometimes the guys yelled to me, but for the most part they forgot I was there, bragging about the overtime they were racking up, or complaining about their tanking house values, or bullshitting about how the River Rats did last weekend. Sometimes I heard snippets of other conversations: "How am I supposed to get past this? I love the kids, shit, I even still love Sue, but I don't know, I just don't know. . . ." "Is she sorry?" "She says she is, I think she is, but . . ." In those situations, I got my stuff together quietly and left. They wouldn't have had the conversation if they'd remembered anyone else could hear it.

I grabbed my purse, my red fuzzy hat, and my wool coat, so long it almost skimmed the ground, pulling things on as I walked out. I waved to Dave, who put his hand over the mouthpiece of his phone: "I'll pick you up at seven. And oh, no uniform tomorrow."

I made my escape. My Saturn was in the back corner of the parking lot. I spied Hale resting against an SUV, its black body and tinted windows making it a formidable vehicle, even in the dark. I was too tired for conversation, especially with him, and walked faster, but Hale intercepted me. So close, and yet so far away.

"Hold up a second, Juniper."

"The only people allowed to call me by that name are my hippie mother and the priest who baptized me. You are neither."

"Sorry, now, June. Just trying to wind you up a little."

He really didn't need to work to annoy me—he did just fine by existing.

"Look," I said, "is there something you needed? I'm ready to drop." I reached my car and yanked at the door, which was glazed over.

"Here, let me," he said. At his third tug the ice cracked, and at the fifth the door came open. Without touching him, I slid around him and turned on the ignition, jacking up the heat after the engine had run a few seconds. I reached under the seat and pulled out both my ice scrapers. "You know how to use this, southern boy?"

"Never heard about my grand New Year's of 2002 on the Great Lakes?" Hale scraped ice off my back window. "Me and Dushawne Wilkes, the two new guys, out on Lake Superior hunting terrorists who might be swimming across to bomb Detroit."

"Was that before or after you stopped talking to us?" I punctuated this with a broad sweep, and ice slithered past the elastic at my wrists.

Hale stopped scraping. "Look now, June, I'm sorry about that. And I'm more sorry than I can say about Kevin. Him being gone, it doesn't seem real."

"Maybe if you responded to a single one of his e-mails you would've known the illness, the cancer, was serious." As I moved around the car, I banged my shin on the bumper.

"Shit," I said, rubbing my leg.

Hale walked toward me, holding his hand in a defensive position as if he thought I might launch myself at him and tear his eyes out, which was a distinct possibility. "I know," he said, "how ugly my behavior with you, with Kevin—"

He stopped speaking as a woman's voice floated across the parking lot.

Last Christmas Eve you hung mistletoe
Right beside the door.
You kissed me under it every night
And said, "Please, baby, more."

Barbara Merry Christmas came toward us, her feet unsteady. No one had ever coaxed her last name out of her, so we all called her by the sixties girl-group Christmas carol she sang all year round. Sometimes she belted the song and sometimes barely whispered it, and I could tell how much heroin she had taken based on the strength of her voice.

And when Christmas passed you kept it hangin',
Kept claiming all my kisses.
By Valentine's you found another girl
And by Easter she was missus.

Today was one of Barbara's good days. Her voice was full, and you could make out the former fun girl underneath the wreckage. She was wearing her lamb's wool jacket and a fox stole around her neck, more holes than fur at this point. Her eyes were lined up to her eyebrows like Cleopatra, and she'd teased the hair on her left side into a bouffant style held in place with a rhinestone barrette. Barbara lived in a basement apartment over on Congress Street, which probably cost her, at most, two hundred a month. Her landlord said she always paid her rent in full and in cash. Barbara's name appeared on the pawnshop lists every so often, selling an engraved cigarette case or a pair of earrings. She never begged for money, but rather *performed*. My dad had tried to get Barbara into Mercy House several times in the seventies and eighties, and I'd enrolled her in a sober-living environment, but her addiction and the demons in her unruly brain always drove her back to the drugs.

Hale seemed torn between helping her and keeping his distance from the obviously crazy woman. "Can we help you, ma'am?"

Barbara didn't respond to his question—she never did—but launched into the next stanza of her song. Her hips did a little shake that was more of a wobble than a shimmy, and she raised her arm over her head and brought it down into a snap.

> *Christmas Eve's come round again,*
> *The mistletoe's up still.*
> *I've got my tree, my popcorn strings,*
> *But I don't have my angel.*

Thank God for Barbara, I thought, and gave her a few dollars just for helping me escape. Barbara clasped my hand as I handed over the money.

"Thank you!" Barbara said. "I'm so honored! Thank you!" as if I had just handed her a Grammy Award.

Hale pulled out his wallet. Barbara turned toward him, her eyelids and knees drooping, seemingly falling asleep where she stood. She was on the nod. Hale reached out, but I knew she wouldn't fall: Barbara had spent the last thirty years on the edge of tipping over but never actually dropping. While Hale's attention was on Barbara I moved around to the side of the de-iced car. Barbara startled and smiled brightly at Hale, and I ducked into the car as Barbara gave her thanks. As she shuffled off, Hale approached. The car wasn't just warm, but hot, and I rolled down my window.

"I gotta confess," Hale said as Barbara walked a series of diagonals across the lot, nodding off again near Pete's Dodge Charger, "I wasn't expecting a junkie population in Hopewell Falls."

I couldn't listen to him for another minute. "We should have no problem working together, because you're a professional and I'm a professional." Relief swept his face. "I do not, however, forgive you. Off hours, I hate your guts."

I didn't roll up my window, but snapped on my seat belt and reversed the car. I drove toward the lot's exit, fishtailing a bit before righting the vehicle. In the rearview mirror, I saw Hale standing in the same spot, and he made me want to play music too loud and drive too fast. The roads, coupled with my practical car, weren't going to allow fast, but I pushed in *London Calling,* turned the volume up to nine, rolled up my window, and closed out Hale, the case, and Hopewell Falls.

CHAPTER 7

So, EX-BOYFRIEND?" DAVE ASKED.

His question barely registered. I hunkered down in the passenger seat, reading through Norm's files before we got to the Brouillettes'. I was studying the body diagrams and Danielle's injuries noted in Norm's tight, neat script. His comments backed up what he'd told us this morning: Danielle was impaled, but prior to that suffered significant trauma. Norm had explained that she was probably struck over the head and stunned, then strangled.

"Petechiae," Norm had said, pulling up the eyelids, exposing cherry red eyes, the blue almost gone. "All the blood vessels in her eyes are blown."

Danielle was a bruised and battered sleeping beauty. I wanted to know this girl who liked to drive too fast with the window open.

"Time of death?" Dave asked.

"Based on the rigor, and taking into account her exposure to the elements, I would say that death was between two and five A.M."

"The congresswoman and the feds are pushing for something more exact," Dave said.

"I know, I know." Norm waved at his instruments, most of which were stacked in a corner because they no longer worked. "And to do that, we need new equipment. But since Albany's got gangbangers, Troy's got prostitutes, and Schenectady has drugs, our little burg, with its five murders a decade and a laughable tax base, will not be funded." He shook his head. "Anyway, rigor is more definitive."

Norm explained all the injuries, and made sure to point out the remains of a tattoo, a heart with the name Jason in it, barely visible thanks to laser surgery. Jason Byrne's name had been called into the tip line—he was her ex-boyfriend—and we would probably be interviewing him this afternoon.

"So, ex-boyfriend?" Dave repeated, his eyes trained on the road in front of him.

"Jason? I can't tell you whether he's a real suspect until the interview. I suppose it's possible."

Dave's voice was casual, but his shoulders were tense. "No, I mean Hale. There's something between the two of you. Like history."

Our one-night stand hardly qualified Hale as a boyfriend, particularly after he blew me off to pursue Missy Fenwick. I decided to hedge. "We haven't talked in years. We were NATs together—"

"Gnats?"

"NATs. New Agent Trainees, at Quantico. He and Kevin were roommates." I hoped that would end this discussion. Most people backed out of conversations about Kevin or my FBI days so fast my head spun. But Dave was trained at getting answers and kept silent until I felt forced to fill the void. "Anyway, we kind of lost touch. I was a dogsbody, going from Missouri to Nevada to L.A. to Oakland. Kevin was in the cybercrime unit in the Bay Area, and Hale did antiterrorism. We never got assigned to the same office."

Hale had been a legacy candidate at a military college—everyone in his family had attended since before the Civil War—and was communications director for the House minority whip before going to Quantico. The FBI allowed him to ever-so-slightly rebel, since his family thought the whole enterprise was in questionable taste. I had trained my whole life for law enforcement, doing admin work at the police station in high school, getting a dual master's in psychology and criminal justice. I considered the FBI a place that would let me take the good work my father did to the next level.

Kevin was the only person I knew in the Bureau who was actively recruited. He started as a black hat, hacking the Pentagon's Web site when he was fifteen. With his midwestern modesty, his sweet black curls and thick black-framed glasses—which he claimed were "punk rock" but in fact were full-on dork—he avoided suspicion. He cut his hair, ditched the glasses, and switched to being a white hat, helping identify security holes in the CDC's Web site. I preferred him with short hair and without the glasses, where you could see his dark blue eyes, like the night sky. The FBI wanted him, and he liked the idea of outsmarting the mob and pornographers. I teased him about the big firefights during the raids on the servers, but he was doing some dangerous assignments, working with Interpol to take down some Russian organized crime figures who posted pictures of teenage "exchange students" who could be bought and shipped anywhere in the world. Those mobsters weren't afraid to kill anyone, including three agents and twenty-two fifteen-year-old girls who were no longer considered "marketable."

I searched through Norm's notes for a topic that would derail Dave from this line of questioning.

"So the last time you saw Hale was when?" Dave asked as he stopped at a light. "Kevin's funeral?"

"No, before that. Kevin was disabled for a long time, and I was the loser who quit when things got to be too much—"

Dave frowned. "I, look . . ."

"—and people more or less washed their hands of us at that point. Or me, since I couldn't hack it."

"Lyons." Dave reached over and grasped my arm, sliding his hand down until his pinky rested against the skin of my wrist. "June, trust me, I know people who cut and run when things get hard. My mom did that. You didn't. You did fantastic, taking care of Kevin and Lucy. I saw you coming in, humping the job, and I couldn't even figure out how you did it."

Dave hit the gas, but he didn't remove his hand. He tended to be casual with his affection, cuffing heads and resting his hand on people's shoulders, so I felt a flash of embarrassment when I realized we were holding hands.

"Do you want off?" he asked.

"No!"

Dave pulled his hand away. My vehemence surprised him, and me, too. "No. I like the work. And hey, this could be a way to get a little of my own back, right?"

"Right. Won't bring it up again." He drummed a little song on the steering wheel. "You, me, and the G-man will have a strong and effective working relationship."

"Yeah, about that . . . ," and I explained my suspicion that Hale was holding back some of the story about Marty's father the enforcer and Danielle's adventures in Los Angeles.

That got Dave's attention. "So you think it is related to the trouble she got into in L.A.?"

"Maybe, although the Abominations shouldn't be discounted— they are nothing but trouble. Marty's patches were stripped—"

"Marty could be faking leaving the gang."

"He could, but bikers take their patches very seriously. To have them stripped, well, bikers have very clear rules that require that a brother be beaten hard; if he survives, he can leave. Marty suffered to get those off, but the gang, and his family, are a dangerous connection."

We turned onto Saint Agnes Cemetery Highway. We passed hundreds of grave sites on the left, many of the stones sunk low, the letters rubbed away. Every relative of mine for generations was buried there. My eye went to where I knew Kevin's grave was, out of sight but not out of mind, and I felt a pull: I never drove past without stopping.

We turned right, and the land opened up, the houses elevated with great views of Vermont. Ahead, I saw a bunch of parked news vans, reporters clustered on the lawn. Dave pulled up to an ungated driveway guarded by two FBI agents who waved us through, cameras pressed to our windows. We drove up to a Tudor-style home, its high painted roof beams rising three stories. Hale paced the length of its long white porch, talking on his phone. He hung up when he saw us, and knocked on the door when we were still three steps down, leaving time for hellos and little else.

The congresswoman's assistant, a young woman with a navy blue suit, fake pearls, and the faintest hint of a Bronx accent, answered the door. She was all brisk solicitousness, introducing herself as Gloria before demanding our coats and then hanging them neatly in the hall closet. Behind an oak door on our right Amanda Brouillette's voice could be heard, rising and falling like the ripples on a pond. Gloria stopped us before we could enter.

"President," she said, as though no further explanation was needed. She was right. Amanda Brouillette was often spoken of as the next candidate for vice president of the United States, so of course the president would extend his condolences.

The young woman paced back and forth in front of the door, forcing us to keep a respectful distance. This gave me quality gawking time, at least of the foyer and what I could glimpse of the living room on my left. The walls of the hallway were creamy white, on the edge of gold, and rose up three stories. I felt child-sized. Not that the house was kid friendly. The living room had furniture upholstered in almost the same goldish white as the walls, the couch sharp-lined and unblemished. In my house it would stay clean for forty minutes before Lucy did something kiddish on it: cutting orange paper into tigers or pulling the cushions onto the floor to make a fort. Above a marble fireplace was a huge painting, nineteenth century, from the Hudson River School, which contrasted rather than clashed with the furniture. I couldn't have said who the painter was but I knew the view: a bend in the river north of Rhinebeck. A designer, rather than the occupant, had chosen the tchotchkes on the side table.

I didn't fantasize about living here.

Overall, this house had a certain substance, with moldings, hardwood floors, and thick doors that separated it from the McMansions that were popping up. And were the floors heated? I wanted to take off my shoes to check, but decided that might lessen my impact as a law enforcement professional.

The study door swung open.

"Hello, hello," Amanda Brouillette said vigorously as the assistant led me and Dave to a leather couch next to the fireplace, while Hale stood behind us, keeping watch out the front window. The congresswoman wore small rimless glasses, a brown tweed skirt with a cream silk blouse, and real pearls, luminous against the freckles that dotted her pale Irish skin and offset her auburn hair. With my wool pants tucked into boots and pilled sweater, I felt like a Cossack.

Rather than sitting with us, the congresswoman took her desk chair and swung it toward us, away from the wide oak desk that faced the backyard.

"I'm sorry to keep you waiting," she said, her voice clear and calm across the several feet that separated us. "I had to take the call. You know how it is." No, I had no idea how a call from the president was. "Gloria, can you grab Phil? He's working on the heavy bag, and I bet he's lost track of time."

"He boxes," she explained, once Gloria had left. "Times, like now, when he doesn't know what to do with himself, he takes himself down to the basement to his home gym and burns off all his extra energy. You'll see, he'll be calm when he gets here."

As introductions were made, I found myself watching the door for Phil Brouillette. In my research, he came off as nothing but your friendly neighborhood multimillionaire. He'd started at what was then Canal Paper at age fifteen as a barker, removing bark and dirt from the wood pulp used in manufacturing. Soon he was overseeing the department and then all operations. Eventually he bought it from the owners, an investment firm that wanted nothing to do with running a paper company after they'd raided the cash assets and retirement accounts. He moved quickly once in charge, turning the company into a digital document management center, and making it profitable for the first time in years. While I personally admired him because the sulfuric scent of paper manufacturing no longer came off the Mohawk River, the business press praised him for his self-taught ability to drag an old manufacturing company into the information age. He was considered a revolutionary; a revolutionary who, from everything I heard, liked to punch people.

Dave had just run through the communications plan when Phil Brouillette hurtled in. He crossed the room to kiss his wife on the cheek before leaning against the desk behind her. He was a fireplug of a man, short with broad shoulders and thick forearms, perspiration stains ringing his sweatshirt—he didn't look like he had the size to take down Marty Jelickson, but the bristle of energy off him made me think he had the will. His shoes and socks were off, the soaked edges of his sweatpants skimming surprisingly fine-boned feet. He reminded me of my uncles, strong men who smelled faintly of cigars and bourbon, and who always had a quarter for a Popsicle.

The congresswoman introduced her husband and offered coffee, trying to give "another social call" mood to our interview, before getting down to business.

"First, I need assurance that everything spoken here stays in this room," she said. "My opponents would love to use this to crucify me politically, and I can't have that." Her voice was even, but she endlessly ran her finger over the edge of her glasses, as if feeling for flaws.

"We can guarantee that, ma'am," Dave said. Amanda waited, I realized, for me, and I nodded assent as well.

Satisfied, she put her glasses back on. "So, what can you tell us about the status of the investigation?"

"Yeah," said Phillip Brouillette. "Who killed our daughter?"

Dave launched into an edited version of the events of the day, leaving out details that even the parents didn't need to know. While he talked, I watched as Amanda sized us up, taking in her opponents. She met my eyes, and I felt like I was in the principal's office, which made sense: Amanda Brouillette was a former schoolteacher. Over the course of fifteen years she had leapfrogged up the ladder, going from municipal council to winning her first congressional term. In her early fifties, she had kept her red hair longer than most women in politics, pulling it into a bun when she needed to get her schoolmarm look on with her fellow representatives.

Dave got to the medical examiner's findings, explaining how, with Danielle's exposure to the elements, we could only narrow her time of death down to a broad window.

"It seems as if these days, with all the advances in science, that we ought to be able to have a more definite time estimate," Amanda Brouillette said. She looked past Dave and me to where Hale stood behind the couch. "Does the FBI have technologies that could aid in that, Special Agent Bascom?"

"Ma'am"—Hale floated forward—"with the weather factor, we couldn't do much better than the local labs."

Amanda's eyes stayed on Hale even as Dave continued sharing the details. Periodically Hale would nod, silently affirming what Dave said; I guess we were lucky that he was backing up our statements. Phil Brouillette seemed to trust Dave, which was good.

Ignored by both Brouillettes, I had a chance to study Phil. His puffy eyes and pale skin showed the wear that comes from lack of sleep, lack of food, or really, just lack. He was waiting for this to be fixed; I knew it never would be. His anger seemed uncontainable, and I thought it might make him dangerous in this interview, but his quiet, controlled wife might be the bigger threat in the long run.

Amanda Brouillette detailed her movements on the night of Danielle's murder: she was in DC for a fund-raiser, which finished after 11:00 P.M.

"And you, Mr. Brouillette?" Dave asked. "Same schedule?"

"You asking because we need alibis?" Phil Brouillette took a step forward.

The congresswoman brushed her hand against her husband, her knuckles barely skimming his leg, and he rested back on the desk like a dog brought to heel. That was a nice trick she had.

"What do you think of Marty Jelickson?" Dave asked. "Know him?"

"I know him." Phil spat out the words. "I know everything about him."

Dave widened his eyes, all innocence. "Spend a lot of time with him?"

Phil choked out a laugh. "Not if I can help it. No, when Dani brought home her 'true love' I did a complete background check, and what that security firm found, it made me sick. Those Abominations don't leave any slimy rock unturned—drug dealing, arms dealing, abusing women, prostitutes. There weren't many things the little scumbag hadn't been involved in, not that Dani listened."

"But you met him in person, before that," I said, hoping to get a little more information on the fight with Marty. "When Danielle left school."

"Can I ask where you heard about that?" the congresswoman said.

"The Jelicksons," Dave said. "But we'd appreciate hearing your version, Danielle's version."

"You know she was asked not to return for the fall semester, I assume," Amanda said.

That was a nice euphemism for *expelled,* I thought. Dave and I nodded.

"What you must understand is that Danielle was blameless. The other young woman stole some of Danielle's medication. Adderall. Danielle got a prescription in high school when we discovered that her low grades were caused by attention deficit disorder. It is, except for the rarest of exceptions, a very safe drug."

This was better than I'd hoped for. Misunderstanding my question, Amanda Brouillette was giving us all information on the incident that got Danielle thrown out of school.

"It seems that the young woman didn't know that she had a heart murmur," Amanda said.

Phil took over. "The girl had a heart attack. Almost died. Did die, for a minute or two. Thank Christ they lived close to the UCLA Medical Center."

"Your daughter and the woman lived together?"

"Nah, Danielle couldn't stand the dorms. Couldn't stand the girl, either, but wouldn't have hurt her." Amanda Brouillette winced, and I wondered if she'd make him pay for stepping out of line, but Phil didn't seem to notice.

"So how did the girl get the pills?"

"They had some classes together. She came over to study and took the bottle out of Danielle's room. And they started to go after Danielle, accusing her of all kind of stuff—drug dealing, can you believe it?" Ignoring me and Hale, he waited until Dave nodded. "Once they found out who my wife was, who I was, and how it was my name on the new law school, they went to town."

Phil described how a multimillion-dollar lawsuit had been filed.

The parents of the other girl had gotten the cops involved, who had lined up witnesses—"all liars," Phil said—claiming his daughter was a drug dealer.

"Obviously, they dropped the charges," Amanda Brouillette said. "There was some confusion early on, but once the police realized that it was a prescription drug overdose, and that Dani had valid scripts from her New York, DC, and California doctors, they were happy to drop the case."

Interesting. Even if they were all legal, Danielle had access to a lot of Adderall and might have seen a way to make some extra cash.

Phil Brouillette picked up the story from his wife. "And the girl's family dropped the case once they received some cash, but it took my lawyer forever to get them to settle. All sorts of shenanigans regarding the timing of the payout and their pack of witnesses, college students who wanted to generate drama. The university backed up the little shit-stirrers. They wanted to pay us back for when we threatened to sue."

"What for?" Dave asked. "Problems with construction?"

"Nah. Some sleazoid graduate TA tried to get Dani to sleep with him in exchange for an A. She turned him down and he gave her a C. He claimed she seduced him, but we had texts from the pervert, and between that and Dani's testimony, he got kicked out of his graduate program. His wife divorced him, too, after we showed her the texts."

"Obviously, the university wanted to avoid controversy," Amanda Brouillette said. "And though neither situation was Danielle's fault, they were not willing to give her the benefit of the doubt, especially with a student hospitalized."

"My lawyer was pretty good," Phil said, "got the family to settle for a quarter of what they asked, but he fucked up one thing. Well, two things. The school still kicked her out, and, worse, he had Danielle go to AA meetings so if this whole thing went to trial, she'd look penitent."

"And there was no need," said the congresswoman. "Danielle never had a substance abuse problem."

"But she got to hang out with the dregs of humanity, and met that cretin of a husband at one of the meetings she went to. And when we were getting ready to move her back and I asked her if she knew any men who could help load up the furniture—not one of those college boys, but someone who could work—she came up with Marty and his friends." Phil jutted out his chin. "He told you what happened?"

"He told us," Dave said.

"Yeah, well, I was tired, tired from moving, tired from trying to manage my business from across the country, tired from the whole thing, and with Danielle screaming blue murder about how I was beating her, I decided to let her go, cool her jets. I certainly didn't expect her to show up six months later married to the mover."

"Her marriage was a surprise to you?"

"We lost touch for a while," said Amanda. "She got a new cell phone number, and it took a bit of time for me to track her down. By the time I did, well, she barely mentioned Marty, honestly. She told me she missed me. She said she wanted to come home, and I told her she would always be welcome."

"And that was when?" Dave asked.

"October," she said. "And she was back two weeks later."

"Husband in tow, and she expected us to take him in with open arms. No way was I letting him and his deadbeat brother in the door." Phil corralled himself, but his anger was seeping through the seams. Hale moved right up with us, perching on the arm of our couch. "Danielle was angry. My little girl wasn't afraid to speak up." Phil Brouillette paused, his hand on his forehead like he was pushing the information out. "That husband was just cold, though. He just left, pulled her out the door behind him without a word. A couple of days later he sent us a wedding album and a letter, a letter on paper, telling us he would do everything he could to make her happy."

Interesting. The picture of Marty I was getting didn't quite jell with his background as a hardened biker. I had no doubt that he had the rage and skill to hurt someone, even kill someone, but it seemed to be paired with an old-fashioned courtliness. He used coasters, took care of those he loved, and sent letters—on paper no less—to his true love's parents.

"Do you have a copy of that letter?" I asked.

"No, I was pissed off. I burned it."

"And the album?"

"Threw it out," Phil said. He balled his hands into fists. "Last pictures of our daughter, alive, and we threw them out."

"No," Amanda said. "We didn't."

She walked over to an oak filing cabinet, the fine wood giving off a warm glow. I would have identified it as an antique until she ran her finger along the edge and punched a security code into some well-hidden keys, releasing the drawer.

She handed us the cream satin album. I slid next to Dave and we flipped through the pages together: Marty and Danielle standing under the entrance to a white tent garlanded with flowers, Marty in a tux and Danielle wearing the same dress that I had seen on Ray's Facebook page. I could see the expensive detail in the fabric and the stitching of her gown, and with the camera not shooting down her cleavage and no flask in her hand, she looked almost demure.

The rest of the shots depicted a pretty traditional wedding, albeit a DIY version. Supermarket flowers stuck in mason jars with ribbon tied around them dotted the tables, and Christmas lights gave the tent a gentle glow. There was no bar, but the food looked amazing: a salad garnished with brightly colored edible flowers, and shrimp skewers resting on rice studded with almonds.

"Looks like they spent their whole budget on food," commented Dave.

"Or her dress," I said. "I didn't see the gown in her closet."

"She returned it," Phil Brouillette said. While we were studying the photos he had moved around the back of the couch, looking at the album over our shoulders. "She bragged to me about it, how she took the seventeen-thousand-dollar dress for one day and returned it, like I would be proud of her for swindling the dress shop."

"And Marty's friend—his sponsor, Marty said in the note—he was a caterer, and did the food for free," Amanda added quickly. "Alcohol was not served."

Thus Danielle and Ray sharing a flask out back. We flipped ahead, to shots of people dancing, the bridesmaids clutching matching sequined bags, Marty with his groomsmen, including Ray, holding out the Leatherman tools that had been their gifts. There was a photo of Ray, his grin sloppy, spinning a white garter on his finger. In the final picture Danielle leaned against Marty's chest, his arms wrapped tightly around her tiny waist, face half hidden in the cascade of her golden hair. They were alone on the dance floor, saying good-bye to their guests.

As we flipped the album closed, Phil Brouillette took it from Dave's hands and walked back to his wife, placing the album behind them. We agreed to let them keep it, for now.

"So you haven't talked to your daughter since then?" Dave asked.

"I saw her on the street a few times," Phil said. "She was a cashier over at the pharmacy. She thought we'd be embarrassed seeing her working for a living." Phil shook his head. "She didn't last. She claimed they didn't have the money to *pay* her. I gave everyone a work ethic except my *daughter*. She fucked everything—"

Amanda Brouillette talked over her husband. "The boy she dated in high school. His parents own the pharmacy."

"Jason Byrne," Hale said.

"Yes." Amanda Brouillette pointed out the west window. "His family lives on the next property over. Good people."

"Yeah, sure, Jason Byrne," Phil said. "That kid's got hustle— you gotta when you're broke. I throw him a few bucks to come over, check on the place when we're in DC."

"Congresswoman, when was the last time *you* saw your daughter?" Dave asked.

"Eight days ago, over at the capitol. Marty worked there as a security guard." Amanda removed her glasses and put them on the desk next to her. Seconds ticked by. "*I* got him the job." The congresswoman picked at an invisible piece of lint on her skirt, waiting for her husband to react. When he didn't she continued. "It had benefits for both of them, medical, dental, everything they needed, so if something happened. . . . That morning I was meeting the state senate majority whip for a strategy breakfast. I had to run to the meeting, so I invited them to dinner." Again she paused, giving her husband a chance to blow. "Danielle made me promise to make my lasagna, but . . . they never showed."

All was silent. Phil traced the rug pattern with his toe.

"That sounds nice," he said finally.

"It does." Amanda reached up, and he took her hand in both of his, cradling it.

Dave flipped back and forth between pages of his notebook, letting the Brouillettes collect themselves. Finally he said, "So do the two of you have any enemies? Any threats come in?"

The congresswoman let go of her husband's hand, reached behind her, and grabbed a stack of papers. She assumed that her daughter's death was about her, which, I realized, it very well might be. "I had Gloria pull together the kook list for you. These people are more than concerned constituents. Agent Bascom, is the FBI aware of any viable threats?"

Hale shook his head, a sharp no. "But we are going over additional intelligence."

"As for my enemies," Phillip Brouillette said, "I'm really goddamned rich. Someone always wants to kill me. I'll call our head of HR, see if we have any pissed-off ex-employees. The crazy environmentalist groups have lain off us since we got out of the paper production business."

"And your daughter?" I asked. "Any enemies?"

"Oh, no," Amanda said. "In high school there were always girls with grudges—they were either best friends or mortal enemies." She dropped her voice, as if sharing a secret. "Danielle was a beautiful girl, you know. But honestly, she was a little young to have provoked serious enemies."

"Except she's dead," Phil said. He pointed his finger at Dave and me. "Thanks to that husband of hers. Why aren't you interviewing him?"

"We did," Dave said.

"Yes, sir," Hale said before I could back up Dave. "He's a person of interest."

"But not an active suspect," I quickly added. The last thing we needed was Phil Brouillette going vigilante. "Can we see her room?"

"It's empty," Phil said.

"There may still be something interesting there, we—"

"As I said, it's empty. I had movers take everything from the room and drop it at their apartment." He raised one arm, as if to make a point, and then a second, as if in supplication. "Look, are we done? We've dragged out all our dirty laundry. Just . . . just, she wasn't a bad girl. Not really. She pushed. She always pushed. But she would have turned things around."

The congresswoman nodded in agreement, and sat forward on her chair. I sat forward as well, trying to bridge the gap across the broad fine-weave carpet.

"She was such a bright, lovable little girl. She would hold teas for me and her stuffed animals, and then play school next to me while I prepared lesson plans, teaching me math and giving me pop quizzes." I smiled at this, as Lucy was currently in a similar phase.

Amanda continued: "She said she wanted to be just like me. Then she hit her teens, and it seemed like nothing was going to make her happy. Maybe I could have paid more attention—I was in the middle of my first national campaign and a little distracted—but

I thought, 'Oh, right. Sixteen.' I remembered breaking little rules, rebelling against my parents, and I guess I missed the point when she crossed the line." Her voice broke, and she hesitated. When she spoke again, she had her politician's voice back. "But she would have turned things around. She never had the chance."

CHAPTER 8

I DIDN'T WANT TO GO IN. I wasn't cold on the porch of McKellison's Funeral Home—it's always warmer when it snows—and the less time I spent at wakes, the better. Kevin's funeral had been more than enough for this lifetime. Mourners arrived: local politicians and a few from the state level, employees from Brouillette Paper Company, and any number of Hopewell Falls residents. My second grade teacher from Saint Patrick's stopped and chatted with me. It turned out she'd taught Phillip Brouillette, too. Hale joined me, and I introduced him to the people who paused to talk. Nobody seemed to realize that I was there on official business, and their glances at Hale probably had more to do with thinking he was my new boyfriend than that he was FBI.

"How 'bout we head inside?" Hale asked, clapping his hands together. Hale's cashmere coat and lined leather gloves had to be warm, but his head was bare, and he was wearing his wingtip shoes. Even the most proper of church ladies and obsequious political toadies knew enough to wear boots in this weather.

Four racks were set up for coats, and the funeral home folks wheeled out a fifth to handle the overflow. The mortuary was a converted house, built over a hundred years earlier for one of the lace-curtain Irish families who managed to clamber out of the mills and make a place for themselves.

People still liked the big houses—the Brouillettes' place proved that—but now the functions were different: instead of sitting rooms and bedrooms, the Brouillettes had offices and home gyms. Still, the size of the Brouillettes' house meant that it had been early afternoon before we completed our search.

Dave and Jerry arrived at McKellison's together. A tired Dave dragged, but Jerry's eager step offset his grave expression: he loved everything this case was doing for his career. Jerry beelined for the Brouillettes. He didn't get far. The condolence line spilled out of the room and snaked into the opposite sitting room and toward the back door. In addition to the friends and neighbors, the lobbyists were there, wanting to make a good impression on the congresswoman. The guy from the dairy industry was first in line. He'd arrived at noon.

I joined the line with Hale and Dave, several people removed from Jerry. Phil wore a gray suit, and in the face of people's grief, he stared at the ground or over their shoulders. Amanda wore a black dress with a small circle pin glinting on her lapel. She pulled people in, accepting their condolences with a warm handshake, never breaking eye contact. Most people made a brief stop in front of Danielle's open casket, and from back in the line she appeared un-injured: She wore a pink dress and artfully applied makeup, making her look young and alive. They'd styled her hair to cover the bruise on her head, and she held a rosary in her left hand. If I hadn't seen the earlier wreckage I would have thought her death had been nat-ural and peaceful.

Dave nudged me, tilting his head to the corner of the room

where Marty and Ray sat. Marty wore a suit, and I was very aware that underneath his navy wool and cuff links a flaming skull was traced on his arm. Ray was again playing dress-up in his brother's clothes: belted chinos, a white shirt that hung halfway down his shoulders, and a tie. In fact, Ray wasn't that small—he was only a few inches shorter than his brother—but he had no substance to him. His body was shooting up, but soon age would settle weight on his frame, bulking him up with muscle or fat. Marty had that solidity—all muscle—and I don't know whether it was his years in the Abominations or Danielle's death that gave him a heaviness of spirit that tethered him tightly to the ground. I bet Marty believed that everything in life had to be hard. I felt the same way after Kevin died, but it seemed an unfair burden for a twenty-five-year-old.

No one talked to the brothers. No one got within three chairs of them. Ray stared at the crowd, his mouth set in a straight line like Lucy figuring out one of her spelling problems. When Ray saw us he elbowed Marty, who nodded and returned to gazing out the window.

Dave, Hale, and I stood at the front of the line now. Dave shook Amanda's hand, and I reached out to Phil.

"I'm here in an official capacity," I said, "but I wanted to say how sorry I am about your daughter, personally."

Phillip nodded, never breaking eye contact with my wrist. I imagine I looked the same after Kevin died. A banking lobbyist shouldered himself in front of Amanda, and we found ourselves pushed in front of the casket.

Hale nodded toward the reception area, where a few hundred people congregated. "I'm going to the reception room, keep an eye on things."

"I'll go with you," Dave said, and then more quietly, "Keep an eye on things in here, okay?"

I made a quick sign of the cross, helpless not to with my Catholic childhood, and approached Marty. A formal acknowledgment of his grief seemed appropriate, even if the rest of the room shunned him. I extended my hand.

"I'm very sorry for your loss. Do you mind if I sit with you?" I eased into the chair next to him. "Have you spoken to Danielle's family?"

We both winced; Marty was Danielle's family, too. We looked to where Danielle's parents stood. Amanda was leaning in, listening to an older woman, but Phil stared straight at us. Marty twisted his body, cocked sideways, his hip lifted off the chair, which gave him the comfort of not accidentally making eye contact with Phil. "Yeah. I offered to bring her favorite dress, for her to be buried in. A short black number. With the coffin, who would have known she was showing some leg?" His mouth quirked up, a half smile. "And I know that somewhere, it would have made her laugh. They said no." Thus the pink dress, I thought. Marty continued. "Tried to pay for the funeral. Said no to that, too, said they'd arranged every-thing, and when I contacted some other funeral homes . . ."—Marty slumped down in the chair and extended his long legs, almost trip-ping a banking industry lobbyist—"no one would take my money."

Ray hurried forward to the mourners' line, almost pushing Susie—as always in her Dunkin' Donuts uniform—into the white carnations of one of the two dozen or so wreaths that lined the walls. Jackie DeGroot and her father stood patiently, and I expected Ray to rush his girlfriend. She was dressed in black, but it was a sort of cocktail dress, sequined gladiolas stitched to the front. Tears welled up in her eyes as Ray approached a young man instead of her, slapping his back and calling him "bro." The man, too, was dressed all in black: a button-down shirt, black pants, motorcycle boots, and a pendant on black leather laced around his neck. He was six feet four or five and towered over most everyone in the room.

"Awesome shit, son." Ray's inappropriate comment carried over the crowd.

Marty watched the two of them through squinted eyes.

"I told him how to behave at a funeral. No yelling, swearing, all that sh——, er, stuff. We were raised in a barn." Marty made a fist, three joints loudly popping. I must have looked alarmed because he apologized. "This weather, old injury starts aching."

"Are your parents here? Your brother said they were coming in today."

"No, the snow in Chicago . . . their plane got canceled. Tomorrow."

"Did they know Danielle?" I asked.

"Yeah, she took herself up there to meet them a week before we left the coast, even though I told her why I cut them out of my life." He stared at Danielle in the casket, as if willing her to explain herself. "She called me from Soledad, told me she went up there to thank them for giving me to her, like they had anything to do with the good. The good stuff, that's all AA. Anyway, it worked out, because she managed to talk them into letting me take Ray with me, which was a . . ." From across the room Ray barked out a laugh, and the room fell quiet. Marty frowned, dropping his voice, and I leaned in close to hear the rest. "Well, they must have liked her, because they didn't *kill* her."

Another young man wedged in the door, blond curly hair and cheeks flushed bright red from the cold. Marty waved. The line of mourners edged forward, and I saw Denise Byrne from the pharmacy. Denise was the same height and shared the man's same fair coloring, although her blond was so bright it had to have come from a box. I would bet that the young man was Danielle's ex-boyfriend Jason.

I had met Denise during Kevin's illness, I couldn't say exactly when. I felt like I visited the pharmacy twice a day back then, picking up medication for the cancer symptoms or, more often, for the effects of the cancer treatment. Denise and her husband were always behind the counter—Byrne's was a mom-and-pop operation running three generations back. Several times she dropped off prescriptions at my house that the doctors had called in late.

"I can't believe you did this. You're a lifesaver," I said the first night I found her at my door.

"Us little guys need to do something to compete with the big chains," Denise said, spinning away before I could get out a "Thanks."

I hadn't discovered until recently that Denise's own husband was sick.

"Oh, he's real bad now," Lorraine told me one day, when I mentioned the favor. "The Lou Gehrig's disease is finishing him fast. I don't know how she does it all—him sick, and having to do all the work at the pharmacy on her own, especially when the chains are trying to eat her lunch. Her son helps her—he's a sweet kid—and he's always cheery, but me, I'd be more like you were."

I was curious. "What was I like?"

"Closed off. Which I don't blame you. I'd be a bitch on wheels if I was going through so much stress. I mean, not that you were a bitch."

"I'm kind of a bitch now."

"Yeah, but no one can stand those chipper types, really." She lowered her voice. "I mean, like Denise. She's sweet, too sweet, and while everyone goes through hard stuff different, we all know Denise's 'Fine!'s' are a lie. But she's tough—it's not that she would ever ask for help." Lorraine paused, head tilted, her shiny coral lips pursed, and considered. "Maybe she's not so different from you."

Ray and the young man in black returned, Ray pointing at me and whispering, "Cop." The young man looked to be about Marty's age, but his calculated swagger made him seem as immature as seventeen-year-old Ray. Jackie tripped along in their wake in too-high heels, skipping her last regards to Danielle.

"Hey, man," the young man said, putting out his hand. Marty

ignored it, reaching around to pull Jackie into the center of the group, thanking her for coming and telling her how pretty she looked.

"Jackie DeGroot, this is Officer June Lyons of the HFPD," Marty said, all formality. Jackie didn't acknowledge me, adjusting her dress to keep the satin from bunching at the waist, with little luck—the dress was about a size too small.

"And this guy is Craig Madigan"—Marty rolled his eyes at me—"the Brouillettes' pilot."

"Not their pilot." Craig shook my hand, holding it a little too long. "I own my own airplane charter company."

Marty snorted. "Your dad owns a charter company, you mean."

Craig stood there, frozen, and Ray jumped in. "Hey, bro. Marty. We're going to take off for a while, go drown our sorrows at Craig's place. Can I go?"

Marty seemed to consider Ray's request. Ray was holding his breath, and surprisingly, Craig and Jackie were, too. Finally Marty nodded.

"All right," he said. "You're going home with Mom and Zeke in a few days, so I guess you can have a last party with his friends."

Tears welled up in Jackie's eyes, but Ray hopped from foot to foot, excited, before catching himself and returning both feet to the ground. "You wanna come, bro?"

"Thought I should stick around," Marty said through gritted teeth, "it being my wife's funeral and all."

The sarcasm was lost on Ray. "Yeah, man, that's cool. Maybe next time." Ray, Craig, and Jackie were in the doorway before Marty called to his brother.

"You got your phone?"

Ray patted all five pockets of his cargo pants before nodding.

"Pick up if I call," Marty said. Ray waved a yes as he walked out the door.

Marty shook his head. "Too late for me to correct his manners."

"Ray seemed wired into his phone when I met with him. I'm surprised you had to remind him."

"I check all his messages, so he leaves the phone home half the time. Probably figures there's no point in texting if he can't be a jackass." At the last word several people shot us glares, and Marty lowered his voice. "Sorry."

I wanted to ask him why he was checking his brother's phone but was afraid anything I said to him might be considered an interrogation, which he really didn't need right now. The smell of carnation wreaths was thick in the room, coating my nose and mouth. Carnations were everywhere when Kevin died. I wanted to spit.

Marty stood up as Jason Byrne approached.

"I'm sorry for your loss, Marty," Jason said, and shook Marty's hand. Jason was wearing a light blue shirt and chinos, shiny with overwashing, a crease ironed into them. "Are you doing okay?"

Marty shook his head at the crowds. "Things are kind of crazy."

"I left some coffee cake my mom made this morning with your brother. Did he give it to you? I know it's kind of stupid, but Mom said we can't afford to send flowers, like I wanted. And I know you have people dropping in on you, and you don't want to have to worry about feeding them, and it's what you do when someone dies. I think." At this he stopped, having talked himself out.

"Well, I'm not much of a flower guy, so your cake, it was great— sorry for not thanking you before. The only people visiting are the cops, like Officer Lyons here." He flicked a thumb at me, crooked from an old injury. "She'll probably want to ask you a few questions."

"Of course. I'm happy to help."

I stood up. "How about after the wake? We don't need to discuss police business here."

He paused, darting a look at Marty. "I'm really sorry, I have to go back to the pharmacy after this. But we close at eight P.M., so I could talk to you after. Unless it's an emergency." His words slowed, and finally halted. He cocked his head. "Which I guess it is."

As he gave me his number, Denise Byrne approached, her arms overflowing with two matching down jackets, a trail of feathers leaking from a ripped seam. "Jason, sweetie, I'm afraid you've taken more than five minutes. Every second here is a second the pharmacy might lose a customer."

Little chance of that when every person in Hopewell Falls was here. "Denise, sorry for holding him up. Will you be available at eight as well? And your husband?"

"My husband?" she said, and Jason cringed. "He's sick these days, and doesn't really talk anymore."

"He can *talk*, Mom." Jason sounded insulted.

"I know, sweetheart. But do you really think it's a good idea, when it wears your dad out so much?" She reached out, ready to smooth back her son's hair, but at his glare her hand dropped. "But of course we don't mind, and we want to help out the investigation any way we can. Tomorrow too late?"

"We can come before work, as early as you'd like."

"Come at seven. Jason, sweetie, let's get going." Jason hustled out the door, brushing past Hale.

Marty touched Denise Byrne's arm, and then quickly pulled away.

"Ma'am"—Marty's proper streak was in full effect—"thank you for the coffee cake. It was delicious. I appreciate it."

"Oh, I didn't realize—I thought it was going to our neighbors, the Brouillettes. But I'm *so glad* you enjoyed it." She slipped from his grip and left the room.

"What am I doing here?" Marty whispered, so quietly only I could hear. He took in the suit he was wearing, the wall of wreaths, and the crowds. His eyes settled on Danielle, and for the first time I saw tears. Before I could reach him he clomped out. Seconds later, the back door hit the wall with a bang.

I twisted through the crowds to the hallway. Dave and Hale were writing down names from the guest book.

"Subtle, guys."

"Oh, you mean like how you provoked the bereaved husband into storming out?" Dave asked. "Nice form, by the way. I decided to stay well out of it once I saw you had things so under control."

A funeral home employee was plowing as I left. He was being thoughtful and discreet, making sure none of the snow blocked in any of the parked cars. The drive home wasn't bad, provided I kept the speed to ten miles an hour.

I was reaching for the lockbox when my daughter ran to the entryway. I quickly stowed my gun. With two parents in the FBI, Lucy had received the gun safety lecture early on, but I wanted to keep her curiosity to a minimum. To date, she'd only noticed my gun once, remarking how small my Hopewell Falls Glock was compared with the Sig Sauer I carried in the FBI.

"I'm the teacher," Lucy called, waving two sheets of paper. She was wearing pink striped tights under a purple striped jumper, with a lime green belt tied around. Dad had lost the clothes battle again.

"Oh, really." I sat down on the steps that led upstairs to wrestle my boots off.

"You have a quiz today," and she showed me the handwritten test that consisted of a series of math problems written in Lucy's six-year-old writing, the ink purple and sparkly.

"Okay. Can I eat dinner first?"

"No!" Lucy yelled and grinned and, holding on to the banister, swept out in wide circles.

"No? But won't Grandpa be lonely?"

"No! It's not Grandpa. He's a student." Lucy was now swinging closer, and making dramatic *whoa-oa!* sounds. As I stood up, my daughter careened into me, grabbing hold of my legs with an *oomph*. With Lucy still attached to my front, I backward frog-marched her into the kitchen, where my father was at the table reading a paper, spaghetti and salad—the greens a pleasant surprise—on the table. He had used my lusterware plates. When I'd moved in, I'd brought out the boxes of Depression-era china I'd collected since I was a teenager. I only had a chance to unpack one box before Kevin's illness worsened and my attention moved back to him, but my dad used the dishes constantly.

Now he peered at me over the top of his glasses. "How'd the wake go? Was every politico in the state there sucking up to our future vice president?"

"More or less."

"I thought I felt a hot wind coming from the direction of the funeral home." My father put down the paper. "And I assume Jerry shook hands with every one of them, right?"

"At least it kept him busy," I said. "He's more of a menace when he thinks he's 'leading' the 'investigation.'"

I inhaled the smell of dinner. Real Italians would sneer at the sauce, and my father still hadn't figured out al dente, but this was the food I grew up with, so I thought it was perfect. I wanted to dive right in, but remembered my manners. "How was your day?"

"Good, good," he answered. He waved a glass of red wine at me. "Done for the night? Want one?"

"Half a glass would be good. I'll slide out of my chair with more."

Lucy chose to ignore dinner. "Mom, Grandpa, take your test."

"Okay, but you have to eat one meatball while we do it," I said. I read through the test, widening my eyes. "Wait, these questions are hard!"

Lucy cackled.

THE REST OF THE evening was peaceful. My father and I took Lucy's tests. He curled his arm around three sides of the paper, guarding his answers. Dad had lost fifty pounds since his heart attack, but he wasn't a small man. He made a big show of cheating off me, going so far as to copy my name in the top space of the sheet. Lucy gave us both a stern lecture on the evils of cheating after correcting our many intentional mistakes.

"I guess that's the trade-off with a girl. Fewer fart jokes, but having someone around who knows what's best for you, and really, really enjoys explaining it to you," he said, pulling the plate I had cleared from the table out of my hands.

"Get outta here," he added.

After working twelve hours, I didn't take much convincing. "Twist my arm."

Lucy and I played poker. I liked cards, liked watching Lucy's reactions to her hand, dark blue eyes peeking out from under her straight black bangs. At bedtime I walked her upstairs to what was my old room. On the day Lucy, Kevin, and I moved in, I discovered that light purple paint had replaced the pale blue walls of my teen-age years, and a big canopy bed now sprawled in the center. More jarring, Dad had moved into my sister Jenny's old room, leaving the master bedroom for Kevin and me.

"Creepy," I said, the first night.

"What?" Kevin said. "It's not like it's their bed."

I reached across and punched him in the arm.

"Very nice. Beat up the guy with cancer."

The room had enough space for a bed and a few favorite things, and I stayed there even after Kevin died. I moved his clothes down into the garage with the rest of our belongings from California, in storage until the day Lucy and I could move out, which considering my finances and the cost of child care, might be never.

I rubbed Lucy's back under the glow of the night-light, making nonsense talk that soothed her into sleep. I took a nice warm shower after that, and wandered downstairs in sweats. Dad was watching some sort of police procedural. He especially enjoyed pointing out everything they did wrong. During the commercial breaks I described the case.

"I don't know," I said. "This doesn't feel like a situation of domestic abuse carried too far. I mean, it might be, I'm not saying Jerry's wrong—"

"Why wouldn't you? He's a moron."

"That's true. But I think Ray's lying about being asleep, and she either had some cash or was playing with someone who had some cash. You should have seen the earrings. . . ."

My cell phone started buzzing. At the same time, the home phone rang. I took the cell, while Dad took the landline.

"June, it's Dave. There's a dead body in the congresswoman's backyard. Hale's boys are securing the scene, but we'll need to get out there fast." The last words were muffled, and it sounded like he was dressing and talking on the phone at the same time.

Dad came in carrying the phone. "It's someone named Hale Bascom. He says it's an emergency."

I coordinated with both of them, one in each ear.

I ARRIVED AT THE Brouillettes' house almost an hour later. The snow was falling faster than the plows could clear it, and I crept along at five miles per hour until I came up on an accident. I stopped. It was Hale.

"God, lucky break," he said as he climbed into the car. He was again underdressed for the weather. I would give him the address for the Army & Navy Surplus in the morning so he could get some real boots, or the Eastern Mountain Sports at the mall if he wanted something stylish. In the interim I cranked the heat.

I concentrated on the road while Hale gave me more details: One of Hale's agents was patrolling the Brouillettes' land. The agent turned on the barnyard lights and that's when he saw the body, an unidentified male. Amanda and Phil Brouillette were now in the house, far away from the crime scene.

We arrived at the Brouillettes' to find a path plowed up the drive. I knew I didn't have the traction to make it even halfway, and I ended up backing out of the driveway and parking on the road. As we got out of the car, Dave arrived. The three of us trudged through the back pasture to the barn, almost a quarter mile away, the blackness of the open field swallowing us whole. We didn't talk, Dave absorbed in forging a way through the rapidly mounting snowdrifts, Hale tucking his chin low in his jacket to keep warm, and me focused on the lights flickering through the falling snow, getting brighter and brighter until we arrived at the barn, which was lit up like daytime.

The place was still, the agents on scene securing the perimeter almost in shadow. Dave, Hale, and I were twenty-five feet from the body when we stopped: The blood spatter was wide. The artery the killer hit with the ax had sprayed the snow in an arc. Pink near the edges of the scene, the snow underneath was black with blood. Blood from the torso and the head saturated the victim's clothes— khakis, white shirt, and a ski jacket. One of the blows to the throat had sliced away his tie. Hit so many times, the victim's head was almost severed, and his face had an ax head lodged in it, obscuring his features.

I shuddered. "That's Ray Jelickson."

CHAPTER 9

IT WAS ONLY FIFTEEN steps between the barn and the crime scene tent, but by step three I had serious doubts about whether I would make it. I was tired and the snow was falling fast, and I could barely make out Annie inside, investigating the scene.

Crime scene tent was perhaps a bit grand a term. With techs slow to respond in the weather, we had constructed a shelter out of items scavenged from the Brouillettes' garage, and Annie was working in an old patio frame with plastic sheeting wrapped around it, held together with duct tape and a prayer. It looked like a snow globe but in reverse, where the world was shaken and only inside the tent was there stillness, peace.

"Stay behind me, tight in my path!" Dave yelled over the wind. "Grab the edge of my jacket and hold on!"

High winds sent ice into my eyes, the only part of me not covered by layers of wool, down, and some space-age fabric that the manufacturers claimed would wick moisture away from my skin;

they lied. I closed my eyes and blindly let Dave pull me toward the shelter, drifting left before being yanked forward two steps.

I was still recovering from the property search. Before being called off on account of the blizzard, everyone we could scrounge from any local, state, and federal agency had searched from the front road, across the field, up to the barn and beyond to the creek, to the arterial road. The search was successful, in a way; some state troopers found the Jelicksons' car as well as a second set of tire tracks, and Hale and I pulled bloody clothes out of the creek. Even with waterproof gloves, the cold from the creek made my fingers ache as I fished out Dickies work clothes, a fleece-lined jean jacket, and utility gloves.

"So our suspect has frostbite," Hale joked.

The killer took the time to submerge the clothes so the DNA evidence would be contaminated, if not destroyed—the lab might profile a trout. Nonetheless, we filled the evidence bags we were carrying, and I even hiked back for more bags at one point.

At the tent, Dave yelled to Annie, but she didn't respond, either because she couldn't hear over the wind or because she was ignoring us. Air gusts wrapped the tent door around Dave's arm twice as he pulled it aside, and he carefully untwisted it. The warmth from the heaters came out of the tent in waves, and even two feet away, I warmed up.

I could see our presence register with Annie, who squared her shoulders and tilted her chin.

"What?" she said.

Dave stepped past Annie into the tent. "Can we come in and do our job?"

"Don't mess up my crime scene."

The three of us pressed as close to the wall as we could without tipping the whole structure over. Stepping into the pink-tinged mess that filled the tent, I made plans to throw out my boots when

I got home. I assumed Annie had donned her waders for dramatic effect, but they were appropriate in this glop.

"Did those people"—Annie's low opinion of the state troopers and FBI agents came through in her tone—"manage to get that phone working?"

Moisture—we weren't sure if it was melted snow or all the blood—had left Ray's phone inoperable. The troopers had managed to get it dry enough to take a charge, but the screen was still watery and unreadable. Personally, I would have dropped it into a bowl of rice, which worked for me when Lucy tried to give mine a bath a couple of years back. Of course, I had been working with a flip phone and not the smart phone Ray had on him.

"They're working on it," Dave said. He cocked his head sideways. "What's going on with this blood spatter pattern?"

"Didn't you get the report from Figuera?" Annie waved in the direction of the barn and the blood spatter analyst graphing her findings inside.

"We did," Dave said. "But why don't you give us the big picture."

I could see Annie struggling between being offended by having to redo the work of someone with lesser skills and reveling in Dave's deferral to her expertise. She went for the reveling.

"Based on the position of the body and the blood spatter"—Annie pointed out where Ray lay crumpled, his feet twisted under his knees, a flashlight visible where his torso bent to the side—"I'd say our killer came up behind him and used the ax to sever his head."

"How'd you know it was an ax?" Dave asked.

Annie gave him one of her best *you're a moron* looks and pointed at the body. "Other than the *ax head* buried in his *face?*"

"I mean, was there a second weapon, a second attacker?"

Annie downgraded her look to *you're possibly a moron.* "We're still sorting out the footprints. Did you all line-dance around the body while you were waiting for me? Near the body, I found only one set. I mean it's *possible* a second killer came along, but if he did, he was only there to cheer the real perp on. They took the weapon"—at this point Annie held an invisible ax over her head—"and swung from the right, sending blood spatter arcing over toward you. You can wait for the M.E. to confirm, but I bet this cut was made first." Annie pointed to the slash that almost took Ray's head off his body. She then traced a cut that split his right temple, eye, and cheekbone. "He was still alive when that one, the second swing, came down. He really, really wasn't going to recover from that. While Ray was on his knees the killer took another whack. That finished him off. A fourth hit sliced the side of the face around the jaw and a fifth slashed along his brow. That's where the ax head detached from the handle and embedded in his face."

"So the only thing that slowed the killer down was a broken ax?" I asked. I angled around to see the face, which was difficult between the blood, the cuts, the ax blade, and Annie's rule that we not mess up her crime scene.

Off in the corner, a piece of wood was emerging from the melting snow. I pointed it out. Annie retraced her steps, stopping two and a half feet short of where an ax handle stuck out of the snow.

"Get out." She pointed toward the door. "I'm not done here. While I appreciate the fact that you need a place to have a tea party, you need to leave."

"C'mon, Annie, we can work together," Dave said.

"Out."

"Fine, fine," I said, pulling an evidence bag out of my pocket. "Give us the ax handle and we'll leave."

Annie folded her arms in front of her chest. "No way. The reason there's only me in here is yes, they wanted the best, but also it's such a small space, we didn't want to miss any trace evidence. Post one of the chuckleheads outside the door of the tent. I'll send it over when I'm done."

"We'd like it now," I said.

"Mmm, good for you. And if this were going to hold you up by twenty-four hours or even two hours, I'd hand it over right now. But it's going to take twenty minutes. I'll send it over after I photograph and bag it and you can have all the alone time you want. I'll even send candles."

We couldn't argue with that logic. The second I stepped outside I was hit with a shower of sleet; I pulled up my hood. The sleet, while more miserable than the snow, was a good sign in that it meant the storm was on its way out. By the time I got home, things would have calmed down enough that Lucy would be ready to turn all this snow into a snowman, or better yet, a snow fort. Just the thought of her made my step quicken. I kept my head low and followed Dave's feet.

With a last push from the wind, we stepped into the relative heat of the barn. Pete waved us down. "Jerry told me to send the two of you into the command center's command center."

"Huh?" Dave said.

"Yeah, Jerry's in with the tools." He waved his hand to a door on the far side of the barn. State troopers sat on one side of it, forced to dart in and out of stalls left over from the property's days as a working farm. On the other side of the door sat Hale and the FBI agents. Hale looked worn out, or rather, his hair did. He had worn a fur-lined hat—with earflaps, no less—and his hair hadn't taken kindly to being in something so unfashionable and was now sticking out in pique. He was briefing four local agents, gesturing at a computer that was propped on a saw bench. I didn't know them, having gone out of my way over the last few years to not meet people from the Albany field office.

"Her? Really?" one of them said as I passed. They all stared, and for the first time in my life I rushed to see Jerry. We found him perched on a chair he had grabbed from the tool bench, a map of the area pinned up behind him, notebooks and pens on a barrel to his left.

"I reviewed the interview with the congresswoman and her husband," Jerry said, waving at a closed pad, "and I think it's pretty clear the husband did it."

"Phillip Brouillette?" I said, surprised.

Jerry rolled his eyes. "No. Marty Jelickson."

"Good thinking, Jerry." Dave said. "But we can't prove that he did it, can't even prove he had an opportunity to do it."

I heard a knock on the door, and Hale walked in, snapping open a folding chair in front of him like a lion tamer.

"Y'all mind if I join you?" he asked, straddling the chair backward.

Jerry shifted back and forth in his seat, back straight, trying to appear taller. "Actually, we're—"

"Or my liaison, Officer Lyons, could brief me right now."

Jerry pursed his mouth so tightly that I could see the outline of his teeth, which made me like Hale a little. What was the old saying: the enemy of my enemy is my friend? Well, I wouldn't go quite that far, but I did appreciate that when Jerry spoke, his mouth barely opened. "You can both stay and brief me. Why don't you go first?"

"That's very generous of you," Hale said, all politeness. "The first bit of news I have is on the phone."

"It's working?" Dave asked.

"Not yet. But we subpoenaed his cell phone records—"

"Already?" I asked. Most of the judges we worked with were fast asleep, and the ones who were awake would want the petition for discovery presented in person for something that could be such a violation of privacy.

"Federal judge."

Federal judges were even slower to issue phone record subpoenas than local ones were, unless it was part of an ongoing investigation. Jerry had other concerns.

"I could have arranged for the subpoena," he said. "This is still our investigation."

"But one less hassle is a good thing," Dave said. "What was in them?"

"We can't get the substance of the messages, not yet," Hale said. "We got a list of who received them, however. It looks like there were a bunch to Danielle, a couple to his folks, and in the few hours before his death, several to an untraceable phone."

"What do you mean it's untraceable?" Jerry asked. "With a little effort, all phones are traceable these days."

"The phone was purchased at a beverage center in Albany. You use up the minutes and throw it away." Jerry looked skeptical, but Hale continued: "We'll check with the owner tomorrow for credit card receipts and videos—you know the drill. Ray's phone was registered in Marty's name, although the bills were still going to an address in California."

"His parents?" Dave asked.

"Very likely. And speaking of the vic's parents, we'll be seeing the whole clan tomorrow."

I had a terrible thought. "Did anyone notify Marty?"

"Patrol car sent," Dave said. "So the Brouillettes . . ." Dave ran his finger down the page, his eyes following his hand. I half expected him to tip over and fall asleep on the floor, and I was ready to curl up next to him. I used one of my old listening tricks, where I focused my eyes on different objects to concentrate on the words. A scythe hung on the wall. Geez, was I seeing things? Who the hell has a scythe?

Dave recited the details of the interview: Phil was distraught, but Amanda Brouillette remained calm.

"The lady doesn't flinch at a thing," Hale said.

"Well, she kind of can't, right?" I said. "Her line of work, she probably can never show emotion or she gets hit for being 'hormonal.' When every day is a big swinging-dick contest." Jerry looked shocked at my statement, Dave smiled, but surprisingly, Hale frowned, his head tilted in concern. He knew I was speaking from experience, and he pitied me. It pissed me off. "Although I would argue that having emotions makes you human, not female."

A soft rap sounded at the door. We sat staring at it until Jerry yelled, "Come!" Pete ducked his head in.

"The FBI pulled the prints off the ax handle. Thought you might want to know."

"Who came up?" Dave asked.

"Who turned it over to the FBI?" Jerry said. He started toward the door, stopping short and turning on Hale. "Was this your move?"

"I'm sure they were just—" began Dave.

"Yes," Hale said. "We have better labs. Even our mobile labs. Plus, ya'll are overloaded."

"Decided that, did you?" Jerry marched out into the main room.

"Give me the ax," he said.

"Will you excuse me?" Hale didn't wait for our response. I peeked around the corner, pulling back quickly. Hale was going to face down both Jerry and Annie, who had got wind of the fact that evidence was going to be removed from her oversight.

"God, that's going to be a bloodbath," Dave said, the flannel lining of his pants sending up a cloud of dust as he patted them.

"I don't know who to root for," I said. "Maybe Annie."

"The prints," Pete said, only continuing when I nodded. "The prints that came off the ax were Phillip Brouillette, Ray Jelickson—"

"Great. Maybe he committed suicide," Dave said.

"—someone named Craig Madigan, and one unidentified."

"Craig Madigan? Really? He's on our list. Tomorrow, right?" Dave asked. "What was he doing with the ax?"

Voices rose from the other room.

"Shouldn't you be out there throwing your weight around?" I asked Dave.

"Eh. Jerry's so much better at throwing my weight around; I'll let him do it."

Jerry yelled, "Support capacity only." I couldn't quite make out

Hale's response, pitched low and deadly. I edged toward the door so I could hear better.

"—and if you think for one moment, sir," Hale said, "that we are going to jeopardize this investigation so that you can play tin-pot dictator, you are very much mistaken."

Dave stifled a laugh from behind me. I pressed close to the shelves lining the wall, feeling them crease my arms. I pulled away and brushed off the shoulder of my sweater. The wool was covered in red powder from one of the one hundred or so flares lined up on the shelf.

"You think you can waltz in here . . . ." Jerry was building up a good head of steam.

The red powder on my sleeve . . . I racked my memory . . . there was something. . . . Scythe. Okay, decorative. Glass containers under the bench. Red flares. And was that ammonia?

I grabbed Dave's arm. "Jesus Christ. We're standing in the middle of a meth lab."

CHAPTER 10

I STOOD IN THE DOORWAY of the barn, wrestling with the toggles on my parka. The toggles were winning.

"Going home to rest on your laurels?" Hale asked.

"Uh, yes?"

The last of my brain cells had shut down fifteen minutes before. The previous six hours had consisted of asking Hale and Jerry to come look at some evidence; shouting for Hale and Jerry to shut the fuck up and look at the bubbling 22s, flares, and ammonia; convincing Jerry the barn was a meth lab; implementing hazmat protocols—which consisted of trekking to the garage to wait for the all clear from Albany's heavy rescue squad and watching the para-medics listen to Jerry's lungs and assure him that no, the ammonia crystals in the barrel he had propped his pens on weren't going to damage his lungs; searching the barn for remains of the drug opera-tion; and finally, watching while Hale and Jerry, with Dave's careful mediation, negotiated jurisdictions. Neither Dave nor I faulted Jerry for collaborating: A single murder was taxing our personnel to the limit. Two murders and a meth lab were going to do us all in.

We reluctantly agreed that Hale could ride along with us, and Hale reluctantly agreed to give the ax handle and phone to Annie for processing. Dave would coordinate the rest of the Ray scene, Hale and I would finish interviews, and the FBI would conduct a second search at the Jelicksons'. Jerry was all for me doing the interviews, which was surprising. I assumed his exhaustion impaired his spite. When I left, Annie was giving Ray's phone a stern talking-to, and it seemed to be responding, the screen light coming on before dying again.

Hale snapped his fingers in front of my face. "Want me to carry you into town?"

I squinted at him sideways, partly from the snow glare and partly because I wondered why he thought we were now friends. I picked up my stuff and made my way down the narrow path. "You need a ride because you crashed your car, don't you?"

"It was a controlled crash—"

"Says someone who has no understanding of black ice."

"Who's a touch more awake than you are, Officer Lyons. If you insist, you can drive, and I'll be there to push the car out of the ditch once you fall asleep behind the wheel." He grinned and held out his hand. "Throw me the keys."

"So they can get lost in a snowdrift? No thanks." I walked over and placed the keys in his hand, folding his fingers around them.

At the car, I pushed the Cheerios littering the seat next to Lucy's booster onto the floor. Hale turned on the engine and grabbed the snow brush.

"You sit tight," he said, popping out of the car.

I climbed in and shut the door. A blast of warm air hit me square in the face. I tried flicking the passenger-side vents but remembered they wouldn't move. At the end of her dad's illness, Lucy had decided he needed some company on his almost daily trips to and from the hospital. She'd shoved one of her Fisher-Price people between the slots—the girl with the yellow ponytail—and no one was able to dislodge it. One day last summer, furious in the humidity and with my inability to do anything about my crap car with the crap air-conditioning, I wrenched the vent closed. I succeeded only in breaking off the tab that shuttered it.

I closed my eyes in order to keep from drying out my eyeballs and drifted in the heat. Maybe I should move back to L.A. with Lucy? My time in Cali, at least before Kevin got sick, had been happy; surprising, considering that I spent my days collecting data on gang killings or doing drug buys in the Palm Desert. I would visit San Francisco once a month or so, and Kevin would come down to L.A., crashing on my couch over the weekend. We e-mailed constantly, and he sent me pictures of bikers he took on his travels around the country, with captions like "The Pagan's (sic) need to bone up on the possessive form." Our weekends consisted of hanging out, surfing (and failing disastrously), and biking.

We didn't just talk shop, but he didn't mind hearing about work when it did come up. Still, he could understand when I had to keep confidences. Of course, I hadn't considered that I might have to keep my love life quiet. For the most part, dating was a nonissue, since I worked seventy hours a week. But when I mentioned over sushi that I'd gone out with a likable graphic designer I'd met in a bookstore, the conversation got strained. No angry words, but Kevin addressed his full attention to separating every piece of ginger on the plate before eating them one by one. I knew I'd made a misstep, but I didn't know how. When we left, half the sushi was still on the plate.

The night was sultry, the day's smog burned off in a startling red sunset, and even downtown we could smell the faintest hint of orange blossoms. Kevin marched silently toward the car, and I got mad: he was carrying the protective friend thing a bit far. This situation was nothing like the one with Hale. I was older, and the graphic designer was a nice guy.

"What's your problem?" I demanded. Kevin was two steps ahead of me and walked faster, so I pushed harder. "Are you mad you haven't vetted him?" He put more distance between us.

"It's not like you're any sort of relationship genius! Your last relationship was with that crazy girl from your hometown, who cheated on you with your second cousin! Who's fifty-three!" I reached out and grabbed his arm.

And suddenly he was in motion, pulling me to him and kissing me. If I was honest with myself, the kiss wasn't very romantic. In my surprise, all I could do was grab hold of his left biceps and try to keep upright. I shut my eyes. His lips were dry but still really soft, and edged with stubble. I opened my mouth and ran my tongue over his lower lip, and his tongue met mine, and . . .

He broke the kiss, holding me at arm's length and panting. I reached out for him again, but before I could touch him he said, "Right. I'm going to the hotel now. Right now. It's for the best," and walked quickly down the street, breaking into a run after fifteen feet.

Was it for the best? I wondered as I sat on the couch in my apartment, looking at his bag, tucked neatly away in the corner of the living room. He didn't take up much space in my life, physically. He did take up a huge amount of space in my mind and my heart: I texted him when I wanted to tell someone about the hummingbird that was skirting the apricot blossoms outside my bedroom window, or the terrible turkey sandwich I had at lunch, or when I didn't feel at home in my own skin after a day when I was June Lyons, FBI agent, rather than June Lyons, person. Although I never consciously thought, *I want Kevin,* I now found my first thought was exactly that.

The front door buzzed. I leaped up to answer, banging my knee on the coffee table in my rush.

"Hi, it's me," Kevin said through the intercom, as if it could have been anyone else. I stood in the hallway, my foot holding the door. He stopped short when he got off the elevator, then marched forward, explaining before he even got to my door.

"Look, I promised myself I'd never force the issue, but I felt more . . . more strongly than I realized. And I can't change it, can't change the way I feel." He wouldn't meet my eyes as he talked, instead professing his feelings to each of my neighbor's doors, the floral arrangement the building's management put at the end of the hall-way, and the lines on the carpet. He almost walked into me, which forced him to meet my eyes. "I understand and respect the fact that you don't feel the same way. I may need to put a little distance be-tween the two of us for a while, but I love you, June, I've loved you for a long time—"

And I kissed him. This time he was the one with his eyes open, but he was quicker on the uptake than I was and he kissed me back. It was good. As we pushed and pulled each other into the apartment, Kevin took his hand away from my hip and backhanded the door shut. We slowed each other down in our haste to get our clothes off, with both of our hands reaching to unbutton his shirt and unzip my skirt. I broke the kiss as we neared the bedroom.

"Yes?" I asked.

"Yes," Kevin said, picking me up and carrying me the rest of the way to bed.

Later, we lay talking.

"I didn't want you to know," Kevin said. "I overstepped the bounds of friendship back there at the restaurant, and I figured you'd never want to see me again."

"That's quite the conversation we had." I smiled at him. "Too bad it only happened in your thick head."

"Yeah"—his breath warm on my shoulder as he laughed—"I was all ready to do the honorable thing and slink back to San Fran-cisco. And have you mail me my socks."

"Honorable? Slinking?"

"It made sense, in a sort of southern gentleman way."

"Which you're incredibly bad at, being from Minnesota."

"Very true. Anyway, I was all set to do the *cowardly* thing when I remembered I'd left the keys to both my car and my apartment here. I had to man up and face you."

"And here we are." I pulled him to me, wanting him closer. "I love you, you know?"

"I didn't know." Kevin went from being pulled into my arms to pushing forward and kissing me, the heat of his body warming me from the inside out.

A BURST OF COLD air broke my reverie as Hale got into the car. There were tears in my eyes. Grief wasn't my whole life, but it could still sneak up on me, leaving me demolished. I didn't know if the tears were because I was thinking of the time when I had Kevin and good work or just plain old exhaustion. I was prepared to play it off with a lie about the vents, but Hale didn't even notice: he climbed in, pushed the driver's seat back to accommodate his long legs, and slammed the door hard.

"Hey now, sleeping already?" Hale said. "Was that on the schedule?" I stared ahead at the approaching minivan, ignoring him. The vehicle slowed and the window rolled down, revealing Denise and Jason Byrne.

"Oh, hello there!" Denise called, cheerful in a way that could only be caffeine induced. "June—Officer Lyons—I'm sorry, my son and I had to go into the pharmacy. We waited as long as we could, but people need their medications and, well, making them wait could be inconsiderate. Inconsiderate and dangerous, you know, the ones who depend on us."

"We had a development in the case," I yelled across Hale.

"Did you arrest that poor girl's killer?"

Jason popped forward at this, waiting eagerly for my response.

"No. But we're working hard on it." Jason slumped back. Relieved or disappointed?

I thought through our schedule. Marty's was our next stop, and I wanted to take my time with him, if I could. Hale's people were already on their way to the Jelicksons' house to find any "evidence missed on the first go-through"—their words—and I figured that we would need two or three hours. I proposed that we stop by the pharmacy at noon.

Denise agreed. "Oh, and before I forget, I made these for you." She got out of the car, a tinfoil package in her hands. "Cranberry orange muffins. Lord knows I don't need them—gotta keep to my training weight." She laughed, patted a nonexistent roll of fat, and shoved the baked goods in the window.

"Thank you, ma'am," Hale said, pinned against his seat by Denise. "These'll keep us going."

"Glad to be of help, Mister . . . ?" Denise smiled at him expectantly. From this angle I could see a missing molar, marring her sweet smile.

"Agent Bascom, ma'am."

"Agent Bascom. I'm glad to help the investigation in any way I can." Denise walked back to her car, her step brisk and light despite the snow on the ground and her thick-soled utility boots. She and Jason sped off, her car skidding toward the shoulder before she did the smart thing and slowed down.

Hale put the car in drive. My ten-year-old Saturn lacked high-performance steering, and he had to pull the wheel hard to make the U-turn.

"Well, she sure is nice," Hale said.

"She really is. I hope we didn't inconvenience her too much."

"Who cares? You managed to unearth a meth lab. A meth superlab. A meth superlab being run out of *a congresswoman's house*." Hale didn't take his eyes off the road. He shook his head in disbelief.

"I would've never believed it. And based on all the crystals we found dumped in the barrels, active for quite a few months."

I thought back to the ranches where noxious fumes seeped through the smell of soybeans and manure. "Those bubbling twenty-twos could produce a huge amount of meth, in the hundreds of thousands of hits."

"Who was cooking?" Hale asked.

I puzzled. Marty? Danielle? Jason? Craig?

"Ray," I said finally. "Or maybe Marty."

"Or both. Maybe their kin hoped to open a new branch of the Abominations' business."

"But someone was distributing it. Who?"

Hale drove, one hand on the wheel, the other resting against his neck. *Lying,* I thought. Before I could call him on it his phone rang.

"Hello," he said as he skidded to the side of the road, the car jerking forward as he put it in park. "Yes. Yes. Estimated time? Good. Update me once you're in. Yes, good."

Hale explained that the weather had done us in again. "They can't get down to the Jelicksons'. Can't get within five blocks, what with the snow. Want me to drop you home?"

"Well, we know where to find the Byrnes. Want to swing by the pharmacy?"

"You could catch a nap. You need it."

"I need to solve this case, and honestly, I won't sleep. Let's go now."

"Yes, ma'am."

A couple of salt spreaders rumbled by, dropping rock salt on the layer of ice missed by the plows' blades. Hale swerved out of the way of an arc of snow, a man with a blower giving back what a plow had pushed into his driveway. Up ahead I saw ninety-year-old Mrs. Primeau attacking her stairs with her great-grandson's kiddy shovel. It was just her size, and she had two of three steps done.

On a day like today, I wished I could be home with Lucy. By this time during the last snow day she had become bored and started to melt her crayons near the fireplace—she didn't enjoy it as much when she and I had to chip off the wax disks that dotted the bricks—but still, it would be more fun than this.

"So, you seem settled in here," Hale said. "And you seem happy. With your family, which makes sense. But if I'm not mistaken, you're enjoying the work, too."

I stifled a laugh. If Hale knew that my work consisted of doing endless patrols during the crappy shifts and leading safety lectures in schools, he wouldn't say that.

"Considering your ambition way back when, June, I'm having a hard time matching you up with the girl I knew at the academy."

"Hale, we haven't been close in ten years. We haven't seen each other at all in eight. Do you think I'm the same person?" I turned to face him, confront him, but his eyes remained glued to the road. "We're developing a good working relationship, a relationship that's helping us solve this case, but I don't want to have a personal conversation with you. Unless we discuss the case, let's not talk. At all."

CHAPTER 11

HALSTON STREET WAS PLOWED, which was surprising—usually side streets weren't cleared until the next day. One of the snowplow drivers must have a girlfriend on this block. Denise Byrne, who was piling garbage bags and empty boxes in the alley at the store's rear, did a double take as we slid past. Up in front, Jason didn't notice us. Headphones in ears that were red from cold, a cord leading down to the pocket of a fleece-lined jean jacket, he was shoveling the front walk, flipping snow to the beat of some tune only he could hear. He seemed to be enjoying his time in his own world.

"June?" Denise called, moving quickly to meet us. She was wearing an HFHS ALL-STAR BASKETBALL GAME sweatshirt, the hood pulled up and her thumbs poking through holes in the wristband. "June, we weren't expecting you for another three hours and I'm afraid you caught us when we're a little behind. We have customers coming, and we have to clear the walk and the trash, and I have a number of prescriptions I need to fill."

"Very sorry, Mrs. Byrne, we had a change in plans," Hale said.

"But we'd be happy to conduct the interviews with you while you prepare for your day," I said. Denise's teeth chattered, her thin lips blue. "Or at least while you go inside and warm up."

Jeff Polito sauntered up the block, slowing as he saw us.

"Can I pick up my prescription, Mrs. Byrne?" he asked.

Denise looked at me. "Would it be okay if I took care of Jeff first? If it's a problem, I guess he could take some aspirin and come back in an hour."

I recognized Jeff from way back. He drove trucks these days, but in high school he was "that guy"—the man in his midtwenties who would let kids come to his house and party. The kids always found one person like that, and Jeff was less creepy than most, although that wouldn't have prevented my father from running Jeff out of town if Dad had found out. Jeff would go to the beverage center with our pooled money and buy beer and my favorite, wine coolers. His only requirement was a twelve-pack for himself, but since he drank Genny Cream Ale, this was no great hardship. He seemed hopelessly cool at the time, with his own apartment and all the free pizza he could bring home from his delivery job.

"June!" He grinned at me. "How's your dad?"

"He's good, he's home with Lucy today. You okay?"

He held up his arm. "Old injury—arm got caught in the rig. Acts up in this weather. It's not an emergency or anything. . . ."

"That sounds terrible," I said, seeing my chance to get Jason alone. "If you're putting the prescription together now, Denise, we can start with Jason. We can talk to him while he works."

"Or even help out," added Hale.

Denise marched toward the front, and with her basketball player legs she quickly outpaced Jeff, Hale, and me. She tapped Jason on the shoulder as she passed, and he scrambled to pull out his earbuds, nodding at everything his mother said. Then he jogged toward us, suggesting we join him in the alley while he took care of the garbage.

"So . . . Danielle," I said. "You guys dated, right?"

"Yeah, back when we were in high school," he said, as if it were a million years ago instead of three. Jason slashed through the tape on the boxes using an X-Acto knife and collapsed the cardboard in on itself, throwing it in the recycling bin, which stood next to the most pristine Dumpster I had ever seen.

"Emma Willard?" Hale asked.

Jason snickered. "No. Not Emma Willard. That's for girls, and superexpensive. We attended Catholic Central over in Troy. We took the bus together. Well, at least until my dad gave me his car."

I asked Jason to describe Danielle. He stopped working and gave it some thought. "She was nice."

This was like pulling teeth, but I didn't take it personally: young men weren't known for their eloquence.

"She was funny, you know, she'd say anything to anyone. Even the teachers. And she dressed cool, which is hard in a school uniform. Her penny loafers had the chunkiest heel I ever saw." He leaned over to pick up another box. I recognized the brand as a shower chair Kevin had used. The pharmacy probably stocked a full set of products that catered to Hopewell Falls's aging population: adjustable beds, walkers, and hospital supplies.

"And she didn't mind that I was quiet, quieter than her, because she said I let her do all the talking."

I smiled. I knew several long-lasting marriages that were based on the fact that one person liked to talk and the other liked to listen, or rather, liked talking less.

"Was she out of control, a little crazy?" Hale asked.

Jason dropped his X-Acto. "What?"

"You know. Hot." Hale picked up the knife and handed it to Jason. "When you guys got it on."

"You shouldn't talk like that about her. We were kids. We just hung out. That's all." Jason shoved the cardboard into the recycling bin so loudly it echoed. I thought he was going to use the box cutter on Hale if I didn't step in, so I picked a nice neutral topic: her interests.

"She liked movies a lot. She said she was going to go out to Hollywood and be an actress, which is why she picked UCLA." Jason stopped, flipping the safety on the box cutter and putting it in his pocket. "That's what got us talking. She never saw any of the old movies, like from the seventies, so I showed her those." From behind Jason, Hale raised an eyebrow. "She really liked *Bonnie and Clyde,* and cried a bunch at the end. Her dad only let her come over to my house when my parents were home, and when the movie finished she had to go right home."

"And you stayed in touch?" I asked.

"I saw her Facebook updates, all the fun in L.A. But we didn't talk or e-mail." He paused. "And we didn't date after high school."

Jason didn't seem like the type to speak ill of the dead, so I asked the next question gently. "Did she ever do anything you didn't like so much?"

"Well . . . ," and Jason seemed to strain under the effort of saying something not so nice, "she sometimes drove too fast and played her music too loud." I stifled a smile remembering my little drive from two nights ago. He furrowed his brow. "She would mouth off to people if they told her what to do. That was maybe a bad idea 'cause she got thrown out of a couple of high schools. And maybe college? I'm not sure what really happened there. Craig said she ran off with Marty and her dad disowned her, but she said she got bored of college, which I can't understand. I mean, I love college."

"Are you in college now, Jason?" I asked.

He paused, picking up another box and breaking it down; he had three left. "Pharmacy school. I was supposed to start the DPharm program last month—"

"The what?" I asked.

"Doctor of Pharmacy program. I took twenty credits a semester and finished undergrad early but . . . with my dad? Things are tight right now. Plus, my mom thinks if I take a couple of months off she can talk me into going to medical school." He shoved the box into the Dumpster with a clang. "That's not happening. Anyway, I guess that's another thing that wasn't so great about Danielle. Her folks, they just *gave* her stuff, and she didn't seem to care. She would throw away the things they gave her, things other people would kill for."

He was on a roll: "I thought she changed out in L.A.—grew up?—but she wrecked college, too. And she wasn't a very good employee here, promising to work hard and then not caring. It's like if you're nice to her, she doesn't try to live up to her side, like she wants to punish you for trusting her. My mom said she couldn't afford to pay for someone, especially someone who was unreliable, and"—he gestured to the alley, the Dumpsters, the snowdrifts—"here I am."

"How about Marty?" I asked. "You guys seemed like good friends."

He put the last box in the bin, and shut and locked it, testing the top to make sure it was secure. "He'd be parked out here, waiting to pick her up after work—she hated the cold, and he tried to make sure she didn't have to spend even a minute outside. The two of them, they were like movie stars, like Faye Dunaway and Warren Beatty, and I"—he shrugged—"well, I'm not. So I was surprised when he invited me over for dinner. He was a cool guy, you know, he'd read Charles Bukowski's poetry. And he always, always watched her when she bounced around, and he always listened to what she said, and got mad if she 'played the dumb blonde.' And he gave her books to read, like Jack Kerouac and Chuck Palahniuk." A blast of cold air seemed to take Jason's breath away. "She didn't read them, so I borrowed them."

"Do any drugs, Jason?" Hale asked.

"What?!" Jason watched the pharmacy's back door. "I don't know what you're talking about."

I touched Jason's arm, petting him like frightened animal. "What Agent Bascom meant to ask was whether drugs were around."

"Well, sometimes pot," Jason blurted softly. "I didn't smoke any. Neither did Marty. Sometimes Dani did, but only outside. Marty hates drugs." He spoke low and quickly, keeping his eye on the back door. "I think his brother, you know, Ray? He smoked it with her sometimes."

"What'd you think of Ray?" I asked.

"He is really juvenile." I stifled my smile at a twenty-one-year-old boy calling a seventeen-year-old juvenile, but he had a point: with his familial and financial responsibilities, Jason was mature beyond his years. "Ray would be around a lot, when me and Marty hung out. Marty said he and Danielle were trying to be real parents to Ray. I guess Marty's family isn't so great. Marty was making sure Ray didn't get into trouble—he was strict, but said Ray needed a firm hand. Danielle was helping Ray study for the GED. Danielle got a GED, you know. She never graduated from high school." Jason took a deep breath. "But Ray, he was okay, I guess."

"So you won't be too broken up to hear he got killed," Hale said.

Jason appraised Hale. "No way. You're lying."

"Jason, we're not," I said, impressed that he had caught on to Hale's shock tactics. Jason's pale eyebrows shot up in surprise, visible only because his face was red with cold. "That's why we were over at the Brouillettes'. We found his body on their property."

"God. Does Marty know? I wouldn't have said those things if I'd . . . God. Poor Ray."

I tapped at my notebook. "Can you tell us where you were last night from eight until midnight? We need to know for our records."

The back door swung open, and Denise Byrne dragged out two huge garbage bags and placed them next to the pile she had brought out earlier. Hale gallantly reached over to pick one up and stumbled; they were heavier than they looked.

"You can leave that for Jason, Agent Bascom." Denise looked from me to Jason. "You almost done out here?"

"I have to do the plastic and glass, Mom, and after I can finish the trash."

"No, I meant the detectives." Denise waved her finger between Jason and me. I felt scolded.

"A few more questions," I said. "Jason, last night?"

"June, I think I misunderstood this discussion." She walked down the steps until she was at ground level, although she still towered over me. "I thought this was just an interview, but you're talking to my son like he is a suspect."

"It's okay, Mom," Jason said. "It's okay. Last night, I watched some videos with my dad. There was a storm, you know?"

"I don't know why you two needed to watch *Star Wars* again. After four hundred watchings you must know all the lines by heart," Denise said, smiling fondly. "You know, I hate to be a pain, June, but we should have our discussion right now, while I have the time."

"I think we're done here," I said. "Jason was a great help." I moved toward the pharmacy door, but Denise stepped sideways and blocked me.

"Oh, no, you can't go in this way, you have to go around to the front door." She moved up the steps and had her hand on the door-knob, as if ready to slam it in our face. "Authorized personnel only, because of the controlled substances. You know how regulators are."

"As a police officer and an FBI agent, we're pretty trustworthy," Hale said. "And it'd be better if we could have the conversation in private."

"Oh, I can definitely understand. Do you want to find a time later?" I shook my head no.

"Jason," Denise said, "when you're done with the trash, you need to clear the walk again. Then don't forget to come in and sweep and mop. People have been tracking snow in all morning."

Once we were around front, out of earshot of Jason, Hale spoke. "I think we aren't going to get her full attention here. Bring her in after work?"

"No." I had an aide named Juliana who came every day when Kevin was in his last few months. Juliana would have stayed around the clock if I'd asked, and I would have been happy to have her if my budget had allowed it. Juliana cheerfully wiped bile off her smock, all the while chatting with Kevin about her childhood in one of the hill towns at the west end of the county, a life filled with an endless supply of summer days and chickens. No, I explained, Denise's husband needed constant care, and we weren't going to pull her in to prove who was boss.

"Good point. That said," Hale said, "I'm frozen through, and do wish we could've done the last interview inside."

"Me, too." I caught Hale's elbow as he slipped sideways against me. "Jason's a blusher, and it would've been interesting to see when he turned red."

"You think he's lying? Could he have been jealous enough to kill her?"

I chose my words carefully. "It's possible, but it's not my first choice." Jason had seemed infatuated, but infatuated with Marty rather than with Danielle.

As we entered the store, Denise Byrne was waiting for us. Perched high on a stool behind the counter at the end of a long aisle lined with cold and flu remedies, she was very like a Roman emperor of the absolute rule rather than the bread and circuses variety. Her sweatshirt was gone, replaced by a pharmacist's smock over a silky pale purple shirt, and her hair had been brushed and sprayed into a thick helmet of gold. Several file folders were lined up next to the register and the glasses repair kits, lip balm, and throat lozenges.

She started speaking while we were several feet away. "I want to keep things friendly, but I feel like we're being treated like suspects rather than witnesses. We want to help. We do! But you would tell me if I needed a lawyer, right?"

"No need for any of that, Mrs. Byrne." Hale seemed to have

decided to go the southern charm route with Denise. He nodded at the files. "Are all of these for us?"

I picked up one and scanned the W-2 statement, Danielle's employment history, and her application.

"I made you extra copies, so you don't have to stay here to read them," Denise said, reaching up to her neck and smoothing down the collar. Up close I could see that the shirt was polyester rather than silk.

"Why'd you hire her?" I said as I read. "She lasted less than two months and doesn't seem to have had any experience."

"My son remained fond of her, and that's the sort of thing I do for neighbors. Plus, she had to make her own way after her parents cut her off. I knew what that was like. I put myself through school on a basketball scholarship."

"But she didn't work out as an employee?" Hale said.

"No."

She didn't elaborate, so I prompted her: "Did she cost too much to pay?"

"No!" Denise exclaimed. "Who's saying things like that?"

I didn't tell her it was her son. Instead I asked, "Did she miss her shifts?"

"Her husband always dropped her off right on time. Probably nothing better to do. Between you and me"—she dropped her voice—"I think he was a deadbeat. He just looks like that type, you know?"

I went direct. "Did she steal from you?"

Jason appeared at the doorway, holding his key chain in front of him. "Mom, I can't find the key for the garbage."

"Jason, I've told you to keep your keys in a safe place, so you don't forget where you put them."

"I did, Mom. I had them. It's—"

Denise sighed loudly, but she smiled at her son. "We'll look at home later, okay, honey? Go back out and clear and salt the walk again."

Denise waited until he was out of earshot before continuing.

"Yes." She nodded, and her bangs fell over one eye. Using two fingers, she precisely slid the hair back in place. "Yes, she stole from me."

"Drugs?" I asked.

"Drugs from up here. All the controlled substance inventories matched up, even the Oxycontin, which is the druggies' first choice. She took cold medicine—three packets a week. And eye drops, although that might have been shoplifted. We always report the losses to the auditor, even the supplies Danielle stole. I made Danielle's thefts anonymous, since I didn't have one hundred percent proof and hadn't wanted to embarrass the congresswoman or her husband. They say Amanda's going to be president, or at least vice president, which I guess would be okay."

Denise straightened a display of earplugs. "We do take precautions against theft. We got a private security system put in. We have cameras out front, and I lock the Dumpsters. And of course I have a gun—and a permit, of course—for when I'm working late. Since my husband got sick, that happens . . . a lot."

Thankfully, this murder hadn't involved a gun. The doorbell rang, and an elderly man walked up the aisle toward us, pushing forward on a walker.

"Is there anything else?" Denise said in her pharmacist's whisper.

Hale collected the files. "No, ma'am, I think this is everything. You sure have been helpful."

"I have a question," I said. "Do you know Ray Jelickson?"

"Only in passing. He was at the wake yesterday, making a lot of noise." Denise Byrne's eye flicked nervously at the customer. "I didn't like my son hanging out with him." She smiled brightly at the man behind me. "You are a hearty one, Mr. Ashby, braving the snow! I'll be with you in a second. Me and June"—she looked at me questioningly—"we're done, right, June?"

MARTY'S BLOCK HAD BEEN plowed. Piles of snow rose against the parked cars, almost burying some of the economy models. Not that they could get out. Right down the middle of the street was a line of black sedans: "Bucars" from the FBI. We pulled in and walked up the narrow shoveled path, no more than a foot wide, that wove between cars, past the gate, and up the walk and the steps. Midway to the door was a huge indentation where someone had fallen.

Before we had the chance to knock, the door opened, an agent holding it wide. We made our way past two more men, who were opening DVD cases. A third was emptying the shelves, shaking books out and dropping them on the floor. Him I recognized: Potreo. When I first arrived in California he had constantly called me and the other female agents "Breast Fed." None of us laughed and he took to pouting.

I slipped on a pile of CD cases, found a helpful hand under my elbow that let go too soon, and flailed to regain my balance. I turned to my pseudohelper, a guy from my last assignment in Oakland. These weren't people Hale had pulled in from the Albany office, they were agents from across the country, all of whom specialized in drug trafficking and gangs. I wondered if any of them would tell me what was really going on. Probably not.

"Report," Hale said.

I looked up. The kitchen had fallen from disrepair into destruction. All the cabinet doors hung open and the contents were strewn across the floor: tea bags soaking in tomato sauce, macaroni fanned out, and dishes smashed roughly, bowls broken in half and glasses splintered into tiny pieces.

An agent picking up broken glass nodded to the back porch. "Not us. Him. Slammed the cabinet open when we told him he couldn't leave for coffee, and a bunch of dishes came down. Accident, I think." He dropped his voice. "The second cabinet he did intentionally."

I stepped over a broken teapot, the rosebud pattern dotting pink across the floor. On the back porch I saw Marty tipped back in a lawn chair, gazing out at his backyard. A three-by-three-foot patch of snow had been roughly cleared to make space. The sound of the door opening didn't draw his eyes from the squirrels skittering across the surface of the snow. He wore a hat but no gloves, and I was alarmed to see his hands, red with cold, brush against the snow that walled in the chair. He was wearing his reclaimed leather vest over a quilted jacket. It looked painful, cutting tightly across his broad shoulders and puffy coat.

Marty still seemed unaware of me. I had experienced that kind of grief, where hours or even months passed without notice. I didn't want to alarm him, and I rested my hand on his shoulder to let him know I was there.

"I only wanted a coffee," he said. He tipped forward. His chair skidded, and I held tighter to steady him. "They wouldn't let me leave. I couldn't get away."

CHAPTER 12

CAN WE LOSE THIS bitch?" Marty said.

He was getting friendly. It took us a while to get him talking—forty-five minutes, two ham sandwiches (the first of which he tossed to the squirrels), and some warmth. He was full of a rage that appeared to be righteous. He was currently sitting on the floor opposite me, leaning against his bed's box spring, which was flipped up against the only wall with a window, blocking out what little natural light there might be on this winter afternoon. The cheesecloth at the bottom of the mattress was torn, and a strip hung down, dusting Marty's elbow. I was propped against his upside-down dresser, its contents dumped onto the floor.

Marty hadn't said anything of value during this conversation, answering half my questions with a shrug and spending the rest of his time picking up random objects from the pile next to us: a pair of socks, a well-worn BLOWFISH SUSHI T-shirt, four or five hair elastics. Periodically he shot sidelong glances at Hale, who loomed above us, leaning against a wall. When Hale told Marty to stop fiddling with the stuff on the floor and answer the questions, Marty called him a bitch.

I could understand the urge, as Hale annoyed me, too. Earlier, to coax him off the deck, I'd told Marty we could go to the station. It would be easier to talk, and he wouldn't have to witness the FBI tossing his house. He was unsure, not trusting the federal agents, but I got him to the point of agreeing when Hale piped up.

"Marty, we are going to need to go through everything here, in detail, even the yard. You are really getting in our way."

"You tar snake. I'm staying."

But Marty agreed to go inside. We wound through the house, stepping over the broken china, squeezing past the refrigerator that had been moved to the middle of the room, and dodging several *Fuck you* looks from agents. Most of them were directed at Marty, but a few were aimed at me. I did get a friendly nod from Jeff Scylla, out of Missouri, and from Sam Bailey. Sam was called "Silent Sam" because of the way he lived the phrase "Speak softly and carry a big stick." A nod from Sam was a big wet kiss from anyone else. In a way, I had a harder time ignoring the friendly faces than the adversarial ones, and both Marty and I stared at the ceiling waiting for Hale to let us know the bedroom was clear.

"Don't want to contaminate evidence," he said.

"I pretty well contaminated things when I took a shower," Marty said.

I'd had enough of their bickering.

"Just give us a time line for last night," I said, sketching out a table in my pad, writing "Time" and "Location" at the top of its two columns. "If you saw your brother and when. I can't promise to get the feds out of here any sooner—they're too busy rechecking my work to listen to me—but at least we can make progress on finding your wife's and brother's killer."

Playing the "us against them" card seemed to be the best way to get Marty to cooperate. And I wasn't lying, not really. I wanted as little to do with the other agents as possible.

"I got home around sevenish. After the wake I went to an AA meeting." He watched me, expecting me to flinch at the mention of AA, but I kept my face bland. He continued. "I was really tired last night—I don't know why—and kind of crashed when I got home, calling my sponsor in L.A., watching TV, chilling. Ray got home around eight or so. Gotta say I was surprised. I mean, he never loses a chance to hang out with his one true love."

"Jackie?" I asked.

"Craig," Marty reached up, grabbed the hanging piece of cheesecloth from the mattress, and pulled down. Half the gauze came away and dust puffed out of the slash. Hale coughed. The fabric wrapped around Marty's wrist, and he shook it, but it tangled. From underneath the pile to the left, a phone started ringing. He grabbed a pair of scissors off the floor, cut the fabric away, and began to hunt through the pile. The ringing stopped just as he pulled the phone free.

He looked at the screen. "Jackie called."

"For you?" I asked. My back was getting cramped leaning against the dresser and I sat forward, sliding the scissors behind me.

"This is Ray's phone." Marty laughed bitterly. "The dumb shit forgot it again."

As Marty flipped through the texts, I glanced at Hale, who raised an eyebrow at me. A second phone. That's how Ray got around Marty's phone monitoring.

"Marty, can I see that?" Marty ignored me. Hale looked ready to grab it out of his hands.

"Marty," I repeated more loudly. "Marty, give me the phone."

He flung the phone on the floor between us. Before I could reach it, Hale had knelt down and grabbed it.

"I want that back," Marty said.

"Craig?" I said to Marty. He didn't answer, watching as Hale walked the phone to the door and handed it to an agent on the other side. I prompted him again. "Oh, yeah, *Craig*. Ray thought Craig was the shit with his plane and the man jewelry he wore."

"At the funeral, I got the sense you're not impressed with Craig."

"You got that right. He was always panting after Danielle like a puppy. And Craig's my age, but he hangs out with the teenagers 'cause they're impressed by his bullshit. Back in L.A., when Phil and I were tussling, Craig just stood there with his thumbs up his ass, watching the whole thing go down. Craig's all talk."

"And your brother. All talk, too?" Hale asked.

Marty clenched his jaw once, twice, before he answered.

"Yeah. Yeah, he was," daring Hale to make a comment.

Hale hadn't informed me he was going to be playing bad cop here. It wasn't needed. Marty thought all cops were bad cops. The locals were less bad than the feds—or maybe less competent and less of a threat—and he trusted me marginally more than he trusted Hale. I needed to keep him talking and asked him to tell us the rest of the details from the night before.

"Ray got home around eight. Settled down. Jason dropped off some submarine sandwiches. He didn't stay. So me and Ray, we ate those."

Jason hadn't mentioned stopping at Marty's last night. I looked at Hale, but he was still in the staring contest with Marty.

"Around nine my brother announces that he needs to go to the grocery store before the storm. Should have known that little shit-head was lying."

"Why?"

I heard a crash from the direction of the living room. Marty cringed, and Hale didn't look happy, either. "He didn't know what groceries were. We had plenty of cheese curls. He was set."

I thought of Ray calling out for grape soda in his too-big biker vest, the vest that now strained across Marty's shoulders.

Marty saw me smile. "What? You like one of those social work-ers?" His voice got high and shrill: "'Just stopping to make sure the boys are eating right.'" He rolled his eyes and his voice dropped back to its bass rumble. "Like you give a fuck."

"No, it's like my daughter," and I explained how I'd gotten soda for Ray a few days ago, and my seven-year-old would have chosen the same kind.

Marty sat forward. "What's her name?"

"Officer Lyons's personal life is off limits," interjected Hale.

Marty rolled his eyes at me. "We really need this clyde here?"

I laughed, confusing Hale. I explained. "A clyde is someone who cuts you off in their cage." My explanation needed an explanation. "Their car."

I had Marty's attention. "You ride?"

I was ready to describe the interesting "neighbors" I had in Cal-ifornia, leaving out the part where I was instrumental in arresting said neighbors, when Hale butted in again.

"Officer Lyons here is one of us," Hale said. "FBI, in California. Probably saw your jacket. And your mom's got a sheet, right?"

Marty shook his head. "Fuckin' fibbies. Entrapment—"

"I *was*," I said, as furious as Marty was. "I *was* in the FBI. I'm out."

Marty paused. "They kick you out?"

"I left." I spun it in my favor. "Couldn't take these assholes anymore."

"Yeah." He rolled one shoulder in a friendly shrug. He pushed the second shoulder back and looked pinned to the wooden slats of the box spring. He rolled his head back and squinted at me. "But once an asshole, always an asshole, right?"

I protested, but he cut me off.

"Thought maybe you wanted to hear the real story. I know why you're here. You don't give a fuck."

"I do."

"You don't. You don't care who killed my brother. You probably think he deserved it. Because me and Ray are the sons . . . no, *I'm* the son"—a fierce pride seemed to ride through him—"the heir apparent, to the Abominations' chief enforcer."

Hale rolled his eyes. "Well, that and your little California meth lab."

I couldn't hide my anger. "Shut it, Hale."

"Spare me, sister," Marty said. "Sitting here, pretending like you don't know, with these shitheads"—and he nodded at Hale—"sorry, these *gentlemen* crawling all over everything."

"Marty," I said, "as far as I'm concerned you are innocent until proven guilty."

"Don't you mean guilty until proven dead?" Marty said.

"Or guilty until proven guiltier," Hale said. "It's not like you were much of a clean liver before."

"Fuck you very much, fed. All the charges, even the RICO stuff, were dropped. My record is clean."

I was completely lost. There was no point in my being there—Hale made sure of that. I would have left, except I might need to break up a fight.

Hale rolled his eyes. "Only because our lead witness—"

"Your rat."

"—was murdered," finished Hale.

Marty smiled. "Never did find his body. Rumor has it he traveled to Costa Rica to open a banana farm."

"And if I were as dumb as you, I'd believe that. What you need to know, Officer Lyons, is that Marty here, from when he was seventeen until we arrested him at the ripe old age of twenty-two, showed a real aptitude for producing and distributing meth. In one of those superlabs. And our friend Marty here got off after he killed our lead witness."

Marty chuckled meanly. "And you can't touch me. Double jeopardy, *friend*. Guess you fucked that up. But the thing that kills me is that you dipshits won't be able to find who killed Danielle"—he swallowed, choking back rage—"because you're so busy pinning this on me. You'll drag crap out of any old evidence locker and splay it out on a table for the press. All the while knowing I. Didn't. Do. It."

"You're a bad guy," Hale said. "Your people are the ones doing drug production and dealing."

"And you need me, my family, my club"—and this was the first time I heard Marty identify himself as a member of the Abominations—"you need us to be major league bad guys so you'll get more taxpayer money for overtime and shiny new equipment. You're prosecuting the old case you lost, who *cares* who killed Danielle and Ray."

I couldn't make out which case they were arguing over—here or in California.

"You guys are all the same," Hale said.

"You mean us Abominations? The best part of this"—and Marty threw his arm wide to take in his tossed room—"I'm not even one of them anymore. I got them to jump me out, and I got the broken ribs to prove it. Broken fingers, broken hand, crushed sinus cavity, fractured clavicle, and a bridge in my mouth to replace the teeth that Zeke personally kicked out. They wouldn't have me. But here's some fun news for you all: Some real Abominations are showing up today. My parents are coming. They'll take Ray out of the morgue. They'll break me out of here. They'll haul ass back to California, and throw a huge fucking funeral." Marty heaved himself up, deftly stepping sideways over the glass lampshade now on the floor. I scrambled up. "My parents arrange a lot of memorials. They're good at it."

Hale rolled his eyes. "You may be putting on a show of being clean and sober, out of the Abominations, but we both know this poison is in your blood. We'll see if you're cracking jokes when we arrest you."

"You aren't going to arrest me, because I didn't do it." Marty dusted himself off. "Now I'm leaving. I'm going to go to the wake."

"The wake's canceled," I said.

That actually brought him up short, but he recovered quickly. "Then I'm going for a walk. Hell, I'm going to go drown myself in the river."

"Marty," I said.

"And if you try to stop me, I'll—"

"You'll what?" Hale said. "C'mon, tell me what you'll do."

"Man, you won't even see me coming. Trust me." And with that, Marty slammed the door behind him.

FOR A FEW SECONDS the slam echoed. We could hear a few of the agents in the main room protesting, and the crash of the front door.

I turned on Hale. "What the hell was that?! Could you have fucked that up for me any more?"

"He needed to understand this was no joke."

"And you don't think he picked that up from the ten guys tossing the living room?"

"June, you deserve respect. You aren't just some Barney Fife—"

"I don't demand respect from a witness and possible suspect who barely trusts us! Really!" I was one step away from name calling, and I worked to get myself back under control, lowering my tone. "Way to misread the situation. You backed him into a corner."

"I was backing you up. We're team."

"No," I said. "We're not team. The fact that you won't tell me what's really going on says it all. We're collaborating, right here and right now. But as several people in the next room would be happy to remind you, I washed out."

"You didn't."

"I did. I am no longer on your team. And you need to respect me in my new role."

"I do."

"You don't." I hated losing control, and I wasn't going to accomplish anything if I couldn't think. "If you respect me so goddamned much you need to follow my lead in these interviews. He didn't trust you. And after this little performance, I'm pretty sure I don't, either."

Hale took a step back, dropping into parade rest, a habit left over from his military school days. "I take full responsibility for what I did."

"So tell me what's really going on."

"June, you don't have clearance—"

I walked quickly out of the room and past the agents tossing the house. No one protested when I left.

CHAPTER 13

I STOPPED HOME BRIEFLY, staying in motion while I was there: shower, clothes, food, admiration of Lucy and her grandpa's paper snowflakes and promises to play later this afternoon, more food, and back to the station. Everyone who could be spared was doing cleanup at the Brouillettes', and the civilians of Hopewell Falls had decided to forgo their life of crime, at least until the streets were plowed.

At the station I found Dave at the conference room table poring over a file. A platter of subs sat in front of him, half picked over. But he'd been doing more than eating and reading. On the wall were two trees of evidence. A picture of healthy and smiling Danielle topped one. She sat in the passenger side of a car, kissing her wedding ring. From there, lines of tape branched off to pictures of the river, the house, and its backyard. At the bottom were autopsy photos, clinical and gray, of her back, her neck, and her torso.

The picture of Ray alive was taken by an FBI agent in the funeral home's parking lot, Ray checking his cell phone while Craig and Jackie walked a few feet ahead. In the corner of the frame Jason Byrne was climbing into a vehicle while Denise Byrne buttoned her bulky jacket, her eyes trained on the back door as if on the lookout to make sure no one saw her wearing such an ugly coat. I hadn't known the FBI was there. Much more gruesome lines threaded from there: a picture of the ax handle, stained red in places; the clothes we found in the creek; Ray's vehicle by the side of the road; Ray's body, twisted in the snow; and several close-ups of his face with the ax head embedded in it. I ran my finger along the tape that connected the picture of Ray's body to the one of him walking. Only a few hours had passed between one point and the next. While the wall helped clarify our thinking, we needed to ensure that no one who loved either of the victims, or even hated them, would see these pictures.

I waved at the room. "Well, this is . . ."

"'Nice' isn't the word."

"No, it's not. You set this up?"

"I needed visual aids."

"Well, it's certainly visual."

There were three loud knocks on the door.

"Come in!" Dave called. The door rattled. Locked. I walked over and opened it, and Annie darted past me, shouting, "What took you so long!" over her shoulder.

"The same might be asked of you," Dave said. "Pokey with that evidence, aren't you?"

"You are about to eat your words," Annie said, shoving the file Dave was reading across the table and thrusting the phone we'd found at the scene of Ray's murder under his nose. "I am a genius."

Dave touched the screen, which came to life, watery but legible. There was a prompt for a password.

"Y-O-L-O," Annie said. Dave entered in the code and breasts greeted us. The face above the shapely torso was cut off, and we were lucky that a few well-positioned icons kept it from being full frontal nudity.

"Whoa," Dave said, blushing slightly. "I really hope that's not Jackie."

"Yes, yes, very exciting," Annie said. "Wait until you see this." She tapped the phone and I watched her flip screens, hit the camera icon, and open the photo album. She punched one picture and handed the phone back.

It was the same photo, but uncropped. This time, our focus was not on the breasts, but instead a smile: Danielle smirking at the camera. Sitting on an unmade bed, crimson sheets twisted around one leg, she held her hair up and loosely back, showing off her breasts and, more important, a pair of diamond earrings.

"Ho-lee . . ." Dave said, his voice trailing off.

"Her breasts aren't *that* nice," Annie said.

"Does this mean what I think it means?" I asked.

"Oh, read the texts," Annie said. "Ray wasn't the suavest lover."

Dave and I read the messages. Ray's were blunt: "I want to fuk u now," "I am hard for u," and more simply and sweetly, "I luv u." Danielle's were more complicated, going from adoring to demanding and back again, messages begging him to slip away, bend her over a table and give her what Marty couldn't, interspersed with commands for him to pick up the beakers at her parents' house and bring them to the new location.

"That came in the night she died," I said. "It's her last message."

There were no texts from Jackie or Marty, and only four other numbers were logged. A number in California—his parents, I guessed—sent a few vaguely worded notes that all said essentially the same thing: "Plans going good?" A Canadian texter sent a sequence of numbers and letters—a code, or possibly a bank account.

Two other contacts were the meth cooks. The first had sent messages in late December, setting up meeting times, listing supplies needed to produce meth, exacting payment of twenty-five thousand dollars before he or she would finish the job. The second started texting a few weeks ago, demanding to know when production would get started and asking for the new location. Yesterday Ray had requested a meeting, with a string of back-and-forths finalizing the plans to meet at the Brouillettes'.

"Our killer," I said.

"Same person as the December texter?" Dave asked. We asked Annie to make a transcription of the texts as soon as possible, and after reminding us that she wasn't our secretary, she left.

I nodded at the closing door. "Ready to go take a crack at Jackie?"

"After all this, I'm exhausted. When it comes to Jackie, it's got to be all you. I'm just going to be furniture." He nodded at the food. "Want some before we leave?"

I shuddered. I hated subs. The only thing worse than subs was leftover subs. The shop's owner was Lorraine and Leslie's brother, so I knew petitioning for pizza or, God forbid, Chinese was a losing battle.

"You can stare down death," Dave cracked, "but pimento loaf brings you to your knees."

"It's against the laws of God and nature," I said. "C'mon, let's get to the DeGroots before they have a chance to toughen up."

"How about we both take our weight class? I'll do Chuck and you do Jackie."

WITH HIS BROAD SHOULDERS and big belly, Chuck DeGroot filled the doorway of his Cape Cod house.

"Jackie!" he yelled up the stairs, and then more quietly to us, "I cleared a space in the dining room."

I cataloged the living room as I walked past. The couch was plaid and covered in plastic. In the corner, closer to the TV, sat a beige recliner, not in plastic and decidedly not protected from stains. A TV tray stood next to the chair, which also included seven remotes. The TV played ESPN classic, some baseball game from the seventies when men were not afraid of mustaches and sideburns.

Chuck apologized as he came into the dining room.

"Jacqueline had a big shock this afternoon, with the boy. Her boy?"

The two of us nodded.

"I told her she could put her face on, but she had to come down—no dodging the cops. Want some coffee? A beer? Some water?"

In a few minutes he returned with our drinks, my water in one hand and two mugs of coffee in the other, his meaty fingers barely fitting through the handles.

"We had those." I pointed to the china cabinet that displayed a set of plates with Washington playing the drum, Lincoln playing the fife, and Franklin carrying a flag, under a "1776–1976" banner. "My dad collected all the grocery receipts for six months and managed to earn the full set from the A&P. They were from the bicentennial."

Chuck smiled. "Those're my mom's. She passed a couple of years back. I haven't got around to moving all her stuff."

"I wondered about the figurines back there," Dave said. "You don't seem like a Hummel kind of guy."

Chuck laughed. "I bought those. For Jackie. Gave her one on every birthday."

The Hummels were all girls with brown ringlets, the younger ones in lederhosen doing things like chasing butterflies, the older girls demurely combing their hair in front of a mirror.

"Jackie's mom around?" Dave asked.

"Eh, sort of," Chuck said. "She lives over in South Albany, but Sandra's got some problems. Cocaine, you know, for fun, when Jackie was a kid. Never could put it down, and once stuff started to get out of control . . . well, now it's crack. She's been ruled unfit."

"That sounds hard," I said.

Chuck shrugged. "Sandra's out of the picture nowadays. Easier than when she was coming and going, but harder now my mom's gone, and Jacqueline being seventeen." Chuck smiled at us. "Should've locked her in the house when I had the chance."

"She in trouble?" Dave asked.

Chuck clasped his hands. "Nothing too bad. You know, boys. And I have to force her to go to school these days. She's not dropping out, not like I did. She saw what happened to me, and she knows there's nothin' you can do without a college degree nowadays."

I pulled out a notepad. "What do you do?"

Chuck described how he'd worked at Brouillette's factory as a dye handler until it stopped producing paper. He was now a stock clerk and cashier at the Freihofer's day-old store.

"No kidding?" Dave said. "My dad delivered bread for Freihofer's for years. I was never short of chocolate chip cookies."

"Oh, lemme get some." Chuck hustled his bulk deftly around the chairs and into the kitchen. He returned and dropped an open box in the middle of the table.

Dave popped a cookie into his mouth whole. "So was it weird, Jackie hanging out with the daughter of your boss?"

"Nah. He wasn't my boss no more, and it's not like Jackie and the girl were friends before that—that girl, Danielle, was expelled from Cohoes High before Jackie was a freshman, and Jackie? She was angry at the Brouillettes from when I got laid off. I was lost for a while, I gotta tell you, and if it weren't for my mom, we would have been homeless. Jackie thought it was all the Brouillettes' fault. But Phil was always decent. He was always willing to pitch in out on the floor, and he put in a good word for me at Freihofer's. It doesn't pay like BPC did, but I get by."

"So Jacqueline got over her anger?" I asked.

"Oh, sure. Until a couple weeks ago now Jackie was over there every day, mostly 'cause of the boy, Ray." Chuck munched a cookie contemplatively. "But the girls were friends. Jackie brung home new clothes every night, boots and dresses Danielle gave her, expensive things. Me and Jackie had it out when she tried to wear the getups to school."

"Afraid her nice new clothes would get ruined?" I asked.

"Nah, but these outfits were too . . . too . . . too mature for a teenage girl." He grabbed another cookie, avoiding eye contact. As a teenager I'd had my own fights with my father, who thought my acid-washed jeans were too tight or my hair was too big. If Jackie was anything like me, she shoved the clothes in a backpack and changed before school.

I grabbed a cookie of my own. "Can you tell us where she was last night, what time she arrived home?"

"Eh, she needed some time with her friends, you know, after the funeral, but ten on school nights is curfew, and she was home by nine thirty. She's got work over at the ice rink, and some special program in the mornings, something for her college applications." Dave tapped my foot under the table. It would seem that Jackie and Ray's early morning trysts had been going on for a while. Chuck continued: "She was in on time, which's good. The roads were pretty snowed under. I'm pretty protective of her since she was meeting the Brouillette girl that time. I mean, that maniac could've killed both of them."

"Which maniac?" Dave asked.

Chuck opened up his interlocked fingers and I was reminded of the game I used to play with Lucy: "Here's the church, and here's the steeple, open the doors, and see all the people." Chuck was at the "people" stage. "That husband. I guess he brung his brother to keep an eye on Dani when he was working, and wouldn't let her go nowhere. Or at least that's what Jackie said."

"And Ray? Was he trouble?"

"He was kind of a dope. But as long as she made her curfew and didn't screw up school, what was I going to do? She's gonna bring home plenty of dumb kids. He spent Christmas here, didja know?" When we shook our heads no, he continued. "Yeah, he showed up here on Christmas Eve, sayin' his brother'd thrown him out. He looked like a stray dog—wet and shaking—and it being Christmas I let him stay. He ate half a ham and told some lame jokes, but

Jacqueline laughed more than she had in a long time. I spent the night sleeping in the hallway, halfway between the living room and Jacqueline's room, but he didn't try nothin'."

I smelled Jackie before I heard her. Her tread was light on the stairs—I bet she was eavesdropping—but she'd soaked herself in some drugstore perfume and gave herself away.

"Anyhow, the brother showed up early, before we opened presents. He ordered Ray outside. I don't like being bossed around, and told Ray he didn't have to go nowhere, but Ray followed his brother. The two of them talked in the driveway for a long time. Oh, and Danielle was there. At one point she pulled Ray into the car with her." Chuck cocked his head—he had picked up on Jackie's approach. "I could see her and Ray talking, and then next thing you know Ray came back and grabbed his clothes. The brother said he was sorry and tried to give me a fruitcake, but who eats that shit? Plus, I got more baked goods than are good for me already."

Jackie walked in, wearing black patent-leather high-heeled knee-high boots covered in tiny buckles. One of Danielle's gifts? She clomped over to the table and slumped bonelessly in a chair as if it was a fainting couch.

"Hi, Jackie." I held out my hand. She shook it, gripping mine limply. "I'm so sorry about Ray."

Jackie nodded, keeping her eyes on the ground and letting her hand drop out of the handshake. She was taking to her role as widow. "I don't know what I'm going to do without him. He was the love of my life."

"I could tell," I said quickly. "We want to figure out what happened to him and bring his killer to justice. Do you have some time to talk?" Jackie didn't answer, looking from Chuck to us.

"Chuck," Dave said, "you mind if we talked to Jackie alone?"

Jackie nodded her head yes vigorously at this. She could rouse herself when it mattered.

"Yeah . . . okay," Chuck said. He went into the other room,

and after a minute we could hear the noise of different channels: sports, game shows, *Judge Judy,* and back to sports. He could hear if he listened closely, so I leaned in and dropped my voice, like a friend sharing a secret. "Jackie, can you tell us the final time you saw Ray?"

"I was the last person to see him alive," Jackie said in a rush. "We were hanging out at Craig's, the three of us. Ray was upset leaving me and moving back to California. He didn't say it, but I could tell—we had, like, a psychic bond. He was a man of action, not words, playing video games, reading comic books, that sort of thing. He gave his heart to me.

"And he really cared about Marty. Probably too much. What my dad told you about Christmas, well, what you need to know is that the accusations about drugs were completely false." Her voice rose and she caught herself, dropping to a low hiss. "I told him he could stay here as long as he needed, even forever. But Ray was the bigger man and forgave his brother."

Chuck hadn't mentioned drugs at all. "What did Marty think Ray did, Jackie?"

"He thought Ray'd smoked meth. Danielle planted the idea in his head, but once she did, Marty was thinking all kinds of crazy things, like he smelled ice on Ray's clothes."

I was surprised that Jackie knew the slang for meth. "Why did Danielle do that?"

"Why did Danielle do anything? She liked to play with people. But playing with her was like playing with razor blades."

"Did she play with you, Jackie?"

Her chin quivered. "No. Never. I was too smart for her. But she convinced Ray . . . she *tried* to convince Ray . . . that he didn't love me."

Danielle had been more persuasive than Jackie realized, but I wasn't going to tell her that.

"How did Ray seem last night?" I asked.

"He was fine. We spent hours together. He didn't want to leave my side."

"Tell me the exact chronology, Jackie. We want to be able to capture Ray's killer."

"Marty called, and we dropped Ray off at his house so he could spend some time with his brother."

"Did you see Marty?" Dave asked. "How did Ray and Marty seem together?"

"I didn't see him. Ray always made me wait outside when Marty was there. And then we came here and Ray dropped me off."

"And did you know he was going to the Brouillettes'?" Dave asked.

"He said Dani left some of her things in the barn. Marty wanted him to go get them. That's all I know." She slid her arms out to full length and laid her head down, her hair fanning out around her, the pietà of Hopewell Falls.

"What time was that?" Dave asked.

"Ray dropped me off at eight thirty," she mumbled into the table.

"That's not what your dad reported," I said.

"What?" Jackie sat up with a start, her hair showering behind her. "Of course he dropped me off. Who else would it be?"

"I don't know Jackie, who would it be?" I asked.

Jackie craned her neck to make sure her dad was still in his chair, and then frantically whispered: "My dad'll kill me if he hears I was with a guy he didn't know."

"So you better tell me fast."

"Craig, okay? Craig drove me home 'cause Ray asked. Ray was always so considerate of me. And I wasn't lying about Ray having to go to Marty. He did, and he was going to be late, so they agreed Craig would drive me home and then go help Ray."

"What time was that?" I asked.

"Seven thirty. He journeyed out into the snow." Jackie made Ray sound like the hero of a romance novel instead of, well, Ray.

"And you and Craig hung out?" Dave asked.

"Yeah. We watched TV."

"What was on?" Dave asked.

"What? Um, a lot of stuff. A movie."

"What movie?"

"It had Bruce Willis and explosions," Jackie said, describing every Bruce Willis movie ever made.

I flipped back through my pad. "And you didn't fool around with Craig?"

"No!" Jackie shouted.

From the living room, the TV muted and we heard the snap of a footrest being lowered.

"Jacqueline?"

"I'm fine, Daddy," she called, her voice, sweet and light, filling with air. The three of us waited until we heard the footrest snap back into place and the football game start up again.

"No. I was in love with Ray and Ray was in love with me. Besides, Danielle was having an affair with Craig."

"You know this for sure?"

"Yes. She was one of those girls, those bitchy ones, who aren't happy unless every boy falls in love with her. Not that Ray did."

"And you didn't mention this before?"

"I didn't want to gossip!" Jackie protested. I doubted any such thing. "And, you know, I never saw anything with my own two eyes. I mean, he's good-looking, if you like big guys with deep eyes and long hair. He'd come over when Marty was working, the four of us would hang out. Danielle and Craig would go into the bedroom to 'talk,' if you know what I mean. Ray said we couldn't disturb them no matter what, not that he cared. He only wanted to be with me."

"And Marty knew?"

"Yeah. He knew. He told Craig not to come around. And I bet he killed Ray because he was mad at Ray for being better than him, having more friends, for being friends with Craig."

"No one else who might have wanted to kill either of them?" I pushed.

"Danielle was a spoiled rich bitch who wasn't as hot as she thought she was—no one liked her. But Ray didn't have any other enemies." Jackie started crying again. "He loved me. And everyone loved him. Everybody."

CHAPTER 14

To BE HONEST, RAY was an annoying little pain in the ass," Craig Madigan said, balancing his beer on the back of the couch. "Oh, would you like to sit?"

He moved to clear the dirty clothes from the corner of the sofa onto the floor. Dave and I'd been there for a good ten minutes, and this was the first time he'd given a thought to the fact that we were standing. Of course, Hale had taken the only decent chair in the place.

"Finished the search and thought I would come on by and support you," Hale had said when he met us at the front door. Currently sandwiched between a beer-can tower and a massive stereo system that was balanced on a series of milk crates, he was penned in. Good.

I wasn't sure I wanted to take Craig up on his offer of a seat on the couch. It was sticky. But really, what was some congealed soda and cigarette ash in the scheme of things? Add some Funyuns stuck between the couch cushions and the place would be exactly like Hale and Kevin's suite at Quantico. I sat.

Dave sank deep into the couch, which seemed to be all cushion and no frame, and I struggled not to fall into him.

"I'm not sure if I'll be able to get out of this again," Dave joked.

Craig laughed. "Yeah, it's pretty comfortable. The ladies love leather."

Hale chuckled, but neither Dave nor I laughed, not that Craig noticed.

"Anyway, Ray, man, he was okay to hang out with, kind of fun. He always had these big plans, stupid plans that were going to force people to show some respect, if you know what I mean."

"No, actually, I don't," I said, and out of the corner of my eye saw Hale tap the armrest twice. Was that a nervous twitch or some sort of code? "You better explain."

"He was always saying how he was a member of the Abominations and people were going to quake in fear when they saw him coming. Mostly I thought he was a dopey little kid who mouthed off." Craig edged closer to me as he talked and I got a good look at the pendant that hung from the leather thong around his neck. It wasn't just jewelry—it was a med-alert necklace, albeit a trendy one in gunmetal and black. "I let him tag along because I had to watch out for Danielle."

"So you and Danielle," Dave said. "The two of you date?"

"What the hell? Who said that? Her husband? He was a suspicious bastard. Danielle took the sacrament of marriage very seriously." Thinking of the pictures on Ray's phone, I somehow doubted that, but I let Craig continue. "That first time I met Marty was when he went berserk on Phil. Don't get me wrong, I could take him, but who knows what he would have done next. The stories Danielle told . . ."

"What stories?" I asked.

"Well, his family was bad news, and Marty, well, he was a chip off that tree." It took me a minute to disentangle the two clichés Craig had just mashed together. "He was violent and kinda lazy." Craig had a satisfied smile on his face. "Danielle wanted someone who was going places, and Marty was not that guy.

"Back in L.A., I kept the peace because Dani and I'd been friends for years. She's always looked up to me, like I'm her cool older brother." He frowned. "Well, maybe not brother. But I was her cool older friend. Cool older *guy* friend. Her dad had me run her back and forth at Thanksgiving when she was out in L.A., and she always showed me the city—it was wild. Back when she was in high school, I'd help keep the peace between her and her dad, giving Dani a heads-up when her dad was planning one of his surprise trips, trying to catch her partying. And I always helped her clean up after her fun, if you know what I mean."

"No. Tell us exactly," I said, thinking of drugs.

"You know, after high school parties, airing out the place, getting rid of empties, rehanging pictures." He swigged off his beer and put the bottle on the table.

"Chopping wood?" I asked.

"Nah. Phil asked me to cut some wood for the fireplace. Why?"

"Well, we found your prints on the ax that killed Ray," Dave said. I wondered if Hale had clued Craig in to that in advance, letting him know his prints had turned up on the murder weapon. I was spending as much time studying Hale as Craig, splitting my attention and seriously throwing myself off my game.

Dave continued. "Did she offer you a special thank-you for the chores?"

Understanding crossed Craig's face. "Oh, wait. You heard this from that girl Jackie." Neither Dave nor I said anything. "God, she chased after Danielle and always had her nose in everything, butting into Danielle's business." Craig didn't need confirmation. "Did she tell you me and Dani would talk together?"

"Spend time in the bedroom alone together," I said. "Danielle's a pretty girl, you're a nice-looking guy. . . ."

Craig laughed, shooting a panicked look at Hale, who shook his head, a quick no. "God, I knew Jackie'd say that. What Danielle and I had went deeper than sex. We were connected in a very deep way. Plus, with her husband and, God, before, that father of hers? Danielle needed a shoulder to cry on. And that was me. I was the only person she could trust."

"And where were you on the night she died?" I asked.

"Flying a round-trip to Montreal." He looked at Hale. "I thought you checked my flight logs."

"We did. They were right as you reported," Hale said. I was ready to shut down this interview right now—Craig was compromised as an informant—but Dave jumped in with a question.

"So when was the last time you saw Ray?"

Pulling his leg up on the couch, Craig faced me directly, touching my shoulder briefly before speaking. He described how Ray had stayed until seven thirty, when his brother called. As he spoke, Craig reached forward and pulled a cigarette out of the pack in front of him and lit up. I couldn't tell him not to smoke in his own house, and Dave, who quit last year, looked ready to ask for one. Craig blew smoke wide into the room, watching it arc.

"And?" I asked.

"And what?" Craig said. "Then I didn't see him again."

Craig was leaving gaps, and if I guessed, I bet it was because Hale coached him not to lie but *to omit*.

"No," I said.

"No what?" Craig took two sharp drags on his cigarette. "I mean, I was supposed to meet him later and help him carry some stuff, over at Dani's. He didn't show."

Dave sat forward, despite the couch's best efforts to immobilize him. "Did he call?"

"No, man, he *didn't call*." Craig pointed at Dave, nearly knocking over the lava lamp propped on the table next to him. "He texted, telling me he'd give me a heads-up when he needed my help."

I usually avoided open-ended questions, but Craig had given some pretty interesting responses.

"Who did you see?" I asked.

"What do you mean? The girl? I didn't touch her, you know. And I even got her home by her curfew." He said the last smugly.

"No, at the Brouillettes'," I said. "You were there, right? That's where you waited for Ray's text."

"Yeah."

"So who did you see?"

Craig hesitated. "No one, man. I sat there for like an hour, freezing my nuts off."

"Until when?" I said.

"Ten thirty. I don't know. I was sitting there waiting for Ray to call me back, but I got the all clear. I drove out, never turning on my lights. I felt like a secret agent, slipping away."

"And who gave you the all clear?" I said.

Hale tapped the chair.

"Hale," Craig said. "He was wearing that crazy-ass hat with the flaps."

Hale sat forward. "I think you might be mistaken, Craig. That wasn't me."

"Ohhh. You're probably right."

Dave stood up and grabbed Craig's cigarette out of his hand. He pounded it into the ashtray, sending butts spilling across the table. He stood over Craig, chest heaving. I had never seen Dave anything approaching angry, and I stood. Hale was up a second later.

"Craig, I'm tired," Dave said. "So rather than spending another thirty minutes with Officer Lyons applying the thumbscrews, why don't you describe the special friendship you and Agent Bascom have."

"Ask me," Hale said from behind Dave.

Dave held up a hand inches from Hale's face, his eyes on Craig. "I trust Craig more. Craig?"

"Shit. Don't you people talk? Hale said if I was ever questioned by the cops to direct them to him." Craig gestured at Hale. "So I'm directing you to him." He stood up, one of the few people who could meet Dave eye to eye, heightwise. He marched to the front door and opened it, all bravado except he wouldn't meet our eyes. "My mouth's shut. I'm no fool."

"Oh, you are," Dave said, and walked out the door. I ran to catch up as he crashed down the stairs, with Hale gliding fast behind me. As we arrived at the first-floor landing, the door flew open and the inhabitant, dirty CREED T-shirt and skin covered with scabs, came out, ready for a confrontation.

"I heard what you said!" the man raved, his snarl revealing black teeth that were rotting out of his mouth. He got lost, drumming his fingers, and I mentally shifted gears from the Craig interview to patrol officer, preparing to take him into custody. He seemed to notice us again and pointed an accusatory finger somewhere to our left: he didn't quite seem to know where we were standing. "Don't think I don't know about your plots!"

I approached him slowly, ready to intercept. I didn't know him, but someone who was that disordered would show up on my radar sooner rather than later. He hadn't actually done anything criminal, but I wanted to get his name, because I knew I would be seeing him sometime soon. I didn't get the chance. The man slammed the door.

The slam was still echoing in the hall when Dave reached past me, grabbed Hale's collar, and swung him around, slamming him against the wall.

"Okay, pretty boy." Dave twisted his hands, drawing the fabric tight across Hale's throat, not enough to choke, but definitely enough to hurt. "You want to tell me what that was? Because I've stayed awake for almost two days straight, and while I am a patient man, I am done with your bullshit."

Hale looked past Dave to me. "You have to understand, there's more going on here than you realize."

I ducked under Dave's arm, putting myself between the two of them. I tapped Dave's arm and he released.

"Meth, obviously," I said to Hale. "But I have to assume that it is FBI level. Big supply? Big distribution? The Abominations? Tell us, Hale."

Hale couldn't meet my eyes. "You don't have clearance, and . . ." He lunged past me. "No!"

I heard, rather than saw, Dave punch the wall. The construction was thick, but there was the sound of bones grinding against flesh, followed by a rain of plaster flaking to the ground.

"Fuck." Dave shook his hand out vigorously. That was a good sign—waving his hand would hurt like murder if he had broken anything. There was banging on the wall. The tenant of apartment one didn't appreciate the noise.

"Hale." Dave's voice didn't have the sharpness and anger of before. He sounded tired. "Hale, I'd like you off the case, but unlike the FBI I'm not willing to cut off my nose to spite my face. We'll liaise. We'll liaise like no one has ever liaised before."

"And we will assume," I added, "that every word out of your mouth is a lie."

"I'm not lying, June," Hale said.

"Fine. We will assume that everything you say is not the complete story."

I was holding the door for Dave when Hale called to us.

"Y'all call me—call the Bureau—if you need some help."

I slammed the door shut on him.

Dave and I walked to the car. This whole case was such a hard slog, with everyone who should be working to get it solved throwing sticks in the spokes, sending me tumbling. I didn't feel beaten, though. I felt mad. I was going to solve this case despite the best efforts of Hale, Jerry, and the Brouillettes. They could try to stop me, but I was moving forward.

"So," I said as we reached the car, "you think Hale's pretty?"

"He's got nice eyes."

Dave marched through the unshoveled drive around to the passenger side. The wood-frame house, now covered in aluminum siding, had been built before the advent of cars, and the single lane that ran between the two buildings was barely wide enough for one vehicle. Dave ended up scraping the door on the opposite house.

He was still mad. "Your idiot FBI friend has been thwarting the investigation the whole time. I may not be able to run them out of town, but I can burn their hotel down. I mean, c'mon."

"I have an idea," I said. "I could go myself, or—"

"Yeah, to get the accelerant down in time we'll need two people."

"Or we could regroup and talk to Hale and company tomorrow. Get some sleep and face them at full power."

"What do you mean? I'm at full power," he said faintly. He crossed his arms and rested his head against the seat belt strap. Within a minute, he was asleep.

I lowered the volume on the police radio, the quiet chatter of Leslie and the fading light of the afternoon cocooning us in the car. I made the executive decision to drive Dave to his house. He lived a few blocks over in a Victorian he was converting in his spare time. I pulled to a stop in front of his house and nudged him.

Dave slept on. The house rehab was going slowly, the time he spent at work leaving little time for construction. Last summer, at the end of his Fourth of July barbecue, Dave and I, mellow with too much beer and too much sun, had talked, the smell of burned charcoal dying away. With his bottle of Rolling Rock he'd gestured down the hill toward the river, which flashed behind a line of tall trees.

"I can never forget where I came from, even up here." He threw out his arms to take in all he surveyed, including his back deck, his yard, and farther down the hill the house where he grew up, on the island in the old Ukrainian section of town. It was the first time the two of us had discussed anything other than police work. Dave had described his life: his father, his brother, his maiden aunts and bachelor uncles, all making sure he didn't even miss his mother after she took off with some guy.

"And look at how far I've made it," he said.

I smiled. While Dave was working his way up through the department, I was across the country doing work I never dreamed possible. Now I found myself at home again, most of my go-getter friends long gone, following the trail of jobs and money to New York City. I had been long gone, too, a country between me and this town and these people who I had thought were going nowhere. I was glad when I found them again, grounded, but having landed where I belonged, at home.

I pushed Dave harder and harder until he woke with a start.

"Hey." He rubbed his eyes, and slapped his cheeks a few times. "This isn't the hotel."

"No, it's the place where I am reliably informed they keep your bed." I wrinkled my nose. "And your shower. Hale will still be able to lie to us in the morning."

Dave raised his finger to make a point and then dropped it. "Okay. Call me if you find the clue that'll crack this case wide open, right?"

I nodded, and he slowly picked up his things, before dropping them next to the gearshift.

"Got your head, or did you drop that, too?"

Dave flipped me the bird and slammed the door. He waded up his unshoveled walk, the snow leaving a ring of white up to his thighs. He reached the porch, where he picked up several papers, and waved good-bye. I pulled out into the street, heading toward home. We needed to be ready for the wake, the FBI, and an outlaw biker gang: whatever got thrown at us and whoever threw it. Considering the number of people pissed off at us, we had to be ready for anything.

CHAPTER 15

THE DAY OF DANIELLE'S funeral, I woke with my legs twisted tight in the comforter and my arm reaching across the bed, across Kevin's side. When had I become a person who took up the whole bed? I had always been a restless cover-hog—Kevin accused me of full-contact sleeping—but my body had always known intuitively where the boundary resided between my side and Kevin's. I pulled my arm back into my blanket cocoon, half for warmth and half to make it up to Kevin, forcing my body to remember him.

It was full dark still, and I couldn't hear anything stirring: no cars half skidding down the street, both my father and my daughter still fast asleep. I closed my eyes and pushed my head deep into the pillow, hoping the warmth of the covers would pull me back under. I inhaled and tried to clear my mind. I stopped when I realized I was searching for Kevin's scent, a combination of hair gel and green grass. Of course it was impossible, it had been more than two years, almost three, but I had found that my husband's phantom smell would show up out of nowhere, either ambushing or comforting me. For so long after he died our bedroom had reeked of ammonia, his odor during those last months no matter how many sponge baths we gave him. My father got a frequent-buyer card at the candle store during that time, bringing home bright pillars in lavender, apple pie, or eggnog. He was searching for the one that might get rid of the smell instead of cover it. They all made me sick. Eventually he stopped.

Lucy didn't seem to notice, climbing into bed with Kevin and pretending to read him stories. She turned the pages of books she knew by heart, flipping them around so he could see all the pictures. She built train tracks with bridges that traveled over Kevin's legs and sent the blue cars careening off the bed; they laughed and did it again. Away from Kevin, Lucy was no angel, with notes coming home from preschool for hitting, and night terrors that woke everyone in the house except Kevin, who slept the sleep of the Oxycontined. All Lucy's bad behavior stopped the minute Kevin died. She became quiet in a way that had only begun to pass in the last few months.

The night before Kevin's funeral, I didn't sleep at all, furious with my father, who had taken all the sheets and blankets and washed them while I was at the wake. Kevin had started to go missing from my life at that point. Secretly I was hoping he might come back. He'd still be sick, sure, but if they changed everything—if my father kept moving Kevin's stuff—then there would be no chance. He would certainly slip away if we pushed him.

Some people seemed to expect me to feel relief after his death, as he was sick for so long and was in a coma for almost a month.

"You said good-bye weeks ago," my mother commented, as though it was supposed to comfort me. Our last night in bed, I told Kevin stories of my day. The final thing coma patients lose is their hearing, so he heard about Lucy's adventures in snow forts and how I'd picked up a pair of oxblood shoes from T.J. Maxx the day before that were a steal. Even in his coma he smiled, my love of hunting out deals a long-running joke between us, and the skin stretched tight across his teeth. I knew he was there, he was with me. He wasn't gone.

And then he was. The people from hospice were almost too efficient, arranging within an hour for his body to be transported to the funeral home. The next few days were nonstop activity: setting up the wake and the service; keeping Lucy close; arranging housing for Kevin's sister; talking my own sister into running interference with our mother so I could avoid her; and a million other things large and small. I kept in constant forward motion, as stopping and thinking would've been pointless: I couldn't think. The next thing I knew it was the day of the funeral, and I was lying awake, condemning my father, and exhausted in every way.

My alarm rang. It was time to get up for Danielle's funeral. I rolled over and hit the clock hard, banging my wrist. I could hear my father in the shower. I pulled the covers back and made the bed, knowing my father had done the same thing: the military trained him and he trained me. I heard him shuffle across the hallway to his room and I made my way to the bathroom, the cold from the wood floors seeping through my socks. My father kept the thermostat low during the night as a way to save money and build character. In another hour the house would be plenty warm. Not so warm a sweater wasn't needed, but warm enough that your fingers didn't turn blue.

My father didn't restrict the hot water, thankfully, and I took a nice long shower. I had so much hair that it pulled my neck back when it was wet: my hairdressers didn't so much style my hair as keep it from achieving critical mass. Maybe after the case was finished I would get my hair cut. And shave my legs again, although there was really no point until spring.

Out of the shower and blown dry, I made a fast dash to my room—cold, cold, cold—and put on the suit I'd laid out the night before. Black and conservative, the skirt hit my knee even when I sat. My little trick was the tailoring, which took the business out of it and made me feel ever so slightly feminine. I had a bunch of these suits, purchased during my FBI days, and had worn this one to Kevin's funeral. I had pulled it out the morning of his service and discovered that it slid down my hips and was a half shoulder too big. I couldn't fix it or buy another, so my jacket slumped sideways through the day, even when I worked to keep my back straight and to meet everyone's eyes and thank them sincerely for their condolences, their cake, their support. It fit again now, even with the Glock holstered under my shoulder, and I finished by pulling my hair up into a French twist, applying some nude lipstick, and fixing pearls around my neck. I looked at myself in the mirror and tried to appear competent, trustworthy. Like a cop.

I went downstairs. I could hear my father in the kitchen, speaking softly.

"I know, right. . . . Uh-huh." As I walked in he raised a cup of coffee to me. "Look, I gotta go." He took a sip from his cup. "Yup . . . take care. . . . Bye."

I put some cinnamon bread in the toaster and poured myself some coffee, and stood against the counter at the opposite side of the kitchen.

"Who was that?" I asked.

"Your mom."

I choked on my coffee, barely avoiding spitting it on my shirt. "Mom?"

"You sound like a sulky teenager. Your mom and I talk. You know that. She's an early riser, probably the only thing we have in common."

"So how often do these little chats happen?"

"I don't keep a calendar," he said, sighing. "When there's news. When something big happens. We've been divorced twenty years, which is enough time to get over things, even for a grumpy bastard like me." He raised his coffee cup to me. "You should try it sometime. It's been what? Three years?"

"Since Kevin died. You know that. I'm a little busy, and she'd probably just tell me to balance my chakras."

"Your aura does seem a little off," Dad said, and then more seriously, "You okay? You look fried."

"Just tired." Not the truth, but I didn't have time for grief over Kevin right now.

"I boiled some eggs for you and cut up some carrots. A few corn muffins are in there, too." My father handed me a paper grocery sack as my phone buzzed. It was Dave.

"There's enough for him, too. And a thermos of coffee." I pulled on my boots and dropped my toast, wrapped in a napkin, into my purse.

I yanked on the front door twice before the glaze of ice that covered it gave way. Halfway down the walk my phone rang again. I patted down all the pockets of my coat as well as my suit, pulling it out of my purse right on the fifth ring.

"Hi," Hale said. "Don't hang up."

"Assuming you're calling regarding our case, I'm not going to hang up."

"The way you laid into me, I figured it was even odds, but in your role of liaison . . ."

I lost the second half of the conversation climbing into Dave's car. "Hale," I mouthed to Dave, who made a face at me before relieving me of the bag of food.

"What?" I said.

"I said that Marty and Ray's folks have boarded their flight, so they'll arrive in plenty of time for the funeral. Phil asked if the Jelicksons could be banned, Marty included."

"No."

"That's what I told him. I'm going to be sticking with the Brouillettes until we get to the church, since they know me and trust me."

I rolled my eyes, and Dave mouthed, "What?"

"Anything else to report?" Hale asked.

"Not for the funeral," I said. "I can brief you on our interview with Jackie and Chuck DeGroot later."

"I've got a second now."

"I don't have time for you right this minute."

Hale sighed. "Debriefing later would be fine. I'll see you directly."

I hung up the phone and broke the news about the Jelicksons' arrival.

"Great," Dave said, his mouth full of egg. "They'll probably firebomb the church and make you one of their old ladies."

"Or they could make you their old man. Mrs. Jelickson's coming, too, don't forget."

"She's going to whisk me away from all this." Dave waved his arm expansively, taking in the gray snowbanks that lined the streets and the old boardinghouses beyond them. "She's going to throw me on the back of a Harley, drive me to sunny California, and support me in the manner I've grown accustomed to."

"I think that's what Danielle was hoping, and look how well that turned out."

Dave pulled into the lot of Saint Agnes, parking close to one of the exits. A half-dozen cars dotted the parking lot, mostly Lincolns and Buicks from the eighties with one white late-model Honda tinged gray from salt and dirt. By the time of Danielle's funeral Mass, the lot would be packed and cars would be parked all the way down the hill. In the shadowy early morning, even the little old ladies who attended funerals for fun were still at home, picking out their black dresses.

The two of us walked across the gravel of the parking lot to the church. I accidentally skidded slightly across the rocks, then skidded intentionally, remembering how much I'd enjoyed it when I used to go to church with my parents.

"Monsignor Ottario told us to cool our heels until Mass was over," Pete called across the parking lot. He gestured over to a white van parked in front of where the Catholic high school once stood. The diocese had demolished it after they figured out it would cost more to keep it closed than to knock it down. "That's the FBI truck. They tried to check IDs for the people going to seven A.M. Mass, but Mrs. Reilly—you know the one? was a union whip?—well, she and a few other old ladies told them to go hang. Monsignor backed 'em up, and the agents let 'em go."

I savored the idea of a few retired seamstresses sticking it to The Man, but realized I was The Man, too, and shouldn't be encouraging that kind of behavior. We heard the organ inside cranking out the recessional, "Now Thank We All Our God," and went out front to intercept Monsignor. The front doors swung wide and Monsignor exited, gesturing two agents off the steps and several feet away. He greeted everyone who came out with a vigorous handshake, leaning over to talk with some and helping the weaker ones down the stairs. A few of the ladies shook hands with the FBI agents and gave them an earful about civil liberties. Norm Finch nodded as he passed.

Monsignor was out of hands to shake and was heading my way.

"So this is what I need to do to get you to church, June," he said. Monsignor Ottario had been Father Ottario through much of my life, coaching my class through our first confession. I had been fearful, my ten-year-old mind coming up with all kinds of sins I'd committed that were unforgivable. Father kept it short and sweet, sidestepping my efforts at self-flagellation. After I had left the pews filled with my classmates and come up to the confessional as slowly as I could, I said the line I had memorized: "Bless me, Father, for I have sinned. This is my first confession."

He seemed to be considering me in all of my sinfulness. "Which team do you want to win the World Series?" he asked.

His line of questioning threw me off. "The Mets?"

"You've nothing to be sorry for. Go in peace," and I wandered in a daze back to my seat.

He had presided over Kevin's funeral, and stopped by three or four times, ostensibly to visit my father but somehow always catching me when I was home. He'd talk church gossip and church business—he was involved in the diocesan investigations into priests' sexual misconduct, which he took seriously. He'd eat stale coffee cake, take my hand, and say a prayer. I hadn't been the praying type for a while, but in my grief I found solace in this person who was a trusted part of my childhood.

Now I needed him to trust me and give me access to the church. "Monsignor, we need to get in there and do a sweep before the Mass. It's an intrusion, a serious intrusion, but until we know who we're dealing with—"

"Sure, c'mon in." He unbuttoned the top of his cassock as we climbed up the stairs, not waiting to see if I would follow. I waved the others into the church and ran to catch up to Monsignor, who threw questions over his shoulder as we hustled up the center aisle about my dad, Lucy, my health, and if I ever spoke to Kristen, my best friend from high school who had moved to California. Although his hair was gray, he moved quickly, and could still catch teenagers skipping school before they knew what hit them. Only the center front pews had the lights on and the church was chilly, two cost-cutting measures to keep it from closing. Monsignor would stop to straighten missals and flip up kneelers, and gave a quick sign of the cross as he passed the altar.

"I need to ask you to put the lights on through the whole church," I said. "And do you want to accompany us when we search the altar?"

"I've got a conference call with the diocesan lawyers at eight and have to get ready for the funeral." He stared past me to where the agents were leading police dogs up and down the pews, flashlights scanning below the seats. "Are there animals in my church?"

"Dogs that are on loan from the state troopers K-9 unit. Don't worry—they're better behaved than most troopers."

"I trust you, June."

"I appreciate that, Monsignor. But I also need a minute of your time to ask you a few questions."

"Later would be better."

I halted in front of a statue of Saint Agnes, a bank of votives before her. "Actually, doing it before the service would be a big help."

Monsignor raised an eyebrow at me, mischief evident in the flickering light of the candles. "Okay, boss, it's your show." He walked back to me. "I can give you a minute."

I flipped to my list so quickly the paper cut across my middle finger. I blotted it on my notebook and soldiered on. "Did you know Danielle?"

"She came to after-school Catholic Ed, so I saw her, but only talked to her at the big events, stuff the teachers brought me in for. It seemed as if she didn't know how to talk to other girls, and they didn't seem like they knew what to do with her, either."

"But she knew how to talk to boys?"

"They went out of their way to talk to her. I heard Jimmy McCollough ask her to fool around in the empty bingo room, but she said, 'Not in a million years,' before I had to step in. I also heard one of the kids' fathers ask her to go to a hotel with him. I was grabbing a smoke out back"—he waved in the direction of the confessionals, and I assume the parking lot beyond. "She said, 'Is the hotel in New York City near Saks?' I shut down that discussion immediately, and that father and I had a long conversation regarding the sanctity of marriage and where teenage girls fit into that equation." Monsignor shook his head. "I told Phil, and he yelled, but not at her. More like *near* her. He aimed most of his anger at me."

"And Danielle's mom? Any sense of how they got along?"

"I know that back in high school Danielle didn't like all her mom's travel, but that was when she was a kid. She was proud of her mom."

"She told you that in confession?"

Monsignor grinned. "Juniper, if the killer himself told me his sins in confession, I wouldn't tell you."

"Fair enough," I said. "So how did you know?"

"She and I got stuck next to each other at an Ancient Order of Hibernians dinner, right after she was thrown out of Catholic High. It seems she liked to time her high school expulsions with her mother's campaigns, when she could get Mom's attention."

I wondered if Danielle had done that last year, when Amanda Brouillétte had been defending her seat. I could imagine how that conversation at the Hibernians' dinner went. I'd found myself confiding in Monsignor Ottario because he made it clear that he'd heard it all before—more than once—and your sins? Kind of boring. While he kept his eyes on the divine, his feet were firmly planted on the ground.

"Did you give her any advice?"

"I suggested she might want to figure out what course she wanted to chart, instead of charting a course against her parents. She had a hopeless attitude, convinced that her parents had all the major accomplishments covered. The Brouillettes emphasized how they were self-made and she should be, too, even as they handed her everything. She felt they cut her off at the knees whenever she tried to stand on her own feet. I tried to explain that money and power were not the only goals one could have in life." He paused, considering his words. "I had hoped that with her move to California and her entrance into UCLA, she was finding her way." He raised his thumb toward the sacristy. "We done?"

"Not quite," I said, and Monsignor gave me a *hurry up* motion with his hand. "Have you seen Danielle recently?"

"She and her husband came to church around Christmastime, for a month or so. Or rather, she came once, and *he* came for a month. Danielle was one of those kids who were confirmed so that they could tell their parents they weren't going to church anymore. I grabbed him once after Mass, and he said he was just checking out a little God. Not bad. Or at least trying not to be bad. I don't think he had much practice at being good."

"And her brother-in-law? Ray Jelickson? You know him?"

"Not at all, but I'm reasonably sure that you could ask Jackie DeGroot, Chuck DeGroot's daughter. They were dating."

I tried to think if I'd missed anything. Above me, Saint Agnes gazed down, looking less like a scared fourteen-year-old virgin martyr than like an assured young woman confident in her belief in God and in alignment with His will. Parishioners believed in her as well, based on the number of people who lit vigil lights to her.

I couldn't think of anything. "You're off the hook, Father, er, Monsignor."

"Oh good, just in time for my conference call." Monsignor stepped close, resting his hands on both my shoulders, an arm's-length hug. "It's nice to have you back, Juniper."

I smiled. "Don't get your hopes up about seeing me at Mass anytime soon."

"What I meant was that we lost our hero, the woman who would push to make sure the world was a more decent place. It's nice to have her back, no longer hiding her candle under a bushel basket. And of course, I'd be happy to see you here along with Miss Lucy—she's quite the conversationalist." I smiled at his very true description of Lucy, and he squeezed both my shoulders and nodded toward the agents who were continuing their sweep. "Don't let them trash the place."

"I'll ask them to clean off any gum they find stuck underneath the seats."

He swept off in a flurry of purple robes. I left the watchful gaze of Saint Agnes and walked down the wide aisle, passing the stained glass window that was my childhood favorite, the one showing the fires of hell. My parents would let me sit next to it, if we could, since I was less fidgety when I could study the devils with pitchforks and the flames licking the damned. It's not like the windows of the saints were any less bloody: from stigmata to bodies pierced with arrows or crushed by wagon wheels, Catholic imagery, at least pre–Vatican II, was hardly known for its restraint. I had gone to church during a time in which they encouraged a folk quartet to sing light rock ballads in an effort to make the church hip and approachable, but my eyes had always studied this window where the wages of sin were writ large.

Moments later, the lights came on.

CHAPTER 16

THE IRISH CATHOLIC IMMIGRANTS had built the church a century ago, greater and higher than any other church in town, overflowing the pews every week with their crowded families. It's a good thing they did, I thought. Danielle's funeral had packed the seats, with more than two thousand people in attendance.

With the light shining down on her auburn hair, Amanda Brouillette gleamed like a copper penny in the front row. She hadn't cried, and no doubt somebody in the audience was concluding that she had killed her daughter and that boy if she didn't even cry. I remembered my own efforts to stiff-upper-lip it through Kevin's funeral. "So strong," my friends commented. "She never really cared," my enemies said. In retrospect, I wasn't fooling anyone—I could barely carry on a conversation in those weeks, and ended up with my clothes inside out more than once—but I needed to grieve in private because my sadness might wash me away.

Against thee only have I sinned, and done this evil in thy sight. . . .

Monsignor paused, the words from the Miserere sinking into the hearts of those witnessing the funeral for Danielle. The Mass was very fire and brimstone. Who had opted for the old-fashioned Mass? Probably Phil Brouillette, who sat next to his wife looking puffy from lack of sleep, too much alcohol, and maybe some crying.

Half hidden behind a pillar was Hale. He didn't fit in, despite his sober clothes and somber expression. His perfectly fitting suit brought out his sharp angles and broad shoulders. He was a viper in with the garden snakes.

I recognized many of the faces, including the parents of grade school friends, diners at Spiak's, perps I'd arrested. I didn't see many people Danielle's age. She either didn't have many friends or the friends she did have were away at college. A sea of lobbyists flooded the pews, identifiable from their pin-striped suits and the smart phones under the sight line of the pew. The guys from the Brouillette plant wore ties tucked into their ski jackets, stood with their hands folded in front of them, and knelt as one when it was time— even if they didn't know the Mass, they understood respect. Chuck and Jackie were within a few pews of the plant guys, and Chuck exchanged nods with several of them.

Jackie kept glancing back at Craig, who stood in the back, the province of young men who wanted to make a quick escape. Shifting from foot to foot, Craig glanced at the door Dave patrolled. I wondered if Craig was watching for the Jelicksons. I know I was. Marty had arrived alone. He wore the same suit he'd worn to the wake, an imprint from the iron on the back of his left sleeve. The congresswoman squeezed his shoulder as she passed, while her husband stared through Marty as if he wasn't there.

Deliver me from bloodguiltiness, O God. . . .

Jason Byrne arrived shortly thereafter with his parents, his mother pushing his father's wheelchair. I was surprised—I expected Mr. Byrne to be too sick to come. Braces around his head, torso, and neck kept him from sliding sideways, but his dull hair, ropy arms, and yellow skin made him appear decades older than his wife—eighty-five rather than forty-five. His brown corduroys had been carefully folded up at the ankles to keep them from getting caught in the wheels. He nodded to a few people, weakly and a beat too slow, but still alert and part of life. Jason raced ahead to Marty, who slid over in his otherwise empty pew. Ten rows back, Denise Byrne slowed and finally stopped, ignoring Jason's wave; then turned, strode around to the side aisle, and parked her husband next to the pillar where Hale stood before she slid into the very end of the row, far away from her son and Marty.

Monsignor Ottario stood up to give the eulogy. He spoke of Danielle in the most general terms, how she was loved as a child of God and would be missed, but I knew he meant it. With a groan from the century-old hinges, the heavy wooden doors opened and the Jelicksons appeared. Zeke Jelickson's hair was slicked back and his beard was trimmed, and he was wearing biker formal wear: polished brown cowboy boots peeked out from under a conservative wool suit. Linda Jelickson could've been any one of the politicians' wives that crowded the first few pews, or even one of the politicians themselves, wearing a black pantsuit with her blond hair pulled back into a chignon. Her face was a little more weathered than the country club set, but her boots were Ferragamo.

I tracked them as they sauntered up the aisle. Dave ambled forward, squinting. Craig stepped sideways, into their line of vision, but they ignored him. Jackie waved, and Denise Byrne stood up and released the brake from her husband's wheelchair before he jerked—a protest—forcing her to sit down again. Marty pushed over in the pew without saying anything, going so far as to hush his mother when she whispered to him.

Monsignor finished his eulogy, enlightening us on the endless love of God and his mysteries. At Kevin's funeral, not much love had been lost between God and me, and as to his ways, well, I didn't want to know. Lines formed to receive Communion, first the Brouillettes and the Jelicksons, and finally the rest of the communicants. The crowd avoided making eye contact when passing either family's pew, with most looking at Danielle's closed casket, hidden beneath the shawl of flowers. A few moments for contemplation followed Communion, the church quiet except for the occasional sob.

From the sea of bowed heads, Hale launched up, his hand to his ear and talking so loudly into his radio that even in the rear of the church I could hear the words "contain the threat." He wasn't running up the aisle, but it was close: the razor-sharp creases of his pant legs flattened against his shins as he hurried toward me. Marty shook off his mother's grabbing hands and walked calmly up the aisle, head down. I stood up, ready to intercept Hale.

Dave opened the door. The gigantic sound he let in caused the whole congregation to turn as one toward the back of the church. He rushed out. Dave never rushed, and I broke into a run. I smashed the door wide and it slammed into the doorstop, almost bouncing back on Hale, who was on my heels.

What I found shocked me: lined up behind the hearse, two by two, was a whole posse of Harley-riding bikers.

In front of the group, Dave waved his arms and yelled. I crossed behind him to the middle of the road, flanking the line midway, around the seventh pair of riders. Hale moved opposite me, and six more agents positioned themselves in a star formation around the group.

I could make out some of Dave's words. "Gentlemen!" he yelled, as well as "cease" and "engines." The gargantuan man at the front of the line rolled his bike forward, within a few inches of Dave's left foot. If he rolled closer, either intentionally or unintentionally, Dave would end up with a fractured leg. It didn't help that the rider wasn't on the smoothest surface, poised on the edge of a pothole with delusions of grandeur—it was almost a crater.

I stood on a crack and was thrown off balance, forcing me to widen my stance. Snow would have improved things, evening out the surface, but public works had taken their job seriously, moving not only the snow off the street but the snowbanks as well; everything plowed onto a truck and dumped onto the frozen river to wait for spring. With the street clear, the hole where the high school used to be looked like the bomb site it was, the demolition experts having used explosives to take down a building that big.

The bikers seemed more amused than fearful of the collection of law enforcement officers that surrounded them.

Dave shouted louder. "Disperse, or you will be under arrest."

Hale approached the stony-faced man closest to him. "You heard what he said! Get out of here, now!"

"Showing our respects," the rider said, nodding toward the FUNERAL stickers pasted below the green MERRIMEN patches. They weren't the Abominations, but I had no idea if the Merrimen were good news or bad. Probably the latter.

The church doors swung wide. Marty emerged, shaking off Pete's grip. He ambled down, straddling the front tire of the lead bike like a cowboy so he could face Dave, his nose inches from Dave's chin. He spoke, and Dave gave a barely perceptible nod before stepping away. Marty took three breaths, his shoulders rising and falling, turned, and faced the gang.

"Brothers," he yelled. "Thank you for the respect for the dead. For Danielle and Ray, and for me."

"Your father," said a guy with big lungs—and big everything else—who had no problem being heard above all the engines' roar. "We're here to pay respect to your father and his family."

The exhaust choked me, but Marty seemed to have no problem getting enough oxygen. "For the funeral of my wife, a congresswoman's daughter—"

"You know where you came from, boy?"

"I know." In his quiet way, he controlled the scene, the bikers, their machines, and law enforcement and our weapons. "I can never forget."

The bells of the church rang out, announcing the end of the funeral Mass. Marty looked at the steeple, covering his eyes against a sun that wasn't there, his wedding band bumping against the skull ring he wore on his middle finger.

He undid his tie. "Merrimen and Abominations, we're blood."

"You're not blood," the leader growled. "Your father. Your brother. For them, we'd die."

"Then for them, we need a little reverence."

The leader of the Merrimen was having none of it. "Reverence? For these people? Respect is better than reverence."

"I know. But the pigs don't. And Danielle's mom, the congress-woman, she don't. And they can fuck things up for us, but good." The Merrimen seemed unimpressed with that argument, and I got ready for things to get ugly. Marty continued. "You know why? They don't understand brotherhood and friendship. Having friends, closer than blood family, who watch your back no matter what. They don't understand and they're fucking envious."

"And you do, turncoat?"

"I do. No matter where I go or what I do, I'm still one of you. Always, always."

I shifted from foot to foot, my legs aching from the effort to stay in place. The agents waited for some signal from Hale.

"And I need the brotherhood right now," Marty continued. "I need you at my back, to find who killed Dani and Ray. To be with me to see Ray off right, to make sure he gets his due. To get justice, our justice, *real justice,* 'cause God knows we can't leave it to the cops." Several heads nodded in agreement and Hale rolled his eyes at me.

"And if you get yourself arrested here for not having a *parade permit*"—Marty shook his head in disgust—"I'm . . . my family's left hangin'. So go back to my place, down on Cataract Street, and we can plan this out right."

The guy at the head of the line tilted his head, seemingly in consideration. Mirrored aviator glasses blacked out the top half of his face and a green bandana obscured the rest, and I had no idea what he was thinking. Seconds ticked by.

Slowly the biker raised his thick arm upward with his index and pinkie finger extended. He held it aloft, and the men revved their engines. Finally he slammed his hand down on the throttle. My eardrums throbbed as sixteen Road Kings accelerated behind him in staggered formation, their tires pelting my skirted legs with gravel.

Two altar boys opened the front doors of the church and stood dazedly in the exit watching the bikes disappear around a corner. Finally, the crowd forming behind them, and a few sharp words from Monsignor Ottario, compelled them to hook the doors open.

Monsignor stood aside and gestured to the young men who were carrying the casket out toward the hearse. The Brouillettes, tightly behind, helped each other down the steps. Phil Brouillette looked ready to yank the box out of the back of the hearse, as did Marty, who stood next to the car's door, touching the casket as it glided past.

"Where'd the rest of the mourners go?" Zeke Jelickson yelled to Marty from the top of the church stairs. At his father's yell Marty turned, letting Danielle go. His mother ran to him and he folded over into a hug. He spoke to his father over his mother's shoulder: "Sent 'em home. I gotta keg, which'll let 'em mourn plenty."

Amanda Brouillette walked up to Marty, stepping in front of his mother and taking his hand. "Thank you for taking care of things." Her voice was even. "Things are so . . . are so . . . terrible."

"Showing proper respect? That's so terrible?" Zeke Jelickson said, his arm thrown wide as if to embrace the congresswoman. She stepped closer to Marty.

"C'mon, Zeke." Marty said. "Danielle's people wanted things proper."

"You're Danielle's people. You're going to let them piss all over you?"

"You asshole." Phil Brouillette stormed toward them. "You may think you can pollute our daughter's memory—"

Hale edged up to Phil Brouillette, although whether to protect him from Zeke Jelickson or to protect Zeke Jelickson from him, I didn't know. Hale nodded to me, and I positioned myself to the right of Zeke. Mourners had begun to stream out of the church but gave our group a wide berth, the grief too sharp on this island. I could smell the faint scent of cigarette smoke coming off Zeke, and brushed the wool of his suit, which was a fine weave, very soft, and no doubt expensive.

"I'm sorry for all our losses," Zeke Jelickson said, grave and serious. "We're all sipping from the same bottle here. This is how our family honors the dead. We have as much say over Danielle as you do."

"No, you're mistaken." The congresswoman sounded like she was making an agriculture policy statement, but her words were harsh, all quaver from her voice gone. "She's mine. Mine and my husband's and Marty's."

"And Marty's ours," Linda Jelickson said. Marty shook his head.

"I don't think so," the congresswoman said. "I think he's mine now." Marty gave an even more vigorous no, but I don't think she noticed. "And this town is mine." The congresswoman stepped forward so that only the people in the tight circle could hear as funeral goers streamed around us. She was right in Zeke Jelickson's face, and I was forced to step backward a few inches when, ever so slightly, he withdrew.

"And before you decide that you're going to cause trouble here, realize that if you cross me, if you defile my town, I will destroy you. I will reach across the country and bring you and your organization under so much scrutiny that you won't so much as be able to blink without my permission. If you think, Mr. and Mrs. Jelickson, you can do things our way, the right way, you are welcome to come over to our house for coffee and cake. If you can't, I will *roll over you*. It will happen so thoroughly and hard that you won't even know what happened."

"Ma'am, I can see where Danielle got her swagger." Zeke Jelickson tipped an imaginary hat. "We'll be seeing you while we're in town, I'm sure, but you'll have to excuse us: we have to go and plan the funeral of our son."

"Which anyone with any class would have said they're sorry for," spat Mrs. Jelickson. She walked toward a Harley that was parked illegally at a fire hydrant, but stopped and called to Marty. "Baby? You coming?"

Marty shook his head. "I need to see Dani buried."

"Marty, would you like to ride with us over to the cemetery?" asked Amanda. Behind her, Phil looked ready to protest.

"No. I don't need that," Marty said. Zeke Jelickson smiled, but his smile faded at what Marty said next. "I'm going to go to work after this."

The congresswoman pulled a slim phone out of her bag. "Let me make a call. There's no reason that you should have to work today."

"No, ma'am, don't," Marty said. "I want to work, get away from all you people." Marty ducked into a limo, his motorcycle boot the last thing visible before he was gone behind a black wall.

"Thanks for having my back there, man," Dave said to Hale once the Brouillettes were safely away.

"No problem," Hale said, lifting his hand to his ear. He wasn't really with us, listening for updates on the Brouillettes or the Merrimen or both. He paused and frowned, the message he was receiving more important than the scene in front of him. He blinked, realizing where he was. "Need help containing the Merrimen?"

"Christ, yes, although it's going to be a manpower stretch."

"We can help with that, you know. We can help you with interviews, too, once this funeral's over."

"Manpower yes, interviews no. We don't—"

"Detective Batko. Officer Lyons." Jerry's voice droned through the crowd. "As soon as I have paid my respects, we are going to have a long talk. Be ready, I'll expect more than the incompetence you have shown to date. Bikers at a funeral? Letting Marty Jelickson walk free? I don't know what you think you are doing, but you clearly have no idea. . . ."

CHAPTER 17

AT MARTY'S HOUSE, DAVE and I found the Merrimen strewn across the front yard, like lawn ornaments of the damned. They moved collectively to block the steps, a wall of bushy beards and green bandanas.

The big guy who led the pack was sitting in a lawn chair in front of the house, a bottle of Jack Daniel's between his legs.

"Private property," he said.

I rolled my eyes. "Uh-huh. Should we call in the FBI to do the interview?"

The big guy, whose patch read TINY, nodded to a young, wiry kid, clearly a probie—a prospect, I corrected myself, a probie was a new cop. The kid slipped inside the house without a word. I found myself shifting from foot to foot while we waited, my panty-hosed legs raw from the cold. I probably should have changed clothes, or at least taken off my pearls, but Dave and I were eager to talk to the Jelicksons before they compared notes with Marty. Good thing Marty was avoiding them.

The Merrimen, in their henleys and leather jackets, seemed impervious to the cold. Three of them circled close, and the warmth came off them in waves. I didn't want their kind of heat and stepped back.

Dave nodded at the bottle propped between Tiny's legs. "You know that alcohol only makes you feel like you're warm, but can induce hypothermia, right?"

"Trying to check out the package of a real man?" Tiny said. The rest of the group laughed like it was the funniest thing ever, holding their guts.

"Faggot," Panhead said. He had a well-trimmed beard and few patches. *Newbie,* I thought.

The front door opened, and the prospect stood half in and half out of the house. "Zeke wants a report from the pigs."

The steps groaned under the combined weight of Dave, me, and the welcome wagon that lined the banisters. The prospect let the door snap shut in Dave's face. I wondered whether we had avoided a fight or were heading for a bigger one.

The living room was barely recognizable from just a few days before. The TV was reoriented to face the recliner rather than the couch, and an ashtray held the remains of a couple dozen cigarettes, the smoke skirting the ceiling. The books and CDs were no longer in spread-out piles, but uneven towers now dotted the room— redecorating provided by the FBI. I stepped carefully, worried that I might send one tumbling.

There didn't seem to be any room for Marty.

Zeke Jelickson sat back in the recliner, swinging his feet up. The footrest scraped my calf, and his steel-toed boot jammed into my knee. I held my ground.

"Find who killed my boy?" Zeke asked.

"Is your wife here?" Dave said. "We were hoping to talk to both of you, bring you up to date on the case."

"She's changing her clothes. We both had to take a shower, get the stink of Danielle's family off us. So if you two want to get going, go back to handing out coupons to people who forgot to put a nickel in the meter, go *right* ahead. You're not gonna do shit to find who killed our boy."

He crossed his arms, resolute. Dave kept talking, explaining the course of the investigation and next steps. I studied the patches that covered Zeke's leather vest. He had a flaming skull, which matched a tattoo on his forearm—the Abominations logo—and a second skull and crossbones that gave the signal that he had maimed, or more likely killed, someone who threatened the club. ENFORCER was sewn to his shoulder, and six IN MEMORY OF patches marked the lower edge. I wondered how many of the dead died of natural causes, how many of motorcycle accidents, and how many were murdered. On his left shoulder was a patch that read PIGFUCKER, and I gave an involuntary shudder. It was a boast to other bikers that he had slept with a cop.

"Like that one, missy?" he said to me, winking. "I should really have three of those, but who wants to look at that many pigs?"

I ignored him. "Your ink. When'd you get the skull and crossbones?"

"Two years ago. Marty did the tattoo. He's got a sure hand and a sharp eye."

Linda Jelickson arrived, made up and blown dry, wearing tight Levi's and a tighter peach sweater. Her skin was pink from the shower and her eyes were red. Dave extended his hand but she ignored it, sitting at the far end of the couch and grabbing her husband's arm.

Dave dropped into a squatting position, so that he was at eye level with the sitting Jelicksons. "I'm very sorry for your loss. I had the chance to meet Ray, spend some time with him. He was the kind of boy I would hope for in a son, forthright and someone who believed in family."

"Bullshit," muttered Zeke, and I tended to agree, but Dave had Linda Jelickson's attention.

Dave continued, "I hate that something happened to your boy, that he will never have a chance to grow up into the man he was becoming."

Linda Jelickson nodded along. "He was a man."

Dave shook his head as he stood up. "He was close to being a man. He had a little more growing up to do. He needed protection to do that, protection from all of us, including me. It's such a waste."

The room was quiet, the shout of "Shit, man!" filtering through the uninsulated window. While there was a wall between us, I was very aware of the threat at my back.

"He was an old soul," Linda Jelickson said. She reached for her pack of Merits, pulling out a cigarette with coral nails, the tips of her fingers stained brown. She lit it and took a deep drag. "He would never rat out anyone, you know. One time, Marty and his buddies were jumping off the roof of the garage, and Ray joined in—he was only five but he wasn't afraid of nothing. All the shaking from those twelve-year-old boys—and Ray—and the shelving units came clean off the walls. The boys knew they would get beat for it. Ray wouldn't lie to me—'I did it, Mama,' he said—but he didn't tell on Marty."

No mother could have looked prouder. "Not snitching" was valued over everything else by the Jelicksons, it seemed.

"Marty got a beat down for that one," Zeke said.

Linda reached out and grabbed her husband's hand. "Marty always needed a firm hand. He had a lot of Jim in him."

"So Marty wasn't your real son, Zeke?" I asked.

Linda looked offended. "He was a real father to Marty after Jim died. Jim Fizzeller." She pointed to one of Zeke's IN MEMORY patches. "Motorcycle accident when Marty was only nine. We had our first rains and California roads get slick. Danielle's funeral today, well, I haven't seen such a big funeral since his."

"And Zeke took care of the fatherless boy?" Dave asked.

"Do either of you have any children?" Linda asked. Dave answered no, and hid his surprise when I said no as well, but no way was Zeke Jelickson going to find out anything about Lucy.

"So what you two will never understand is the bond that develops between a boy and his father. No boy could have asked for better."

"I stand up for my blood and the brotherhood," Zeke said. "Something you know fuck all about."

Linda cut him off. "Zeke was a brother . . . a close friend . . . of Jim, Jim and me. And a year later I had Ray"—so no long mourning period, I thought—"and well, marrying Zeke was the best thing for everyone. No one had a better family than those boys, and they knew it. The boys still called us all the time."

Somehow I doubted that Marty was the one picking up the phone.

A tear slipped from the corner of Linda Jelickson's eye, and she flicked it with a nail, perfectly preserving her eye makeup. "Ray called me when he needed his mom. And sometimes he called Zeke, for a father's wisdom."

Or advice on making meth, I thought.

"Could you tell us the phone number you called Ray on?"

Linda immediately went on the offensive. "Why do you need to know that?"

"We're checking phone records, and want to rule certain numbers out."

Linda folded her arms. "Likely story."

"Ma'am, it's obvious that you loved your son, and we would never suspect either you or your husband in these murders," Dave said.

Zeke Jelickson stared at Dave, his eyes in a permanent squint from glaring at other people. "And the fact that we weren't in the fucking state proves it. You want phone records? Get a warrant."

"Please, Mr. Jelickson," Dave said. "You're not a suspect." Dave unbuttoned his coat, and I wanted to follow suit—the heat of four people talking and the smoke filling the room was getting uncomfortable.

Zeke scoffed. "I'm always a suspect."

"No," Dave said. "Really. You loved your boy, and were, as you said, on the other side of the country. Did you ever meet Danielle?"

"In passing." Zeke watched me as he answered Dave's question, absently fingering the rim of his beer bottle. We all sat there quietly, the lie hanging over the room like the cloud of cigarette smoke.

"Well, there was that one time." Linda scrunched up her face as if trying to recall something from fifty years ago, when in fact it had been barely five months. "Right before the boys moved east." She talked to Dave. "She came up, spent the weekend. She and Ray had become like family, and she wanted to say good-bye to him. That's before Ray decided to move."

Zeke frowned as Linda depicted the weekend, which sounded more like a sorority reunion than time spent with an outlaw motorcycle gang. Linda described giving Danielle a tour of the family home, Danielle gushing over Marty's bedroom as well as the "social club"—a sweet term for the Abominations' den.

"Ray took Dani out for a ride, and she loved it Danielle belonged on the back of a bike," Linda said. "And when she asked if she could bring Ray with them, keeping Marty's connection with home, how could we say no?"

"Didn't like her, Zeke?" I asked.

"No. I liked her fine."

I stepped forward, putting myself between Dave and Jelickson. "You and she talked?"

"She was kin. Of course we talked."

"What did you chat about?"

"Nothing."

"Family business?" I asked.

"Don't know nothin' 'bout making paper."

"I mean your family business, Zeke," I said.

"I don't think I want to answer that question. That 'family business' crack, I know what you're insinuating. Come tomorrow when you got no one to pin it on, you'll take my words and twist them and find a way to pin it on me." Zeke's eyes were flat as a dead leaf trapped under the frozen river. "Bitch."

"Please don't talk to Officer Lyons like that," Dave said.

"I can talk to that *bitch* any way I want to," Zeke said. "It's my freedom of speech."

"He's correct on that." I smiled at Dave reassuringly. "There's no one better versed on constitutional law than bikers, Dave."

Zeke took a swig of his beer. "So tell me this, when are you going to get off your lazy asses and release our son's body so we can bury him properly?"

"Zeke only gets a week off for bereavement from the DMV," Linda added.

Zeke Jelickson, chief enforcer for the Abominations, worked for the DMV? I was stunned.

"I thought you owned a garage," Dave said.

"I have twenty years' service in the Department of Motor Vehicles. Much like yourselves, I'm a civil servant. The garage is just a hobby I share with some other weekend motorcycle enthusiasts," an interesting euphemism for the Abominations if I ever heard one. "Like the gentlemen out front. Who are going to make sure that Ray gets sent off in style."

"Obviously we want to release him," Dave said. "But until the coroner is done—"

"You can't keep him." Linda Jelickson stamped out her cigarette, ash from the tray spraying out onto her jeans. "We have rights."

"I know, ma'am, but we need to complete the autopsy so that we can solve this crime."

"Like you're going to find his killer," Zeke Jelickson spat. "I wouldn't trust you to track down a lost dog, but at least you might try *real hard* if Fido belonged to Amanda Brouillette. You have no interest, no interest at all, in finding the killer of my boy. Unless you can pin it on me."

Zeke Jelickson got up from his seat. He walked slowly, his stance wide in his steel-toed boots.

"Zeke . . ." Linda Jelickson said.

Zeke seemed to be considering his beer bottle carefully. He paused, a foot from Dave. And then he swung.

I dove forward, jamming Jelickson's arm sideways in midswing. The beer from the bottle sprayed wide, hitting Dave, but the bottle missed his face. Using momentum, I pinned Jelickson's arm around his back and held it.

Linda Jelickson leaped out of her seat, sending a tower of CDs crashing down. Dave straddled the coffee table, his foot hitting one of the ashtrays and spilling its contents across the off-white—now off-off-white—carpet, and grabbed her arm.

"This is how you treat a grieving father!" Linda Jelickson yelled, trying to pull out of Dave's grasp. "You people!"

"I didn't mean to spill my beer on you, Officer," Zeke said, but I felt his arm flex, the flaming skull tattoo moving under my hand, and Jelickson's face slid sideways, mashing against an M. C. Escher poster. It tore against his cheek. Being shorter than Zeke had its advantages here. I used my lower angle to pull his arm tighter, but this wouldn't last—the second I let him go he would pound me into the ground.

"Wrong," I said. The patches on his back were easy to read: ABOMINATIONS, 1%, and COPPERHEAD, which must be his club name. "You were *trying* to hit him with the bottle."

"Why, I wasn't trying to hit him with anything." The saccharine tone of Zeke's jagged voice was more insulting than if he'd told us to fuck off and die. "An accident, I swear, Officer."

"He's right, Officer Lyons." Dave spoke only to Linda Jelickson. "Zeke's mind wasn't clear after he heard the news that we might not be able to put together a case because people are withholding evidence."

Linda Jelickson stopped pushing against Dave, and as she re-laxed, I released my hold on Zeke.

Zeke Jelickson shook out his arm. "I don't know who might have been 'withholding evidence,' but the congresswoman is all twisted up, warped inside with all the power she's got. That woman, and her husband, too, they're users, no doubt about it."

Linda Jelickson nodded. "I'm a mother, and I can tell. Amanda Brouillette's got no mother's love, and neither does this bitch here. Any idiot could see it."

"We're done," Dave said at last. "But consider this, today, a free-bie. You are grieving parents, and you aren't," he emphasized, "sus-pects. But you take a swing at me or anyone else in this town and you will be locked up. And if you don't keep the boys outside on a leash, you will be locked out. Am I clear?"

Linda Jelickson didn't reply, going to the door and holding it open for us. Jackie's voice could be heard from the porch, trying to talk her way past the gauntlet. The requirements for her entrance were different than those for Dave and me.

"Show us your puppies," a guy was saying, gesturing for her to lift her shirt.

"Jackie," I asked, "does your father know you're here?"

Jackie squared her shoulders. "The Jelicksons are expecting me."

"We are," and Linda Jelickson opened the door wide, gesturing Jackie in with her cigarette. "Jackie dear, come in, come in."

Jackie slid past the men, but stepped back when Linda tried to hug her.

"Can you put out the cigarette? It's not, it's not . . . healthy."

Linda Jelickson flicked the cigarette over the porch railing where it burned out in the snow. "Do you want a soda, Jackie?" She threw her hair over her shoulder. "Of course, it's family only."

CHAPTER 18

OW, FUCK." DAVE GINGERLY pulled the blue cloth away from his body and winced. "I think my chest hair is freezing to my shirt."

"Now, now," I said. "Zeke didn't mean to spill beer on you. I'm sure he's very sorry."

"Because he wasted beer. He wasn't sorry that the wasted beer ended up on *me*."

I bumped Dave's shoulder with my own to adjust his course as he ran up the steps of the police station—he was going to run into the frieze next to the entrance rather than through the door itself. The carving depicted Justice, her scales and sword at the ready, with a beaver, the official New York State animal, nestled at her feet. It had probably seemed like a good idea at the time.

"Please hold," we heard Lorraine say as we pushed open the door. She raised an eyebrow at Dave. "You know you smell like a bar mat, right? And while that's not a problem most days, today you should get yourself cleaned up. Jerry called, and the chief and him are out of their meeting with the governor. Jerry said, and I quote,

'The governor handed out so much pain, there's more than enough to go around.' Unquote. Always the big talker, Jerry. They'll be here in fifteen minutes or so. Plus, you got an FBI agent waiting for you in Room Two."

"Oh, joy," I said.

Dave grabbed a shirt out of his desk drawer and jogged toward the locker room. "Please let me solve this case before I run out of clean shirts. Hey," he called over his shoulder, "don't kill the G-man before I get back."

Hale sat at the far side of the table in Interview Two. Two files and a stack of papers were at his right hand, and a recorder? a camera?—I was no longer up-to-date on the latest surveillance technology—at his left. Behind him was carnage: bloody pictures of Ray and the bloodless pictures of Danielle.

"You willing to hear me out?" Hale said, his black suit picking up the faintest layer of dust as he spread his arms wide on the table.

"Dave might. My bullshit detector is still in place."

"That might change once you hear what I have to say."

"Doubtful." I pulled a chair from the corner so we had seats for five.

"I—"

"Let's wait for Dave, shall we?"

We sat in silence. Hale turned sideways, keeping one eye on me while he studied the wall of evidence. I could see him follow the ribbons that led from one photo to the next. He seemed calm, unflappable under my scrutiny until he made eye contact. He then, ever so slightly, blushed.

Behind me the door opened, the chill air hitting my neck. I continued to stare Hale down, trusting Dave at my back.

"Sorry it took me so long," Dave said finally. "I bathed."

He collapsed next to me, the steam of the shower still clinging to his clothes, radiating out.

I slanted a glance at him. "Didn't have time to towel off?"

"I'm solving a murder here. At least I'm no longer going to pass out from alcohol fumes." Dave crossed his arms across his broad chest. "So what's up?"

"Something . . . something big." Hale gestured at the recording device.

"Something big enough that you waved Craig off the crime scene?"

Hale froze. "Wait. No. You don't believe I'd do that."

"He *knew* you. He described what you were wearing, your stupid hat."

"The boy was snow-blind." Hale leaned forward on the table. "He was mistaken."

"No one in law enforcement," I said, "no trooper, no one from the sheriff's department—no one would wave away someone from the crime scene."

"No one in law enforcement includes me."

"Really?" I said. Dave shifted, and his leg pressed against mine under the table, whether to give support or calm me down I didn't know. And I didn't care. "You're protecting Craig, who very well might have murdered two people."

"June, you as much as anyone knows an agent has only two things: his reputation and his confidential informants. Craig wouldn't—"

"Means, motive, opportunity," I ticked off on my fingers.

"We track him constantly."

"Constantly. Really? So you knew he was at the scene?"

"Constantly might be too strong a word."

I had a full head of steam built up. "Well, whether you are lying—"

"I'm not."

"—or not, which we have no way of proving, why don't you

describe this big investigation so (a) I don't haul your CI in and hold him, and (b) you restore some of your beloved reputation. Because right now? You look pretty dirty."

"No," Hale said. "Let's settle this, for good. I wouldn't compromise the investigation. Until I know you believe that, we can't move forward."

"I believe you," Dave said.

"Really?" Hale said.

"What?" I said.

"I do." Dave grabbed his neck, an exaggerated version of Hale's tell, and gave me a meaningful look. "I don't believe that he would wave Craig off."

I stifled a smile.

"I *might* believe that you didn't lie," I said to Hale, "but to build my trust, why don't you tell us everything that made you compromise two murder investigations."

Hale didn't say anything, instead pressing the tiny button on the small machine that lay next to him.

"So I'm trying," Zeke Jelickson's voice roared out, and Hale lowered the volume, "to get a handle on things."

"Well, sheeyit," said a man's voice with a southern accent. Texas, I thought. "What're ya doin?"

"Funeral for the girl. And Ray's body—"

"Brother, you have my deepest sympathy. Lost my own boy young."

"Ray lived a righteous life, and I plan to stick it to the cowards who murdered him, so that his death is paid back. Paid back in full." Zeke breathed deeply. "In the meantime, we got to take care of business."

"Your girl took care of the wire transfer. She was just full of surprises—it was those Orientals in Canada tipped us off that she had paid in full. If I didn't know how close you were to your boys, I might have been worried that she was gettin' ready to cut us out of the sugar. Such a shame she passed on. She was a firecracker." There was a pause. "And they told me you got her pilot lined up. He's solid, right?"

"Hold on a sec." In the background Linda Jelickson could be heard saying, "Watch out for that cabinet there. It makes me nervous; it could tip over and kill someone. Do you want a soda?" And Jackie answered, "Yes, please."

Static crackled until finally Jelickson spoke. "He's solid. We're locked down, and we got the Merrimen in for protection since the Mongols are across the river, and the Angels are up north."

"Tiny's a good man, and he knows how to play ball," the voice said. "Does Marty?"

"Marty's back in the bosom of his family," Jelickson said quickly.

Huh? Was the break between the father and son a fake-out?

"That's good. When you lose kin, draw the family you got tighter." The man hung up.

The sound of a phone being dialed filled the room. "Marty, I'll keep this . . . short. Quit the act. Get your ass home."

Hale flicked off the machine. "Thank you kindly, by the way. We've had a wiretap on that phone for two months, and this is the first time someone has used it."

Dave nodded graciously, all noblesse oblige. "Lyons made him whimper."

"I know." Hale laughed. "But your consideration and, I'll say, kindness completely threw him off. He panicked, and made a phone call. You're a good cop."

I was unconvinced by Hale's ass kissing. "How much surveillance do you have?"

"We couldn't bug the place, but we got ourselves a wiretap."

"How'd you get a judge to approve that?" Dave asked.

"And how'd we not hear about it until now?" I added.

"A federal judge gave it to us, under seal. This investigation has already spread to six states, and this murder—"

"These two murders," I pointed out.

"These two murders might be the ticket to shut down the Abominations for good."

Hale explained how they had been running surveillance on a ring down south. Mexico was the source, but Missouri was the distribution center.

"And we were monitoring the buys down there, when Craig rolled into town. We stopped him at the airport with a cargo load of pseudoephedrine, and told him we were going to arrest him and seize all his father's assets, and well, let's just say the boy would have sold his grandma out to get off. He started spouting out names like Jelickson, and we knew this was going to be big if we could line it all up just right.

"Craig was sweating bullets, completely freaked out. His father is a hard man, plus Craig was real upset about letting down Danielle. He blurted everything out, sure if we heard about Danielle's desperate plight, we would help him rescue her."

"Rescue her?" I asked. "By distributing meth?"

"By Craig's logic—and I will admit I had a hard time following it myself—Danielle needed the money to free her from her controlling husband and his violent family. Craig seemed to forget that Danielle already had a rich father who would pay a hefty sum to send his son-in-law away, preferably to hell."

"So Craig wasn't lying when he denied sleeping with Danielle?" I asked, thinking of the photos on Ray's extra phone.

"Craig claims that she took her marriage vows so seriously that she wouldn't even consider cheating on her husband, despite Marty being a rat bastard. Based on our background check"—Hale flipped through a few of the papers on the desk—"Danielle was overstating her reverence for marriage, at least other people's. In addition to that TA Phil told you about—who had been happy to be seduced by Danielle up until she laid waste to his career and his marriage—there was also a married anthropology professor who paid for her trip to Fiji on a research project that took place entirely inside the walls of a hotel." Hale flipped a few more pages. "There was also a movie producer. He did small-scale projects, TV movies and the like, and again, very married. Danielle used his credit card to buy her wedding dress, which she then returned for cash. He wrote off the dress as script research, which the IRS found very interesting."

We told him about the photos we'd found on Ray's phone, fleshing out Annie's report, which Hale had read.

"The thing is"—and Hale opened the first folder—"Craig had to work hard to deny that Danielle was an operator."

In the first photo he showed us, Ray held an open box in front of Danielle while she fastened a diamond hoop in her ears. The earrings were Ray's Valentine's Day gift, it seemed. The next picture had Danielle and Ray on their back porch kissing passionately, his hands on either side of her face. The photographer had caught them when they had blocked out the rest of the world, even Jackie and Craig, who could be seen, backlit, in the kitchen. Two motives for murder, right there.

"Of course, Craig claimed that it was all an act, that she was leading Ray on so he wouldn't tip off his brother. Craig seemed to think of himself as her white knight, when honestly, he was her whipping boy. That didn't prevent him from telling us everything he knew about the drug operation in an effort to 'save' her."

"No lawyer?" I said.

"Craig was not yet in custody, so no reason to read him his rights. His strategy consisted of blurting out everything he knew, which would then convince us to let him and Danielle go free. He also seemed to think that he would get buckets of money for his trouble."

I raised an eyebrow at him. "And he got that impression from . . ."

"He came up with it all on his own, and, well, perhaps I didn't enlighten him about his misunderstanding. He seemed very concerned that Danielle would find out he'd screwed up—more so than even his dad—and was in a hurry to get back. Craig gave up the entire meth ring, from Ray, Danielle, and Marty, all the way up to the Jelicksons, in less than sixty minutes." Hale tipped his chair back on two legs—he seemed to be savoring the memory. "Well, what he knew. It seems as if the Jelicksons didn't tell Craig a whole lot." Hale dropped back onto four legs, jerking forward. "We sent him on his way, but before we did we took a load of pictures, so he knew we had him dead to rights. He flew back to Hopewell Falls thinking that he and Danielle would walk into the sunset together, free of charges and with enough money to buy a fleet of charter planes, and that Marty would go to prison and never bother Danielle again."

Hale explained that the Albany field office had watched as Craig landed. The agents documented that a woman and a young man, who were later identified as Danielle and Ray, loaded the pseudo-ephedrine into the Brouillettes' Jeep.

"And do you have pictures of that?" I asked.

"We do. But look, I need you to promise to keep this info quiet."

"Have you thought that maybe you are doing a little too good of a job of keeping this quiet? Maybe being a little more forthcoming with information might help us out here."

"Which is why I'm showing you these." He opened the folder and slid three eight-by-ten surveillance shots across the table: Danielle on the phone, deep in conversation; Craig and Ray loading sacks into the back of the Jeep while Danielle kept watch; and a third of the truck driving out of the parking lot.

"That's it?" I asked. "And why didn't you bust them right then?"

"Well, you see, this was an on-the-fly operation, put together in a few hours without full manpower. . . ."

"Danielle and Ray lost the tail," I said.

Hale nodded. "Unfortunately, yes. And while we tried to get Craig to ask some leading questions—with a wire, of course—Danielle gave up nothing, just telling him to stand by for the next pickup."

"Which was when?" I asked. Hale seemed to have no concern for the fact that the drugs were out there, poisoning people, while he and his boys got their act together.

"Which will be *tomorrow*. And the next supply is coming through Canada. With the south eating up all the pseudo before it has the chance to cross the Mason-Dixon, Danielle decided she needed something bigger. The thing is, I'm not sure she clued in her in-laws. You heard that phone call. Danielle was making her own deals, independent of the Abominations." From the folder he pulled out more pictures, surveillance shots, grainy, done in the dark, at strange angles: Ray carrying huge glass containers into a warehouse, glaring at Craig, who was gripping the head of one of the massive beakers, the rest of the container lying broken at his feet.

"That's an old glove factory downtown, by the way. Until June spotted the stuff stashed at the barn, we had no idea where it came from. Our one mistake"—Hale saw me glare—"our one *big* mistake was not having someone on Danielle that night."

"Anyone poking around the meth lab?" Dave asked.

"No, and we haven't heard anything from our informants in other parts of the distribution chain as to when the next supply is coming."

"Distribution?" I asked. "Bikers?"

"Bikers to truckers and back to the bikers again. They've got a pretty tight lock on it, and yeah, it's the Abominations. If Danielle and Ray had lived, I'm not sure how things would have played out. I suspect, based on some other intelligence we have, that the two of them and Marty were splintering off, trying to set up their own score."

I wanted to keep Hale talking. "So who was running the show?"

"Well, Danielle wore the britches in that family, but she had no experience making meth. Ray had the family connections, but was hardly a criminal mastermind. But Marty, he gets my vote, mostly because this is how it went down last time. Hands off, let the others take the fall, a move he learned at Daddy's feet, when Daddy was willing to let him take the hit on that lab." Hale checked his notes. "Which is why I wanted to keep him out there on the streets, although with Daddy in town, the operation may have a new boss. And lo and behold, Craig got a text from a burner phone telling him to pick up the drugs as planned tomorrow night."

"The wire transfer the guy mentioned," Dave said. "Danielle already paid for everything?"

"She did. The Abominations have a long relationship with the gangs in Mexico, but Danielle was making her own deal on her own terms with groups with ties to Asia—to build credit, in a way. She had to prove she could be trusted."

"Like you're doing now?" I said. Everything he was saying fit with what I knew, and Hale seemed like he was playing ball, very probably with spitballs.

Before he could answer, Jerry walked in, acting, as he always did, like he owned the place.

"Let's start," Jerry said, tapping the edge of the table like a gavel.

"The chief?" Dave asked as Donnelly entered, carrying a cup of coffee.

The chief sighed the sigh of the deeply put upon. "Did you solve the murders? The governor is ready to make this a state operation."

"And I tend to agree," Jerry said. "Both of your careers are ruined. Not that you"—and he smirked at me—"had much of one to destroy."

Dave cleared his throat. "Well, it appears we have an international drug operation moving into Hopewell Falls."

Jerry rolled his eyes. "Tell us something we don't know."

Hale picked up on Dave's lead. "I don't believe that you understand the scale of this. We're talking about an operation to rival the Juarez cartel. Or the Hells Angels in the eighties." Hale leaned back in his seat. "Did I ever tell you about Marty's daddy?"

"Jim Fizzeller," I added, helpfully. "Used to run the Abominations."

"Until he had his 'accident.'" Dave could use air quotes with the best of them, and made the three of us seem like we were in the know.

"Yeah, tragic how that happened as Zeke and Jim were coming back from that meeting where they set up the roach coach distribution," Hale said.

"Roach coaches?" asked the chief, appalled.

"They were carts," I explained. "Vans actually, where they sold good cheap food. Sometimes Mexican. Great tacos." The chief wasn't convinced. He was raised on boiled beef and cabbage, so even really good Mexican food held no appeal. I pulled out the rough outlines of the operation from my long-ago memory. "Instead of ordering a number fourteen—carne asada tacos—you could order a number seventy-seven and get some crank. The Abominations supplied all the drugs until five or six years ago."

"So they lost out to the competition?" Jerry asked, as if he expected outlaw bikers to be up on the laws of economics.

"In a way," Hale said. "The Hells Angels firebombed them when they got a little too friendly with folks in Oakland. This"—Hale emphasized each word with a sharp tap on the table—"was supposed to be their big comeback. Unless Danielle, Ray, and Marty cut them out." Hale explained his suspicion that the three were making their own deals.

"And it goes down tomorrow. We get the Abominations, there will be more RICO indictments than we've seen since the Teamsters."

Chief Donnelly shifted in his chair. "Agent Bascom, I was on patrol when heroin showed up in the seventies." He seemed lost in thought. "That tore up lives, and good folks . . . they lost their souls. And we still can't get that out of here." He stood up, collecting his pad and coffee cup. "I'll give you twenty-four hours."

"But the governor will need to be briefed," Jerry added.

"Sir"—and unlike the times when Hale had called Jerry "sir"

before, this time he sounded respectful—"this information needs to stay in this room."

Dave leaned forward, and got right in Jerry's face. "I trust Hale. He had our back at the Jelicksons' today"—which I knew was patently untrue. But Dave knew what I did. We needed Hale. Not just the resources of the FBI, but him, and his headstrong, headlong ways.

"We need to take down this drug ring. Don't you think that's best, Jerry?" Dave asked.

Dave's magic worked.

"I will give my okay, but only"—Jerry glanced at the chief—"for another forty-eight hours."

The chief nodded. "For you, I'll stall them for an extra day. C'mon, Jerry, let's go have another conference call."

Jerry stood up, and Hale extended his hand. Jerry seemed confused, but after a moment shook it. He shook Dave's readily. He ignored mine. I didn't care. Jerry could ignore me all he wanted as long as we had the time we needed to solve this case.

"YOU HAVE A LAPTOP in the laptop terminal?" Dave said from the passenger seat of Hale's big-ass SUV. "I thought that space was just a good place to rest a pizza slice."

"Oh, I do that, too," Hale said. "I put it on top of the laptop."

We were on our way to the capitol to visit Marty Jelickson at work. Hale seemed to know his way through South Albany. The streets were empty. During the day, tens of thousands of state workers flooded the area, crunching numbers, sending out tax notices, eating hotdogs for lunch because they didn't work for the state for the salary, they worked for the benefits. The Egg reflected the moonlight, Rockefeller's avant-garde half dome squatting like a spaceship among the Hellenic columns and ornate cornices of the Victorian buildings that surrounded it. I'd taken Lucy to see *Peter Pan* in its theater, but she was much more interested in trying to figure out how the two little poles kept up the bowl of cement. I didn't have an answer for her.

We drove to the front gate of the capitol, which was chained shut, with a sign telling us to enter via the garage, and Hale put out an official tag, letting us park right in front. Apparently that's what it took to get parking in downtown Albany.

We walked around and down the garage ramp, ducking under the security gate, which at this hour required a state ID. The garage was empty of vehicles except for a couple of clusters: one near the elevators, and all the official state cars at the edge of the lot. In the middle of the structure was a glassed-in security desk.

With no Marty.

Hale darted ahead, almost running up to the door, but I grabbed his arm before he could enter. *Another crime scene,* I thought. We stood in the doorway. The room had windows on all sides. The guards probably didn't look out much, because mounted on the ceiling was a wall of security screens, flicking from picture to picture: the front entrance with the locks in place, a darkened hallway, and Marty sitting behind the security desk monitoring the cameras.

Wait. What?

The views on the screens flicked again. Another hallway, light spilling from one of the offices, the majority leader's suite still brightly lit with people working late, and a maintenance man mopping a hallway. Flick. The first scenes returned: the hallway, the front entrance, and Marty sitting at the desk, a desk that was now empty. The three of us were nowhere to be seen on the screens.

Someone had doctored the security feed.

CHAPTER 19

THE RIDE BACK TO Hopewell Falls was quiet. Dave and I floated past the Watervliet Arsenal, spiked gates and cannons keeping the site safe from long-deposed foes. Of course, those were just for show—the best-in-class tanks behind those walls could hit a target in Pennsylvania.

"Marty's our man," Dave said. We were on our way home to catch a few hours' sleep. Hale had dropped us off at the station before going to meet Craig at the airport for a preflight check.

"So it seems," I said. As we crossed the Watervliet/Hopewell Falls border, progress seemed to stop. We were in the same old rotting economy filled with a bunch of falling-down buildings.

"He was at the crime scene—"

"He had the *means* to be there. We have no confirmation."

"Fine. But why'd he go to all that trouble? He was one motivated man."

Dave had a point—our visit to the capitol more or less confirmed Marty as a suspect. A few clicks and Hale was able to find the source file that was endlessly looping, showing Marty, diligent and alert, at his desk. It was located between the incident reports of February 14—a couple having a loud, angry fight on the plaza—and February 15—when one young man assaulted another young man with a meatball sub.

"He's been doing this since February fourteenth," Hale said, and began to unplug the desktop so the FBI's computer labs could do a complete search. Stan Shay, the manager of security at Building Two of the capitol, was *not* happy to see that, once he arrived, but got over it when we told him we were going to take a close look at his recordkeeping for the last few months. Stan loved keeping records.

"The problem, of course, is vehicle 12992," Stan said. He was reviewing, for the fourth time, the complete list of state vehicles that were currently in stock.

"It's missing?" My voice echoed through the concrete garage.

Stan stopped, flipped the pad back three pages, and wrote down my question. He recorded every question we asked, including "Where's the bathroom?" He flipped back to his pad before answering.

"No," he said.

I was having a hard time keeping my attention on Stan and his ponderous ways. The nature of security was to check and double-check—and triple-check and quadruple-check—and Stan was missing nothing. Next to me Dave was on high alert, and Hale kept walking away, looking behind pillars, under cars, all the while within earshot.

"But the plate on the Cobalt isn't a state plate. ALB792 . . ."

"Thank God he did something illegal," Dave said. "We can get him and hold him." He hopped on the radio, putting out an APB for a 1992 Honda with state plates. Hale opened his phone, jogging toward the exit ramp. The garage carried sound, and even from the gate I could hear him repeating the information.

"Geez," Stan said, once the two of us were alone. "I'm going to have to cover the rest of his shift, and with no computer. I knew that kid was trouble from the very start."

"Why'd you hire him?" I said.

"The congresswoman *asked*. He's her son-in-law? Or he was. She said we could fire him if he didn't do right by us."

"Any problems with him before?"

"One time I showed up early, and he came back in a rush, he said from a patrol. Protocol says we should call in the Albany police first thing, but sometimes you observe someone or something, and it's easier to go check it out yourself, 'cause it's usually nothing. We used to always have two guys on at one time, even at night, but once they got the cameras and card reader there"—he pointed to a swipe machine that was next to the elevator—"well, you couldn't get into the building at night unless you had a pass, and the guys had to sit in their seat and do their job. I mean, we have to give the guys on the night shift a break so they can go to the can since that's their human right, but anything more than a few minutes and they'd get written up. They knew I reviewed the video every morning."

With the feed loop of him sitting at his desk, Marty could be away for longer than a bathroom run. "Any other times he wasn't where he was supposed to be?" I asked.

"The cleaning staff said they saw him regular. They get out of here around one, though, so maybe after? We can pull the scan card records for the last month."

"Last three months," I said. "His whole employment history."

"Last three months." He wrote it down. "You know, I wouldn't have tagged him as a problem employee. He'd cover all sorts of shifts. He kept good notes, and did good recordkeeping." He tapped his pad with his eraser. "That's half the battle with these guys—most of them can't write in complete sentences. He could and he did." He cheered up. "So maybe he didn't murder her."

LORRAINE'S VOICE RANG THROUGH Dave's car. "C-1 and C-12, what is your 10-20?"

"You C-1?" I asked Dave. He was. I radioed Lorraine our location.

"C-12, I need you at a 10-53P . . ."

Why in the world wouldn't she send one of the on-duty patrol cars for a vehicular accident that only involved property?

". . . related to cases 13-478 and 13-484 . . ."

Danielle's and Ray's cases? I listened closely.

"At the corner of Vesey and Halston."

I signed off and turned to Dave. "Get to the pharmacy. Fast."

WE ARRIVED AT THE alley behind the pharmacy to find twisted metal and smoke: the snowplow operator puffing away on a cigarette next to an idling plow, which was filling the air with exhaust, and a Dumpster, crushed sideways across the alley, with its contents spilling out into the snow. *Finally, some luck,* I thought as I spotted the bloody boots and hat with earflaps the driver had called in. Our luck ended there, as Denise Byrne, inside filling some emergency prescriptions, came out to check on the ruckus.

She was now pleading her case to me, while Dave took the snowplow driver's statement.

"I don't understand how this happened," she said. "It's impossible. People trust us not to let outsiders tamper with their medical information . . . even . . . especially, the police. You know you're making a mistake."

I was willing to let Denise Byrne complain a bit. It wasn't going to change anything. What Denise didn't realize was that privacy wasn't our primary concern. The murder was. Tired from another all-nighter, I needed to save my energy for the real fights. I was going on hour twenty-four in the same outfit, and the way it was itching, my skirt was as sick of me as I was of it.

"Denise, I cannot believe that you wouldn't follow all regulatory guidelines to a T."

"No, we're compliant in every way," she said. "But we struggle to compete with the chains, and if it got out we broke confidentiality, well, I couldn't show my face!"

I tried to calm her down. "Privacy, not confidentiality."

"Same difference."

"No. It's not." I pointed to several crushed pill bottles in a fan pattern in the snow. "I bet there's no way to see who used those or even what was in them. You would never improperly dispose of pharmaceuticals."

Her pale eyebrows shot up. "Of course not."

"Because you plan ahead. You're careful. The fact that your patients use medicine isn't a secret."

She seemed to consider this. The light sprinkling of snow coming down dusted her gold hair, curls releasing themselves from their tight blowout into soft waves. "I want to help, June, I really do, but you need to understand, my reputation's on the line. People will say, 'Oh, those Byrnes. You know how they are, you can't trust them.' It would kill my husband if we lost this business. The pharmacy has been in his family for three generations, I can't lose it."

"I promise you, Denise, we'll do everything to make sure you aren't pulled into this investigation unnecessarily." She smiled triumphantly, but her smile disappeared as I continued. "But we are investigating. We're thinking, unless you can explain otherwise, that those boots are related to the murder of Ray Jelickson. Now we need to discuss how they got there."

The crime scene unit's van whipped around the corner and screeched to a halt. Annie clambered out of the driver's side. She didn't acknowledge any of us, disappearing behind the back of the van. I was happy to see her—Annie wasn't going to miss a thing. She was also going to complain a lot, and she needed to be kept far away from Denise Byrne.

"Is there somewhere we can have some privacy?" I asked Denise.

We agreed to go inside. I signaled to Dave and checked in with Annie.

"Oh, it's you." Annie snapped her rubber gloves like a mad scientist. "You don't need to tell me to maintain biohazard protocols or to sweep the entire alley. I know."

"The snowplow operator—"

"A snowplow? I would never have known."

"The boots and hat are the most obvious find, but more—"

"Yes, yes. For kicks, I'll go ahead and catalog everything." Annie's words were muffled as she pulled the biohazard suit over her head. "And I'll get the gorilla and his machine on his way as soon as possible. And I'll do my job, which I'd bet, although I can't promise, that I can do better than you. And we'll get this case solved, and hopefully not have to trudge through snow searching for clues for months. Sound good?"

"Sounds good, Annie."

Annie rolled her eyes.

DENISE LOCKED THE THREE dead bolts behind me. Just as we were getting settled—Denise propped on her Roman emperor stool and me on a folding chair—my radio beeped.

"C-12," Dave said, "can you join me outside for a second?"

I was surprised when Dave met me at the front of the store rather than in the alley. He kept his voice low, monitoring for anyone who might be trying to listen. "They picked up Marty Jelickson. At the Canadian border. Or rather, near the Canadian border."

"Canada?" The pharmacy's security cameras tracked us. I doubted they had audio, but I dropped my voice further, just in case. "To do business?"

"He headed right up the Northway, and was trying to find a way into Canada where he wouldn't need a passport. Some state troopers are driving him down now, and he should be here in another two or three hours." Dave hopped twice, I think from glee. "We can charge him for stealing the plates and spend as much time as we want with him."

Jeff Polito walked slowly past the accident, trudging up the walk toward us.

"I should get back to the crime scene," Dave said. "Annie has things well in hand, but she probably misses me."

Back inside, I called to Denise. "I think you have a customer."

Denise peered down the aisle. When she saw Jeff she waved a *one minute* finger and raced to the back.

When she returned, she had on her pharmacist's smock. It flowed behind her as she raced to the door, unlocked it, and shoved a paper bag into Jeff's hands. She whispered, "You can owe me," and slammed the door shut on him. I followed Denise to the back, where she reperched on her stool.

"So the tan boots and hat in the bin," I said. "Are they yours?"

"Oh, no. They're a bit masculine for me."

"How about Jason? Look like something he owns?"

"No." I stayed silent, and Denise crossed her long legs, and then crossed them again—she could find no comfortable position. Finally she said, "He might have a pair of those boots. But I'm sure his are a different size."

Something was not right here. "And the key to the bin?"

"Jason and I shared one, but it's missing. We had it the day before you stopped by, and the next day, it was gone."

"Gone?" I thought of the sandwiches Jason had dropped off at Marty's. "Was there anyplace it could have been lost?"

"No. I went straight home. Although . . ." She seemed to be searching for words or for a memory, rubbing her forehead. The years of handling chemicals and medications had left her hands dotted with scars and discoloration. "My son did drop off some sandwiches for the Jelickson brothers. I told him the coffee cake was enough, but he decided he wanted to be nice."

"And he had the one key with him."

"Yes. Before, we had a second key, but it disappeared."

"When was that, Denise? Two weeks ago? Two years?"

"A few months. Right when Danielle got fired. The hauling company is sending two more keys. That's two hundred dollars down the drain, right there. Thanks to that idiot I have to buy a whole new box."

"Could I have their number?" I asked. Denise pulled the Rolodex out from a shelf underneath the register.

"Jason knew the schedule for pickup, I assume." I waited until Denise nodded, her attention still on the business cards. "And when was that?"

"Two days ago. Although they didn't come . . . the storm."

"I'm going to need to talk to him again. He had a key—"

"The key was gone." Denise continued to flip through the cards.

"And he stopped by Marty Jelickson's the night of Ray's murder."

"My son had no reason to kill those people."

It took me a minute to pick up the card she extended, trying to puzzle out Denise's logic. "What makes you say that, Denise?"

"Lots of reasons." Denise ticked off the points on her fingers. "First, I raised my son right. But also, the key was missing, remember, and Marty Jelickson very well might've stolen it. Did you see his parents at the funeral?" she asked, and I nodded. "He's not a decent person; his whole family is bad news."

"And Danielle? Did she come from bad people?"

"No . . . but you know that." Denise stomped around the counter. She rearranged the vitamins, slotting vitamin K after iron, and putting ginseng on another shelf altogether. She glanced quickly around the store, like someone might have overheard. When she next spoke, her voice was gentle. "My son's a good man, generous to a fault. He wouldn't cross that line."

"Well, we'll find out when we question him."

"It won't be today," Denise said with authority. "Celia called in sick, and he's the primary caregiver today. I won't allow it."

"Allow or not allow isn't in question," I said. "He's not a minor. And we have to find Danielle and Ray's killer."

"I understand. I do. It's just, he works so hard here, and with his dad . . . I want to give him a break. His first girlfriend got killed, and I want him to not have to . . . to go through this." She slumped against the counter, staring at the floor. She seemed overwhelmed by everything: the store, her sick husband, her son's possible involvement in two deaths, and me.

"We'll work with him," I said. "Make it as easy as we can. We'll visit him at home."

I meant it. When Kevin was sick, I wasn't able to manage everything I needed to do, let alone wanted to do. I wanted to give Jason a break. I wanted to give Denise a break.

"That's good, that's good," Denise said. "This whole thing has been so awful. You know, you work to give your kids a better life, or at least the life they want, and there's nothing Jason wants more than to take over this stupid old pharmacy." Her chin trembled. "And my husband, he doesn't have long now, and for his family's business to fail, well, I can't let that happen." She drew herself up, craning her neck to peer through the front window. "Are we done? A customer's waiting."

"You're done." I followed her up front, where Dave's smiling face peered through the window.

"Officer Batko," she said. "What now?"

CHAPTER 20

THE SUN WAS SHINING. Not peeking out, not radiating from behind a wall of snow, not hidden behind a bank of clouds, but shining. While it wasn't warm, I could imagine heat for the first time in months. The shops that remained as going concerns were opening, including the bank, a check-cashing place, the Wishing Well Coin Laundry, a second check-cashing place, and the Knicker-bocker Diner, the only business that could be described as "busy." They deserved to be—their home fries were life changing.

"Let's get some breakfast before we go back to the station," I said. In the window of the diner I saw the owner, Salina Jacobs, raise her coffeepot at me. I think she'd set up a pancake-powered homing beacon inside the diner and knew we couldn't resist. "We can discuss police business and it will be like we never stopped working."

Dave didn't answer, sliding sideways between two cars and jay-walking toward the diner. I was in the middle of the street when the doors of the bank crashed open. Out came a beast with three backs: Phil Brouillette and Zeke Jelickson clenched together, a third person

I couldn't make out, big as the two of them put together, forcing them to the ground.

The three dropped behind a car, out of my view. Jelickson gained his footing first, pulling himself out of the brawl far enough that he could draw his arm back and take a swing at Phil Brouillette. Brouillette ducked and cut Jelickson off at the knees before punching him squarely in the jaw. Brouillette had the build and attitude of a street fighter. I banged my shins on a bumper when I cut the turn close, but as I got nearer I was able to identify the third person: Chuck DeGroot. He was winding up to kick Jelickson—hard.

Dave grabbed Chuck before he could follow through, using Chuck's momentum to force him up against the window. I pinned Phil against a lamppost, putting my hand on the back of his neck and pulling his arm around and against his shoulder blades. He fought, and I shoved my knee in behind his own, forcing him off balance and closer against the pole. He stopped struggling.

Jelickson moved to his knees, but Dave let go of Chuck to push Jelickson back against the concrete. He pointed to Chuck.

"Don't move," he said.

A crowd of faces pressed against the doors of the bank, with an elderly bank guard holding them inside. They watched Dave handcuff Jelickson as I patted down Brouillette. I froze.

He had a gun. I kept my voice calm, not wanting to send either of the other men into fight-or-flight, or alarm the crowd forming in front of the diner across the street.

"Sorry, man," Dave said as he cuffed DeGroot.

I nodded Dave over and pulled a Smith & Wesson out of Brouillette's back holster.

"Very nice," Dave said. "You better have a concealed carry permit, Mr. Brouillette, or you're going to be in more trouble than anyone."

"I have a permit," Brouillette mumbled against the metal post. "It's a registered gun."

"He's carrying, and you're going to jack me up?" Jelickson demanded.

"We let you off last time, Zeke, but not now," I said. "Both of you are going in for disorderly conduct, and that's just for starters."

With Pete documenting some last details at the snowplow scene and Bill out on Route 9 investigating a barking dog, we were on our own. We could call in someone off duty, or the troopers, who were honestly not so bad to work with, even if they did consider themselves a bunch of badasses. After much discussion between Dave and me ("Is this legal?" "I missed breakfast. I don't care.") we made a parade of it.

Jelickson protested. "Do we have to do a perp walk in front of the whole town?"

"Well, you could continue to kneel on the cold ground on the main street until we can free someone to pick us up," I said.

"You could let us go. Or at least the two of us," Brouillette said, nodding at Chuck.

In the end we deputized the guard. Forty years on the job, the guard had sharp eyes but a slow gait, and the two-minute walk ended up taking closer to fifteen. Jelickson went first, his hands cuffed behind his back, chin up, daring anyone to say anything. I saw a boy aim a camera phone at the group, but before I could order him to put it away, Jelickson growled, and the boy ran back to a giggling group of kids.

I followed Jelickson. Then came Chuck DeGroot, the guard, Phil Brouillette, and finally Dave, "the clown car in this parade," as he put it.

Phil Brouillette called to Chuck—"I'll get you some representation"—but when Dave asked him if he was waiving his rights, he quieted right down. Once we arrived at the station we booked and separated the three of them, immediately moving Jelickson and Brouillette into cells, for their own safety. We sat Chuck in the chief's office, handcuffed to a chair, while we took the bank guard's statement.

According to the guard, Chuck DeGroot and Jelickson were in line, a few people between them. Chuck always came in on Thursday mornings to deposit his paycheck, so nothing weird there. They were either ignoring each other or didn't know each other. Brouillette arrived and lined up behind Chuck, and the two started talking, "but Brouillette was watching Jelickson the whole time." Jelickson dropped back to talk to them, at which point the guard could hear Brouillette say, "Stay the hell away from me. I'm not talking to someone like you." Brouillette and Jelickson started to tussle, and DeGroot wedged himself between them. It seemed to break up. The guard moved into position—"although who knows what I'd do with three fighting men at my age"—whereupon he heard Jelickson say, "You should be on my side, we're practically family," followed by something that was lost as Chuck let go of Brouillette and took a swing at Jelickson. Jelickson ducked, but Brouillette hit him in the side, seemingly in coordination with Chuck.

"Sorry I couldn't be more help with everything," the guard, Charlie, said. "With the bank closing, they don't want to go to the trouble of hiring someone new. I should have been able to defuse it, used to be able to, but I'm a little too old for even that, I guess. I mean, pulling the out-of-towner aside would have solved everyone's problems."

Dave and I let the guard go back to the bank and decided to work on Chuck next. Since arriving, he had made one call—to his job—and sat quietly. When we walked into the room he was reading the paper, running the finger of his free hand across the basketball stats.

Dave uncuffed Chuck and straddled the seat opposite him. "So?"

"Man, I don't know what happened back there. I mean, *I know.*

Brouillette's crazy with grief, which, if something happened to Jackie . . . well. And there's Jelickson, but even he just lost his son."

"So you got pulled in when you were breaking up a fight?" I asked.

"Sure."

Chuck agreed a little too readily for my taste.

"But you threw a punch. Why?"

"Phil needed help. You know how that goes."

"And Jelickson didn't say something to you, make you mad?" Dave asked.

"I'd advise you not to speak," said a voice from the doorway. I found myself facing R. Michael Fitzgerald. He had a minion at his side, and both men were suited up and ready for a fight.

"Did you even read him his rights?" asked Fitzgerald, coming to stand next to Chuck and resting his hand on his shoulder.

"They did," Chuck said.

"Then as your lawyer I would advise you to make the most of yours and remain silent."

"Huh?" Chuck said. "I didn't hire you. I can't *afford* you."

Rather than speaking to Chuck, Fitzgerald addressed Dave and me. "Phil Brouillette said you were an innocent bystander, Chuck, as was he. As you both were caught up in Jelickson's lawlessness, the Brouillettes felt that you should be represented alongside Phil. My associate is going to speak with Mr. Brouillette, to make sure he wasn't mishandled, but as you seem to be under the most *duress* right now, I'm going to work with you to see this situation doesn't escalate."

Fitzgerald talked as if he ran the whole shebang, a quality that made him a good defense lawyer. In the two cases in which I had given evidence against one of his clients, Fitzgerald had managed to get one guy off and the second convicted of lesser charges. His trick was to convince juries that he believed absolutely in his clients' innocence, and the juries, in turn, should trust him. He always had a minion who would jump up and object to everything and anything, but Fitzgerald seemed without fear that his client might face conviction. Fitzgerald floated into court on a cloud of righteousness, and floated out without letting judge or jury see that he'd stuck the prosecution with a shiv.

"We were going to take his statement and release him," Dave said.

"Oh, yes, I'm *sure* that's what you were planning. Mr. DeGroot, don't believe that for a minute."

"If that's the case," Dave said, "I'm going to see if we can move Chuck into a cell while we wait." Dave stormed out with Fitzgerald following, leaving Chuck and me alone.

"That your lawyer?"

"Guess so. Although I'm not sure if I'm allowed to speak to you." He shrugged. "I wish I didn't have to be put in the cells. I haven't been in there in twenty years. Got picked up on a drunk driving charge before the laws got tough. They still cold and damp?"

"Well, it is jail," I said with a smile. "We don't want to make it too enjoyable."

"Urgh. I was hoping to have this all done before tonight so I didn't miss another day of work, and maybe get out of here in time to cook dinner for Jacqueline if . . . after . . . she comes home."

From the squad room, I could hear the sharp tones of Mrs. Jelickson along with another voice asking how long his client would be held. The other side's cavalry had arrived.

I continued our friendly conversation. "Do you cook dinner every night?"

"Mostly. Jacqueline's always telling me she ate before, but I think she's not eating, not wanting to get fat. The doctor says she's healthy. . . ." He trailed off, lost in his own thoughts.

"Girls at that age don't realize how beautiful they are," I said.

"She is beautiful, isn't she?" He frowned suddenly, as Jackie's voice rose above the din in the next room.

"Let me see my father," she demanded.

I stepped into the hallway. Jackie was with Mrs. Jelickson and a lawyer. The guy didn't have a pin-striped suit on, but the casual loafers with jeans ensemble gave away his lawyerliness.

"What do you mean, DeGroot already has representation?" the lawyer was saying, the flatness of his *a*'s more Connecticut Yankee than upstate New York. "Some public defender?"

I recognized Charles Van Schoon from the society pages. I didn't read them, but they were right next to the obituaries, which my dad read religiously. The guy was some big-shot New York City corporate lawyer who had a "weekend place" in Columbia County. He and his wife would go to all the social events when the Saratoga track was open, avoiding the lawn-chaired masses to sit next to the Whitneys in their box.

"No, me," Fitzgerald said, coming from Chief Donnelly's office.

"Oh, Mike," the man said. "Didn't realize . . ."

I caught Jackie's eye and waved her over. I stood in the doorway, trying to slow her down, but she barreled past and ran to her father. I did stop Mrs. Jelickson.

"Family only." I shut the door in Linda Jelickson's face.

Chuck held Jackie at arm's length; her fingers caught in his sleeve. He turned his back on her, and tears welled in Jackie's eyes. It was not the happy reunion I was expecting.

"It wasn't like that, but with the baby . . ."

A baby, I thought. That explained so much.

"And I told you I'd help," Chuck said. "It's my grandkid."

"The Jelicksons' grandkid, too." Jackie's voice was high and frantic as she blurted her reasons. "They're pretty rich. And they're in California."

"And I'm your father. You didn't come home last night—"

"I was talking with the Jelicksons. They're like family. They understand what it's like to miss Ray. Miss Ray so much I want to die, to be with him." She looked down, tears rolling down her face, her jewel-studded hoops glinting softly. Were those Danielle's earrings? No, they were pastel stones and didn't glint quite as brightly. "You don't even want me to have this baby," she said.

"No, I want you to have this baby." His eye caught mine and his voice dropped low, but I heard everything. "But I don't want you to drop out of school, ruin your life. Like your mom. Like me."

"I won't ruin my life!" Jackie yelled through angry tears. "This baby will be the best thing that ever happened to me. And I will love it so much, and be the best mother you ever saw, and this baby will love me and no one else. You don't want me to have his baby, or go with his parents. You want me to be a loser like you, being grateful for the scraps they drop like we're dogs!" Chuck looked stung, but Jackie didn't notice. She crossed her arms in front of her, the fabric pulling taut against a small, but visible, baby bump. "But I'll be eighteen in three weeks. I can leave the state. You can't stop me."

Mrs. Jelickson's screech sounded faintly through the door. Chuck reached out, and despite her angry tears, Jackie let him put his arms around her and pull her close.

I cleared my throat. "Chuck, can I trust the two of you to stay put?" He didn't respond, and I left. The brightness of the main room blinded me, and I almost ended up running into R. Michael Fitzgerald's right-hand man.

Barely out of school, he had patronizing *down*. "Of course, now that Mr. DeGroot has counsel, anything said since then isn't admissible."

"Oh, shut up," I said.

The more things progressed, the more I—and the whole police department—were being cut off at the knees. The people we couldn't question, the information withheld by the congresswoman, the FBI. And I was tired and missed my daughter a lot. I decided a quick phone call was in order. Lucy was still in school, and my father knew I was working through the night and wasn't going to be worrying, but I needed to reconnect with real life, with a life outside cops and killers and murdered kids.

I sat down at my desk. No one noticed me. I dialed home, and as the phone rang, I bounced my Dude Lebowski bobblehead, his beard brushing against his blue bathrobe.

Dad picked up and immediately dropped the phone. I could hear it bounce off a chair and land on the floor.

"Jesus, Mary, and Joseph," I heard from a distance.

"Long day?" I asked, once he was on the line.

"I think that's what I should be asking you. You into double time yet?" He was a cop through and through, one who wanted to solve the case and catch the bad guy and who understood the value of overtime.

"Flipped into double time somewhere around Tuesday. How's Lucy?"

"Okay. I received a long speech about how I'm boring and how I comb her hair too hard."

"Which you do," I said, smiling even though he couldn't see me.

"Yeah, okay. You're not bald, though, and I'm sure she'll live. Anyway, I couldn't do anything right, which means she misses you."

"I miss her, too." I did, in a bone-deep way. Instead of cheering me up, this conversation was exhausting me. I needed something happy to look forward to. "Hey, let Lucy know that when I get home tonight, we can go ice-skating."

"That'll keep our girl happy."

"She's probably angrier at me than you."

"Nah. You know, Luce brought home pictures of you fighting crime. In a cape, no less. She's good."

"And you're good. You're a live-in babysitter when you were all set to enjoy your retirement."

"Eh, I had to retire. No way I was going to *enjoy* it. Plus, now I'm a grandpa." His tone was warm. "You seem to be enjoying yourself. Monsignor Ottario said you worked him over yesterday."

I laughed. "Maybe I'm enjoying it a little. Still, I miss her." I looked down at my desk, pretending to study a report. The only thing keeping me from tearing up was the knowledge that two Jelicksons, two lawyers, and Lorraine were ten feet away.

"I know. I remember. But Hopewell Falls has one murder a year, tops, and generally it's solved fast. This one's a big one. I think the last time we had one this rough was back in the eighties, where the father chopped up his family and made them disappear. If you ever figure out where he stashed those bodies, I'll sleep better. You'll solve this case, I know you, and you'll come home and spend more time with your daughter than you even knew you wanted. Okay?"

"Can I have a nap between now and then?" I asked, feeling better.

"The way you slept as a teenager, I'm amazed you managed to ever wake up. Now go finish up and be back in time for dinner," he said. "Or so help me, I'll make sloppy joes again."

I hung up and sank back in my chair, my body wanting rest, my mind tracing the room. Under the fluorescents everyone looked like they belonged in a wanted poster, including Dave and Lorraine, who were in intense conversations with the lawyers. Fitzgerald kept cutting off anyone who made a comment, and Charles Van Schoon's WASPy dignity couldn't cover the disgusted look that crossed his face whenever he scrutinized the station, Dave, Lorraine, or particularly Mrs. Jelickson.

I glanced into the chief's office. Chuck stood at the window. To be fair, Hopewell Falls crime was more of this type—folks getting into a tussle in public and needing to calm down under the watchful eye of the police. Admittedly, the tusslers weren't usually suspects in a high-profile murder. Still, the mundane police work had been what I needed when Kevin was sick, and even more now I was a single parent. The decision to return had been painful, but for the first time in my adult life—"First time in your whole life, you mean," Dad later said—I needed help. Kevin had been the one to argue most against giving up my work with the FBI, but I knew I had to give up something I wanted for what I needed.

"LYONS," DAVE SAID, STANDING right in front of me. I was so out of it I completely missed his approach. "Got a minute?"

"For you? Sure." I followed him into the interrogation room, where Hale was waiting. I hadn't even realized he was back.

"After consultation with the fine people of the State of New York—okay, Amanda Brouillette—Jerry has decided not to press charges," Dave said. "He says he doesn't have enough evidence, claims that it's a misunderstanding. I disagree, so I get to spend a few hours on a conference call, explaining why one of the state's most prominent citizens was arrested on such a nuisance charge."

"Tell those folks y'all were responding to a public disturbance this morning. You were just being neighborly. And you can't give them any details because I'm a controlling pain in the ass." Hale's southernness always shone through when he was tired, drunk, or talking to his mama. The accent was out in force.

"I'll bet my firstborn," Dave said, "that Amanda Brouillette instigated this phone call and will be listening in. Clearly, if she's wasting our time that way, she doesn't want her husband sprung from jail that quickly." Dave sat down in a chair, tipping it back against the wall. "Since we're in no rush, I think Lyons, here, should go have that talk with Jason Byrne, track down those boots and what happened to the key. You, too." He nodded at Hale. "Go see if you can get Byrne to confess to the whole thing so I can go home." His eyes drooped closed.

"Are we dismissed?" I asked loudly.

Dave didn't open his eyes, just waved us out. "Be gone."

CHAPTER 21

GREG BYRNE WAS NOT willing to go quietly. While amyotrophic lateral sclerosis, or Lou Gehrig's disease, had taken away many things, when we asked to question Jason, Greg Byrne had no problem speaking his mind, albeit slowly, with a voice scratchy from disuse.

"Need to stop Jason," he said, "from selling self down river."

Jason grinned as he set up folding chairs next to his father's bed, which sat in the corner. The room was cramped, less of a living room than a well-decorated hospital room. While the Byrnes were near neighbors of the Brouillettes, the Byrnes' house had been built twenty years earlier, smaller in size and intention, with narrow windows that received no afternoon light. The room was adorned with pink and gray pastel couches and a glass-top coffee table, the 51-inch flat-screen TV crammed in opposite Greg Byrne's bed a modern luxury out of place in the 1980s decor. Needless to say, I'd guess decorating was low down on their list of priorities, below keeping Greg Byrne breathing and keeping the drugstore afloat.

I had deep misgivings about doing the interview with Greg

Byrne present. Jason was an adult in every sense of the word, so no parent was needed, and his missing key was probably the only way anyone else might have accessed the medical-waste Dumpster. Why someone chose to dump the boots and hat at the pharmacy rather than in one of the empty lots around here didn't make sense, unless like Marty they hadn't been here long enough to know what areas were abandoned and what areas just looked that way. Jason didn't think much of Danielle and clearly admired Marty, and I wondered how far he would go to protect his friend. Despite his earnest demeanor and eagerness to please, I didn't trust Jason.

We settled in, knees bumping and "Excuse me's" all around. Hale, energized by a sixteen-ounce coffee and his discomfort at being around someone so sick, jittered his leg on one side of me. Jason's leg bounced up and down on the other side of me, his arm poked through the bars on his father's hospital bed, unashamedly holding his father's hand. I was surprised that a young man—any man—would be that openly affectionate.

I started the questioning. "So, Jason, we'd like to again go over your movements two nights ago."

"That's easy. I was home all night, watching movies with Dad."

"And before that?"

He looked puzzled. "Before that I was at work."

"And you weren't anywhere else?"

He darted a look at his father before answering. "No. Nowhere."

"Marty says otherwise," I said. I flipped back through my notebook. "Marty said you stopped at his place with food. Your mom says the same thing. How come you didn't mention that when we talked to you before?"

"But I didn't go in." A flush ran up his neck to his cheeks, making him look very young. "I would have told you that. I dropped stuff off and I came home."

"I don't know." I read my pad as if I didn't have these facts memorized. "What time was that?"

"Around six or so," he said, and stopped. "What?"

A small movement gave away what was going on—Greg Byrne was squeezing Jason's hand, signaling.

"We can continue this questioning back at the station if you'd like," I said.

"I don't have anything to hide." Jason pulled his hand from his father's. "I arrived home around six thirty. I hung out with Dad."

"Your dad awake the whole time?" Hale asked.

Jason opened his mouth but said nothing as Greg Byrne cleared his throat.

"Yes, awake," Greg said, each word deliberate, an effort. "Questions for me, ask me."

It was quiet for a moment, all of us waiting for more. He slumped back on the pillow, and I asked my next question. "So you got home at six thirty, with the key to the Dumpster in hand, I assume?"

Jason looked relieved. "Mom told me you'd ask that, because of the boots and the hat you found. Yes. I came home with the key." He absently grabbed his father's hand. It was their best mode of communication. "Actually, that's why I didn't remember Marty's, didn't remember it as important, because I had the key the whole time. I'm sure I remember coming home and putting it on the hook that night. I'm pretty sure. I do it every single night, so I don't know why I wouldn't have. My mom came in to talk when she got back from the pharmacy right at the end of the first movie, when Luke was destroying the Death Star, and told me if Celia managed to show up I'd need to come in to the pharmacy to work, including throwing some of the trash out, 'cause the guys were supposed to come, the waste disposal guys, either the next day or the day after, since they had missed the week before. Because of snow. Anyway, I got up when the movie was over, and grabbed it so I wouldn't forget it. I do stupid things sometimes."

Another hand squeeze. Next to me Jason's knee stilled.

Hale's leg pressed against mine. I was so used to working with

Dave, I thought he was signaling me, but realized his touch was inadvertent. I shifted away into the TV that was wedged against the couch. I tried to stay still, not wanting to destroy their one nice thing.

Hale leaned forward, elbows resting on his knees, filling up the space in the middle. "Tell us, Jason, did you give the key to Marty? Or did he steal it?"

"No, I told you already. I didn't even go in. I didn't give it to him. And he didn't get it away from me." Another hand squeeze. "Even I'm not that incompetent."

"So I'd be grateful," Hale said, "if you could explain why we found your DNA all over the bloody boots and hat in the Dumpster this morning."

"I don't . . . I throw a lot of stuff in that Dumpster." Jason's cheeks stained red. "So the boots are definitely . . . ?" He stopped as his father squeezed his hand.

His father was again moved to speak. "No way DNA from this morning. Lying."

He was right. As police officers we could lie in the call of duty, although we couldn't withhold evidence. Hale was caught. The room went silent. "What Hale meant was the clothes. We found your DNA all over the clothes. Along with all the compounds that go into meth." Greg Byrne squeezed Jason's hand through the whole statement.

"I'm going to remain silent, I think," Jason said, and then more forcefully, "I choose to remain silent."

"And you are not going to explain what happened to the key?" Hale said. "Or how those boots and hat got in there?"

Jason shook his head firmly, an emphatic no.

I flipped my notebook shut. "Call your mother, Jason, you're under arrest."

"What?" He was up and out of his seat. "I've been nothing but nice during this whole thing."

"Nice isn't what we want, Jason," I said. "We want honest."

Too many paths were leading back to Jason. He was in the middle of this in some way. The box and the key were too big to ignore, and he was in Marty's pocket.

Jason pulled his hand away from his father's and spoke directly to us. "Okay. Let me call my mother. Again." The next words might have come directly out of Denise Byrne's mouth. "We hoped you'd be decent."

He paced as he talked on the phone, the steady stream of words making it clear he was leaving a message rather than talking to a real person. I caught Greg Byrne watching me.

"Do you mind if I ask you again?" I said. "Are you sure you didn't fall asleep?"

"No sleep. I'm awake." He paused. "It hurts."

Hale approached the bed. "Are you in much pain, sir? Can we fetch you anything?"

"I am . . ."—Greg Byrne caught his breath—"used to work. Pharmacy. Used to live. Used to be dad."

Jason finished his phone call and walked to the fireplace mantle, which was topped with twenty or thirty pill bottles, quickly scanned them, and grabbed one. He had been listening the whole time. He filled a cup from a plastic pitcher on the coffee table, leaving behind a water ring on the *Pharmacy Today* magazine.

Jason smiled as he shoved the pill into his father's mouth and moved a straw to his lips. "No more bendy ones."

We heard the back door open. Denise Byrne didn't call in from the kitchen, but appeared in the doorway, bundled up in a coat, a hat, a pale blue scarf, and matching gloves. She moved to Jason and clutched him fiercely.

"Hi, Mom," Jason said, quickly disentangling himself. Holding hands with his father was communication, but hugs from Mom were embarrassing.

"They need to take me in to the station," he whispered.

Denise pushed her son behind her, and pointed a finger at me. "June, do you realize what a big mistake this is? My son has done nothing."

I walked toward mother and son. Jason moved his mother aside, despite her protest, and I took his arm.

"We're going to have to handcuff you," I said.

"What?!" Denise protested. "You are not arresting him."

"Yes, we are. I think he intentionally omitted information about his whereabouts the night Ray Jelickson died—"

Denise put her hand to her chest.

"—and we have a strong suspicion that he was involved in a conspiracy to commit murder, either as an accomplice or something more. We're taking him in." I spoke quickly to Jason. "You want to put your jacket on first?"

"Let me get it," Hale said. Denise pointed in the direction of the kitchen. "Shouldn't you go, too?" she said to me. I refused, and she turned her back to me, her height and bulky coat creating a wall between me and Jason, with whom she had a whispered conversation.

"I'll be fine, Mom," Jason said gently. His voice dropped more as Hale returned. "Dad gave me good advice, and remember, I didn't do anything. Neither did Marty, for that matter."

"Jason, listen to me—"

"No, Mom. Listen to me. Get me a lawyer. In the meantime I'm going to follow Dad's advice to not rock the boat and to keep my mouth shut."

"Jason, do you really think that's a good idea? I—"

"I do think it's a good idea. And I would suggest you do the same."

Denise looked stunned, but closed her mouth. The room was silent. This far out of town there were few cars, and the snow and cold deadened the scrape of trees and the sounds of animals. I approached Jason, preparing to read him his rights, when Denise rushed me. She was taller and bigger, propelling herself past me to her husband. She heaved the table out of the way, pulled Greg forward, took his face in her hands, forced open his mouth, and reached in with one finger. She tugged out a pill, wet with saliva. Greg gasped, taking sharp wheezing breaths. His throat muscles were so weak and constricted that he hadn't been able to swallow, and the capsule had blocked off air to his lungs.

Jason's bravery was gone. "Oh, God, I'm sorry."

Greg Byrne coughed softly. "No problem."

Denise Byrne was furious. "No, it's a problem. These people come in here, and, and . . ." She threw up her hands. "I thought you, more than anyone, would understand, June. I did you favors."

"I'm not sure if I ever got a chance to thank you for that," I said, knowing I hadn't. Denise Byrne hadn't let me. "You saved my husband a lot of pain. Thank you."

"Can't you show us the same consideration? Do you have to arrest my son?"

Hale seemed to expect some sort of response from me, some sort of outrage or anger at what Denise said. But I was a professional. This situation, so close to my own, wasn't mine.

I left Denise Byrne's accusation in the air, unanswered. I went up to Jason and rested my hand on his arm. "You ready to go?"

"Yes," he said. He took his fleece-lined jean jacket from Hale. Once dressed, he leaned over and hugged his father.

"Sorry."

"Nothing sorry."

Jason straightened, holding his wrists in front of him.

"Turn around," I said. I tightened his arms around his back, cuffing him, while Hale gave Denise Byrne the time line and our contact information. I guided Jason down the hallway, the two of us and Hale walking single file in order to work around the dusty motorized wheelchair that rested along one wall. We continued past the spotless kitchen, a pot of something delicious bubbling on the stove, metal canisters of sugar and flour on the counter, and a medication schedule written out neatly on graph paper taped to the cabinets, outlining the hour and amount of drugs that would need to be dispensed. It took up three doors.

"Jason, I'll call a lawyer," Denise shouted over Hale's head. "He'll meet you there. Don't say anything until you see him."

"Thanks, Mom. And remember to pull the chili off the burner in twenty minutes." Jason stopped at the door of the mudroom, pulling me up short. He nodded at the switch next to the door. "Wanna hit that? We'll crack our heads open on the shoes otherwise."

I flicked it on. The porch was a jumble of coats on pegs. Rock salt and two shovels were tucked in the corner, and a dozen pairs of shoes—a jumble of boots, sneakers, and slippers—were on the floor. On the wall, right at my eye line, hung a key caddy.

"You sure the key to the bin is missing?" I asked.

"Yes, I'm sure," Jason said. "Those two sets of car keys are for the van. Then there are the ones for the Toyota, which was my dad's. We sold that a while ago. The next are for the Brouillettes' garage. They like me to go and turn the cars on and off when they're gone for a while, keep them running in the cold weather. Then those"—he nodded at a ring with three keys—"are the keys to the pharmacy door locks. Normally the Dumpster key is on there, too."

"Denise," I called, "do you have another set of keys to the pharmacy?"

"You going to seize our business, too?!"

I couldn't see her, but called out, beyond Hale, into the kitchen. "No, but I'm taking these into evidence, and didn't want to leave you in the lurch." I pulled out an evidence bag, dropping them in.

"What's that last set of keys, there?" Hale asked Jason.

"That's for my locker at college. I'm taking a semester off, so we don't need that, either."

I reached around him to open the door. Unlocked. "Let me go first," I said, and checked for ice patches. Hale eased Jason down the steps and then pulled the door shut behind him. He jiggled the knob, checking if an outsider might have had access. The door gave way.

As we passed the Brouillettes', I glanced up at the house, dark except for one light upstairs: Danielle's long-empty room.

"Is Amanda Brouillette at home?" I asked.

"The Brouillettes are steering clear of their property since it's a hazardous waste site, from, well, you know." Hale nodded toward Jason in the backseat.

"Oh."

Then maybe it was a security system. The light winked out and was gone.

CHAPTER 22

Jason's lawyer, a personal injury shyster with an 800 number—promising on his billboard that he would represent people "For Free!!!!"—seemed unhappy that Jason had given us his name.

"Don't answer *anything* without me present. These people want nothing more than to hang the whole thing on you. Did they even read you your rights?"

Jason nodded, having taken to heart the order to remain silent.

The lawyer humphed, frowning at Hale and me. "Can I have a moment alone with my client?"

At this point, the station was running out of room for lawyers. Worse, we were running out of room for suspects.

Lorraine sent Chuck on his way with a wink and a "We'll be calling!" and processed Jelickson's paperwork slowly, per Dave. Van Schoon was discreetly impressing upon Lorraine that Jelickson's driver's license was in no way a counterfeit, but rather, Californian. He was used to doing deals in carpeted offices behind thick mahogany doors with people who spoke in reasonable tones, and seemed unmoored in this wide-open room. Finally, in the face of Lorraine's willful denseness—I had no idea she was such a spectacular actress—Van Schoon decided that discretion was impossible.

"You!" Van Schoon pointed at Dave, who was writing a message to me that read, "Do you think Van Schoon gets all blotchy when he gets mad?"

"Hmm?" Dave said.

"Are you going to enjoy the harassment suit that I'll be filing on behalf of my client?" Van Schoon said. "You hicks are obstructing things. Get that FBI agent out here."

Lorraine, at the use of the word *hicks,* produced an emery board and began to file her nails. I could have kissed her.

"He's in a meeting," I said, as seriously as I could manage. In reality, Hale was napping in his car until Marty got there.

My radio blasted. Pete talked loud, although not fast. He never talked fast.

"June. You got a situation. Those Merrimen? The biker guys? They're on the front steps of the police station."

A predatory grin spread across Zeke Jelickson's face.

"And that wouldn't be a problem," Pete added, "except the troopers need a parking spot to bring in your prisoner."

That would knock the smile off Zeke's face fast enough.

"Bring him in the prisoner transport security entrance," I said authoritatively as I marched to the back.

"The back door?" asked Pete. Linda Jelickson burst out laughing.

"Yeah. The back door." I was trying to make our jail sound impressive, but our "prisoner transport security entrance" was little more than a steel-reinforced door. That said, the door had done a fine job for over a century, certainly better than the new jail across the river where there had been a recent break. There, some prisoners were "tussling" in the laundry when a misplaced punch perforated unreinforced drywall put up by a contractor trying to shave a few bucks off the costs. The gentlemen put aside their differences and pummeled their way out, resulting in a manhunt that ended when the prisoners were found in an off-season hunting shack, still within county limits.

"Finally," Amanda Brouillette said, stepping away from her husband's cell bars. She hadn't been sitting vigil for her daughter, but for her husband.

I brushed past. "Not yet."

"You let that criminal out and not me?" Brouillette protested. "I'm going to sue for wrongful arrest."

Amanda Brouillette tried to bridge the gap between us. "There is no reason Jelickson, and Chuck, for that matter, should have been released before my husband."

Dave shrugged. "Yeah, but they didn't get picked up with a gun that wasn't theirs."

Brouillette sputtered. "That-that-that gun is mine."

"You have a Lady Smith & Wesson?"

"Huh?" Brouillette recovered quickly. "That's my wife's gun. They must have been swapped in the safe. We have licenses for both."

"Which your lawyer's explaining right now. You'll no doubt be released soon, but you can bet that you're going to lose your concealed carry permit *tout de suite*." The last words were lost as the door groaned open. A state trooper waited on the other side, as casual as one could be in a military stance. "You need any help with the Merrimen?" the trooper asked as Dave scribbled his name on several pieces of paperwork. "New Hampshire says they're pretty small time, and they don't cross state lines that often."

"They're afraid of Vermont," I said. "They might cross the border and have their choppers magically transformed into Volvos."

He laughed. "Actually, I might be a little afraid of Vermont, too."

The trooper craned so far forward his windburned neck extended out of his gray collar. The second he saw the congresswoman and her husband he snapped back, like a turtle into a shell.

"Here's his property, his clothes." He handed a bag to me. "His vehicle is at the trooper barracks near Potsdam, and will be transported tomorrow. Pictures of the whole thing from the chassis on up will be e-mailed shortly."

We covered Marty's head as he ducked out of the vehicle, and he kept his face tucked as he approached, chin touching his chest, arms cuffed behind him, dressed in orange scrubs. Crossing the threshold into the jail, he looked up and spotted the Brouillettes. He stopped for a moment, and then lunged. I dropped his clothes so I could grip him with both hands.

"You?" Marty cried. "I knew you killed her, you sick fuck."

"Bastard!" Brouillette's shoulder pressed against the bars as he jammed his finger at Marty. "I'm in here because of you, your family. You people foul everything you touch. You're disgusting."

Marty tried to break away, but Dave and I held him tight, letting him thrash until the fight left him.

"Marty, Brouillette was brawling in public. With your father," Dave said. "Who is, by the way, out front."

"Of course." Marty shook his head and laughed bitterly at the ceiling. This close, I could see him swallow, choking. With nothing to slump against, he collapsed in on himself.

"C'mon, bucko," Dave said, snagging up the bag of Marty's property and pulling him along, Marty's feet half sliding and half dragging against the blue-flecked linoleum.

"Marty," the congresswoman called as we got to the squad room door, "why did you run? If you didn't kill my daughter, Marty, why leave?"

"Ma'am," he said, but didn't turn around, "no offense, but you have no idea. They've got me tagged as some scumfuck, and if I even breathe wrong, they roll me up. I ran to get away from the cops, and my parents, and, no offense, to get away from you."

Marty battered his way forward, an unstoppable force. He ran smack into an immovable object.

"Baby!" His mother threw her arms around him.

"Mom," and he placed his forehead on her shoulder, like Lucy did when she was up past her bedtime.

Dave untwisted Linda from her son. "Ma'am, if you could give me some room."

She let go. As she did, Jackie put Marty in a tight squeeze, locking his arms behind him.

One side of Marty's mouth quirked down. "Uh, hi, Jackie."

She pulled away, blushing. "We're practically related."

The only one who hadn't rushed up for a family reunion was Zeke Jelickson, who lingered near the front entrance. He stared down his son. Marty wouldn't play, looking at the fans bolted to the ceiling in the corners, the recycling bin next to Lorraine's desk, and the line of doors; everywhere but his father. Zeke's lawyer ended the staring contest—or the "not-staring" contest, in the case of Marty—when he handed Zeke his walking papers.

Zeke put out his leathery hand, pumping his lawyer's pale one. "Nice work, Charles. Talk to you on next week's conference call about that Chinese intellectual property thing."

"You don't want me to stay?" asked Van Schoon. "I was helping you out until a real criminal lawyer got here, but obviously the firm and I are more than happy to do the same for your son."

"I'd appreciate that—"

"I decline!" Marty announced. "I'm not using the Abominations' lawyer. I'm not taking anything from you, Zeke."

Zeke leaned over, whispering something to the lawyer.

"You're the boss," Van Schoon said. The lawyer pulled out his card and gave it to Zeke. "It's not public, but that number there is my cell."

Zeke pocketed the card as the lawyer left.

"Linda. Jackie. We're done."

"Marty," Linda Jelickson whispered, "we'll post bail."

"I don't want you to bail me out," Marty said, not unkindly.

"And he won't get it, ma'am." Dave handcuffed Marty to a chair. "He's a flight risk. Officer Lyons here will process the paperwork."

"Linda," barked Zeke.

"Jesus, Zeke, I'll be there in a minute!"

Zeke left. I began the paperwork, while Hale and Dave disappeared into the evidence room with Marty's belongings. Marty answered my questions, giving his age, "Twenty-five," and his full name, "Martin Fizzeller Jelickson."

His mother was spelling out "Fizzeller" for me when Marty snarled, "Go, Mom. I don't want you here."

Linda Jelickson stepped back. "Okay, baby. You need a little time to sort this out in your head, to brood. I know my son." She smiled sweetly and hissed: "Just don't open your mouth between now and when you come to your senses."

"Was Ray a brooder?" asked Jackie as Linda guided her to the door, one hand at the small of Jackie's back. The doors swung closed behind them, and quiet reigned.

I breathed in the silence, waiting patiently for the computers to load the next screen. Finally I was able to enter the codes for the different charges. Petty larceny. Stealing of state property. Not murder, not yet.

"You want to make your phone call now?" I asked.

Marty rolled his eyes. "Who am I going to call? My dad's lawyer?"

"A lawyer, sure, or I thought you might want to call your sponsor."

Marty looked at the ground.

"No," he said.

I was walking to the printer for the paperwork when Dave dragged me into Interview Two. A laptop was open on the table. Hale sat in front of it, clicking, again and again.

"Ta-da!" Dave said. "The crack team at the FBI was able to pull some digital photos out of Marty's work computer."

"Some special FBI decryption software?" I asked.

"Left in the recycle bin," Hale said, not looking up. "The photos were sitting there waiting for us. The guys made us a copy."

Hale clicked. The first two pictures were of Marty: one reading a Don DeLillo book on his couch, and another looking up from the same book with an arched brow, beckoning the person taking the picture to him with a sly smile. Hale clicked again.

Solo shots of Danielle followed. They captured her beauty, but more important, they captured her aliveness. In one, a twist of smoke from her cigarette traced the pathway her hand made when she was gesturing grandly toward Ray, who was doubled over with laughter.

The picture that followed looked familiar: Ray could be seen carrying huge beakers into a building. Painted on a wall behind him a pale hand curled around a red rose, now pink all these years later. I knew exactly where that photo was taken.

"How did he get copies of your surveillance shots?" I said to Hale.

"He didn't," Hale said.

"Different night?" Dave asked.

"No." Hale looked angry. "Marty was there when we were there. I'll be having a conversation with the agents on how, exactly, we missed him. At least we have proof that he was there the night Danielle was killed. Are we done?"

He clicked. The next shots were of Craig, Ray, and Danielle: Danielle gesturing angrily at Craig, her iridescent red nails glinting dangerously close to his face; Ray and Craig giving each other a fist bump in front of Marty's house, Danielle on the porch and almost out of the shot; Danielle and Craig hugging at the doorway, his face buried in her gold hair.

Finally Hale spoke: "Spy anything, June?"

I hesitated.

"What?" Hale twisted around, looking at me. "What's your instinct?"

"I have an idea," I said, appalled at what I was about to suggest. Dave frowned, but Hale smiled, like a shark tasting blood.

"Let's do it," he said.

CHAPTER 23

I SAT ACROSS THE TABLE from Marty in Interview Two. With his eyes focused on the wall over my shoulder I had all the time I wanted to take him in. He'd lost a little weight in the last few days, his features were sharper, more wolflike. If I didn't know they weren't blood, I would have sworn he was Zeke's. Marty's eyes darted around the wall: Danielle alive, Ray at the funeral, Ray in the bloody snow, Ray and Danielle kissing on the back porch, Danielle after her autopsy, pale and still, like a pearl covered with frost. Marty's eyes shot back to Ray and Danielle kissing—it had been Dave's idea to post that one—and then back to Danielle after her autopsy. Again, Danielle after her autopsy. Again, Danielle. Again.

I had felt excited as Dave and I led him to the room, my stomach knotting. I explained to Marty that with Phil Brouillette's release in process and Jason being interviewed in Room One, he'd have to cool his heels.

"Jason?" he said. "For what?"

"An accessory to murder, guy," Dave said. "The murder you committed."

"I knew you guys couldn't tell your ass from your elbows, but Jason? That's fuckin' idiotic." As he ambled toward the room, Marty's orange pants slipped down an inch, revealing his flat stomach and the slide of his hip bones. His hands cuffed, I hitched up the waistband.

"Hel-lo, Officer." Marty winked at me, Danielle and Ray seemingly forgotten. "Trying to take advantage?"

He remembered Danielle and Ray fast when I opened the door, revealing the murder wall.

"Oh, hell no."

"Oh, yes," Dave said, handcuffing Marty to the table and walking out.

I now sat opposite him, steeling myself. Not illegal, but that's the only line I wasn't crossing. I spoke low and firm. "Marty, I understand. Marriage is an important thing." I thought of Kevin, for whom I would have done anything to keep alive, and Danielle, whom Marty might have killed. "It's supposed to be forever."

He didn't respond, and I adjusted course.

"She must've loved you a lot, considering she didn't have to marry you. I mean, she wasn't pregnant." At this he shook his head, participating in the conversation nonverbally. He would talk soon.

"And she had choices, her parents made sure. Sure, UCLA didn't work out, but she wasn't going to be stuck in a dead-end mill town, wearing a smock and stocking cigarettes at the minimart on the eleven-to-seven shift, always on the lookout for someone who's going to rob her. Her parents would've made sure she earned a degree, bribed her way into a second- or third-tier school somewhere far away, someplace where Jesuits could give her a solid education so she could be a teacher, or a newscaster. She was pretty enough to do that."

"Don't forget smart."

A response. I was on the right track. I continued my story. "And she'd marry someone nice, someone who'd appreciate the connections she provided. Being the daughter of a congresswoman had its perks."

Marty joined me in telling my fairy tale, far away from an interrogation room in Hopewell Falls, New York, with, if I had to guess, everyone he loved dead. "And Phil's got weight. Weight he could throw around. If he wanted to."

I knew the "if he wanted to" part was the part that stung. Phil didn't want to help Marty. "So she must've loved you," I said. "Or you must've had something she wanted."

He nodded at the pictures on the wall. "Like my brother?"

"So that was it?" I leaned forward. "You were stopping her from going behind your back?" I continued to tell the story. "I think you were setting up something nice for yourself here. You brought your brother out as your second. You ran the operation the way you ran the operation in California, your wife stealing amphetamines from her job until she got fired."

"They didn't have the money to pay her. . . ."

"Fine, if you say so. The Byrnes were broke." I pushed at the edges of Marty's control. "So you, your brother, and your wife were the first wave in the Abominations' move to New York, and she was the perfect cover—the daughter of a congresswoman and a millionaire—"

"Multimillionaire," he corrected.

"—who could fix things if you got in a jam. You just repeated the operation you had set up in California: Get the supplies through the Abominations' connections. Cook at the Brouillettes'. You were the one with years of experience running a meth lab. Produce enough meth to blanket upstate and Pennsylvania and maybe Ohio—did you have enough? But then, you caught the brother and the wife—caught them on camera—trying to edge you out."

"When they weren't fucking." He nodded to the picture of Danielle and Ray kissing. "Don't forget that."

"That couldn't have been a surprise." I was ready to tip him over. "Yeah, they figured out you'd lost your edge—lost it when you got sober. He bought her diamond earrings, and you bought her a tea set."

He exploded. "She liked that tea set. She liked it *fine*. She always talked about how she and her mom would have tea parties, and I wanted to give her back a little of what she had . . . something nice. She used it the night she died—I came home, and she wasn't there, and two cups were in the drying rack. Two cups you fuckheads broke, thank you—"

"Submit a receipt, Marty. Let me finish my story, and after you can tell me yours." I had him talking, and discussing Ray's diamond earrings had him off balance. "So an old and boring gift made clear you didn't have enough brass to run the show, and they were going to do it themselves, do it better. You had to punish them for the run-around, what they'd done. I can understand. I can. You build something up, you make your own way, away from your family, and you get screwed. So you did what you did last time. You killed them."

He nodded along. "One problem. My brother was a squid, and—"

"Squid?" I asked.

"I thought you were little miss gang task force. Big surprise, you know shit. A squid is . . . a guy, a kid, who has no fucking idea how to ride a bike . . . has no respect for his machine or the road. Ray couldn't cook a clean batch of crystal to save his life, and unless Danielle was taking lessons"—he hesitated, cocking his head, as if considering the same thing I was: did she learn to cook? He shook his head and continued—"if I was running the show, I'd be hard to push out." His wrist wrenched against the cuff as he pointed at me, and it would be red and bruised in an hour. "Except I wasn't. I didn't pull them in. Into the life." He hissed at me the same way his mother had, warning and threatening at the same time. "I've seen what crank does. Taking it, cooking it. What I did, before, in Cali? I had no choice."

I got up and walked around the table, never breaking eye contact as I circled. "Marty, you're the person who knows more than anyone. You know why someone might've killed Ray. You know what Danielle wanted to do, what she did. You know why someone killed her."

I placed my hand on Marty's shoulder and leaned close, so that I could look up at the wall of evidence—the wall of blood, and death, and so much cold—from the same angle. "People wanted them dead. Like Danielle, there. Cut right through her middle, almost in half. And Ray's head wasn't really attached to his body. Someone hated him."

"Someone like me?" He didn't meet my eyes.

"Someone like you," I agreed. "Did you do it, Marty?"

He was silent.

"Marty?"

"No." He breathed deeply. "But Dani and Ray, those stupid, stupid . . . and I didn't stop them. I didn't protect them."

"From who?" I edged my shoulder against him, trying to be a still presence, even as my legs shook from holding the crouch. The room was warm, and a trickle of sweat ran the line of my spine, but I remained steady.

"Not the dealers. Abominations've got the dealers by the nuts."

"Which dealers?"

"Truckers, mostly."

"Which truckers?"

"I don't have their *names*. And maybe the Mongols found out too soon, but no, I don't think so. But the cook or the suppliers . . ."

He stared at the wall in front of him. When he looked at me his pupils were wide, blacking out most of his blue eyes.

"Craig," he said. "He was supplying them, must have been their partner."

I stood, processing what Marty had said. It didn't match up with what Craig was claiming at all, presenting himself as an innocent—or rather, dumb—sidekick.

"He flew a bunch of shit up from the South. He was going to fly more sometime soon."

"The image there, with Ray"—I pointed to Ray going into the glove factory. "Bigger facilities? Were they doing a little downtown redevelopment?"

"Yeah. I was gonna go down there and bust up the deal, but then Danielle . . ."

"When was that picture taken?"

He paused. "I have to keep her name clean. I went to work after the funeral to get rid of them all, so no one would see them."

"You didn't do a very good job, Marty. You didn't do a very good job with any of this. Deaths wouldn't have happened."

"I brought those deaths."

"Marty, when was it taken?" I asked gently.

"The picture was from that night. The night she died. Ray grabbing the supplies from the Brouillettes' barn and making Craig move all the shit to their new cook spot. I figured I'd get proof on that dumbfuck."

"Sure you weren't keeping tabs on your employees?" I asked.

"Would you listen to me for a second?!" he shouted. "That's not me anymore!" He tried to cross his arms, but the handcuffs prevented it. "It never was, not really. It was the life my parents shoved me into, twisting me into a person they could use. And I finally figured out they were doing the same thing to Ray."

"When?"

"Valentine's Day."

"Not Christmas?" I asked. "I heard about how you threw him out. Very Hallmark Special of you."

"That was different. I smelled meth in the house. You know how noxious it is?" I did, unfortunately, like cat urine or rotten eggs. "Well, that was on his clothes. And I got so mad at that shit-for-brains that I threw him out. Danielle talked me out of it the next day, said to give him another chance. She said"—the words caught in his throat—"that she felt like a mother to him, and that we didn't want him to go through what I went through and get into bigger trouble by sending him back to the Abominations." He shook his head at the memory. "Danielle wanted to get him into bigger trouble out here."

"So Valentine's Day?" I asked.

"The earrings. I never saw them until you forced Ray to hand them over, but I knew they existed. Ray got some certificate of authenticity in the mail from the jeweler, laying out how much they were worth. I opened it. I thought he was throwing money away on Jackie, kept expecting her to show up wearing the earrings. Now I know they were for my wife." Marty shut his eyes and took three deep breaths. I let him have a moment of peace.

"In either case, I knew Ray had money—too much money. And coming from our family, I knew there was one way he would make it." Anger crept into Marty's voice. "He didn't know. Dumbass thought our people, Zeke, he thought it's the way to live, that making meth was an honorable profession. He had no fucking idea being a gangster involved being a real bad guy."

"And did you know what it took?"

His eye went to the photo with the 22s, the beakers, the chemicals. He looked poisoned. "I did. I didn't want to know, but I did. And the weird thing I figured out?" He laughed. "So did Danielle. She heard my story in AA. Heard what drugs did to me, heard where they were taking me: jails, institutions, death. When she and I got together . . . I thought she wanted me in spite of it." A grayness settled over him, which I thought would never leave. "No. She wanted me *because* of it."

"And Ray gave her what you wouldn't. And he did what she told him?"

"Like that was hard. I tried . . . I tried to show him how a man lives. A real man, who gets up in the morning and goes out into the world and does the right thing. AA taught me how to live, and I was going to teach him how to live, save him from my path. I got a job and was going to maybe buy a place later this year. I had my eye on a sweet place on Cayuga, been for sale forever." I knew the place Marty was describing, a two-story white wooden house with almost two acres of land around it. It even had a picket fence.

"Real estate is for cheap around here, you know?" Marty continued. "That's why we were living in that shit-hole, so I could save money."

I thought of my father's house, neat and clean, and worth just what he paid for it in 1970. "What happened to all the money from the last deal?"

"Danielle, she's her father's daughter. She invested in the business, the next stage. That night, at the factory? Craig dropped a bubbling 22. And what does Ray say? 'Danielle is going to kill you.'"

"Did they take any money from you? Any other source?"

Marty pointed to pictures of his parents. "Them. The Abominations. I think that little 'get to know you' visit before we left was her making the deal. They wouldn't trust Ray with milk money, but they always wanted a chance to go national. Danielle was their in—in to the Northeast and a chance to tie me to the family."

I wound up for my last push. "Marty, you had access to the car. You had plenty of reason to hate Danielle, to hate Ray. Hell, you might have done it for the money."

"I loved them."

"Well, sometimes people kill out of love. Pained love. Twisted love. When the people you love stab you in the back."

He stood up, the table jerking, the floor screws straining. "Fuck you. I walked away, I gave up everything I had—my fucking birth-right. Three years in the desert, no family, no connections, and then Danielle. And I could see where she was going with that dealing

Adderall bullshit, and Ray, he couldn't wait to get patched. I was trying to help them, save them! Instead, I brought them together." His voice broke, and he crumpled back in his seat. "I killed them both. That may be who I am. I destroy stuff. Like Zeke. But I didn't do it. Is that what you wanted to hear?"

"I just want the truth."

"Well, you got it. I won't profess my innocence. 'Cause I'm not innocent. I brought death to their door." He stared at the wall of photos. "Are we done?"

"Let me make sure we have a cell open for you." I exited into the hallway. Dave high-fived me. To my surprise Jerry, on the phone, gave me a thumbs-up from across the squad room.

"You know that wasn't a confession, right?" I said.

"I know," Dave said. "Everything but. He told us why he did it. He gave us the motive. We know he had opportunity. It's enough to arraign him on charges. Hale is off corroborating details with Craig."

"Charging him would be stupid. We can't physically place him at either murder, it's all circumstantial." I hesitated before my next statement, but I knew I was right. "He didn't do it."

The smile fell halfway off Dave's face. "Well, I think he did. And so does Jerry."

"I don't."

Dave crossed his arms in front of him. "Look, Lyons, type up your report and go home now."

"Are you dismissing me?!"

"No!" he yelled back, and then more gently, "It's just . . . I think there isn't anything either of us can do tonight. I'm going to go home, and Jerry can't take it in front of a grand jury until tomorrow, at the earliest. Maybe we can get some more evidence, prove how very right I am. June, we both need to get ready to play cops and robbers with the feds tomorrow. And while that drug deal tomorrow will line up the Abominations for Hale, I think we got our killer."

I didn't feel like things were solved. At all. But I knew they weren't going to be solved tonight. Seeing Jerry approaching, I braced myself for something worse than Jerry's criticism: his praise.

"June," Jerry said. "Great policing in there!"

I let his positive words, like his negative ones, wash away, disappear under my thoughts of Marty, and Danielle and Ray, drugs and family, too much money, and not enough. Marty had given me the key—who was underwriting this venture? who was the cook?—but I couldn't yet unlock the door.

CHAPTER 24

I PLODDED UP THE SIDEWALK to where my father sat on the steps. Even in the low light, he was reading, a newspaper in his hand opened to coverage of Danielle's funeral, a cup of coffee beside him, still steaming.

"Lucy?" I asked when I was halfway up the walk.

Still focused on his paper, he gave an almost imperceptible nod toward the far end of the yard. Lucy popped out from behind what had once been a formidable snow fort, now brought low by higher temperatures. She disappeared, surfaced again, and threw a snowball, which flew three feet and dropped into the snow. She raced up to it and dug it out—she had no problem discerning her ball of snow from the drifts that surrounded it—and threw it again. It sailed high and to the left. Lucy raced to where it landed and, again, dug it out. She ran up, her face filled with harsh determination, completely focused on the snowball. She suddenly realized how close she was to me and stopped, only a foot away. Instead of throwing herself into my arms, she whaled the snowball right into my chest.

I gasped slightly, from the shock as much as from the icy ball. Lucy darted back behind the wall of her snow fortress.

"Shouldn't have missed ice-skating," Dad said, taking a sip from his coffee as he continued to read his paper.

I was as sorry to miss ice-skating as Lucy was. After a day spent in crowded rooms that closed in on me, death plastered to the wall, I had been anticipating the clean air and open space and the *speed* of ice-skating. Not that I could really go that fast, being so out of practice. Maybe a snowball fight would be good for us. I gathered up my own ball of snow and ran within her throwing range. Unlike my daughter, I fought fair, although she was seven and gave me plenty of warning on the attack, albeit unintentionally.

Her aim and control had evidently improved. The next snowball missed my head, but only because I ducked. As Lucy leaned over to grab another, I gently threw my own loosely packed snowball, which disintegrated before impact, sprinkling white against the purple of Lucy's snowsuit.

Lucy ran up and threw another snowball from her stash, and I dropped a shower of snow over her, where it spilled over the pompom and earflaps of the dark blue cap and made Lucy laugh.

Until it went down her back. She rubbed the snow that was on her head and neck and ended up smearing even more snow past the edge of her elastic collar.

"It's in my back!" Lucy cried.

"C'mon, honey." I pulled her to me, but she flapped me away. I held my hands out as I might with an angry suspect, proving I wasn't armed, and dropped my voice low. "Let me get that out. Or maybe we should go inside and get warm? I know I'm freezing."

"It's cold, Mom," she said through tears. "It burns."

I knew my daughter was too distraught to make the decision to let me help, so I snatched her up in my arms and walked into the house, my father shutting the door behind us. I sat down on the staircase and pulled her into my lap, interspersing hugs between removing her hat, snowsuit, and boots and dropping them all on the paper grocery bags that lined the hallway in the winter months. Lucy went limp in my lap, the tears stopped. I kissed my daughter's temple and held her close, taking advantage of her rare stillness.

"Mom, stop." Lucy giggled as I hugged her close.

I spoke into the top of Lucy's head. "I missed you so much. And I'm sorry I missed ice-skating."

"Grandpa told me." Lucy wriggled around, turning left and then right, her blue eyes—Kevin's blue eyes—still wet with tears. "Plus, he said you were sorry you missed the quiz I gave him last night. I saved it for you to take tonight."

I made a big show of rolling my eyes. "Lucky me. Lucky, lucky me. May I change into my play clothes first?"

"You may," she said, like she was granting an audience with the queen. I gently pushed her off my knees and trudged up the stairs. I bent over the railing and yelled to my father in the kitchen that I would be down to help in a minute.

"Take your time," he called. "The Internet says I need to let the lasagna rest, whatever the hell that means."

I popped into the shower and scrubbed myself down, then pulled on some sweatpants and a fleece, which was as close to pajamas as I could get without actually wearing them to the dinner table. While I wanted nothing more than to slide under the covers now, I needed to see Lucy and to let her see me, to do normal things. As I finished throwing my laundry in the bin and storing my pearls, Lucy came into the bedroom, in the middle of a conversation with me for which I hadn't even been present. Trying to make it up to her, I listened closely as she explained what she had learned in school— the parts of a flower and what they did—and had me explain dry cleaning in great detail, and why some things like socks didn't need it, while other things like suits did.

"Maybe someday we can take one of my dresses to the dry cleaner?" Lucy asked hopefully.

I struggled to keep from laughing. "Maybe, if you're very lucky."

The doorbell rang. I listened from the top of the stairs, Lucy gripping my hand, as my father opened the door and—damn it— Hale said hello. I let Lucy hold me at the top of the stairs, hiding from Hale so that I might not have to go out into the cold and investigate something: death, or chemicals, or drugs.

". . . just a second, let me get her," I heard my father say to Hale, and then his voice, louder. "June!"

"Thank you, sir," I heard Hale say as I walked down the stairs. Lucy let go of my hand, shy with a new person in our house, and stayed one step behind me the whole way down.

"You eaten?" Dad asked.

"Well, sir, I'm not very good company right this minute. I need sleep almost as much as June." As he spoke he looked from my father to the stairs, and he beamed. I felt like a prom queen until I realized the smile was directed at Lucy.

"Well, hello there!" Hale's voice as sweet as his smile.

I arrived at the bottom of the stairs with Lucy twisted around me. I dragged her to the front and introduced her to Hale.

"It's a pleasure to meet you, Miss Lucy," he said.

"Hello, Mr. Bascom." Lucy stuck out her hand. "Not Miss. Just Lucy."

"Okay, Lucy. Call me Hale."

"Coming?" Dad called from the doorway, waving a spatula like a billy club. Lucy broke the handshake and ran into the kitchen.

"I'd hate to impose on your family time," Hale said. "I wanted—"

"Why don't you stay?" I surprised both of us with my goodwill, which was a mix of happiness that he wasn't there to drag me back into the cold and a tiny bit of our restarted friendship exerting itself.

"Suuure." Like he didn't really believe me. He filled me in while he unbuttoned his coat. "I stopped by the station to brief y'all in person, but you were gone. Craig denied almost everything that Marty said."

"But the pictures—"

"Remember, we knew about everything Craig did in the pictures, everything illegal, that is. For now, I told him to mind his p's and q's, and as a bonus, though he doesn't know this, he's under surveillance. I stopped by the glove factory, and hey, I forgot to tell you a fun fact—Phil Brouillette has title to the building. Things there are locked up tight." He gave a mock shudder. "That glove factory is creepy. Do you know we found a room filled with wooden hands?"

He gave me a brief rundown on the schedule for tomorrow. Dave and I would be part of the team working the drug bust. They had a sizable number of people in town, but were keeping a low profile.

"And you'll know at least some of the folks there tomorrow. Ernesto Aguilar is on the team."

"Ernie?" And suddenly I *was* excited for tomorrow. I'd worked with Ernie on the desert meth operation. I would gladly spend six weeks in a tin shack with him. Ernie was team.

Hale stopped speaking.

"That's it?" I asked.

"I believe so. Yes?"

"Thank God. I thought you'd showed up with another catastrophe. C'mon," and I led him into the kitchen. "Dinnertime."

As we sat down, Lucy was telling the story of the boy in her class who could roll his eyeballs back.

"That's not going to be funny when his face freezes that way," my father said.

Lucy considered. "It might be."

The dinner was relaxed, and I found myself laughing for the first time in days. Hale ended up taking my test for me.

"Addition of three numbers," he whispered loudly. "This is tough stuff."

"No talking," Lucy said.

I ate two pieces of lasagna. Dinner was beyond good, bordering on excellent. I expressed this with more surprise than Dad appreciated.

"What? I can read." He shrugged his shoulders. "And I used canned sauce."

Even the iceberg lettuce in the salad was delicious after eating nothing but vending machine coffee and subs for two days. And doing the dishes was a pleasure, safe and warm at home.

My hands wet, I joined everyone in the living room, where Lucy was playing poker with Hale on the coffee table. She was kneeling forward against the edge, trying to peek at his cards. Hale was loose, his jacket off, resting with his back against the couch, one leg drawn up to rest his hand with the cards, the second leg spread wide. Hale gave Lucy a few easy ones until he began to lose, whereupon he played in earnest. Lucy wiped the decks with him handily.

They played three hands, during which my father would point to a newspaper article on the case and hand it over without comment, practicing the same discretion with Lucy that he used to practice with me when I was a child. I found myself in a bit of a domestic reverie, enjoying the back-and-forth between Hale and Lucy and missing Kevin, but only a little, an ache rather than a raw tear. I almost lost track of time.

"Okay, Luce, fifteen minutes until you have to wash up and get ready for bed."

"Nooo," Lucy whined, which is what I expected. Lucy said no each consecutive time I told her, until the last time, when her no was followed by "Can Hale read me a story?"

I smarted. That was mine. Hale chose that moment to pick himself up.

"I need to get home, sweet pea," he said. "But let's see if I can get my coat and my hat on faster than you can get ready for bed." He checked his watch. "Ready? Go."

Lucy hesitated, realizing that this was an adult "going to bed" trick, but her competitiveness took over, and she raced for the stairs.

Hale said his good-byes to my father, who was pretending to be awake in his chair, and ambled to the front door. He took his time, stopping to look at pictures of me in my high school graduation gown, my sister adjusting my tassel; my father and Kevin snapping a wishbone at Christmas the year before Kevin died; a picture of my sister with her kids and husband behind her, all in red sweaters, each with a hand on her shoulder, which must be the fashion in Ohio. He stalled, giving Lucy a chance to win. I was pulling his coat out of the closet when we heard all of the water pipes quiet at once and the stomp of feet from the bathroom. Lucy stood at the top of the stairs, wearing her favorite purple nightgown—she couldn't sleep without it—over a pair of yellow footy pajamas.

"I won!" she said.

Hale nodded. "That you did. I'm pretty poky."

"You're not so slow. I'm fast. Want to listen to the story?"

Hale smiled up at her, and the smile was still on his face when he looked at me. God, he was still handsome.

"*Charlotte's Web?*" I asked him.

"I've overstayed my welcome."

"You aren't imposing."

"C'mon," Lucy said.

Lucy climbed into bed, arranging her pillows so that her head was directly below her dream catcher. Lucy had been plagued by nightmares—night terrors, really—when Kevin was at the end of his illness. She would wake, terrified that her father had been kidnapped or swept out to sea. We tried soothing music, back rubs, warm baths, and night-lights, but nothing worked. My father must have mentioned it to my mother, because the next thing I knew this gift arrived in the mail.

"To guide you through your night's journey," my mother's note to Lucy said. Lucy had no idea what that meant.

"To catch your bad dreams," I explained. I figured Lucy liked the feathers, beads, and purple latticework, but my mother's hippie weirdness worked. Since then, Lucy had developed a nightly ritual—touching the feather and positioning herself carefully underneath—that she still followed even now, three years later. The willow frame had started to crack, and I might be forced to ask my mother to buy a replacement. I was not looking forward to that day.

I read through the creation of the "Some Pig" web, turning the book so that both Hale and Lucy could see the pictures. Lucy was fast asleep in midchapter, and the two of us crept out by the glow of the night-light.

"She's beautiful," Hale said as he wrapped the scarf around his neck. "She's a long drink of water, just like her momma. And with the black hair and those big blue eyes, she's the image of Kevin. That must be nice." He winced. "I mean, I assume—I imagine that it'd be a good thing, but it might also pain you."

"No, it's good. I like to remember my time with him."

Hale unclenched his jaw. He seemed as nervous as I was about restarting our friendship. I realized that he was intentionally not breaking eye contact, giving me all the signals that we learned at Quantico to show he wasn't lying. "I owe you an apology. You and Kevin. I was young and stupid, and hurt that you two left me on the outside."

"As I recall, you were the one who opted out of our friendship," I said, but with no bite in it. I dropped my voice. "And other things."

"It sure didn't feel that way. At training, the two of you were always in each other's orbits, crazy in love."

"We weren't even dating," I protested.

"Kevin thought you hung the moon. Any fool could see it."

I laughed. "As I recall, you were the one I had a fling with, not Kevin."

Hale blushed. "Well, perhaps I was wrong. You were both so confident being agents, I figured you were sure about everything. Kevin was going to raise hell, break things wide open. You were going to set things right, and restore order. You were the stars."

"You did well for yourself."

"You think? Most folks figured it for a little hobby, something I'd put aside when I started in the family business."

"Being rich is the family business?"

"The way my people do it. When I visited home for Christmas the year we were at Quantico, Momma strewed blondes around the house. She thought the right woman could correct my ways. My father cornered me after his fourth highball and said, 'If you wanted to carry a gun, you could have joined the hunt club like a gentleman.'"

"I didn't know," I said, thinking of how I had imagined Hale spending that winter break. It involved blondes and highballs, but in my mind, he was enjoying it.

"Your family seemed to be all for a career in law enforcement," he said. I glanced around the corner at my father, sleeping away. Hale stood close to me, his voice husky. "And you . . . you were made for this life. When Kevin got sick and you left the service . . . I didn't believe it." He paused, and seemed to be thinking over his next question. "Do you regret leaving?"

I breathed in the scent clinging to his clothes, gun oil and the dust from the glove factory, and underneath it, Hale.

"I don't regret anything." I realized this was true. "What I gave up, where I landed, what I did, how I lived . . . it let me have the best things in a way I couldn't have otherwise."

"You ever think about rejoining us, now that things have settled down?"

"This is calm?"

He shrugged. "Calm in your personal life."

"I don't think that's a road that's open to me."

He tilted his head, considering me. "Let's have this conversation again next week."

We both reached for the door at the same time. He pulled his hand away and let me open it for him. He was over the threshold before he stepped back and hauled me into a hug. I hugged him back.

"I'll be seeing you, June Lyons." He kissed my cheek, his mouth brushing my hair before pulling away. He walked down the path, out of the range of light from the porch. I shut the door and turned out lamps, finally stopping in front of my father, who never would admit that he wasn't watching. He would always be a cop. So would I. Tomorrow I would work to finish off this case, keeping the world, big and small, a little safer. I convinced my father to go to bed—he was awake, he swore—and went to find sleep of my own.

CHAPTER 25

From my perch atop the mill's roof, I had a view of the whole neighborhood. Despite the rain, through my binoculars I could see the details not only of the buildings, but of the neighbors' lives: a couple tearing into a pizza, a family watching a reality TV show that seemed to involve people racing up a beach with buckets on their heads, an elderly woman drinking daintily from a teacup, which she refilled from a bottle of scotch. I could watch the actions of everyone within sight of my binoculars.

Except for the FBI's. The surveillance that blanketed the neighborhood was evident to me because I knew where to look: the FBI listening equipment housed in a van right underneath me on the Old Mill Parkway, and an assault team parked a straight shot down Silliman Street, at the end of the alley that ran behind the Jelicksons', shiny with rain. Farther still was the Mohawk River, where Danielle was thrown, if not to her death, then to her impaling.

But that's not where my attention was focused. The dealer—the killer—had told Craig to drop the drugs in a tiny park that ran between the east side of the neighborhood and the cliffs that dropped into the Hudson River. A quarter-mile long and twenty feet wide, the undeveloped land had been too unstable for heavy industry during Hopewell Falls's boom times. Craig was instructed to slide the drugs to the center of a ring of benches a few feet from the parking area, a Ladies' Garment Workers' Union tribute to the women killed in the looms or mangled by machines. The seats were high and curved, taller than I was, and from my post the four solid ellipses formed an Irish knot, open yet impregnable. I had spent many days there the summer after Kevin died. I would lose track of time, letting the sounds of the river wash over me, drowning out the roar of the voice in my head reminding me that there would never be a time without grief. Never placid, in winter the current of air could sometimes make you feel like it would pick you up and drop you off the cliff into the water below. Inside the circle you were protected from some, though not all, of the winds.

My eyes flitted to the Jelicksons' on Cataract Street. The Merrimen had lit two oil drum fires, and the block was bright. The flames had been festive, almost pretty, when they were confined to the Jelicksons' front yard, but now they'd dragged the second barrel into the street. When they lit it, the tinder and the gasoline sent flames shooting up two stories like a Roman candle. Then the fire dropped to a low, hellish glow and seemed to be contained, but they were blatantly breaking the law and deserved to be arrested. I felt as if Hale was shrugging at me through the radio when I suggested we call in the locals: "As far as they know, the investigation is closed. Let's not give ourselves away."

It's not like the day had started out all that great. Reporters showed at 8:00 A.M. for Jerry's announcement of the indictment against Marty, which was—surprise, surprise—just in time for the national morning talk shows to pick up. The chief and Dave stood grimly behind Jerry while he explained how justice was being served against the killer of such a fine young woman. He didn't mention Ray.

"The people of Hopewell Falls and the Capital District"—Jerry trying to invoke gravitas, but instead sounding nasally—"everyone in the Empire State can sleep better knowing that this murderer, this craven killer, will face justice."

The TV folks stuck around to do their establishing shots on the jailhouse steps. They seemed to think everyone wanted the attention Jerry was chasing, and took my "no comment" as the start of a discussion. At ten, Dave and I reached our breaking point, and gave the chief the heads-up that we were on our way over to the Kelly Suites to "liaise." That's where the federal agents were holed up, planning their stakeout. As Dave and I escaped out the prisoner transport entrance we saw Denise Byrne bundling her son into a minivan. With Jerry not willing to indict Jason without more evidence, we had had to cut him loose.

The Kelly Suites was a hotel of opportunity. Travelers would check in when they couldn't drive another mile up the Northway. With its faded olive and harvest gold color scheme that couldn't muster any optimism, and the half-fallen poster announcing FREE COFFEE EN SUITE, the place appeared to be slumping into bankruptcy. The only thing that didn't fit was the lit NO in front of the neon VACANCY sign.

The back of the hotel told the true story. As Dave and I walked up the steps to the second floor, we watched a half-dozen buzz-cut guys in DEA windbreakers and white-jumpsuited techs rushing around loading up hoses, tents, ventilators—meth labs could produce enormous amounts of corrosive gases and chemicals—as well as mobile kits.

"You're trying to poison me?" A voice rose above the din in the parking lot. It came from the masked tech who stood glaring at us from under the balcony. Though not currently visible, a scowl was assumed.

"Hi, Annie!" Dave leaned over the balcony. It creaked under his weight, and he pulled back. "I knew you liked to work closely with me—"

"Shut up!" Annie whipped off her mask. "I've logged more overtime in the last two weeks than I have in the last two years, and you want to make sure I die before I get paid?"

"Annie, what are you doing here?" I asked.

"My boss assigned me to do 'interjurisdictional cooperation,' which means I get to die with all the *professionals*." I could make out Annie's air quotes even through the sanitary mittens. "I don't know whether my boss hates me or the FBI more. Probably me."

"Well, I'll feel safer knowing you're on the team," Dave said. "We've got a meeting—"

"You think I came over here just to make pleasant conversation with you?" Annie seemed to like interrupting Dave more than most people. "No. I came to tell you that I should have the testing done on the clothes and the boots later today. The FBI agreed to let me use some of their equipment while we're wasting the next six hours waiting for you all to get your act in gear."

I grinned. "Annie, did you volunteer for this operation so that you could get us our results faster?"

"I didn't volunteer! My boss insisted and I . . . agreed. I found a silver lining to this black oppressive cloud that is my life."

A couple of other techs called her to help load some cabling. "Gotta go!" She zipped across the lot and grabbed the end of the ropy metal, the force of her small body providing what they needed to get the cable wrapped around a large spool.

"Take my calls tonight!" followed us as we entered the hotel room.

We could barely get in the door. Agents took up every chair in the living/dining room, with several more milling around, restless and weary of waiting. Plans filled every available wall space: maps of the neighborhood, broad aerial shots, as well as detailed photos of the riverside drop site and the Jelicksons' property, all posted and diagrammed. The evidence wasn't covering any sort of spectacular decorating: the main room's furniture was inoffensive, pastel and bolted down. The room had empty soda cans stacked into a tower in one corner and squared piles of warrants and chain-of-custody forms in rows on the couch, ready to be served. With no access to this room for several days, housekeeping must be freaking out. Little did the housekeepers realize that the people monopolizing these rooms made their beds with hospital corners, although the agents did skip decoratively fanning out the toilet paper.

A couple of men from the Jelicksons' case, three guys from the Albany office, and some people from the gang details in both California and Missouri were there. From across the room I spotted Ernesto Aguilar. Ernie! He sprang up, going around, under, practically over people to get to me. I was equally eager, but a huge chest blocked my path. Potreo, who had been so helpful when I almost fell at Marty's, ignored my "Excuse me's," smirking. I used my elbows.

"Attention, all!" Hale yelled from the head of the table as Dave and I found a spot of wall to lean against. "We have a raid to plan tonight."

"Officer Lyons"—Hale pointed to Harmony Mills on the map— "you will be here, part of the roof surveillance team, along with Agents Potreo, Zulietski, and Aguilar."

I fist-bumped Ernie surreptitiously.

"Detective Batko, you and Agent Bailey will be assault team Bravo." Dave got a nod from Silent Sam Bailey, tight braids brushing his shoulders. This was probably the extent of the small talk Dave would get for the duration of the operation.

With no concern for FBI hierarchy, Dave spoke up. "I'm not with my partner? Don't you want us working at our best?"

"We need our local guides," Hale said, "to be in different places, to show us the back ways and shortcuts. We have maps, and we have run over every square inch, but if our suspects, the Jelicksons, *anyone,* zigs, we need to make sure we don't zag. Tonight's going to be tight. We're going to nail our meth cook, and we are going to stop ice from breaking on a large scale in the Northeast."

He was hyping up the troops. I silently added to his list. We'll catch the killer—or was it killers?—of Danielle and Ray, and we'll stop the black hole of drugs and crime from sucking up everything good that was left in this town.

Hale explained that Craig would be dropping the pseudoephedrine behind a ring of benches. Dave and Sam Bailey would tail him after the drop.

"Y'all park over here behind this fish fry place"—Frank's Fish Fry: my father had picked up dinner there every Friday until the place closed fifteen years ago "because no one observed goddamned Catholicism anymore," Frank said, with a shake of his head.

"The surveillance van will be right under Sierra 4." He nodded at me, and pointed to two agents who could have been Kevin's brothers. One of them was wearing a hipster band T-shirt under his button-down, and both had the wide, bloodshot eyes of people who stared at computers all day.

We would then spring the trap, monitoring the only roads in, and more important, blocking off any exits. Whoever it was—including the Jelicksons—might be able to pick up the stuff, but they weren't going to be able to get it out of the neighborhood.

Once Hale summarized the timing of the evening, we calibrated our watches.

"Really? You do that?" Dave asked.

In the kitchenette, pistols, semiautomatics, and a few high-powered rifles were lined up on the breakfast bar like kindergarteners on their first day of school. They offered Dave a Sig Sauer, but he decided to stick with his Glock.

"It fits in my hand," he said.

I breathed in. To me, the scent of gun oil was what baking bread was to others. An agent with a clipboard inspected the bulletproof vests. And the ammo? I couldn't see that as I peeked over the counter. Probably in the refrigerator.

Eyeing one of the M-15 sniper rifles, I asked which one I'd be getting. The tech took his time searching through the list. Finally he said, "It doesn't look like you have one assigned, but we assumed you would have your service revolver?" My disappointment must have shown on my face because he quickly added, "From your position, you should be surveillance only. We do have some binoculars for you—very high powered. And a bulletproof vest."

Ernie consoled me on my lack of firepower and I helped him with his bulletproof vest.

"You hear about Bear?" he asked as I pulled the strap of his vest so that the last gap behind his shoulder closed.

I had just been thinking of the third member of Lyons, and Tigger, and Bear. "No. How's he doing?"

"Yeah, two cases back the Mara Salvatrucha made him. We found him . . ."—and I swallowed down the bile rising in my throat as he talked—"we found him with his guts, his intestines . . . unwound across an acre of land. They think he was alive when it happened. At the start, at least." Ernie stopped talking, briefly, his ever-animated face frozen in grief.

"Ernie," I said quietly, so only he could hear.

"We got the guys. We got them all"—Ernie's nice-guy nature nowhere in evidence. He sighed. "Another distribution network popped up the next day."

"Good. *Good.* I'm glad you got 'em," I said. The insult of not carrying a rifle suddenly seemed a lot less important. I dropped the vest over my head. The latest technology, it felt about twenty pounds lighter than the ones issued by Hopewell Falls. "Can you help me with the strap?"

Up on the roof, I discovered that the ninja wear hadn't changed in one key respect—it still trapped cold sweat everywhere it touched my body. "Just rain," Hale said. Freezing rain was as miserable as you could get. I would have preferred snow. Snow, and the chance to be more in the middle of the action of this operation. I was *action adjacent,* which didn't quite count.

Hale's voice sounded in my ear, so free of static it seemed as if he were standing behind me. "Sierra 4, report."

From the main road, Craig's SUV approached. Dave and Bailey's car followed at a safe distance.

"Sierra 4 to Alpha," I said. "CI's vehicle passing checkpoint one."

Craig turned left into the alley, and Dave and Sam veered right into Frank's parking lot, their headlights going dark.

Over the radio, Craig was complaining how much his arms hurt from lifting all the pseudoephedrine onto the truck.

"You just had to push a button, Craig," Hale said. "The truck has a hydraulic lift."

"But I had to arrange it all. And we've got eight hundred pounds of that stuff, and I didn't want to get it on me. I could have a heart attack or something. At least the drug dealers in Canada helped me carry stuff."

"Craig, don't clog the channels with chatter," Hale said.

Craig didn't take the hint, continuing the running commentary. That was a good thing, as far as I was concerned. While I could see his truck and the stone benches, I couldn't see him, too low and too far left.

"Shit! It's sleeting!" Craig said. "Did you guys know it was sleeting?"

"Affirmative, Craig," Hale said.

"What?" Craig said.

"Yes," Hale said, and I could hear a snicker, quickly muted.

"So you really just want me to back up and slide the pseudoephedrine down?"

"Yes, Craig," Hale said.

"Are you sure? What if a bag breaks? There are eighteen of them, you know."

"The bags won't break. Drop the load, Craig."

"I am, I am," Craig said. "Hold your horses."

The radio was mostly silent, with brief grunts from Craig. No one approached from any direction. The only movement on the street came from the Merrimen. The fires were contained, but the men swung farther and farther away from the Jelicksons' property, like moons breaking away from a planet's orbit, tossing rocks at one of the streetlights until it broke.

"Okay. I'm done. And I'm texting whoever to let them know," Craig said. "Okay. He's telling me there's a box for me in the entry-way of Saint Patrick's?" Saint Patrick's was where I'd been baptized, but it had closed before Craig was born. I gave him directions.

"Craig, tell the person that if the money isn't waiting for you, you are going to come back and kick his ass," Hale said.

"Done," Craig said. "They're responding. 'Shut it or . . . ur . . . dead."

"Don't give it a second thought, Craig," Hale said. "We won't let him kill you."

Craig drove under my position on his way out to the main road. The rain hit the back of my neck as I craned over, and the SUV's slick roof glinted unevenly, the elements having worn away the finish, the rust running dull, the rest shining. Craig continued to the main road and stopped at Saint Patrick's.

"I've picked up the money, the box," Craig said. "I'm heading toward Mohawk Street."

"Charlie to Alpha. A subject has exited rear of Jelicksons'," came a voice, chattering teeth clicking over the radio. "Over the fence." I craned my neck, but the backyard of the Jelicksons' was completely beyond my view.

"Charlie to Alpha. We've got an ID. It's Jackie DeGroot."

CHAPTER 26

ALPHA TO CHARLIE. REPORT on DeGroot," Hale demanded. I was eager, too. Not being able to see or act was driving me crazy. Jackie was a wild card in this, an emotional teenager who knew her beloved boyfriend had cheated on her.

"Charlie" narrated Jackie's every move. "DeGroot's at the side of the alley. Subject is crouching down."

A vehicle approached on Mohawk Street and sped past Craig, who was headed in the other direction.

"Sierra 4 to Alpha," I said. "Vehicle passing checkpoint, Chevy half ton." I trained my binoculars on the driver's side until I could make an ID. "DeGroot's father."

"Foxtrot to Alpha. Vehicle slowing. Vehicle's stopped. Jackie DeGroot is running toward the vehicle . . . and she's in."

"And the vehicle's away," came Hale's voice. "It's heading your way, Lima."

"Lima to Alpha, confirmed." The truck came out of the alley

going around sixty. It didn't turn down the Jelicksons' block, but again made the turn right off Mill Way.

"Thank God she's out of there," came Dave's voice.

"Alpha to Lima, tail the DeGroots."

A low black car, driving with its lights off, slid past.

"Alpha to Echo," Hale said. "Cover Lima position."

"Can I talk?" Craig asked.

"Yes, Craig," Hale said.

"Look, dude, this box is too light. There's no money. I should check."

"No," Hale said. "Drive to the meeting place. The agents who are tailing you—"

"What?!" Craig said. "I don't see them! Shit, with all this rain—" He sounded like he was having a full-blown panic attack.

"They're behind you. Trust me. Gentlemen, do you have Master Craig here in view?"

"We do." Dave's voice came over the radio. "Hi, Craig."

Craig didn't answer, and Hale spoke again. "See now, Craig, all taken care of. Continue with the original plan—"

Dave broke in, sharp and short. "He took the wrong road."

I craned my neck, watching for headlights. On the river road I saw a flash through the trees, a second set of headlights shining through a moment later. The gap closed between the second vehicle and the first, until Dave and Bailey's headlights illuminated the bumper of Craig's car. The river road was an easy route to the highway, letting people get out of town fast without having to negotiate the rutted, tight streets of downtown. Did he have a bigger plan or was he just stupid?

"Correct course, Craig," Hale said evenly. I wondered if he really had faith in Craig or whether he was keeping everyone, including the other agents, calm. "Craig, please acknowledge."

Nothing for ten seconds. Then fifteen. Finally Hale spoke, his voice hard.

"Alpha to Bravo, intercept the vehicle."

"Bravo to Alpha. Affirmative," said Bailey.

"Alpha to Foxtrot, provide backup for the agents in pursuit."

Mike Tran, who was well respected for his work on New York City gang kidnappings and was up here for this operation, gave an affirmative for team Foxtrot. A black car parked at the end of the Jelicksons' block started up and raced off.

"Alpha to Sierra 3 and Sierra 4, report."

"All clear," Ernie said.

Dave's voice blasted across the radio before I could answer. "He keeps cutting us off. He's weaving back and forth across the road. He presents a danger to us and oncoming traffic."

"Use any necessary force," Hale said.

"Oh, shit," Dave said. "He's run off the road on his own. Shit, shit." In the background I could hear grinding metal. "He's crashed through one of the concrete barriers, and stopped."

My teeth chattered—the rain was sliding into the small gaps in my clothes—and I clamped them shut so I could hear everything: Dave's door opened and closed, and then a second door slammed. They were now on foot. They were voices in the night, remote in space, and I wanted to be there.

"Craig's out of his car and he's . . . he's . . ." Dave panted. "Craig's fallen."

"Approach with care," Hale said.

"He's injured," Bailey reported. "Batko! He might be armed!"

"It's going to be okay, Craig"—Dave's voice now, low and soothing. "C'mon. Okay? You can hear me, right? You did such a good job tonight, you were a pro, c'mon, hang on." Gentle and sweet, and then frantically to someone else. "Get an ambulance here. He's going into shock. He's not breathing."

"Foxtrot to Alpha," came a voice. *Tran,* I thought. "We've radioed for an ambulance."

"Alpha to Foxtrot, are you on scene?" demanded Hale.

"Affirmative. First-aid kit being delivered to Officer Batko, and I'm directing traffic, directing the ambulance to the scene."

"Step away from that boy, Batko," growled Bailey. "I'm not kidding."

"I can't, I can't," Dave said. "Do you see—"

"I'm not dicking around here." And if Sam was slipping into profanity on official channels things *were* bad. "Bravo to Alpha, we've got a biohazard situation here. Yellow dust all over the vehicle. Craig opened the box."

My mind raced, thinking of what it might be. Anthrax? Ricin? Chemical or biological? And Dave was right there, exposed.

"I can't leave," Dave said. "He's . . . I've got to intubate him. He's not breathing."

I smacked the bricks next to me, furious that Dave was without me in this.

"I'm exposed. The yellow stuff's on me—my hands, my face"—and now Dave was breathing harshly. Were his lungs shutting down already?

"Drop the first-aid kit right there—there!—and get back!" I was relieved to hear him shout.

I could see the lights from an emergency vehicle right on the edge of town. The city couldn't afford its own ambulance service and so relied on the surrounding cities to provide emergency support. This one was coming in from Watervliet. The radio was filled with the sounds of everyone in crisis mode: estimated time of arrival on the ambulance; communications with EMTs that they should bring their protective clothing and respirators; Hale ordering half the folks at the decontamination unit set up at the glove factory to drive to the scene and isolate Craig's car posthaste, and demanding reports from all the agents still on post in quick succession; and Dave trying desperately, frantically, to keep Craig alive.

"The tube, it's stopped," Dave said. "I can't push it farther. ETA on the ambulance?"

"Sixty seconds," said Tran.

I broke in over the radio, desperate to do something. "Is he still wearing his med-alert necklace?"

"June! Lyons. Yeah, it's here. It's engraved. I can't . . . I can't read it."

I could hear the sound of the ambulance in the background and the shouts of the EMT personnel, close and telling Dave to clear out.

"Any idea what our toxin is?"

"No idea," Dave said. "I'm not reacting, and I've been exposed as long as he was when he went down."

I listened as Dave narrated the action to Hale. His voice was steady, no giveaway wheeze or cough, and I refrained from demanding he give me updates on his own health: "They did a tracheotomy. They got a tube down. They're moving out with him and he's not breathing on his own."

"Alpha to Foxtrot. What's the status of antiterrorism team?" Hale asked.

"Albany office has deployed their WMD coordinator," Tran said.

"Bailey to Alpha. Texts came in on Madigan's phone. Text one from Jackie DeGroot, asking for a ride, and text two from Ray Jelickson . . ."

We have Ray's phone, I thought, and then remembered the one Marty had kept. I listened for the rest, but the siren on the ambulance roared up in the background, making it impossible to hear.

"Alpha to Sierra 4, switch over to channel 3."

I hit my earpiece.

"Hello!" Annie said. "Hello, is someone there?"

After listening in on the FBI radios all evening, the hiss of Annie's cell phone was jarring, bringing me crashing back to earth.

"Annie, you're on Craig?"

"On my way. They packed us into the back of this van—we don't all have seat belts!—and hustled us off to a bioterror site."

"Annie, Dave's at that scene."

"What? Is he exposed?"

"Yes."

"Dave has made me want to stab myself in the head less than most people. I'll do everything I can."

I relaxed the smallest bit. Knowing that Annie would be there, charging through social niceties to solve the case, was oddly comforting.

"I obtained some DNA results on your clothes and boots."

I held the phone close to my head—the static on Annie's cell phone coupled with the sound of rain made it so I was sure I heard wrong.

"Wait. Boots, too?" I said. "They were found yesterday."

"I could've had them sooner, but I got secondary confirmation. Even though he's second rate, he's not so stupid he can't check my work."

"Tell me."

"The clothes found at the Brouillettes' and the hat found in the Dumpster? The DNA was the same, and both matched the guy."

I felt a jolt. Maybe I'd been wrong. "Marty?" I asked.

"The other one. Jason."

"What?" I said, and heard a low "No way" from Hale. I hadn't thought that anyone who had a tell like Jason's—he blushed if he even *thought* something uncharitable—would be able to snow everyone.

"I *said* one of the sets matched Jason. But some other hair, a longer hair, was recovered, too. Did Jason ever have long hair?"

"No. Not his." I ran over the people I thought of as suspects in the case: Craig's touched his shoulders, as did Chuck's, and then there were Jackie and the congresswoman. I asked her to clarify. "What color is the hair?"

"Jelickson's blood saturated the strand, but color was in the range of dark blond to light red."

"And the boots? Was his DNA on the boots?"

"That's the other thing. I identified some skin cells, not Ray's, on the edge, on the lip of the boot. Not Jason. A woman."

"So our killer is a woman?"

"Figuring that out is your job. My job is to confirm that yes, a woman wore the boots." I heard her panting.

"All right. I'm here!" she yelled.

"Annie, can you hold on a second?"

"No. I've got to go save Dave. We're done."

I hesitated before switching the channel, listening to the streets below. I could hear the shouts of the Merrimen, bouncing off all the close buildings, becoming wilder, angrier, the result of drink and, probably, meth.

I inhaled, the wind rushing into my lungs. Over the men's shouts I caught the sound of something sweeter. A song.

> *And when Christmas passed you kept it hangin',*
> *Kept claiming all my kisses.*
> *But by Valentine's you found another girl*
> *And by Easter she was missus.*

I raised the binoculars to my eyes and began searching for Barbara, methodically tracing up and down the line of streets. I heard where she was before I saw her.

"Hey there, old lady," yelled the big biker, Tiny. I pinpointed him in my sight, catching the patches on his jacket, the knife in his belt, and his boots, steel toed and more than capable of crushing a skull. He grabbed his crotch. "I got your Valentine right here. C'mere."

Barbara Merry Christmas went.

CHAPTER 27

I TRIED TO STAY IN position. *I tried.* My eyes scanned back and forth, from the ring of benches glowing white even in the pitch black, to where Barbara was approaching the bikers and their fiery pits. One of the bikers fished out a few coals from his barrel with his leather-gloved hands and whipped them at Barbara, aiming for her face. He missed, but hit her coat.

I skidded across the roof and threw open the mill's door. In the face of the endless blackness of the inside of the mill, I switched on my flashlight.

"Sierra 4 to Alpha," I said as I ran down the lightless stairs two at a time. The radio was loud in my ear, Hale alerting everyone to keep an eye out for Jason Byrne, and relaying the text to Craig from a California number that read, "U have something that belongs to us." I was at the first floor before he answered.

"We have a civilian . . . a citizen . . . in danger," I said. I moved more cautiously now that I was on the ground floor. "The Merrimen are throwing hot coals on Barbara Merry Christmas." While the second floor and the roof were empty, the first floor was littered with things too out of date to be sold, too big to be moved, or too small to be of notice. I clipped my hip on the big iron loom that sat in the middle of the floor, tearing a gash in my black canvas pants and nicking my skin. The line was quiet, and I realized that Hale was waiting for me to speak.

"Sierra 4 to Alpha, permission to assist?" I asked.

I worried that Hale would say no. And then what? I wasn't an agent anymore, and while the FBI might be pissed, what were they going to do, fire me?

"Alpha to Sierra 4," Hale said, finally. "Do not give away the scope of the operation. And make it fast. We're going to need you."

My beam of light flitted across a pair of old wooden double doors that led out to the loading dock, a more direct route to the Jelicksons'. I dropped my fancy earpiece into my pocket.

I felt my way along the wall to the door, the brickwork crumbling under my touch, and slid it open as quietly as I could. I jumped the few feet from the loading dock onto the ground, skidding on the uneven pavement. A few stumbling steps and I was out into the hesitant glow of the streetlights, able to see everything. I tried to project *Officer Friendly out for an evening stroll.* Full-out running, I wasn't doing a very good job of it. The freezing rain kept people indoors, and the streets were empty except for the FBI. I saw a flash of night-vision goggles watching me pass.

I turned the corner, ready for anything. I was happy to see Barbara brushing the last of the coals off the fur trim on her jacket, still singing, her hand out, expecting a "gift" from the men who were trying to set her on fire. God looks out for children and fools; junkies are included in that second category. I wasn't, however, going to count on Barbara staying safe without a little earthbound intervention, and sped up, not lifting my feet from the ground but *shushing* along, half skating and half walking. I barely felt the cold at all.

Tiny beckoned Barbara, one hand coaxing her over, the other holding a bottle of whiskey. Barbara stumbled forward, singing and brushing ash. He was a foot taller than she was and had four times her bulk. He grabbed at her. Without losing her smile, Barbara leaned over and bit him on the wrist.

"You stupid bitch!" he said, holding his wrist close.

He took the bottle and swung at Barbara, missing. The gold liquid arced wide, hissing when it hit the fire. He was about to crack the bottle down on Barbara's head when I barreled into him, sending him sprawling ass-first onto the street, where he skidded along the ice before stopping.

"Stay down." I made my voice big and aimed my Glock at Tiny, then the group, and then Tiny again. I had surprise on my side, but that was changing fast. The men clumped together in what would be a nice social gathering if I didn't think they were massing for attack. The light from the fires seemed to hide as well as illuminate, with four guys on my right periphery slipping in and out of shadow, and one disappearing into the house. I couldn't stop him. I didn't even know if I had backup.

"C'mon, Barbara, let's go. You can sing for some friends of mine and get a nice prize." I pulled at her sleeve, the fabric on the lamb's wool coat coming apart under my fingers. I gripped Barbara's bony wrist and pulled harder, and finally Barbara moved. Unfortunately, so did the bikers.

"Stay! Down!" I yelled at Tiny, who pushed himself up on his elbows. Too late—two of the other bikers jumped the fence. I pushed Barbara behind me and she drifted away from the threat, not in motion, just no longer at rest.

"Okay, you two. You are going to join Tiny on the ground there." They kept advancing and I moved my finger to the trigger. That stopped them, but two others swung wide into the dark. Five men were now out of my line of sight. I backed up, I hoped not into one of them.

"Gentlemen." The growl came from the porch. I hadn't seen Zeke come out, and he was invisible now behind the sheet of rain except for the glow of his cigarette as he sucked in a breath.

"Zeke, call off your dogs." I kept my attention on a ten-foot perimeter. "Call them off or I haul all of you in for assaulting a police officer."

"You and what army?"

"Hear that?" I said. I knew Hale and the rest of the agents were out in the darkness but didn't know if they would come to my aid. Ambulances and police were racing Craig to the hospital, and that was enough for me to bluff. "*Sirens,* Zeke. They're on their way. Unless you clear off the street, you and your boys going to jail, and no Wall Street lawyer is going to get you off."

"Gentlemen, let the good officer go. We don't need you all pulled in on petty mayhem charges. We need you to help avenge our son and our daughter. Me and my wife. And our son, who these dogs are persecuting, needs you. They can't give justice, but we can."

Zeke Jelickson had, perhaps unwittingly, given the same speech that Marty had at the funeral. Was father like son or was son like father?

"You need to step behind the gate," I said. "Get back behind property lines."

The bikers didn't move.

"Linda made some of her world-famous chili." Zeke was a hulking blackness, blocking out the light that spilled from the apartment. He was going in, but called over his shoulder. "Come in for a bowl. It's a little tight, but we can break down some walls and make some room if we have to. And we can talk about our plans for the future. It is *glorious.*"

Zeke Jelickson's voice dripped of acid, and the men responded to his hate. He didn't stay to see if they'd follow. I waited until they were all in the house before walking backward toward Barbara, who hadn't yet made it down to the end of the block, drifting on an invisible current.

I pulled my radio from my pocket and slid it into my ear. "Sierra 4 to Alpha. All clear."

"Saw the whole thing," Hale said.

"From your car?" I asked.

"We have a camera in the nativity scene." The people in the corner house were diligent about putting up their nativity scene—glowing nutcrackers guarding the perimeter of baby Jesus' birth—but less diligent about taking it down. It had been up until July, last year. "Ray Jelickson's phone sent another text while Zeke was making his speech. Any visual confirmation on Linda Jelickson?"

"Negative. I'm going to secure Barbara in my car and retake my position."

I listened for mentions of Dave in the radio chatter: he was breathing, he was oxygenated, and he'd been swabbed for toxins. I choked off a laugh. Dave had to live because I needed to be able to tease him about getting swabbed for toxins. I focused my mind on business, listening closely to the radio: Craig was breathing with the help of the ventilator, and our dealer hadn't approached. I grabbed Barbara's arm to hustle her along a little bit. The rain was coming down hard now, and my clothes were soaked through, the hole in my pants letting in a steady stream of wet. The little fur that remained on Barbara's coat fuzzed. She veered away at my touch, walking parallel with me at arm's length along the path that ran against the mill. I steered her through inference; she didn't want me close but didn't want me far, either. Barbara was singing a girl group song, low and sweet.

> I gave you my crimson scarf to wear.
> I kissed you with a sigh.
> You took your mark, your engine roared.
> It was our last good-bye.

It was the first new song Barbara had sung in thirty years.

"You okay, Barbara?" I said softly, not touching her even as she tipped sideways, scraping the bricks of the building. I worried that she was sinking deeper into her dark places until she piped up with a very shaky version of her Christmas chestnut. A little steadier on her feet now, she was able to move fairly quickly along the two hundred feet next to the mill.

"This way," I said as we reached the lot at the far side. All the FBI agents had driven beater cars, dented and scratched models chosen specifically to fit in perfectly with the other abandoned junkers scattered around the lot. In our Dodge, Dave and I arrived pre-beatered. I guided Barbara, gradually adjusting my own course to push rather than pull her into the car.

"Sit here," I said, easing her inside. My soaked clothes chafed as I stretched wide to buckle her in. This close, I got the full effect of Barbara's scent: wet fur, hair spray, and the sweetish smell of heroin. Not wanting to disconcert her with eye contact, I kept my eyes on her lap. Barbara jumped every time drips of cold rain rolled off me and hit her. She stopped singing, but touched her fingers to her thumb in some internal rhythm—one-two-three-four, four-three-two-one—until they stilled. When I took a step back, I discovered that she'd nodded off in the half minute it took to buckle her in.

"Sierra 4 to Alpha, returning to position," I said into the radio. The chatter had quieted considerably.

"Sierra 3 to Sierra 4," Ernie said. "You have missed nothing other than me losing my nose from the cold."

"Can we knock off the chatter?" Potreo's voice said snidely. I would have told him to go fuck himself, but currently that wasn't essential information. Later, I planned to give him that information, in great detail.

I reached the door of the mill. The entrance was marked MEN, remarkable for a business where most of the employees had been un-married young women. The mill's Victorian owners had strived, in their true muscular Christian way, to improve their lessers. They'd put in a chapel upstairs and kept away any men who might compromise the women's virtue or, worse, marry them and take them away from the mill.

I opened the door slowly, keeping the rusted hinges from making too much noise. All was quiet, and I gave my eyes a moment to adjust, taking a deep, calming breath. The dust in the room hit my throat, and I couldn't help but cough. I held my mouth against the crook of my elbow and constricted my throat muscles, muffling it, but was unsuccessful. The sound bounced around the room, echoing.

Except it wasn't an echo. I listened, opening my mouth to breathe more quietly. It tasted like one hundred years of oil and cotton dust. The sound of the rain was low but insistent, drumming a rhythm that my heart sped up to match. My sodden clothes left me heavy and graceless. I needed to go outside, get help, and guard the exits—it might have been a homeless person looking for a break from the weather, but it might be more.

I took a step and stopped. Heard the low beat of the rain plus something new and harsh, a rhythmic clank that seemed to be everywhere: from behind, from the front, from *above*. I swung my pistol wildly. It wasn't until it was right on top of me that I saw the plunging iron hook.

I darted left, but not fast enough: The hook smashed into my shoulder, its weight driving me against the far wall. The chain crashed above me, bouncing wide, hitting a post, and boomeranging back on me. I dodged it, barely, my head pounded against the bricks. The clang repeated endlessly. I tried to stand, but the sharp pain in my shoulder left me unable to keep my balance, and I sank to the floor, the cement scraping against my skin where my pants had torn before, a pipe digging into my tailbone when I landed. I reached out for my Glock with my left hand, brushing the cracked floor. My shoulder screamed. It was dislocated. I reached around with my right hand, the stretch pushing my far shoulder painfully tight against the wall. I touched my ear. The radio wasn't there, dislodged when I fell.

I pulled myself in tight, making myself small. I couldn't see my assailant, and maybe he or she couldn't see me, either. From the blackness I heard a click, the hammer being cocked, and the pulled trigger—even through my fear, my well-trained brain noted *revolver*—and after, nothing.

The gun failed to fire.

My hand rested on the pipe underneath me. I tugged at it, pain shooting through me, making me weak and afraid to move.

A second snap, the revolver jamming again. I jerked hard at the pipe and it gave way, the rust letting me break it from the wall. All I could hear was the harsh breathing of my assailant, probably a foot in front of me. I screwed myself right, my useless arm flopping to my side, lifted the pipe with my right arm, and with a last burst of energy swung out, screaming in pain as the swing forced my left shoulder roughly back into the socket.

My assailant's scream almost drowned out my own, the sound low and guttural, injured. A clatter followed, the gun dropping. Collapsed against the cold bricks, soaked in cold sweat and colder rain, I prepared to be kicked or punched, but nothing came. My assailant was moving away from me, and as the door swung open, I could make out the bare outline of my attacker in the doorway: five feet ten or eleven, wearing a knit cap, and kitted out with big boots and a thermal jacket. A huge backpack turtled out behind.

I felt shaky, and my muscles wouldn't support me. Still sitting, I skidded the pipe in my hand back and forth on the floor in wider and wider circles, skimming for my gun. It hit something solid and I crawled over. Not a gun, but night-vision goggles. I put them on, the possibility of collecting DNA secondary to finding my firearm. I gathered the energy to move onto my hands and knees and crawled over to my gun. With a last push, I got myself upright, barely, and lurched out the exit.

Sweat ran off my head and across my eyes, mixing with the freezing rain. I shivered. I pulled off the goggles, stuffing them into my pocket. From the far corner of the lot one of the "abandoned" cars started up, skidding briefly before righting itself and speeding toward the exit. I put my gun into firing position and then lowered it—no way could I make that shot from here. I concentrated on the black sedan, trying to ID it, using my eyes when I couldn't use my gun.

A BMW. And the only people in town with one of those were the Brouillettes.

I ran toward the Dodge, which sat with the door gaping wide, Barbara nowhere in sight, and crashed down on the passenger seat, using my good arm to shut the door. I slid across and started the car. No way was I going to put a seat belt across this shoulder. Shaking violently with cold I cranked the heat first thing.

I hit the HFPD radio, calling out to Lorraine as I slammed the car into reverse. The Dodge swung wide, and I only barely avoided hitting another car as Lorraine's voice filled the interior. I pulled aspirin out of the glove compartment, opening the bottle with my teeth, and swallowed down four, the acid of pills scraping my already dry throat raw.

"Where are you? Those agents want you to answer your radio."

"First, put out an APB on a black BMW. It's the Brouillettes', pull the plates. Then get a message to the FBI. I had my radio knocked out."

I concentrated all my strength on turning the wheel and keeping the BMW within sight. Shortly before it reached the Brouillette Paper Company, it turned onto one of the side streets. I swung left onto the same street, catching a glimpse of the car as it crested the hill.

"June. Report." Lorraine's bored monotone was nowhere in evidence, proof of how bad this whole situation was. "June!"

"I'm here, I'm here!" I slowed but didn't stop at the red light that was over the ridge of the hill. The BMW was almost beyond my sight. "I was in the mill—"

"Just a second," Lorraine said. "I've got Hale on the other line. Let me patch him through so we can all hear."

Hale's voice was harsh. "I'd be interested in hearing your interpretation of 'stay in radio communication,' Sierra 4."

I didn't have time for a lecture from Hale. I told the story of my run-in with the killer.

"Get an ID?" he asked.

"It's the Brouillettes' car."

"Phil?"

"It might be Amanda. And Jason has a key." Ahead, the BMW made a quick right. I turned just as it made a left.

"I'm in pursuit," I said.

"I'm securing the drugs and setting up checkpoints around the neighborhoods, but Delta, Golf, Hotel, and India teams will be there shortly."

I made the next right and paused. The rain coming down made visibility difficult, and I waited for the clear views that came for a few seconds after the wiper flapped. I sped up, zooming toward Simmons Avenue, the main drag around here. I turned, and saw the BMW swerve into view six blocks ahead. I slowed, but couldn't hide. Simmons was a straight shot.

"APB is out to all local, county, and state authorities," Lorraine said, flat and direct, as I gave my report.

"Tell them to approach with caution. Suspect has a firearm."

I slowed slightly as an ambulance approached from the other direction, speeding back up to sixty once it passed. I barely kept pace.

Hale came back on the line. "One bag gone, seventeen remaining. They've got thirty-five pounds of pseudoephedrine. The rest still at the benches." He seemed surprised. "They just left it."

"Is it secure?" I asked.

"It's secure. Four guys are locking it down and the rest of us are on the move. Don't approach whoever is in the vehicle until we're there."

"I'll stay clear," I said, even as I sped up. The vehicle made a turn onto Saint Agnes Cemetery Highway and I wondered if they knew I was following. As I reached the intersection, I hesitated, wondering how close I should get. If I turned onto the street, the lights would give away my presence.

I switched off the headlights. There were no sidewalks this far out and worse, no streetlights. My radio seemed louder in the dark, crackling with Lorraine passing on messages from the FBI, the emergency vehicles, updates from the hospital, and notices from the sheriff's office. My windshield wipers thumped unevenly, and in the streaked window all I could see was the broken yellow line of the road.

I turned.

CHAPTER 28

THE ROAD WAS EMPTY. The BMW was gone.

I skidded up the road. The Dodge veered toward the shoulder and I quickly righted it, driving right down the yellow line, figuring oncoming traffic wouldn't be stupid enough to drive without lights. Only I was that stupid.

I lowered my already absurdly slow pace as I approached the Brouillettes', and midway up the drive I spotted the BMW. Behind it loomed the house, dark except for a light in Danielle's room.

I called it in, craning my neck over my shoulder to keep the vehicle in view.

"What?" Lorraine said. "I can't hear you, June."

Once I parked at the cemetery's entrance, I started my third re-telling, but Lorraine cut me off.

"Patching Hale through."

"Sierra 4." Hale's use of my call name let me know he was still broadcasting on multiple frequencies. "We're ten minutes from scene. Do not engage." He paused. "I mean it."

"Sierra 4 to Alpha. Acknowledged." Even if I were willing to go it alone, my left arm was aching and close to useless. "I'm going to hit the perimeter but I promise not to get any closer."

I pushed open the door with my foot and pulled myself out of the car with my good arm. I dragged myself up the road. It was quiet out here, the crunch of my boots in the snow the loudest sound. Light flickered in the front room of the Byrnes', candlelight or, more likely, the TV, looking cozy and warm. Their minivan sat in the driveway, parked near the back door. I pushed farther, until I was midway between the properties, an old-growth beech tree grove keeping both houses invisible from where I stood on the road midway between them. I edged closer to the Brouillettes' property line, body low and gun drawn. Every step sent a painful jolt through my shoulder, reminding me of what this person would do.

Lorraine came back on the line, low and urgent.

"The silent alarm at the Brouillettes' house was triggered. The security company is trying to reach the Brouillettes by phone." Lorraine continued: "They're reporting . . . that they've reached Phil Brouillette at his office. They're reporting . . . that they can't reach Amanda Brouillette."

Lorraine was quiet, and I moved forward, stopping on the edge of the driveway. I counted my breaths, the air sharp in my lungs, the vapor rolling out, and was at twelve when two gunshots echoed through the trees.

I was in motion.

"Shots fired," I reported to Lorraine. Twice I slid backward, the tread of my boots no match for the thick layer of ice. Squares of light from the Brouillettes' window checkerboarded across the snow, and I swung wide—I didn't know what I would find when I arrived, but surprise might be my only advantage. A shadow approached, the light from the porch throwing it into high relief.

"Stop, police!" I yelled. The figure lurched up the steps to the house and I raised my gun. Spotlights came on, painfully bright, illuminating the yard. On the top step of the porch stood Amanda Brouillette. The congresswoman was in crimson men's-style pajamas and a camel coat. Pale as her daughter had been, with blood running across her face from a head wound. I didn't lower my gun.

"I saw the killer creeping up the drive, and I slipped out and stopped them in their tracks. But you need to stop that monster!" Amanda Brouillette ordered, pointing at the trees behind me. I didn't turn around, taking in the yard and the footprints that crisscrossed the snow. In the middle of it sat a backpack, almost a duffel. The pseudoephedrine.

"That *person,* the person who killed my girl, came back. They shot at me!" Amanda Brouillette was almost pleading. "I'll go. I'll find them and kill them if you don't!" She started off the steps.

"Don't move!" I said. I took in the congresswoman, small in her pajamas and her too-big coat. A trail of blood led away from the pack and up the steps—her path. A second distinct trail of blood led toward the trees. Amanda Brouillette wasn't my killer.

"Who was it?" I asked, turning toward the trees.

"I couldn't see. It was dark and they had a sort of mask. A ski mask."

"We need another ambulance," I said into the radio urgently, turning toward the beech grove. "Amanda Brouillette's injured."

"Copy that," Lorraine said. "Three minutes out."

The Brouillettes' floodlights cut through the trees, sharp fingers of light helping me see the trail of blood and where it led. I paused. Continuing on was probably more than I could do with an injured shoulder, and I felt brain tired, my thoughts slow and heavy. But if I waited, the killer would have the chance to do this again, set up a drug deal or hurt someone else.

"I'm going to keep the suspect in view," I said. Lorraine protested as I spoke to Amanda Brouillette: "Stay here. Stay safe."

I crashed forward. Branches pulled at my jacket. With the spotlight behind me, the shadow I cast was long. I wished I were as tall and as large as it made me out to be.

The beech trees were strong and solid. Some of them grew straight up, but many tilted at odd angles, swinging on their axes. As I got deeper into the darkness the trees seemed to glow silver against the off-white of the snow. The chatter from the radio was a tether to the real world as I followed the trail of blood as far as it went. Sirens wailed in the distance. Was the killer heading toward the Saint Agnes Cemetery? The road behind the house, where he'd made his escape before? Toward the Byrnes'? I didn't know. I turned the radio as low as it would go, flipped my flashlight off, and dropped close to the ground to see the trail and hide my position.

I approached a tree that was almost horizontal, using it as cover until the very last minute. I peeked over, and a gun fired, a bullet whizzing past my ear, missing me only by inches. In the brief moment of the muzzle flash I saw the shooter: Denise Byrne.

Denise Byrne? She took another shot, which illuminated her, face pale, blood running down her cheek from a gash in her forehead.

She was ahead and to the right, crouched low behind the crook of two fallen trees.

I dropped behind the tree. I rested my body against it, soaking in some of its warmth through my damp clothes and trying to think.

"Denise Byrne," I called, loud enough so that they could hear me over the radio. I had difficulty forming words. To my ears, my voice sounded loud and harsh. "Denise, it's over."

I nestled my flashlight in the curve of a tree trunk, propping it straight with my gun hand. It shook, and I realized that I might be at the very beginnings of hypothermia, the wet as dangerous as the cold. I edged my hand so that the beam would shine exactly where I thought Denise might be, and turned on my light. It hit her square in the face.

Denise fired again from behind the tree. I ducked. That was the fifth bullet.

"Don't do that!" Denise yelled. "No light in my eyes."

The light is the problem right now? In times of stress, people focused on odd things. I dropped the light so that it shone at Denise's feet. I kept an eye on where she was, even if I couldn't hit any targets right now, the mental fog that came with hypothermia dropping over me fast. The flashlight felt like it weighed two thousand pounds, and with little to no muscle control, it swung in a wide arc, hitting Denise's feet, the trees, the ground.

I decided to appeal to her practical nature. "Denise, I want to get you out of this alive."

"Really? To what kind of life?"

"A life with your husband, your son."

"Please. Are they going to visit me in jail? My son wheeling my husband in on visitor's day?" Denise's voice sounded cruel. "You have no idea what it's like."

"I know what that's like." I worked hard to keep my words focused and clear. If Denise knew I was slipping she would move in and kill me. "I know too well. That feeling, like you're bricked in, no choices."

"Most folks don't. They don't care."

I tried to keep her talking. "Well, I had people like you. You brought me those painkillers for Kevin. You didn't have to. But I can tell you, he was in so much pain that it hurt me, and you fixed that. You helped me."

In the far distance I heard sirens. I wasn't sure how much time had passed—a few seconds or a few minutes.

"You do have choices," I said. "C'mon, Denise. You can choose to walk out of here."

"Where there's hope there's life, huh?" Denise growled. "That's a nice little platitude. But the congresswoman got the last of my hope of a clean getaway, a clean getaway with money, back there when we tussled in the backyard. She wasn't even supposed to be there, the newspapers going on and on about how toxic the land was. And then you had to come along." Denise made it sound as if what I had done was impolite, rather than the breakup of a crime.

"I know." My body sagged a little. I half shoved and half fell away from the trunk, slumping—I couldn't hold a crouch for long.

Denise was talking. "My future is in the bag in her backyard." She sounded calmer. "But that's okay because I got my gun."

"No hope? Ish tha—" I concentrated, and made my words clear, while bracing myself. If Denise fixed her eyes on the light, then I might be able to surprise her. If I kept her talking. "Is that why you killed Danielle and Ray?"

"Oh, Danielle, a little hood rat. Thinking she was street smart. She certainly didn't get that from this street."

I moved myself to a point where the trunk dipped. I would be exposed, but it put me within six feet of Denise.

"So why did you kill her?" I asked.

"She was greedy. She told me over *tea* that she 'didn't need my services anymore,' like if she was civilized I wouldn't mind. Like five thousand dollars would make it all right. And when I got mad, she said that if I didn't keep my mouth shut she was going to tell everyone I cooked meth."

"She made you mad," I said. "It wasn't premeditated. Your lawyer could plead you down."

"Plead down for the death of a congresswoman's daughter?" Her laugh was harsh, echoing off the trees. "Like that would happen. Plus Ray. My life is worth less than nothing if his family gets ahold of me. He couldn't even cook meth, wasn't smart enough to look on the Internet to figure it out, which is how I learned. He sent a text to my phone—didn't even know who he was sending it to—telling me where the drop was and asking me to cook it for him. I guess all his low-life family are really proud of their meth-making skills, and he wanted to keep face. The coward cried when I hit him, so I hit him again and shut him up." She paused. "At least the girl was smart."

"Stupid and greedy and young is a bad combination." I thought of poor Ray, with his grape soda and video games and his unborn child.

"I wasn't greedy," Denise said. I held my position. I could hear help arriving, but the sirens sounded distorted and hard to place, as though they were bouncing through water. Should I stay or should I go? Denise was agitated, her Smith & Wesson flashing in and out of the light as wildly as she was talking.

"I just took enough tonight so that I could dig out. I was going to pay off our debts on the store, pay off the mortgage we took on our shitty house. I wanted my little piece. Not like Danielle. She wanted everything."

"That is greedy," I said.

I edged the light higher so that it reached Denise's waist.

"I was going to let you have the glory, you know," Denise continued. "Going to call in the rest of the junk, let you find it, be the hero. I didn't want that in my community. Did you know how much they were going to make?"

"But you can still help me be a hero. Please, let's make it so we can both get out of this alive. Jason's safe. So is Greg. . . . So are you."

"We don't have anything now that I've lost my reputation. I don't have anything to give them. I can never escape this." Denise's gun hand dropped into the light, gesturing, making her point. "Don't you understand?"

She raised the gun and took aim. Without thinking, I jumped. I hit her middle, throwing her off balance. Denise twisted in midfall, and I found myself half underneath her, my injured arm pinned. The pain gave me a burst of adrenaline to roll her.

Now Denise lay half buried in the snow. I gripped her gun hand at the wrist, but my right was weak, and Denise was bucking. I lifted up, restraining Denise's free arm under my knee. I had her for a second, but she wrenched away, putting me off balance, and raised the gun straight up, inches from my head. I propelled the arm down, pressing it against her chest. She closed her eyes and pushed up.

The gun fired.

Blood poured from Denise's chin and neck, crimson spattering the beech tree behind her.

I pulled off my scarf, staunching the blood with it. The wound spurted sideways, soaking into the snow, into my clothes, a brief bit of warmth before the coldness, the wetness, overwhelmed the feeling. I struggled to stay upright. In the distance I could hear Lorraine calling for me to report, report now! Jason could be heard over all of them.

"Mom! Mom!" he cried. "Mom! Are you there?"

"Your son is calling for you," I said. The last thing the dying lose is their hearing, and maybe if the tiniest bit of life was still in her, Denise could hear me. "He loves you. He will miss you so much."

Denise Byrne's answer was a terrible silence. The cold got deeper. I reached into the darkness.

"I'm here," I croaked, my voice weak. Then, into the radio, "I'm here. I'm alive."

CHAPTER 29

Mom, mom, mom!" lucy yelled from across the ice. "Mom, look!"

I stopped in midcircuit, the winter temperatures of the rink washing over me the second I stopped moving. Outside it was warm, at least relatively; in the forties. I watched as my daughter skated in reverse. Well, perhaps skated was too generous a word. Lucy was doing little more than walking backward, but her form was perfect. Get a little force behind her and she had the making of a wonderful figure skater, if I said so myself. I clapped wildly and raced over to congratulate her.

"That was excellent, honey," I called. I sped up, the tendrils that escaped from my ponytail whipping across my eyes as I turned. With these new skates—thank you, overtime!—I sped up and twisted, sending a spray of ice across Lucy's boots. She laughed and tried it, twisting her hips and then, ten seconds later, her skates. She succeeded only in throwing herself off balance. I reached for her and pulled her back into standing position.

Keeping her hands in mine, I decided to show her what speed felt like. I skated backward, towing her.

"Glide, sweetheart," I said, when Lucy ran on the ice to make us go faster. "Gliiide."

"I can do it, Mom. Let go now."

"You sure?"

"Yes."

"You're not tired?"

"I'm not tired," Lucy said. "Why do you keep asking me that?"

Perhaps because I *was*. The "murder of the century," as Jerry called it, had taken almost everything out of me, and doing the paperwork almost finished me off. Even after a month, the pain and exhaustion would still creep up on me.

When I was brought out of the woods I wasn't in good shape. I called out to Hale, to Dave, to anybody, to come help me.

"We're coming," Lorraine said in my ear. "Keep talking to me, June. Stay awake! Talk to me so you don't lose consciousness."

Light threaded through the trees, shining closer and closer. Sleepy and light-headed from the cold, I stopped trying to yell. Freezing rain washed down my chest. I could feel wetness but not the cold. Hale and three other agents—Ernie! I thought, but my mouth wouldn't form the word—were first on scene.

"Officer down." Hale spoke rapidly into the radio, dropping next to me as Ernie and two other agents swept the area.

"Where?" Hale demanded. "Where's the injury?"

It took a while for me to understand his question, and even longer to speak.

"Not me," I said.

"June," Hale said. Ernie radioed our location to the helicopters that circled overhead. A spotlight wiped away the grove's shadows, exposing the misery. Hale put his jacket over my shoulders and wrapped his arms around me, sending shocks of pain through my whole body.

The paramedics arrived and strapped me onto their immobilizing board. They carried me quickly toward the Brouillettes' property, weaving through the grove, twisting left and right and at points lifting me over the trees. At this angle, with my soaked-through clothes, I felt like I was at the bottom of a lifeboat. The combination of the motion, my injury, and the bright lights from the helicopters made me nauseous.

"Her first," I said, as we passed the congresswoman. Amanda Brouillette sat on the porch surrounded by three police officers and four paramedics. She didn't seem to notice them, clinging to her husband. They were both crying, with Phil rocking Amanda back and forth.

"She's conscious and aware, and has refused to go to the hospital," the paramedic said. "You're the top priority, little miss hero."

I closed my eyes to stop the motion sickness and to keep myself from telling the nice man who was carrying me not to refer to me as *little* or *miss* again. I figured I could enjoy the word *hero* for a minute, but images of Danielle, Ray, and Denise wiped that pleasure out quickly.

I woke up in the hospital, the emergency room personnel going to a lot of trouble to warm me up. Through the fog I was able to catch bits of the news station from the TV bolted into the upper corner of the emergency room. As I waited to be x-rayed I watched Marty's release. He made no statement, but his mother made plenty. I propped myself up on the bed so that I could better hear Linda Jelickson.

"An eye for an eye," Linda said. "And a life for a life. Revenge has been served, and Marty, an innocent man wrongly accused, is now free."

In the background, Marty leaned close and whispered something to Zeke. Zeke smiled wide. I shivered, and had to explain to the nice emergency room doctor that yes, really, I was warming up considerably.

"Yeah, you can't remember warm," he said.

I asked for another pillow, and he brought me another blanket. I was about to complain when the pillow and a bear hug arrived, care of Dave. He gave off warmth like an electric heater, and unlike the staff who'd slipped the little hand warmers over my fingers, he was willing to share his coffee.

"Sure you're not contagious?" I teased. He looked as healthy as a horse.

"That yellow dust isn't going to hurt anyone. Unless you are allergic to bees, like Craig. It was pollen."

"Pollen?"

"Bee pollen. Some kind of vitamin that the pharmacy stocks in bulk. Denise knew his medical history, what with having filled his past prescriptions, and hit him where she knew he'd hurt."

"Is he going to be okay?"

"Not sure yet. We're lucky they got to him when they did. He had a second reaction, but they ventilated him."

"And you?"

"Me? I'm healthy and strong. Which is more than I can say for you." He ran his hand over my head. He was probably checking for bumps, not stroking my hair.

"You okay?" he asked.

I didn't know what to say. I'd seen people die before, but all I could think was *What a waste.* Not only Danielle and Ray but also Denise. Denise had worried what Jason and Greg would do without her for good reason. They kept Jason away until the body was removed, but I doubt that they removed the snow, red and telling. Denise hadn't considered the loss she created in people's lives when she killed young Ray and Danielle, but still. Jason would miss his mother.

I let myself sink back into the pillow. I felt as far from a hero as you could get.

My doctor wasn't going to let me out even after the X-ray proved I didn't have a broken arm, just a dislocated one, and only relented once I was in a sling and my father promised to take care of me.

"I can open a goddamned can of soup," he said. His conversation with Shirley, an RN he went to high school with, sealed the deal.

Dave wheeled me out to my father's waiting car, where he tucked a blanket over the sling holding my arm in place, keeping me warm in the hospital scrubs. They had cut off my bloody clothes and bagged them as evidence.

"I'm going to keep Craig company. He's a lot more fun to hang out with when he can't talk," Dave said with a jaunty wave. "Plus, he was brave, in a very complaining way."

I was a little disappointed that Lucy wasn't in the car.

"I didn't know how you'd . . . look." My father kept his eyes glued to the road in front of us. He was going three miles an hour all the way, swerving to avoid potholes. You couldn't really see them in the predawn light; he had them all memorized.

"I wanted to get you stowed in bed before she saw you. Jeannette from next door came over. It might be hard for, for . . . someone"— and his voice broke, but he got it under control quickly—"for someone who loves you to see you like this."

"Sorry," I said. I never thought my father the cop might worry.

"Nothing to be sorry for. You did the job. We're lucky that things like this only happen once every fifty years in Hopewell Falls. You'll have retired as chief before it happens again."

The next week was spent at half speed, with Lucy physically attached to me most of the time. I cleaned up before she saw me, leaving only the sling, but Lucy was pretty freaked out nonetheless. To her, a sick parent meant death. I made sure I put on clothes every morning and came downstairs, even if all I was able to do was nap on the couch while pretending to watch TV. Dave brought reports of Craig ("Fully recovered. Whining at full volume") and the Byrnes ("Store's shut up, with a sign telling people to go to the

CVS"). Hale brought reports of the Brouillettes ("They thank you for your diligent efforts in finding their daughter's killer") and Jeff Polito.

"You're kidding me," I said. "Jeff was the drug distribution network? He was going to move two million hits of meth?"

"Only a few hundred thousand. He was Denise's guy, not Danielle's."

"Still. That's quite a leap from buying beer for high schoolers."

"He's a trucker," Hale said. "They don't call meth 'trucker speed' for nothin'."

"Was he connected to the Abominations?"

"Nope. Just helping Denise out on her project. It happened after Danielle died. He moved a little that she made out of store stock, but I don't know if he transported any, or simply had intent."

Neither of them brought word of Marty. After ten days, I returned to the station and spent three days doing paperwork. I was supposed to be staying off the streets, leaving the heavy lifting at the Byrnes' house and the pharmacy to people who could still lift things. Everyone seemed to be done with the excitement, particularly once the Jelickson parents, along with Ray's body, left town in a blaze of exhaust. Behind Ray's hearse rode the Merrimen, the first of a long line of outlaw gangs that would honor Ray on his route back to California. The Abominations would pick them up in the lower Midwest, following through Arizona and California. An honor guard, of sorts.

Still, Marty stayed, and I visited him, hoping to shake his hand now that he was cleared.

"What?" Answering my knock wearing jeans and a wifebeater, Marty opened the door a foot and blocked the whole entrance with his body. The tattoo on his right arm of a skull with flames coming out of the eye sockets was in full relief.

"Back to bust me? Or maybe show me pictures of my dead wife and brother?"

"Marty, can I come in?" I looked for the young man I had met before, who spoke of living an honorable life, but that Marty had disappeared behind tired, bloodshot eyes. "I'd like to apologize personally."

"Aww. Think I'll sue? Or maybe you'll claim that the party I had last night was a cartel, and bring me up on RICO charges. You bumped titties with me, sister, tried to pin it on me. I get it; it's what you pigs do." He was closing the door on me as he spoke. "But we're even."

I shoved my foot inside. The door bounced hard off my boot, and the vibrations ricocheted through my body, making my shoulder throb, fresh and bright. The pain must have shown on my face because Marty stopped, leaving those last few inches open—his core of decency and honor was still there. I grabbed my chance.

"I'll leave you alone." I held my sling close, easing the ache and giving me a second to figure out how to say what I came to tell him. "But I want to ask you—to ask your family, the Abominations, not to take revenge on the Byrnes. Jason and Greg were innocent—"

"No shit. I told *you* that, remember?"

"I remember."

"My family won't be a concern." He spoke slowly, concentrating on every word, and I wondered if he had been drinking. "We made a deal: Jason and his family . . . his father . . . can live."

I didn't want to know the answer to my next question. "What do your parents get?"

"In exchange? Me." He held his arms wide like a game show host, kicking over a pile of empty beer bottles that stood next to the door. "And ain't I a prize? Going back to the loving bosom of my family. Where I belong."

"You could belong here."

He shook his head, disgusted. "Jesus, you sound like Jason. Pair of half-wits. Told him to never show his *fucking* face here again or I'd kill him, and the same goes for you."

I was afraid to ask the next question. "Marty, have you been drinking?"

"No! And if I was? It's not *illegal*."

"But your sobriety—"

"My sobriety is my business, not yours. Not yours, not Jason's, not anyone's in this town. God, Hopewell Falls is a shit-hole. I have to finish up some business, and I'm gone. You won't need to worry that I'll seduce any more sweethearts of the city. Unless, of course"—his smile was feral—"my dad thinks there's some growth opportunity here. And I'm a pretty good tattoo artist, one of the best, and lord knows this state could use some good ink. And I'll have family here to visit—Jackie's kid should know his uncle. I might come back."

"Marty—"

"That's it. I'm gone." He slammed the door.

And he was, three days later, when I visited to drop off his security badge from the capitol and a huge ring of keys, which he had left at the station.

"Cleared out of here yesterday," Marty's neighbor said when he saw me peering in the window. I peeked again. The house looked occupied, fully furnished, with dirty dishes and ashtrays across the table. The neighbor kept talking. "Said I could keep everything. Not much worth anything, mostly a bunch of books. The gaming system will bring some money. And he gave me his car."

"His car?" I found that hard to believe.

"Yeah. And before you say anything, he signed the deed over to me, so it's mine fair and square. 'Didn't need no cage anymore,' he said. Rode a motorcycle right out of here, only had the clothes on his back."

I didn't know if I ever wanted to see Marty again. He'd lost hope, and that made him dangerous. I would see him at Jeff Polito's trial, if we even had one. But that was months away, months when Marty would be living and working with his family.

The next week was a blur of cleanup, having my sling removed, and avoiding reporters trying to "understand the woman behind the badge." The craziness continued until Chief Donnelly ordered Dave and me to take five days off.

"Get out of here. Now that our murders are solved, I again have no money to pay you two overtime, although that may change: the mayor received a call from the governor who got a call from the congresswoman's office, and we may not only have money for overtime but for a whole additional detective."

Detective, I thought.

"Of course, it's still in discussion, but let's just say you"—he pointed at me—"impressed the right people. Who control the purse strings. Now be gone, both of you."

I made it all the way into the ladies' locker room before jumping up and down and squealing. I stopped when I knocked a chair into one of the lockers.

"I can hear you, Officer Dignified," called Dave through the hole.

Today, the first day of my vacation, I was up early, making breakfast for my father and daughter before running out to the hardware store to pick up paint. I was going to redo my bedroom: brighten the white on three walls and paint one wall a nice brick red. On the way home I stopped at the cemetery. The grave was almost pretty, the marble slab glowing gold under the sunlight, glossy with melted snow.

"Are you going to stay? After I die?" Kevin had asked one day, lying sideways on the bed, pillows propped under his head and his swollen stomach.

"Here? With my dad?" I said, breathing hard. I was hauling boxes of books up from the basement. Kevin and I had both been readers and I realized that the room didn't feel like home without books in it. "Hopewell Falls is home. I know this place."

"You're part of it. I want to be part of it, too. You should bury me here."

I met his eyes. I'd gotten better at not flinching when we talked about his death. "Gray marble slab over in Saint Agnes?"

"Yeah. Pick out what you want. Pick out something Lucy won't be afraid of. I don't want her to be afraid of me, ever."

"You might end up with something purple."

"Purple's good. Or a nice 'safety orange,'" he said wryly, grasping my hand in his cold fingers. "We ought to let people know they should consider avoiding cancer."

I sat on the edge of the bed and let him hold my hand, appreciating the comfort he was offering even though he was too weak to put his arms around me.

"I wish this wasn't true," I said, after a while.

"Me, too." He yawned. "But I'm glad we were . . . we." He fell asleep.

In the days after the funeral, when we were waiting for the ground to thaw enough to bury Kevin, I asked Lucy what sort of headstone she wanted. Lucy wanted something like the sun, and we picked a yellow marble. By the spring, Lucy could trace the carved rays with her fingers, talking to me, talking to Kevin, talking to the dandelions that sprouted up around the grave. These days, I no longer had the running conversations with him, but I still saved up things to tell him. He answered back less and less.

As I squatted beside the grave, Hale's SUV approached. He parked right behind my car and turned off the engine but didn't get out. As his car ticked away, I walked toward him. He got out when I was almost at his door but stood there, unsure of himself in a way I had never seen.

"Hey there, June."

"Hey, yourself."

"This okay, me stopping over here?"

"Don't be stupid." I stood on my toes and pulled him down into a hug. He came gladly, lifting me up briefly before putting me down. He kissed my cheek, a quick bit of warmth against my skin.

He gazed beyond me to the grave, as if he wanted a formal introduction. His southern gentleman came out at the oddest moments.

"It's fine," I said, taking his hand and pulling him over to Kevin. "I visit all the time. Unless you want some time alone? If so, we can catch up later. I have an ice-skating date that I can't miss."

"No . . . It's not . . . That's not why I dropped by. Today's shaping up to be busy, what with going back to DC, but, well . . . June, I have something to discuss. Work related."

I waited. His eyes darted to the grave.

"We would've talked business in front of Kevin before," I said.

"Fair enough." He pushed his toe in the gravel of the drive before catching himself and standing at attention. "Look here, they need a new ASAIC in Albany."

I played along. "In charge of everything from western Vermont through Syracuse. That does sound glamorous. Anyone I know?"

"The powers that be like that I know the area," he said modestly. "And it would make a whole lot of sense, careerwise, for me."

"That's great!" At a grave five plots over an older man jolted up, and I dropped my voice.

"Really," I whispered. "Congratulations."

He shrugged his shoulder, but a smile broke through. "Thank you kindly. I'm pleased." He leaned in close. "But I'd like to talk to you about coming back in."

My mouth dropped open.

"Me and the Bureau, we parted ways," I stammered out. "They don't want me."

"Now then, don't forget, you left them. Your service record is exemplary."

"That would be . . ."

"Yes?"

"Wonderful," I said.

He grinned broadly, the hard angles of his face dissolving.

"But," I said, and Hale's smile dimmed, "but I can't. With Lucy, I can't pick up and move every two years."

"I see." Hale squared his shoulders. "Roots are important."

"That's part of it. But even this current job, where nothing happens—"

Hale laughed.

"Where nothing *usually* happens," I went on, "it wouldn't be possible without my dad. Back in L.A., during big cases all my plants would die. What would happen to Lucy if I got transferred to Missouri? Or was on a stakeout for two weeks?"

"There's administrative."

"Hale, I appreciate what you're trying to do. But I would prefer to roust drunks and go on calls for old ladies who heard a noise in the night than do paperwork."

"Consulting?" he asked. He tugged at the sleeve of my sweatshirt. "Just think on it. I need at least one ally up among the Yankees. And I'll need to be introduced to all the hot spots."

"I think you'll need a different tour director." I laughed. "The library is the only hot spot I know. Great kids' section and a mastodon. They took the bones they found at the bottom of the falls in the 1870s, covered them in fake fur, and added eyes that follow you."

"Well, that sounds very . . . educational." Hale took a step onto the lawn, sinking a half inch into the mud. He hugged me, and I smelled clean dirt and the first hint of grass.

"Glad to have you back," he said into my ear.

"Glad to be back." I disentangled myself from the hug, unstuck my shoes from the ground, and walked toward the car. "But if I work for you, no hugs. Now I've got to go ice-skate. Someone pulled some strings for me, arranged for Lucy and me to have some private time. But I'll see you in court if not before."

"Count on it." He winked. I blushed, much like I did all those years ago at Quantico.

Sitting in the car, I watched Hale lope over, stopping ten feet away from the grave. He squared his shoulders and walked the last few feet. Overhead, the sun was high in the sky. In my rearview, I saw him trace the rays that were carved in the headstone, like Lucy would.

Lucy was now slinging herself across the ice toward the exit. She still didn't understand the concept of gliding and was frustrated by the distance between her and the hot chocolate. I was as excited as she was, the powdered variety somehow tasting better at an ice rink, but I chose a few more laps. Our time was almost up, and soon tinny pop music would be blaring and open skate starting up.

Jackie brought the chocolate, holding up two cups in victory and grinning before putting them on the bench next to the rink's exit. She placed her hands on her lower back as she waddled toward the exit, a pose I remembered from when I was pregnant. Of course, I was eight months pregnant at the time and Jackie couldn't be out of her first trimester. You couldn't really tell exactly how pregnant she was under the maternity clothes she insisted on wearing.

"Thank you!" I called over my shoulder, picking up speed as I rolled into the turn. I cut through the air, no resistance. This was going to be the last go-round, and I wanted to make it good.

"My pleasure," yelled Jackie. "I owe you my life! Me and the baby."

I laughed as I whizzed past. I came out of the other turn and sped into the straightaway, wanting height as well as speed. My muscles anticipated the jump, and I was up and spinning. My lungs filled with air; I expanded.

I came out of the jump too far back on my blade. The first thing I learned in skating was how to fall safely. I landed on my butt and slowed to a halt, laughing.

"Mom, that was really high!" Lucy called. "Do it again."

I got up and started another circuit around the rink. Maybe I did have another in me.

ACKNOWLEDGMENTS

I AM SO GRATEFUL TO my editor, Rachel Kahan, whose enthusiasm and brilliance challenged and encouraged me to write a better book, and who has been a tireless advocate. My publisher has been amazing, and I'd like to thank assistant editor Trish Daly, copy editor Brenda Woodward, production editor Lorie Young, and designer Jamie Kerner, as well as the stellar marketing and publicity group, including publicity director Danielle Bartlett, publicist Camille Collins, marketing director Kaitlin Harri, and the whole team at William Morrow.

Endless thanks go to my agent, Lisa Gallagher. Her wit, wisdom, and instincts for good storytelling, which she shared with me with such kindness, nurtured this book from its inception. I know, absolutely, that this couldn't have happened without her.

Thanks to those who provided advice and expertise, including my writing group, Kate Curry, Nita Gill, Maggie King, Colleen Olle, and Carole Pollard, without whom I would have abused the word *actually;* my early readers, Lisa DeLange, John McEneny,

Kristen Sunkes, and Michele Tepper; and my law enforcement reviewers, Frank Hagg and John Aspinwall, who helped me understand how police officers think, speak, and even walk. Any errors you find are all mine.

Upstate New York deserves special mention. I'm so proud to have been raised there, and it doesn't deserve the pain and suffering I've inflicted upon it. Residents of the Capital District will no doubt be able to identify the fictional Hopewell Falls, but do know that the people and events are complete fiction.

Thank you to the relatives and friends who supported and encouraged me, including my mother, Maureen Kelly Cooley, and sisters, Bridget and Mary, as well as Vicky and David Baron, Jackie Dion, Michelle Ginthner, Megan Griffith, Rik Nicholson, Kathy Riggins, Deane Shokes, Daryl Sprehn, and so many others.

Read on for an excerpt from
M. P. Cooley's next June Lyons thriller,

FLAME OUT

Coming in May 2015

CHAPTER 1

THE RAIN WAS UNFORGIVING.

Dave was doing a lousy job of holding up his half of the house. My arms strained under the weight of his niece's birthday gift—a large backyard playhouse—and it was slow going back to my car. The spring rain had soaked through the layers of cardboard, and my knuckles scraped against the hard red plastic panels where the box disintegrated.

"You know," I said, "That spin-art kit would've fit in the back seat with room to spare." I hefted the playhouse, shoving it hard, but it jammed against my trunk's lockbox, which held my service revolver. "And I bet Tara would've had a lot of fun with the costume trunk."

"My niece isn't a princess-dress kind of girl."

I stopped short as a red Subaru sped past, spraying the back of my legs with water. "The kit included fake mustaches and Groucho eyebrows. She could've worn those with the glittery pink sandals."

"Until she trips and breaks her skull. Blood. Everywhere." He reversed, backing the box into the trunk. "Can you lift your left side a little higher?" I raised it up to my shoulders.

"That's the trick," he said.

It wasn't the trick, and the edge slipped out of my hand and dropped to the ground.

"You. Out of my way," I said. He stepped aside, defeated. The steady rain flattened his black curls, and the wet white box smeared the arms of his Jets windbreaker with saturated cardboard. I balanced one side of the box on the edge of the trunk, and using leverage, shoved most of it in. The trunk wouldn't close, so I bungeed the top to protect it from the rain, not that it mattered at this point. I ran around front and climbed into my dry car, starting the engine to get the heat going, and unlocked the door for Dave, who made a distinct squelching side as he dropped into the passenger seat.

"I hate to tell you," I said as I backed the car out of the spot, "but Tara won't be very impressed with a big soggy box."

"She'll be *very* impressed with a big soggy box, because she and her dad will have a project," Dave said. "Is it too late to go back to get the kiddie tool set?"

"Yes." I pulled out, bouncing through a pothole. My thirteen-year-old Saturn was close to the end of its life. "Yes, it is."

"Yeah, and she wouldn't go for the kiddie version anyway. I should remember to buy her gift at Home Depot next year."

I drove slowly out of the packed lot and negotiated the traffic circle, passing the exits for Colonie, Latham, and Cohoes. I missed the Hopewell Falls exit and was forced to loop around a second time. Dave snorted.

On the outskirts of town we passed St. Agnes Cemetery, where my husband lay buried. In the first year after he died I would've insisted we stop. In the second year, I would've taken the drive through the cemetery so I could see his grave. This year, I thought a message to him: "Miss you, babe. See you on Thursday. Wait until you hear Lucy's theory on where babies come from. She's definitely your daughter." I would never cut the thread to Kevin.

The landscape crested, dropping into the city below. Hopewell Falls was all downhill. The Mohawk River bounded the city on the east and the Hudson on the south, the waterfall that formed where the two rivers met giving the town its name. Through newly sprouting trees and mist from the rain, I could make out my own house in the distance. Dad was babysitting Lucy while I helped Dave and worked the three to eleven p.m. patrol. In this weather, I wished I were at home. There would be plenty of car accidents tonight, but the bigger threat were those people trapped inside on a Saturday with their "loved ones," drunk, and if I was very unlucky, armed.

The streets got twisty the closer we got to the river. We stopped at a light, waiting to cross Interstate 787 and beyond that, the short bridge that spanned a small waterway, the last remains of the Mohawk River before it joined the mighty Hudson.

Dave was frowning, his eyes on the Ukrainian church, its gold and sky-blue dome bright against the gloomy afternoon sky.

I touched his arm. "You OK?"

"Never better, Lyons." He shook off my hand. Something must be wrong—I spent most of my time extricating myself from the hugs, pats, and leans Dave used with everyone, but especially me.

"You sure? It's only a birthday party. You're too late to be forced into pin the tail on the donkey. And if you really wanted to escape, you could take my shift for me . . . put on the blues, drive around for eight hours."

"Uh, huh."

"And your brother's doing better." His brother, Lucas, had been unemployed for a while and had divorced again for the fourth time last year, leading to a drunk-and-disorderly charge outside his most recent ex-wife's house. Thankfully, the arrest scared Lucas straight.

"Lucas is doing great, although his plan is to score points off his ex today. I guess Felicia threw a roller-skating extravaganza for Tara's school friends, and Lucas insisted on throwing a second party for all the kids from the church. I'm expecting balloon animals."

"So?"

"So what?"

"So why are you tense?"

HE DIDN'T ANSWER. THE LIGHT CHANGED TO GREEN, AND IN LESS than ten seconds we had crossed the highway and the bridge from the mainland to the Island.

"It's just, the Island's so closed off," Dave said finally. I stifled a laugh. Annexed by the same Dutch settler who farmed Hopewell Falls back in the sixteenth century, DeWulf Island was hardly some isolated outpost. The channel separating the mainland from the Island was narrow enough that I could probably cross it with a running jump, and if I followed the main thoroughfare we'd be in Troy in another half mile. Instead of taking the straight shot across the Hudson, I veered right, passing a series of side-by-sides, apartments built by the Ukrainian and Polish immigrants who had fled first the Soviets, then the Nazis, and then the Soviets again. The remains of the Golden Wheat bakery, burned down two years ago, lay on our left, and we passed a small Polish grocery that sold Cheetos, Cokes, frozen pierogies, and pickled beets.

"Left here," Dave said, and we turned onto a street populated with more trees than houses, plants lush with the recent spring rains. The street dead-ended at a modest home surrounded by several acres of land. The façade was brick with a white porch and black shutters. Purple balloons swung wildly in the breeze, and four cars were parked out front. The bench on the front porch was freshly painted, and a lilac bush sprang up on the lawn, trimmed and blooming. We were at Lucas's house. Or rather, his Aunt Natalya's.

Dave and I wrestled the playhouse up the narrow walk to the front door and rang the bell. Lucas greeted us, beer in hand.

"Jesus, Davey. Did you have to be so late?" he said. "And Aunt Natalya'll kill you if you sprinkle dirty cardboard through the house. Oh, hi, June." He stepped outside and dropped his beer on the arm of the bench, picking up my end of the box. He got a good look at the contents for the first time and grimaced.

"Oh, wonderful. A construction project of my very own."

Matching Dave's 6'4", Lucas was fairer than his brother, his light brown hair sporting some gray, straight, and almost fine.

He'd worked construction for over twenty years until suffering a vague injury involving a lot of Vicodin. His new work as a bartender agreed with him. The two men bickered about the gift as they walked around the house to the backyard, where the party was in full swing.

Yard was perhaps an understatement. Dave jokingly called it the back forty, and it wasn't a complete exaggeration, the lot extending back three acres. The lawn had room for a two-tiered bouncy house and a swing set. Beyond that was a garden that could produce enough fruits and vegetables to feed everyone on the Island, with sunflowers sprouting along the border between the cultivated plot and the meadow near the property's far border.

Despite all the wide-open space, the adults were grilling and eating on the porch, clustered under the small green tin awning to stay out of the rain. The bouncy castle's turret listed to the left, the weight of the water pooling on the roof about to send the structure sideways. A bunch of kids flinging themselves against the sides didn't help. I was pretty sure this birthday party was going to end in tears, either with the puffed-up monstrosity tipping sideways or the kids being told no, really, they needed to come in.

"Dad!" the birthday girl shouted, "The roof's caving in!"

Lucas Batko handed the box back to me. "This is going to be a disaster," he said as he jogged across the lawn to the castle that was wiggling like a basket of puppies. On the way he picked up a toy axe lying on the ground outside the door. Squeals sounded as he entered the inflatable structure, and the castle surged and rolled as Lucas trudged across the inflated floor, designed for a 50-pound child, not a 200-pound man. He took the axe handle and pressed up on the roof, sending the water from the first turret splashing over the side. Dave and I maneuvered up the steps to the porch.

Dave's aunt intercepted us, moving rapidly despite her pronounced limp, twisting her left hip forward before propelling the right foot in front.

"David, how could you! Forcing June to march through muddy

grass with heavy box." Dave told me she had been in the US since the late 1940s but her Ukrainian accent hung heavy on the edge of her words, her g's lapsing into h's, dropping articles left and right. Small and sharp eyed, her black hair laced with gray, Natalya rested her hands on her uneven hips, the left a few inches higher than the right. "You are no gentleman."

Dave had to fold in half to give his aunt a kiss. "That's not news to Lyons, Teta."

Dave and I dropped the house on the ground in front of the gift table, and Dave took a green polka-dotted bow out of his pocket and slapped it on the corner. Natalya frowned, but it wasn't at the gift-wrapping.

"Showing up your brother with your big gift?"

Dave held up his hands in surrender. "Can't compete with a bike, Teta."

Despite being almost eighty, Natalya yanked me toward her, pulling me into a hug. I could smell hairspray and powder, the two things that kept her fresh and presentable in the damp weather.

"Food now," she said. "The children stuff themselves with junk Lucas purchased," she said, eyeing the pizza rolls with distaste, "but I grilled sausage and have salad from greens I picked myself."

Dave hooked Natalya's hand through his arm. "Good idea. Lyons starts busting stuff up if you don't feed her."

Dave prepared our lunches under Natalya's careful direction. He came back with two plates piled with perfectly grilled kielbasa, dumpling, and salad, a pizza roll balanced on top, with a beer in his hand and a bottle of water tucked in his elbow. We settled in a few chairs near the edge of the porch.

"Hail the conquering hero," Dave said to his brother as he returned, tipping his beer at him. Lucas reached out and grabbed it, taking a swig. Dave's protests were hard to make out with the dumpling shoved in his mouth.

"Good, right?" Dave said. It was delicious. The pierogies were homemade, and the sausage, grilled perfectly, came from a local butcher who made his own. Heavy fare, but delicious.

Dave said between mouthfuls of dumpling, "Aunt Natalya picked out the best food on the table for you."

"Yeah," Lucas said. "She's always trying to butter up Dave's girl-friends."

Dave choked on his pierogi. "I have no idea where she got that idea."

"Wishful thinking on her part." Lucas pulled out a lighter. "I'd better go. We were holding the cake until Tara's favorite uncle got here"—Dave saluted as Lucas continued—"and since he's deigned to grace us with his presence, I better try to get the candles lit before her next birthday."

"Get me another beer, will ya?" Dave called to his brother, but Lucas was already inside. Dave knocked his knuckles against mine. "You're going on shift, but you want one?"

At my no, Dave went to grab one for himself. I dug into my meal.

I was almost done when Dave broke my food reverie. "Me and Special Agent Bascom grabbed a beer last night."

"You and Hale?" I said.

"Yep. I invited the G-man over today. Once I told him about the bouncy house, he signed right up."

I wiped my mouth, preparing to escape before Hale arrived.

"What's your hurry? You two buried the hatchet."

"Mostly." I collected my trash and stood to go. "He's still a shark, but a friendly one." What I didn't want to tell Dave was that I was avoiding Hale because he was chasing me for an answer: Was I or was I not rejoining the FBI? It had been almost four years since I left, and I wasn't sure if I wanted to rejoin, and what's more, I couldn't figure out why they would want me. Why Hale might want me.

As I was about to say my good-byes, Lucas came out with the biggest cake I'd seen this side of my wedding. Scratch that, it was bigger. A princess sat on top, the highest tier making up her skirt, pink and detailed with icing and candy, surrounded by four birthday candles. Below lay her kingdom, the tiers decorated with characters from the *Dora the Explorer* TV show.

"Tara, come up and blow out your candles!" Lucas called. The kids were slow to leave the bouncy house, and Lucas started to pace, beer in hand, checking to see that the candles were still lit while yelling for Tara to hurry.

"Calm down a little," Dave said to his brother. "Let me get her."

Dave pretended to be a giant and said he was going to eat slow children, and the kids came running up the steps and were corralled into singing. At first deliriously happy, the birthday girl began to cry when they went to cut the cake.

"But it's pretty!" Tara said. I worried that Lucas would get upset by the tears but instead he scooped her into his arms, kissing her on both cheeks, and promised to cut *around* the toys dotting the top.

Natalya intercepted me as I was leaving. "You must take leftovers to your friends at police station."

She wasn't kidding about leftovers. By the time I got the four trays loaded into my trunk, I only had forty-five minutes until my shift. Between changing into my uniform, getting a shift report, spreading out the food in the break room, and fighting my way past the crush of people who heard that Dave's aunt had sent some of her homemade dumplings, time ended up being tight. Once I got people started on their food coma, I hit the road.

There were no calls, and I kept my eyes on the sidewalk as much as the roads as I drove, watching for irregularities. In the past, I'd caught a fair number of criminals at or leaving the scene—I'd stopped someone trying to haul two meat slicers and a peppered ham from the butcher shop on Thursday of last week. Paying attention was my business.

As I turned onto Reed Way, the cruiser skidded gently on the pebbled road. I smelled the problem first, an odor of gasoline dampening out the scent of spring grass. As I approached the long-dormant Sleep-Tite Factory, it got worse. Unfortunately, arson was a too-common occurrence in this area. There's nothing to steal—

the companies went bankrupt or moved to China decades ago—but bored teenagers or professional firebugs chasing an insurance payment regularly set them on fire. No private industry had replaced the factories, and cities razed them for public safety, paving over the land. I called it in as a fire, because if it wasn't one, it would be soon. I sped up and pulled into the parking lot, far enough away that any fire wouldn't destroy the cruiser if this thing got big.

I ran toward the factory through a Day-Glo blue-green slick of gasoline that trailed over the lawn and the sidewalk, across the street, and toward the river, fire extinguisher in hand. Smoke was light, bare wisps lacing the air, but the air was heavy with fuel, and I adjusted my breathing so I wouldn't get lightheaded. My cruiser became obscure—the gasoline fumes warping the late-afternoon light. Even the sirens, hazy in the distance, sounded distorted, their rise and fall hiccupping, half caught behind the veil of gasoline fumes. From my radio, I could hear Lorraine, the dispatcher, calling out for emergency responders: police, ambulances, fire trucks, everyone.

"10-50," Lorraine said, steady and insistent, giving the code for fire. "10-50."

The factory had closed twenty-five years before, long enough that the boards used to cover the holes in the windows had holes themselves. One of the regular places on my beat, it was usually locked. Today the chain hung loose from a door handle, the padlock cut. There were two fifteen-foot sliding metal doors. I pushed them wide, and they slid easily, opening up onto the factory floor.

The room was empty except for a still-running van, which had "CAR F" stenciled across its door in what looked like primer paint. The vehicle's back door flung wide, a path of gasoline splashed from the back of the truck, across the floor, to the far door. Fire engulfed the far side of the building, a burning mattress now blazing, fed by the oxygen coming from the holes in the ceiling and the roof beyond. The blaze followed a distinct route where a trail of gasoline wound across a floor white with pigeon droppings, the path sparking and then dying swiftly without any kindling. Gasoline fires burn fast and bright, dying almost as soon as they spark, but the flames advanced toward the van and beyond that, a pile of textiles, fabric discarded by the last tenants. It was beyond me and my fire extinguisher.

Based on the volume of the sirens, the fire trucks were a few blocks away, and I backed away from the entrance. The flames darted under the van, scorching the edge but otherwise leaving it untouched. The fire reached the fabric pile. I could see the edges spark before the whole thing caught fire, flames shooting straight up twenty feet, hitting the wooden ceiling beams. It sent out a painful blast of heat, singing my hair even twenty feet away. A whooshing sound blew through, the fire consuming the oxygen, followed almost immediately by a scream.

Out of the flames rose a woman.

She stepped out of the heart of the blaze and spun frantically left and then right, trying to get free of the flames encircling her, the bright light mapping her thrashing in the air. I ran toward her. The smoke got heavy. I ducked low and pulled off my coat, ready to extinguish the flames. I needn't have bothered—by the time I reached her, her clothes had almost completely burned away, and she stood in front of me tiny and exposed, red skin blackened with soot, hair burned off. Through the smoke, the factory's doors appeared distant and almost unreachable, and I picked her up and moved toward the faint light shining from the exit. She screamed, loud and long.

"I'm sorry, I'm sorry, ma'am," I said. No question she weighed less than a hundred pounds, but my knees strained, and I had to break left as the fire broke right. Under the crackle of the flames I could make out the drip of gasoline down through the wood floors below us, the steady trickle counting off every second I stayed in the building. I gave a heave and went faster.

With the smoke and her screaming I'd missed the firefighters' arrival. Four were dragging a hose into the building. Two broke away and came to me, lifting the woman off my shoulder and running toward two trucks of waiting paramedics, gently placing her on a gurney.

"Make it stop!" the woman cried before breaking down in a coughing spell. After seeing her go up in flames, it seemed impossible that she was alive, let alone talking. Even out here, out of the fire, I couldn't tell how much damage had been done, but underneath the soot I could make out her bright red skin and the beginning of blisters running across her face. The paramedic cut off the string of elastic, the last that remained of her clothes, and tried to run an IV.

"It hurts," she said weakly, going silent as one of the paramedics threaded a cannula under her nose, force-feeding her oxygen.

"I can't get a vein," the second paramedic said in a low voice, a bad sign: the more dangerous the situation, the quieter the paramedics, their calmness balancing the hysteria around them. "The burns, I can't get a vein. Let's get her to Memorial."

They secured the woman and lifted her into the van, and I watched them pull away, sirens blaring.

A hand clasped my arm.

"Hey, Lyons," said Greg, a paramedic I'd worked with on countless calls. "Come with us."

After listening to my lungs and checking my exposed skin, Greg diagnosed me as "singed," telling me I'd be coughing for a while and that my hair needed the ends trimmed. I refused to go to the hospital so they insisted on oxygenating me there. From the back of their truck I watched as a half-dozen firefighters pushed farther into the fire, dark smoke engulfing them. The smell of acrid burning filled the air, and flames licked up, heavenward, leaping and grabbing for oxygen, tinder—whatever it could take.

It would take everything.

CHAPTER 2

THE FIRE BURNED FAST, FIREFIGHTERS RETREATING AS THE building lost the first floor. By this time, responders had arrived from Waterford, Colonie, Half Moon, and Troy, and backup was speeding our way from Menands and Albany. Hoses doused the main level, and firefighters on ladders rained water on the second floor. A helicopter from the New York Bureau of State Land Management sped toward us, filled with flame retardant. Two trucks of firefighters soaked the Harmony Mill across the street, keeping any sparks from sending the mill up, too. The heavy rains worked in our favor, however, with the gasoline slick sliding down the hill toward the Hudson; with all the buildings so close together, putting out the blaze took an enormous amount of effort.

The sun had set, and the fire appeared even more hellish, casting red, orange, and yellow shadows against the hills rising up behind it, making it look like the whole town was ablaze. Working traffic control over a block away, the heat sent sweat streaming down my back.

Lisa Jones, the fire chief from Menands who was supervising the flames along the western perimeter, filled me in: "A lot of these old mills, they're like a lumberyard surrounded by four walls. You know, Type III construction." I had no idea what Type III construction was and said so.

"The old wood frame construction. Wood floors, wood ceilings, wood beams, wood everything except the walls. With the industrial chemical buildup soaked into the walls, they burn fast."

"And with the gasoline?"

"Unstoppable."

Not that the firefighters stopped trying. For almost an hour they poured everything they had onto it. I worked crowd and traffic control, stopping to slide on a pair of boots lent to me by one of the fire companies, so big I could fit my foot with the shoe still on into the boot. They were awkward but necessary, as my gasoline-soaked shoes would create a pyre for me if any sparks hit. Dave arrived on the scene, waving before running up to reroute traffic two streets above. The flames stretched higher, and we had to secure the whole hill.

The chief pulled up next to me in one of the squad cars.

"The burned woman our firebug?" he asked.

"Didn't see anyone else on scene, and no one"—I scanned the mob of people, as arsonists often liked to watch their own handiwork—"who's taking exceptional interest in the fire."

"This fire brought out the crowd," the chief said. "Probably imagining it's the ghost of Luisa Lawler."

Most people thought the Sleep-Tite factory was cursed. It had been owned by Bernie Lawler, a name especially important in my house. Back in 1983, Bernie Lawler had killed his wife, Luisa, and three-year-old son, Teddy. They never found the bodies but there was loads of circumstantial evidence: reports of abuse, blood spatter across the basement walls, and worst of all, bloody handprints along the underside of Bernie's trunk where Luisa had tried and failed to escape. Thanks to my dad, they caught Bernie, and he was sent to prison. He was still there.

From a few miles away I watched as a helicopter landed on the roof of Memorial Hospital, ready to take my victim on a ten-minute ride to the regional burn center in Albany. From reports, Memorial had gotten a line into her and pumped her full of fluids. They diagnosed her with "second- and third-degree burns" but beyond that were vague, leaving the thorough diagnosis to the experts in Albany.

As I watched the sky, I saw a spotlight shining over the Hudson, approaching fast, a helicopter sent by the Bureau of State Land Management. The fire-retardant chemicals on the helicopter represented our best hope for relief. There'd be red foam over the building, the whole block, and the crowd if I didn't back them up.

I'd moved them about fifteen feet—a couple hundred people watching a large-scale disaster were hard to motivate. The fire shot up, a roman candle shining bright, before disappearing from view. The building groaned, a dying dinosaur, and the roof came down, followed by a crash as the roof and the second floor piled into the first, and then a boom echoing like thunder as all three crashed into the basement below. Sparks shot up brightly, and dust coated my mouth. I spat and watched as the walls of the building, with no support, wavered and then collapsed inward, the two walls closest to the hill going first, and the street-facing walls falling a minute later.

And the fire was dead. Not completely out, but manageable. The helicopter dropped its load, the red foam splatting dead center, and all the fire companies moved in on it, dousing spots where flames poked through the field of bricks, the fire reduced to a slow smoldering.

IT ENDED WITH A BANG AND A WHIMPER.

Once we got the bulk of the crowd dispersed, troopers arrived to take over traffic duty, and Dave and I took the opportunity to go over to the regional burn center in Albany to try to talk to our victim.

"I should call my brother. Lucas'll lead the parade," Dave said, exiting off 787 toward St. Peter's Hospital.

"Parade?"

"His worked at Sleep-Tite and did everything he could to get out of it. Indoor jobs make him nuts."

"So he must love being a bartender."

"Well, he loves booze more than he loved being outside." He smiled. "He worked the early shift at Sleep-Tite, and I can't tell you how many times I woke up to my dad knocking on his door, telling Lucas to get his lazy ass out of bed. Of course, my dad would never use that kind of language. He swore in Ukrainian."

We stopped at an intersection, the faux-gothic cathedral on our left, the too-modern state towers on our right. "Was your dad trying to teach him a good work ethic?"

"Yes, but also . . . Mom worked the nights at Sleep-Tite, and my Dad didn't like to leave her waiting after her shift. He was worried she'd get bored, and when that happened, she'd wreck her life just to watch it crash. He was right. That last time she took off, she left from work. Went on a bender somewhere, stole Aunt Natalya's car, and hit the road." He pulled into the parking lot of St. Peter's Hospital, rolled down his window, and punched a button. A ticket popped out. Dave tucked it in his visor. "I guess I hate Sleep-Tite a little, too."

I tensed up as we walked through the halls of St. Peter's. I'd managed to avoid hospitals during the end stages of Kevin's illness. Before things became hopeless, my husband's days were filled with a constant array of doctor's appointments: oncologists, pulmonary specialists, pain specialists, and all of the diagnostic machinery, MRI's, X-rays, blood tests—the list was endless.

We arrived at the burn unit, a sign on the door instructing us to report to the nurses' station. Once there, we explained to a nurse in all-white scrubs who we were and why we were visiting.

"I paged Gayle. That's her patient," he said. "I assume you'll want to see the patient?"

"For a few questions."

He handed us paper scrubs, shoe guards, and a cap. "Go on. Put these on."

A nurse in her mid-fifties rushed out of one of the rooms. She too wore the white scrubs of the rest of the nurses on the floor, and her crocs squeaked with every step.

"Here about our mystery patient?" she asked.

I reached under my scrubs to pull out my badge.

"Like I couldn't tell you were cops from down the hall," she said. "How can we help you?"

"The burn victim's in a lot of pain. We know that." I said. "But we need to ask her a few questions."

"We've barely gotten her stabilized. Her blood pressure's still all over the place—"

"One question," Dave said. "Her name."

"She's unconscious," Gayle said. "Has been since she got here."

"Compromising her health is the last thing we want," I said. "But could you maybe roll back some of the meds? We need to wake her up for one minute, get her name, maybe who to contact."

A light went on over one of the patient's doors, followed by a low ping.

"Dan, can you answer that call?" Gayle said.

The young man agreed, pulling on a cap and tying on a face mask as he hurried to the patient.

"Look," Gayle says, "This isn't some sort of medically induced coma. Yes, she's on pain meds, but the deal is, her body decided to shut down all nonessential functions. Burn shock. All of her skin, including the surface of her lungs, is struggling to heal right now, and we're pumping her with fluids without swamping her lungs and drowning her. She might wake up—"

"A picture," I say. "Can we take a picture of her in case we get any missing persons reports?"

Gayle considered. "That'd be OK, I guess."

The victim lay on the single bed, her lips pale under the venti-lator, her hair gone. The visible skin glistened, slathered in lotion meant to replace some of the moisture she was losing. She lay naked under a tent, a gauzy fabric draped a foot off her body. That said, she looked surprisingly good, the injuries no worse than a bad sunburn, blisters streaking across her face.

"You get them out of crisis and clean off soot and ash, they start looking a little healthier. Systemically, though . . . skin's one of our biggest organs, and burns like this, it's like she got stabbed in the kidneys," Gayle said.

Dave pulled out a camera. "OK?" Gayle agreed.

"So what's her prognosis?" I asked

Gayle explained how the woman had burns of different severity over parts of her body. A few areas remained untouched, or the burns were first degree—"Her feet, oddly enough"—but most of her body had second-degree burns, where the top layer of skin burned away.

"Gasoline burns fast," she said. "Her clothes, slower, which is where we see the third-degree burns."

I tried to figure out where the woman was severely burned. "How much of this is third degree?"

"Twenty percent. Around her shoulders, and across her lower torso. Thank God for natural fibers, which burn faster than synthetic or, God forbid, plastic." A grim look passed over her face. "Plastic can be a mess."

"So twenty percent," Dave said, putting his camera away. "That's not too bad, right?"

"Oh, it's bad. Especially for a person her age."

"Her age?" I asked. "Do you know how old she is?"

"Well, based on the osteoporosis we detected when we did X-rays, I'd put her in her mid-fifties, possibly her mid-sixties. While it's not hard and fast, a rule of thumb is that if you add a person's age to the amount of their body burned to the third degree, you get the percent chance someone might die: If she's in her fifties, it might be a seventy-five percent chance of death, and if she's in her sixties, closer to eight-five." Dave's face fell. Gayle plowed on. "And any comorbidities—diabetes, heart disease, asthma—might mean worse odds."

The woman's breathing got heavy. I didn't see any blips on the monitors, but Gayle picked up her catheter bag and examined the urine critically.

"We're over-hydrating her," she said. "We might be drowning her right now. You need to go, I'm afraid. I'll be sure to call you if she wakes up, and if I get her, even for a second, I promise, I'll get a name." Gayle adjusted the woman's IV, lowering her fluid. "We want to find out who our friend is as much as you do."